Harry Love
Contract for Murder

– DAPHNE E MACHON –

Printed and bound in England by www.printondemand-worldwide.com

http://www.fast-print.net/bookshop

Harry Love – Contract for Murder
Copyright © Daphne E Machon 2018

A catalogue record for this book is available from the British Library

ISBN 978-178456-580-0

First published 2018 by
FASTPRINT PUBLISHING
Peterborough, England.

For my friends at
The Innovation Centre Market Harborough.

Chapter One

HARRY LOVE Contract for Murder

George Blackwell locked his office door, nodded to his secretary who was clearing her desk in the outer office, and strode down the stairs smiling to himself. It was Friday and nearly four o'clock and he had things to do. He didn't usually work this late, and certainly not on a Friday, he liked to be away by three. But today he had one or two loose ends to clear up before the weekend, things that would produce a nice little income. It had been another excellent week with a very positive outcome to at least one of his investments. His large, pock-marked face, small dark eyes and bulbous nose gave him a rather sinister appearance, but then he was well known for his nasty ways and devious negotiations, so perhaps this was a fair description of the big man. He was a good six feet three with an ample girth and thinning hair making him look a great deal older than his fifty-three years. In the main reception area downstairs, he nodded to the security man by the main door, who touched his forehead in return. The two women sitting at their computers didn't bother to look up, they disliked Blackwell and were offended by his treatment of women and his general rudeness to people.

'Night, Mr Blackwell,' called the security officer, receiving no reply in return. He pulled a face at the disappearing back of the man.

Blackwell left the building, went down the steps and round the side of the building to the business car park. It was already getting dark with it being November, but he liked the dark, it swallowed him up, allowing him to be secretive, private. Unlocking his BMW, he slid behind the wheel and started the engine. He looked up startled when there was a knock on the car window. He pressed the button to lower the window and scowled at the man standing there. He was no one he knew! 'I'm in a hurry, what do you want?' he snapped.

'Not a lot,' replied the man pointing a gun in his face.

Blackwell opened his mouth to reply but no sound was forth coming. The "phut" from the weapon was barely audible and a small red spot appeared in the centre of Blackwell's forehead as he slumped down in his seat. Dead.

The man standing by the car slipped the gun into his overcoat pocket and calmly walked away.

A little red Lotus Elite drove into the Pegasus House carpark and pulled up a few metres from the group of people standing shocked by the side of a large black BMW. Superintendent Harriet Love, head of Torreston Police Station, climbed from the car and made for the gathering where two offices in uniform were keeping the stunned spectators back from the scene. The tall, elegant, senior officer dressed in a navy trouser suit with a crisp white blouse looking more like a model than a police officer, flicked a strand of auburn hair from her eyes as she approached them.

'What have we got?' she asked, peering into the car her sharp green eyes taking in the scene.

'The guy's been shot in the head, ma'am,' replied the first officer.

'Do we have a name?' asked Harriet.

'George Blackwell, head of the Blackwell Corporation here in the Pegasus Building'.

A Saab screeched to a halt behind them and the tall, blond-haired Chief Inspector Charlie Marlow jumped out and hurried across to join them. 'Morning, Harry,' he said coming up to his boss, 'do we have a murder?'

'We do,' replied Harriet, 'I've contacted Stacey and SOCO and they should be here any minute. We need statements taking from these people when the rest of our team get here, Charlie.'

'I'll see to it,' replied Charlie.

Doctor Stacey Boston and several CID officers were soon busy going about their various jobs. Sergeant Philip Hewitt head of Scene of Crime was already searching the area around the BMW, while another member of SOCO was taking photographs of the body and the car. Both CID and uniform officers were scouring the ground for an ejected bullet or anything that might give them a clue as to who the killer might be. Sergeant Sally Pringle and DC Narinder Pancholi, her friend and house mate were systematically taking down the names of all those people present and turning to Sergeant Duncan McAllister, Sally offered to start at one end of the group if he would organise the statement taking at the other.

'I'll get Ben and Luke onto it as well,' said Duncan taking out his note pad, 'I'll just check with the boss if we can let these people go once we've taken their statements.' He hurried off to speak to Harriet who was talking to the pathologist.

'What can you tell me, Stacey?' she was asking.

'He's been shot at point blank range and less than half an hour go.'

'And obviously through the open window,' said Charlie.

'Perhaps it was someone he knew,' said Harriet, 'if he wound down the window to speak to his killer.'

'Here's his mobile phone, wallet and some keys,' said Stacey handing the objects to Harriet, 'I'll be able to tell you more about his death when I get him back to the morgue. There's no exit hole so the bullet is still in the skull, that should at least help you in determining the weapon used. I'll let Sergeant Hewitt know as I think his men are searching for the bullet casing. I'll do the post-mortem tomorrow at ten, Harry,' she added. 'As its Saturday we won't start as early as usual.'

'Thank you, Stacey,' said Harriet, 'I'll see you in the morning.'

'No DI Cassells today?' asked the pathologist.

'He's off this weekend,' replied Harriet, 'it's his mother's seventieth birthday and he and his wife have gone to Lincolnshire for the celebration.'

'He'll be back on Monday,' said Charlie, 'nice surprise for him to come back to a murder.'

Stacey smiled. 'I think by now he's getting used to surprises, being a member of this team; he seems to have settled in very well.' She turned back to the body. 'See you both tomorrow.'

The coroner's van pulled up alongside the BMW and Stacey organised the removal of the body from the car and the placing of it in the van. The vehicle drove off closely followed by the pathologist in her own car. Duncan stepped forward to speak to Harriet, and Charlie went over to the officers collecting statements. Sally was checking off each person interviewed making sure that no one had been overlooked.

'Everyone accounted for, sir,' she said as Charlie came up, 'not that anyone saw or heard anything.'

'Of course they didn't,' said Charlie, 'who discovered the body?'

'A Mrs Jimson, one of the secretarial staff,' replied Sally, 'the woman over there in the red coat.'

'I'll have a quick word with her,' said Charlie moving away, 'and would you make sure someone speaks to the security guy in the Pegasus building.'

Mavis Jimson was standing with two other women all three of them looking pale and concerned. Charlie went over to them.

'Mrs Jimson?' he said to the woman in the red coat.

Mavis nodded.

'I believe you discovered the body of George Blackwell,' said Charlie.

'Yes I did, it was such a shock.'

'What time was this?'

'Four thirty, we leave early on a Friday.'

'Did you see anyone in the carpark when you arrived?' asked Charlie.

'Not a soul. Most people leave early on a Friday and when I saw Mr Blackwell in his car I went over to say goodnight to him, not that I can think why I did as he rarely replies'.

'He's a rude, ignorant pig', said a young woman standing beside Mavis, 'and none of us like him, or rather liked him, and we're not surprised someone has bumped him off.'

'And you are?' asked Charlie.

'Phyllis Goldsmith, I work in the general office with Mavis.'

The third woman was dabbing her eyes with a handkerchief. 'I'm Mr Blackwell's personal secretary, Sophie Gilbert,' she said, 'and I don't know why I'm upset, he was the rudest person I've ever worked for, but it's still a dreadful shock to learn that he's been killed.'

'Had he any known enemies?' asked Charlie.

'Dozens I should think, I was always having to apologise to people for his behaviour and I was actually thinking of resigning and moving on.'

'We'll need to look over his office,' said Charlie, 'have you got a key?'

'Yes, I had just locked up and left the office less than thirty minutes after him.' She pulled a key from her pocket and handed it to Charlie. 'I'll show you the Blackwell offices and Mr Blackwell's personal room.'

Charlie took the key and went over to Harriet to explain what he was about to do.

'I'll join you,' said Harriet, and following the young secretary they made for the main building.

Chapter Two

At Torreston Police Station Sergeant Jack Fuller was at his computer when the call had come in about the body at Pegasus House car park, Harriet had asked him to stay at his computer and she would contact him as soon as she had a name for the victim. She and other members of CID had headed off for the crime scene and Jack had waited. The plump old-time officer swept a strand of his thinning hair over his balding head and took out his note book and ballpoint pen in readiness.

Superintendent Love telephoned him forty minutes later with the name George Blackwell, asking him to dig up anything he could on the man and now he was busily scrolling through all the files on the police website to see just what they knew about him. Jack was well aware of Blackwell; he was a well-known property developer and bully and in the past the police had received complaints about his aggressive behaviour but in all cases the complaints had been dropped before coming to court. It was suspected that Blackwell's thugs had put pressure on the complainants but nothing came to light and the cases were closed. Jack read the information on the police data-base. Blackwell had been interviewed on several occasions and an eye was being kept on him with regards dubious dealings with him buying up failing businesses and moving them on at exorbitant prices. According to the records, Blackwell was suspected of being the cause of some of the businesses failing in the first place and his cronies of being strong armed bullies applying pressure to make the owners sell up. So far the police had been unable to find enough evidence to bring charges against Blackwell but the man was being kept under surveillance. He was married to an Ursula Hemmingway who was a wealthy woman in her own right. They had been married for twenty years and there were no children. Jack jotted down some notes and then pulled up the details of the Blackwell business onto his screen. He began reading again.

Harriet and Charlie entered Pegasus House with the secretary and followed her up the stairs.

'This is Mr Blackwell's office,' said Sophie stopping outside one of the doors.

'Give Chief Inspector Marlow your address and telephone number and then you can go home, Sophie,' said Harriet, 'we can manage from here. As its Saturday tomorrow the premises will be closed I suppose?'

'Yes, the whole building is locked at the weekend although people with an office have their own keys to the side door so that they can come and go if they need to.'

'How many businesses are in this building?' asked Charlie.

'Oh, several, forty plus, the place was purpose built and modelled on Innovation in Market Harborough. We're not as big as them but the place is doing pretty well. The main reception will have all the company names and there's a large board on the wall downstairs naming everyone.'

'Good, thanks,' replied Charlie, 'we will need Blackwell's home address before you go. I take it he was married?'

'Yes, his wife's called Ursula.'

Charlie took his notepad from his pocket. 'And the address?' he asked.

'Copper Beeches, Newham Drive Torreston.'

'And is there a safe somewhere?' asked Charlie.

'Oh, yes it's here in Mr Blackwell's office.'

'And do you have the combination?'

'No, I'm sorry,' replied Sophie, 'Mr Blackwell was the only person who had access to the safe.'

'Thank you,' said Harriet, 'you should be able to return to work on Monday, but if there's a problem with that there will be a police officer here to advise you otherwise.'

Sophie Gilbert nodded and turned away heading for the stairs. Charlie took the key from his pocket and unlocked the door with the brass plate George Blackwell Director. The Blackwell Corporation had three rooms on the third floor and the office of George Blackwell was the largest of these rooms. A huge ornate desk was placed under the window and there was a large swivel chair behind it and a couple of straight back chairs facing. The desk was somewhat bare, with only a tray holding some ball-point pens, a container of pencils, a telephone, a lap-top and a silver photograph frame containing a picture of a heavily made up, blonde-haired, brown- eyed woman with a rather fleshy face. Harriet picked the photograph up.

'Mrs Blackwell, I presume,' she said.

Charlie gave a wry smile. 'You have to hope it is, she's a bit over the top mind. We'll have to get over to their place to inform her of her husband's death before she hears it on the news.'

'We'll do that as soon as we've finished here,' replied Harriet, 'check his desk and then take the lap-top and anything else that might throw a light on his killing.'

'The guy didn't sound too popular with the clerical staff,' said Charlie, 'they suggest he may well have enemies as he upset so many people.'

They set about looking through the desk drawers and the cupboards but found nothing of any significance other than a diary that Charlie put in his pocket. Harriet opened a wall cupboard and found a safe set in the wall. She called over to Charlie. 'Here's the safe, but I don't suppose any of his keys will open it.' She took the bunch of keys from her pocket that Stacey had handed her and flicked through them. 'Nothing here that looks like a safe key,' she said, 'but anyway it has a combination that we don't have.' She held up a large key. 'This is the key to his office door and there are several others on the ring that we don't know what they are for.'

'Who would know the safe combination do you think?' asked Charlie.

'His secretary didn't, so I doubt if anyone does?' said Harriet.

'We'll ask his wife when we see her,' said Charlie picking up the laptop, 'there's not much more we can do here.'

'We'll put tape across the door,' said Harriet, 'and see what we can do about the safe before we let anyone return.'

'I'll do that,' said Charlie as they left the room. Putting down the laptop and taking a roll of blue tape from his pocket it took only a few minutes for him to put it across the office door, then picking up the laptop again he said; 'Ready to go, Harry?'

'Yes, let's hope Doctor Chong can find something on the laptop,' said Harriet. She had picked up a large folder from one of the drawers in the desk and showed it to Charlie. 'We'll take this as well and get Jack to go through it carefully; there might be something in it that gives us a clue.'

Charlie locked the office door behind them and they made their way to the ground floor using the stairs. 'I don't like lifts,' said Harriet as she descended, 'I'm a bit claustrophobic.'

'How do you cope with aeroplanes?' asked Charlie.

'Badly, I hate flying.'

Charlie chuckled. 'And you flew all that way on your honeymoon.'

'I hung on to Ed, but I can't say I enjoyed it.'

'How is Ed?' asked Charlie, 'I haven't seen him for a while we really ought to get together sometime.'

Harriet's husband Ed Harrington was Chief Inspector over at Central station and although he and Harriet had recently married Harriet was keeping her mother's maiden name of Love to allay any confusion of having two senior officers with the same name in the same force. She had avoided using her father's name of Fitzwilliam as he was a high court judge and she wished to avoid any suggestion that she had been appointed because of her family connection.

'I'll organise something,' said Harriet, 'you'll have to let me know which evenings Liz has off from the hospital so that I can book a table somewhere.'

'Okay, I'll speak to Liz this evening.'

They reached the ground floor where Duncan was speaking to a thick set, middle-aged man by the main doorway. The two senior officers went over to the woman at the reception desk and Charlie asked her name.

'Ann Peters,' replied the woman with just the hint of a central European accent. She was in her fifties, smartly dressed with her dark hair tied back in a chignon. She had equally dark eyes which at this moment looked anxious.

'Such a dreadful business,' she said in a quiet voice. 'I know Mr Blackwell wasn't the most popular of men but he didn't deserve this.'

'Can you tell us who left the building at the same time as Mr Blackwell?' asked Harriet.

'Just secretarial staff about thirty minutes later,' replied the woman. 'Was it they who found Mr Blackwell?'

'Yes it was,' replied Harriet.

'How awful, but they were the only people who left the building after Mr Blackwell.'

'How many staff are there here in the reception area?' asked Harriet'

'Just four, three secretarial and the manager Mr Winston, who isn't here today.'

'Where is he?' asked Charlie.

'On business in Market Harborough.'

'Thank you,' said Harriet.

'Could we have your address and a phone number, please,'

said Charlie, 'Just in case we need to speak to you later, although I presume we can always contact you here.'

'Of course, I'm usually last to leave with Alf Brooks, the security man, that's him over there talking to one of the officers, we lock the building together usually about five.'

'Right, thank you,' said Charlie writing down the address the woman gave him.

They left Pegasus House and returned to the car park where several officers were still there. Blue tape was round the BMW and a notice stating Police Aware was on the windscreen. Philip Hewitt was winding down his team's activities.

'Anything, Philip?' asked Harriet going over to him.

'Nothing, ma'am,' replied the sergeant pushing his large glasses back up his nose. 'No bullet of course and no casing, and nothing to show there was anyone else here; whoever did this was no amateur.'

'Quite frankly,' said Charlie running his hand through his short, blond hair, 'this looks like a professional hit.'

'Good lord,' said Harriet, 'surely not, a hitman in Torreston?'

'Why not,' replied Charlie, 'the killer obviously knew what he was doing, no evidence left and no bullet shell.'

Harriet exhaled loudly. 'Right! Then we need to delve into Blackwell's business very closely to find out who might want the man dead.'

'I'll give this lap-top and diary to Duncan to take back to headquarters,' said Charlie, 'if we're going to visit Mrs Blackwell.'

'Give him the folder as well,' said Harriet, 'and the mobile phone; ask him to give them to Jack. He can get the lap-top down to Doctor Chong; the sooner we find something incriminating the sooner we can track down our killer.'

'Follow me will you, Harry,' said Charlie going over to his car, 'I know the way to Newham Drive.'

'I'm right behind you,' replied Harriet slipping behind the wheel of her car.

Chapter Three

Newham Drive was a leafy avenue of large expensive houses. Some of the buildings were rather ostentatious with palatial pillars at the front, brightly painted shutters and in some cases even a flagpole supporting a fluttering union flag. Harriet followed Charlie's car looking for the beech trees that she supposed would announce the house they were looking for. There did not appear to be any numbers on the houses but many of them had elaborate name plates on the gate or pillar at the bottom of the drive. Ahead of Harriet, Charlie's car suddenly winked left and pulled into a gateway. Harriet followed. She watched as Charlie got out of his car and went to the gates which he pushed open before coming over to speak to her.

'No beech trees,' he said, 'but the nameplate tells us this is the house.' He returned to his car and set off up the drive with Harriet following in her little red Lotus.

Standing at the front door Harriet cast her eyes over the large house. 'It's all very quiet,' she said, 'do you suppose Mrs Blackwell works.'

'I doubt that very much replied,' Charlie, 'but let's see.' He knocked loudly on the door using the ornate lion's head knocker, and they waited.

There was no movement from inside the building and Charlie knocked again.

'There's no one at home, Charlie,' said Harriet. 'You have Blackwell's secretary's phone number, give her a ring and ask if she knows where Mrs Blackwell might be.'

Charlie nodded and took his notebook from his pocket. He checked Sophie's phone number and then punched it into his mobile phone. She answered almost immediately. Having spoken for a few minutes Charlie closed down and turned to Harriet.

'She doesn't know where Mrs Blackmore is but says she often visits her sister, a Connie Hemmingway who lives in Leicester. I have her address, but I'll have to trace the phone number.'

'Do that, Charlie,' said Harriet, 'we do need to speak to the dead man's wife.'

Charlie rang Jack at headquarters and requested the number of Connie Hemmingway and staying on the line Charlie waited. It took Jack barely two minutes to come up with the number and having read it out Jack told Charlie that Hemmingway was the maiden name of Ursula Blackwell.

'Yes, it's her sister,' replied Charlie, 'she obviously hasn't married but thanks for doing that, Jack we may have to go to Leicester to speak to Mrs Blackwell. Don't stay at the station all night we'll sort out the plan of action in the morning.'

'Duncan and the others have returned,' said Jack 'and I've sent the laptop down to Chong, I'm going through the numbers on the dead man's mobile and Sally and Narinder are checking the diary. Duncan's doing the file. I'll tell them all to get off home in a bit and we'll start again in the morning.'

'Good,' replied Charlie, 'see you tomorrow, Jack.' He ended the call and dialled Connie Hemmingway's number.

Connie Hemmingway told Charlie that her sister had spent the day with her and would be returning home to Torreston after dinner that evening.

'I need to speak to Mrs Blackwell,' said Charlie having explained to the sister that he was a police officer. 'So if you'll ask her to remain with you, I and my colleague will come to Leicester.'

'Has something happened?' asked Connie.

'Nothing that I can discuss over the phone, I have your address and we should be with you within the hour.'

Charlie closed his phone and turned to Harriet. 'If we stop off at the station on our way to Leicester you can leave your car there and we'll go in mine. If that's okay with you?' he added hastily.

Harriet smiled. 'That will be fine, Charlie, and while I'm changing cars I'll give Ed a call and let him know I'll be late home; its already after seven. Right, I'll follow you back to the station.'

Having left her car at headquarters Harriet joined Charlie in his car. The drive to Leicester took ninety minutes and they arrived at the house in Oadby just before nine. The house on The Broadway was large, white and elegant. Leaving the car on the roadside they walked up the short drive to the front door which opened before they could knock. The woman they recognised from the photograph in Blackwell's office stood on the doorstep pale and anxious. She had very blonde hair piled up on top of her head and was heavily made up. She wore a very tight black skirt and a voluminous white silk blouse.

'What's happened?' she asked wringing her hands. 'Is it George? Has something happened to him?'

'Shall we go inside,' suggested Harriet. 'I'm Superintendent Love and this is my colleague Chief Inspector Marlow.'

Connie Hemmingway stepped forward and took her sister's arm. 'Come and sit down, Ursula,' she said, 'and then the officers can tell us what this is all about.' She guided her into a room off the main passageway and Harriet and Charlie followed. Once they were all sitting down Harriet spoke.

'There's no easy way of saying this, Mrs Blackwell,' she said quietly, 'but I'm afraid your husband is dead, he was found shot in his car in the Pegasus House car park this afternoon.'

Ursula Blackwell squealed, and her sister let out a loud gasp.

Holding her head in her hands Mrs Blackwell rocked from side to side muttering no, oh no! Her sister went over to her and put her arms around her. 'What exactly happened?' she asked Harriet.

'It seems he was shot through his car window before he left the car park,' replied Harriet.

'You say your sister has been with you all day?' said Charlie, 'what time did she arrive?'

'About ten this morning, she often spends the day with me and goes home later in the evening after we've eaten.'

Ursula lifted a tear-stained face. 'Do you know who did this?' she asked.

'Not yet,' answered Harriet, 'but if you know of anyone who might have a grudge against your husband or anyone who might want him dead, it might help us.'

'There's no one who would want to harm George, he was a lovely man and such a devoted husband; what am I going to do without him?'

'Can your sister stay with you tonight?' asked Charlie turning to Connie, 'It might be a good idea if she kept away from Torreston; the press will be on the warpath for a story.'

'Of course she can stay,' said Connie, 'and you know where she is if you need her.'

'Thank you,' said Harriet, 'we'll leave you to look after your sister and we'll be in touch if there's any development.'

'I'll see you to the door,' said Connie getting to her feet.

'Just one thing more,' said Harriet rising, 'do you know the combination of your husband's safe?'

Ursula shook her head. 'I had nothing to do with George's business, I know absolutely nothing about it.'

'Never mind,' replied Harriet. She and Charlie followed Connie to the front door which she opened and then paused turning to face them. 'My sister is very loyal,' she said quietly, 'she and George were devoted to each other. I know he could be pretty tough in his business at times and I'm sure there were people who disliked him, but he was a decent sort really.'

'I take it you liked him?' suggested Charlie.

'Oh, yes he was always charming whenever he and Ursula came here. I think he was just a different person when he was at work. He liked money and was certainly very good at making it, and he spoiled Ursula rotten. A tear ran down her cheek and quickly she wiped it away. 'I don't know what my sister will do without him, but she can stay here as long as she likes. I'll look after her, don't worry,' she added.

Harriet and Charlie left the house and returned to the car in silence. Charlie started the engine. 'Blackwell sounds like a different person to the one his colleagues describe,' he said.

Harriet nodded. 'I think we're going to discover that there are people who would like to see him dead, and those, like his wife who thought him wonderful. Just to be on the safe side get the local police to check with the neighbours of Mrs Hemmingway that she and her sister were here all day.' she said.

'I'd thought of doing that,' said Charlie, 'but you don't think Ursula Blackwell had anything to do with her husband's death, do you?'

'I think we're going to have our work cut out tracking down the actual killer,' replied Harriet.

Charlie looked at his watch. 'It's gone eight thirty, Harry, let's get back.' He did a three-point turn in the road and headed back to Torreston.

Chapter Four

When Duncan had returned to headquarters he immediately handed Jack the diary and folder from Blackwell's office. 'The boss thought you'd have a field day searching through this little lot,' he said, 'I'm to take the laptop to Doctor Chong.'

'If anyone can get into computers, its Henry,' replied Jack, 'and I think I'll get Narinder involved in searching through these documents, we all know how she likes ferreting.' He grinned, he had a soft spot for the DC and admired her tenacity and determination. He opened the folder and began taking out the papers; he would get Narinder involved as soon as she returned.

It was a quarter to ten when Harriet finally reached home. Ed hugged her as she came through the front door and helped her take off her coat.

'Poor old you,' he said, 'hectic day?'

'You could say that, we've had a business man shot in his car outside his premises and it looks as if he had plenty of enemies any of whom might be the culprit.'

'That'll be George Blackwell,' said Ed, 'it was the main story on the news and according to the report it was some sort of gangland hit.'

'Well we don't know that at present,' replied Harriet, 'but it was certainly a calculated killing; a shot to the head at close quarters.'

'We don't have much gun-crime in Torreston,' said Ed, 'but when you trace the bullet and the make of gun you should have a lead.'

'We can but hope. I take it you've eaten, Ed?'

'Fraid so, but I've saved you some of the casserole.'

Harriet pulled a face. 'It's so late, Ed I really don't think I could eat something like that, it would keep me awake all night.'

'You must eat something, Harry, suppose I make you a light omelette?'

'Thank you,' said Harriet, 'that would be lovely. Have you fed Feather?'

'I have, and she's asleep in her basket. Now sit down and I'll do the honours.'

Harriet in fact slept soundly that night and standing at the front of the CID room with Charlie beside her next morning she explained to the team what had occurred the evening before.

'We think it might be a professional hit,' said Charlie, 'and until the post-mortem is carried out this morning we won't know what sort of weapon was used.'

'According to Dr Boston there is no exit wound in Blackwell's head,' said Harriet, 'so she presumes the bullet is still inside the skull. When we have that we'll start tracking people who might own such a weapon.'

'Are there any known hitmen in the area?' asked Duncan who was a firearms expert and a member of the Fast Response Armed Unit.

'I don't know about hitmen,' replied Harriet, 'but there are some characters we know of who have used guns in the past. Jack, if you're not too busy with the Blackwell paperwork, could you start the search on these people when briefing is over and try and discover where they are at the present time.'

'I can do that, ma'am,' replied Jack, 'I've sought the help of DC Pancholi with the folder and diary I was given, so we should be done very soon.'

'Have you found anything of significance?' asked Harriet.

'Not really, ma'am, several names of Blackwell's clients and paperwork on the deals he made, but nothing you could pinpoint as bent.'

'Keep with it, Jack and write down all those names for me so that they can be interviewed.'

'And, Narinder?' asked Harriet, 'anything from the diary?'

'Plenty of dates with meetings arranged,' replied Narinder, 'and I'm writing them all down too, ma'am so that we can check them later.'

'Good,' said Harriet, 'we'll turn up something sooner or later. Duncan, any news from Doctor Chong and the laptop?'

'I'm waiting to hear from him, ma'am, but I do know he has cracked the password and is into Blackwell's emails.'

'Brilliant, we're getting somewhere at last. We need to get Blackwell's safe open and that might throw some light on what has happened.'

'The rest of you need to start questioning the people known to have had disputes with Blackwell,' said Charlie. 'Sally has the names and addresses of the clerical staff at Pegasus House and they will need to be spoken to again; they were rather in shock yesterday and might be a bit more forthcoming this morning. You will have to visit them at home as it's Saturday.'

'There are a few other thing's in the pipeline,' said Harriet, 'which can't be dismissed even though we have a murder to solve. There has been a spate of house burglaries which all appear to have happened at houses where there has been a death reported in the paper or notification of someone being very ill and taken to hospital; again, reported in the paper. Uniform have been alerted to this and are keeping a watch on houses unoccupied because of these occurrences but they can't be around the whole time. Motor patrol also have been notified and will drive by these premises whenever possible.'

'We've also had a couple of complaints from two young women with long hair who have reported having their hair cut off whilst on the bus,' said Charlie. 'This may well be a one-off incident and never happen again, but we have to show compassion and the women need to be visited.'

This statement was greeted by sniggers and smiles. 'It might appear funny,' said Harriet, 'but these women have been very distressed to find their hair cut when they arrive home. The one similarity is that it happened when they were on the X7 bus.'

'Were they on the same bus at the same time?' asked Sally.

'That I don't know,' replied Harriet, 'but we do need to speak to them both.'

'Have they any suspicions as to who the culprit might be?' asked Narinder fingering her long black hair which at this moment was tied back in a ponytail. 'And please, sir,' she said looking at Charlie, 'don't ask me to spend days riding on busses to see if someone will have a go at me.'

Laughter rang round the room and Charlie grinned. 'No, Narinder I won't ask you to do that,' he said. 'And in answer to your question, the women had no idea their hair had been cut until they arrived home, and no they have no idea who might have done it.

'Do the two women know each other?' asked Sally.

'As the first incident was dealt with by uniform,' said Harriet, 'the hair cutting only reached our attention when the second one was reported so we don't have all the facts. I'll leave it to you to chase that up; we don't want to look as if we don't care.'

'I don't think there's much more we can do about the hair cutting at the moment,' said Charlie, 'but we will interview the victims nevertheless. Uniform are on the alert and if there is another incident reported we'll have to think again about what we do.'

'It's possibly just a silly prank,' said Harriet, 'and there won't be any further hair cutting, we'll see how it goes.'

'Let's hope,' said Charlie. 'Right, we have a great deal to do so let's get cracking. I'd like a volunteer to visit the two women who've had their hair cut and the rest of you can start interviewing the staff from Pegasus House and looking into the house burglaries. Good luck everyone, let's get going.'

Sally and Narinder decided they would speak to the two women as soon as they had finished going through the diary and suggested this to Charlie.

'If I help Narinder with the diary we'll be done within the hour,' said Sally.

'That sounds sensible,' agreed Charlie, 'continue with that then, and when you're done visit these young women. Get back as soon as you can.'

'The interviews shouldn't take long,' said Sally, 'and then we'll get on with the more serious matter of a murder.'

'Hey,' said Narinder poking her friend, 'having your hair cut by some creep is a very serious matter. I'd be really upset if it happened to me.'

'I didn't mean it like that,' replied Sally, 'I'm sure these women are very upset, but nobody died.'

'I think you're digging a hole, Sally,' said Charlie with a grin. 'Just get on with the diary and then go and speak to the women. Report back to me when you return, and I'll suggest who you interview in the Blackwell case.'

Harriet and Charlie arrived at the mortuary at ten to find Stacey waiting for them and pulling on their "greens" and white boots they joined her in the cold, forbidding, white tiled post- mortem room. Blackwell was already on the table and as always Harriet shivered as she stood beside Charlie close to where the action was to take place. The sound of the electric saw alone made her flesh creep and the cutting into the body made her feel physically sick.

Stacey pulled back the white sheet disclosing the dead man, stark white with motley blue patches and with a clear red hole in the middle of his forehead. With her recording system activated and a mouth piece attached to the front of her gown she began her examination of the body.

'We have here a large, overweight man in his late fifties,' she began, 'and the noticeable, obvious cause of death appears to be a gunshot wound to the front of the head. As there is no exit wound I am expecting to discover the bullet inside the skull. I shall therefore open the skull first.' She picked up the electric saw and Harriet swallowed hard and clenched her fists.

Chapter Five

Sally and Narinder completed the scrutiny of Blackwell's diary writing down any dates they thought significant together with the names of whoever was being met by the dead man. Giving Jack the list they had compiled they left the Incident Room and headed for Sally's car. Sally drove to Northampton where they called at the address of the woman who had, had her hair cut on the bus. The young woman's name was Christine Shepherd. She was in her early twenties, of medium height and build with fair hair cut short and was the first of the two young women who had reported having been assaulted on the X7.

The officers showed their warrant cards and asked if they could come in. The young woman nodded and opened the door for them to enter. In the living room Sally spoke.

'You reported your hair being cut whilst travelling on the X7,' said Sally, 'I see it's now short, I take it you had to do this after the assault.'

Christine nodded. 'I couldn't believe what had happened when I met my friend at The Coffeepot in Torreston and she asked me what I'd done to my hair. My ponytail had just been slashed and what was left looked ridiculous. I had coffee and then went to a hairdresser and asked if they could cut my hair.'

'It looks jolly nice,' said Narinder, 'but we're sorry to hear what happened on the bus.'

'You travelled on the X7 from Northampton,' said Sally,

'Yes, from Northampton to Torreston. Parking is so dreadful and also costs quite a bit so I often use the bus.'

24

'And this happened Friday morning,' said Narinder looking at her notes.

Christine nodded. 'Yes, it was my day off and my friend was on the late shift at the restaurant where she works, so we arranged to meet for coffee.'

'Can you remember who sat immediately behind you on the bus?' asked Sally.

Christine shook her head. 'The bus was pretty full, and I can't imagine how anyone could have cut my hair and not be seen.'

'You're the second person to report such an incident,' said Sally, 'and this other person was on the X7 too.'

'Good heavens! So there's a nutter out there travelling on the bus cutting hair.'

'Both of you had long hair,' said Narinder, 'so he or she, might just be interested in young women with ponytails.'

The officers asked a few more questions before leaving the house and returning to the car. 'This other woman was on the X7 going to Market Harborough,' said Sally, 'and she lives in Torreston so we'll head back and have a word with her.'

'Was her hair cut on the same day?' asked Narinder. Sally looked at her notes. 'Yes, but in the evening.'

The second woman was Millie Walters and she like Christine was in her twenties with dark hair and again like the first victim her hair was now short. She told the same story. She was on the X7 going to Market Harborough from Torreston and on arriving at her destination was asked by her friend what on earth had happened to her hair. It was then that Millie discovered that one of her bunches had been removed.

'I burst into tears,' said Millie. 'We were supposed to be meeting friends at Ascoughs where we were booked to have dinner, but I looked such a sight I said I wouldn't go.'

'Can you remember who was sitting behind you on the bus?' asked Sally.

Millie shook her head. 'The bus was quite full, but I can't remember anyone in particular.'

'When did you have your hair cut properly?' asked Narinder.

'Saturday morning. I was staying over at my friend's house in Harborough Friday night and luckily she has a friend who is a hairdresser and she asked her if she could fit me in. She explained to her what had happened and this friend, Sharron, agreed to see me at Jelly Beanz at eight o'clock as a favour.'

'Well she made a good job of your hair,' said Narinder

'We'll keep you informed of any progress,' said Sally, 'and although this won't help your case we can tell you that you are not the only person to suffer with having your hair cut on the X7.'

'Good gracious,' gasped Millie, 'how awful.'

The interview over, Sally and Narinder returned to headquarters to discover a woman with a sobbing teenage girl in the foyer with Sergeant Pete Yates. They went over to see what the problem was but on getting close they could see that the girl, who was about thirteen had one long pigtail and the second had been cut off close to her head. Another victim of the rogue hair cutter?

'Ah, Sergeant,' said Pete Yates as Sally approached. 'This young lady has had her hair cut whilst travelling on the X7, can I leave you to deal with it?'

'Yes, we'll take over,' said Sally, 'come with us,' she said turning to the woman and teenager.

Once in an interview room Sally invited them to sit down and Narinder took out her note book and asked for their names.

'I'm Mrs Chadwick and this is my daughter Karen,' said the woman with her arm around her daughter. 'Karen's pride and joy is her long hair,' she said desperately trying to console her daughter. 'We go to Market Harborough every Saturday morning on the X7 for Karen's piano lesson and you can imagine my horror when we arrived back in Torreston a short time ago and I saw she had only one plait; as you can see the other one has been chopped off.'

'And this happened on the bus?' asked Sally.

'Must have done, she definitely had two plaits when we got on the bus to come back because I got on behind her, and one was gone when we arrived back in Torreston. We came straight here to the police station.'

The girl looked up and pressed her hands to her eyes. 'It's taken me years to grow my hair,' she wailed, 'who could have done this to me.'

'You're the third young lady to have had her hair cut on the X7,' said Narinder.

'No!' gasped Mrs Chadwick, 'have you any idea who has done this?'

'Not at the moment,' replied Sally, 'but we're working on it.'

'We have your address if we need you,' said Narinder, 'and we're very sorry for your distress.'

'We'll be in touch if we discover anything,' added Sally. 'I suppose you'll be going to a hairdresser to have Karen's hair cut now.'

Karen began to howl again, and her mother put her arms around her. 'It'll grow again, darling,' she said, 'come along, we'll see if Orlando will fit us in.'

Once they had gone Sally and Narinder climbed the stairs to the CID block. 'I'm glad I don't have to use the bus,' said Narinder, 'cos you can bet your bottom dollar I'd lose my hair.'

'The difference being that you'd catch the blighter,' said Sally grinning.

'Well, it's hard to believe that someone can sneak up behind you and cut your hair,' said Narinder, 'and on a busy bus at that.'

'Well we'll see what we can do about the hair-cutter, but for now we'll try and help with this murder,' said Sally opening the door to CID. 'On Monday we'll have a word with the bus drivers to see if they can remember any regular customer who was on the

X7 at the times of the hair cutting,'

'We'd better find DCI Marlow and discover who we have to speak to about the Blackwell killing,' said Narinder, 'he and the boss should be back from the PM soon.'

Doctor Boston concluded the post-mortem telling Harriet and Charlie that there was little more she could tell them other than Blackwell had been killed by a single gunshot to the head. The bullet had been extracted from the skull and put in an evidence pot which Charlie had taken. This would go immediately to Forensics for close examination to give them the type of gun used in the murder. Harriet informed Stacey that if there were no complications then the body could be released for burial. Thanking her they left the mortuary to return to headquarters.

Narinder pounced on Charlie the minute he appeared in the Incident Room. She told him what she and Sally had done in relation to the hair-cutter and that they would keep an eye on the situation. Charlie agreed there wasn't a great deal more they could do at the moment and advised them to join in the interviewing of people in the Blackwell murder. In her office Harriet telephoned Ursula Blackwell at her sister's house and told her of the result of the post- mortem and that she could have the body of her husband collected by the undertaker and arrangements for his funeral could be started. Loud sobbing could be heard over the telephone and Harriet wasn't sure what she could say at distance to comfort the widow. Eventually the crying subsided and Harriet told Ursula how sorry she was at the death of her husband and if there was anything the police could do to help she was to contact her personally.

'Just catch the bastard who did this,' replied Ursula, and then she hung up.'

Harriet wrinkled her nose and replaced the receiver.

Chapter Six

Monday morning was cold and very foggy; November weather was taking over. Harriet wrapped her thick scarf around her neck and kissed Ed goodbye. 'I'll do my best not to be too late home tonight,' she said, 'what about you?'

'We're pretty slack at the moment,' replied Ed, 'but we are investigating this spate of house burglaries in homes where someone elderly has been reported taken to hospital or died.'

'Yes, we're onto that as well,' said Harriet, 'we've had a couple on our patch.'

'Pretty low-life criminals to target people like that,' said Ed, 'but with luck we'll catch them. There are no further break-ins reported in this morning's paper, but your murder is on the front page.'

'I haven't looked at the paper this morning,' said Harriet, 'I'll read it when I get to the station.'

'Drive carefully in this fog,' said Ed, 'it's pretty thick. I should be able to get off at a reasonable time tonight, how about we eat at the Red Lion, it seems a long time since we were there.'

'Great idea,' replied Harriet, 'and I'll check if Charlie and Liz can make it too. If they can I'll book a table for seven o'clock.'

'Good, text me when you know what's happening.'

Charlie was already at the station when Harriet arrived, and she found him in the Incident Room making sure they had everything necessary for a murder investigation. 'Thought I'd get the place sorted out before everyone arrived,' he said as Harriet came into the room.

'Yes, we'll need it now we have a murder on our hands,' agreed Harriet.

'The newspaper is over there,' said Charlie, 'if you want to read about Blackwell's murder. Mrs Blackwell has given an interview to the press and there's a tearful photograph of her on the front page with her sister.'

'Thanks, Charlie, I'll read it later. On another subject, are you and Liz able to join Ed and me at the Red Lion tonight?'

'Unbelievingly,' replied Charlie grinning, 'Liz suggested just that last night as she has the day off tomorrow and is on the early shift today. So yes, that would be great.'

'Right, I'll book a table for seven o'clock,' said Harriet, 'something to look forward to if we're to have a busy day. I'll text Ed straight away to let him know.'

Officers began arriving and the newest member of the team, Inspector Earl Cassells came over to Harriet and thanked her for allowing him to have the weekend off and how his mother had appreciated him being there for her birthday.

'I'm glad all went well,' said Harriet, 'but we now have a murder on our hands, so you may well not get another for some time.'

'Who's been killed?' asked Cassells.

Harriet explained about the shooting of Blackwell and then called the team to order for briefing.

'We will have the results of the bullet back this morning,' she said, 'giving us the type of weapon used. We then need to track anyone who might own such a gun.'

'Trouble is,' said Charlie, 'the killer may own such a gun, but it may well not be registered.'

'It appears to be a professional hit,' said Harriet, 'which is rather disturbing. We're not used to this sort of thing happening here in Torreston.' She continued. 'SOCO found nothing at the crime scene that might help us in our investigation, so your interviews with the staff at Pegasus House could prove valuable. Did anyone turn up anything that might help us?'

'No one seems to have liked Blackwell,' said Duncan, 'in fact the people I spoke to hated him.'

'Who were these people you spoke to?' asked Harriet.

'His personal secretary, Sophie Gilbert who was thinking of leaving as she found him so obnoxious.'

'We had the same response,' said Ben, a young DC. 'The staff in the main foyer all loathed him'.

'But none of these were likely to kill him, were they,' said Charlie.

'So it's more likely the killer was someone he'd done business with,' suggested Harriet, 'and most probably cheated them.'

'From all accounts there are several of those, 'said Jack. 'I have here the name of an Antonio Romano who publicly threatened to deal with Blackwell after shouting at him in the foyer of Pegasus House and calling him a crook. He actually said he'd kill him if he didn't repay the money he'd paid for some business that turned out to be worthless.'

'His name turned up in the diary,' said Narinder, 'Blackwell had several meetings with him. Sergeant Fuller has our report from the diary with a list of names and dates of his meetings.'

'Good,' said Harriet, 'and has this man Romano been spoken to yet?'

'No, ma'am,' replied Jack, 'he's been in Italy over the weekend according to a neighbour, but this could be a cover for an alibi. Perhaps he's a member of the Mafia, which would account for the shooting.'

'Let's hope not,' said Harriet, 'we can do without a Mafia hitman on the loose in Torreston. But thank you, Jack, Chief Inspector Marlow and I will speak to him today if he's back.'

'The neighbour said he and his wife would be back this morning,' said Jack, 'here's his address, ma'am.' He handed Harriet a slip of paper which she put in her pocket.

'And does someone have the list of Blackwell's other clients?' asked Charlie.

'I have the names we were given at Pegasus House,' said Duncan, 'Sophie Gilbert gave them to me and she's marked the ones he fell out with. I presume they'll match the ones in his diary. We also have access to his laptop now, thanks to Doctor Chong, and we've printed off his bank statements.'

'Good,' said Charlie, 'let me have the list of clients and his bank statements as soon as briefing's over, we also need to speak to the manager of Pegasus House he was away on Friday.'

'On another matter,' said Harriet, 'Central are also dealing with the house burglaries of elderly people who have been reported in the local paper as having died or been taken to hospital, so this is something else we need to keep an eye on. Inspector Cassells,' she said turning to Earl, 'can I put you in charge of this investigation, Jack has the names of the victims on our patch and by all means speak to DCI Harrington at Central so that you can compare notes.'

'Yes, ma'am,' said Earl.

'Any further news on the hair-cutter?' asked Charlie looking at Sally.

'Nothing more to add to what I told you yesterday, sir,' replied the sergeant, 'there have been three now. We spoke to the two whose names we'd been given and then when we returned to the station we discovered a teenager in tears having had one of her plaits cut off.'

'And again, on the X7,' added Narinder.

'None of the victims can remember anyone in particular sitting behind them on the bus,' said Sally 'so we thought we'd have a word with the drivers this morning.'

'Yes, do that,' agreed Harriet, 'and check to see if there are any CCTV cameras at the bus station. You might spot the same person getting on the bus at the times of the incidents.'

'We'll do that,' replied Sally.

'We have two officers from Tech going to Blackwell's office this morning,' said Charlie, 'they will be opening the safe, and that should prove interesting if they succeed.'

'It will be forced,' added Harriet, 'as no keys have been found and no one seems to know the combination. We do need to see what the man has tucked away inside. Right,' she said turning to Charlie, 'I'll leave you to sort out the day then meet me in my office and we'll visit this Antonio Romano.' She left the Incident Room and made her way down the passage.

Chapter Seven

In her office Harriet picked up the newspaper and looked at the picture on the front page. Ursula Blackwell was standing with her sister on the front steps of Connie Hemmingway's house. Connie had an arm around her sister's shoulders and both women were tearfully dabbing their eyes. Beneath the photograph was the story of the shooting of George Blackwell. The report stated that the victim was well known in the area and had a reputation for some suspect deals and had appeared in court in the past for illegal transactions and alleged money laundering. In all cases Blackwell had been cleared and reading the name of his solicitor Harriet was not surprised. Humphrey Bardwell-Fox was well known as a supporter of shady characters and in the profession thought to be bent. Certainly, the police were wary of him and never too happy when criminals in custody named him as their solicitor. Harriet was relieved to read that there was no mention of the killing being done by a hit-man and secretly hoped that in fact this was not the case. Charlie arrived carrying a cafetière of coffee and a jug of milk.

'Thought you'd be ready for this,' he said grinning, 'I presume you still keep your china mugs in your desk cupboard?'

'I do indeed,' replied Harriet taking them out and placing them on her desk.

Charlie pressed the plunger. 'Have you reserved a table at The Red Lion for tonight?' he asked.

'I have, for seven o'clock and I've sent a text to Ed.'

'Excellent I'll do the same to Liz.'

Harriet held the newspaper up. 'The Blackwell murder is front page news,' she said.

'That's not surprising,' answered Charlie, 'we rarely have

shootings on our patch after all.'

'We should hear from Forensics this morning as to the bullet that was used.'

'We then have to match it to a weapon, and there won't be any such weapon registered, I bet,' said Charlie.

'We'll have coffee and then go over to the address of Antonio Romano,' said Harriet, 'I've asked Jack to see if we have this man on file.'

'I've never heard of him,' said Charlie, 'but if he is a crook perhaps he's never been caught.' He poured the coffee and handed Harriet a mug. 'We'll spread the word among our informants to see if any of them know of any shooters in the area.'

'Worth a try,' agreed Harriet, taking a sip of her coffee. 'Hmm, this always makes me feel better, thank you, Charlie.'

Sally and Narinder arrived at Northampton bus station and made for the X7 stand. Two drivers were standing by the bus they were interested in and Sally showed her warrant card. 'There have been a few incidents of young women having their hair cut while travelling on the X7,' she said, 'I don't suppose you've seen anything strange on the bus that might be a cover for someone doing this?'

'Blimey,' said one of the men, 'now I've heard everything.'

'Were either of you driving the bus to Market Harborough, Friday morning at nine or the return trip from Harborough on Saturday morning around ten?' asked Narinder.

'I did the Saturday run out,' said the second man, 'then I went on to Kibworth. What time did the hair cutting happen?'

'The teenager got on the X7 in Harborough at ten,' said Sally, 'and the mother thinks that's when her daughter's hair was cut.'

The second man nodded furiously. 'Yes, I drove that bus back, but I can't say I saw anything weird happening on board.'

'Can we ask you to keep an eye open?' asked Narinder, 'the victims have long hair either a ponytail or plaits as in the case of this teenager who was terribly upset to discover one missing when she got off the bus.'

'It's some nutter,' said the first driver, 'but we'll keep a look out for anyone lurking behind women with long hair. Trouble is you have to keep your eye on the road, there are some pretty crazy drivers out there.'

'Thank you,' said Sally. 'We're going to have a look at the CCTV images to see if we spot the same person getting on the X7 at the times of the incidents.'

'Good luck with that one,' said the second driver, 'the cameras here haven't worked since the new station opened. Perhaps if you made a fuss they'll rectify that.' He looked at his watch. 'Got to go, I'm due out in two minutes.'

Sally and Narinder left the bus station having been told that unfortunately the CCTV wasn't yet working and decided that they had better join the rest of the team at Pegasus House. Arriving at the business park twenty minutes later they found the place a hive of activity. Duncan came up to them as they entered the building. 'We're speaking to everyone possible,' he said, 'definitely all those who worked for Blackwell but anyone else we can. We're ticking their name off on this list when we've spoken to them.' He held up a sheet of paper. 'Pick a name that hasn't been ticked,' he continued, 'and off you go.'

Sally looked at the list. 'How about this guy who has the office next door to Blackwell?' she said, 'neighbours often see and hear things.'

'Good thinking,' said Duncan, 'tick him off, and after that could you speak to Conrad Winston, the manager'

'Will do,' said Sally.

'There's a small coffee shop over there so have a coffee before you start,' said Duncan

'I'm gasping for one,' said Narinder, 'let's do that.'

'This place is just like Innovations in Market Harborough,' said

Sally as they walked through the foyer, 'not as big and not as plush but very similar.'

'How do you know that?' asked Narinder.

'Gerry has a friend who has an office there and I've been with him a couple of times. The café there is pretty special, it's owned by a young woman called Karen who makes the cakes herself and they're excellent.'

'Let's hope it's the same here then,' replied Narinder, 'I quite fancy a homemade cake.'

They made their way to the café area and dumped their bags on a chair at a small table before going to the counter to order.

Harriet and Charlie arrived at the address Jack had given them. The house was a converted barn and appeared to be made of mainly glass on the ground floor. The interior was plainly visible to those outside the building and looked rather like an advertisement from some glossy magazine. There were lights on in every downstairs room encouraging the onlooker to take stock of the elaborate furnishings and huge paintings on the walls that were not totally glass. Charlie rang the bell at the all glass front door and they stood and gazed down the long passageway inside the house.

'So much for privacy,' said Charlie, 'this is a bit like living in a greenhouse.'

'Each to their own,' replied Harriet, 'not that this is my cup of tea.'

Charlie rang the bell again and this time they were rewarded by the appearance of a large man striding down the corridor. The door was opened by a stocky man with a substantial black beard and piercing dark eyes. He scowled at them.

'Yes?' he demanded.

Harriet held up her warrant card. 'Superintendent Love,' she announced, 'and this is my colleague Chief Inspector Marlow. Are you Antonio Romano?'

The man nodded. 'Yes.'

Charlie flashed his card. 'We're investigating the murder of George Blackwell,' he said, 'and we would like a word with you.'

The man continued to scowl. 'What's this about? I had a bust up with that creep and threatened to kill the shit, but I assure you it wasn't me who finally got him.'

'Could we come in?' asked Harriet, 'we can hardly discuss this on the doorstep.'

Romano opened the door and stood to one side to allow them to pass. They were shown into a large, rather bare room, sparsely furnished and with one whole side of it glass. They were invited to sit down. For all his size Romano had a strangely soft voice with barely the trace of a foreign accent. Facing the officers, he asked them what exactly had happened to Blackwell.

'He was shot in the head at close range as he sat in his car,' said Charlie.

'And this was on Friday afternoon?'

Charlie nodded. 'Could you tell us where you were on Friday at five o'clock?'

Romano smiled showing a set of perfect white teeth. 'I was in Milan with my wife, we returned home on Saturday.'

At that moment the door opened and a petite, dark haired woman entered the room. She was in her forties with large dark eyes and beautifully arranged hair in a coil on top of her head. She was elegantly dressed in an obviously expensive purple dress and matching shoes.

'My wife, Arianna,' announced Romano proudly. He walked over to her and put an arm around her waist. 'These are police officers,' he said, 'and they would like to know where we were on Friday afternoon.'

Mrs Romano nodded but she didn't smile. 'I heard you mention Mr Blackwell,' she said, her Italian accent much more pronounced than her husbands. 'He was a bad man, and I am not sorry he is dead, he cheated us out of a great deal of money as he did other people so it is not surprising someone killed him.'

'If he was shot,' said Romano, 'I can tell you now I have no gun and never have had a gun, but I will show you our travel documents and the receipt from the hotel we stayed at in Milan.'

'Thank you,' said Harriet, 'that would be ideal, we do have to eliminate everyone who had dealings with Blackwell, from our enquiries.'

'I will get the paperwork,' said Mrs Romano, and she left the room.

As they left the Romano house ten minutes later, Harriet suggested to Charlie that he get someone to check the flights to and from Milan to make sure the Romano's were actually on them. 'We have to be absolutely sure all our suspects who give us alibis are genuinely in the clear,' she said.

'I'll get Jack onto it straight away,' said Charlie opening the door of his car for Harriet, 'he thrives on doing that sort of thing.'

Chapter Eight

The company renting the office next door to Blackwell was Clarity Accountants, the director being Graham Gulliver. Although the offices of Blackwell were still cordoned off Harriet had allowed the other companies to continue working and knocking on the door marked "Clarity Accountants" Sally and Narinder entered without waiting for a response. A young man, no more than twenty-five or six sat at a desk facing the door. He jumped to his feet as the two women came in.

'Can I help you?' he asked looking somewhat nervous.

Sally showed her warrant card. 'Sergeant Pringle,' she said with a smile, 'and this is my colleague DC Pancholi. I take it you are Graham Gulliver.'

'Ah, police,' said the young man sitting down again, 'yes, I'm Gulliver, this must be about George Blackwell.'

'It is indeed,' replied Sally, 'what can you tell us about him?'

'Other than he's, or was, a loud-mouthed bully, not a lot.'

'Did you have dealings with him?' asked Narinder.

'Not if I could help it. I kept out of his way. He's the only person in the building with more than one room, and no one is sure how he managed it. The place is supposed to be for new businesses getting started and we each have a single office or shared office, which we pay rent to the council for. Blackwell comes along and hey-presto he has three rooms and already has a flourishing business. You explain that to me. '

'You think there was corruption, somewhere do you?' asked

Sally.

'Had to be, how else does he get three rooms and already had an on-going business. He was certainly no beginner just starting out like the rest of us.'

'We'll look into it,' said Sally, 'but all a bit late as the guy is dead.'

'But you can weed out whoever it was taking a handout from him,' said Gulliver.

'We'll certainly have a go,' said Narinder, 'we like digging for dirt, Mr Gulliver.'

The young man suddenly smiled allowing his thin, pale face to lighten up. 'Call me Geegee,' he said somewhat sheepishly, 'everyone does, and I promise you I have no connection to horses.'

Sally handed Gulliver her card and asked him to call should he think of anything that might help them in the investigation into Blackwell's death. The two women left the office and went to the next door on that floor where Sally knocked, and they entered. Here there were four desks in the room each with a computer in place but with only two of them occupied. The two men sitting behind their computers looked up. One immediately stood but the other glanced briefly at the two women and then dropped his head and continued to tap away at the keys.

'Police,' said Sally holding up her warrant card.

'I guessed as much,' said the young man who was standing.

The other man, who like the first was in his late twenties or early thirties, lifted his head.

'I presume you're here about that shit Blackwell,' he growled. 'Good riddance I say, it's no surprise someone knocked him off.'

'You didn't like him then,' said Narinder with a wry smile.

'You could say that!'

Sally turned to the man standing. 'I take it you feel the same?' she asked.

'Absolutely, he was pretty obnoxious and treated the younger members in Pegasus House like trash.'

'And strictly speaking,' snapped the other man, 'we are the true business people who should be housed here. Blackwell was the intruder and should never have been allowed to rent rooms here in the first place. Pegasus House was set up to get new businesses running, and most of us as you can imagine are run by youngish people. No way did Blackwell fit the profile so we all knew something fishy was going on.'

'And not only that,' said the first man, 'but the agreement clearly states that you may only have one office space and most of these are in shared rooms, like ours.'

'So how the hell did Blackwell end up with three rooms,' fumed the young man sitting behind his desk, 'and only he can afford a personal secretary.'

'We're going to look into it,' said Narinder.

'About time someone did,' said the first man, 'we've been complaining for months.'

'Who is the person you complained to?' asked Narinder.

'Councillor Frank Abbot,' they replied in unison.

'And the manager here, Mr Winston,' added one of the men.

Narinder wrote the names in her note book. 'Thanks, we'll pay the councillor a visit and have a word with Mr Winston.'

'If you would give us your names and business cards we'll keep you informed of what progress we make,' said Sally.

Both men handed over business cards and Sally and Narinder left. Outside the door they paused. 'A strong smell of corruption,' said Sally wrinkling her nose, 'if this Blackwell was as powerful as it seems, he would have had no problem putting pressure on a councillor to give him favours.'

'Especially with a hefty backhander,' added Narinder.

'We'll tell the boss about this and see if she wants us to dig deeper at the council offices.'

'And knowing the boss, she will,' replied Narinder with a grin.

'Come on,' said Sally, 'we'll speak to the manager and then check with Duncan to see if all the interviews here have been completed. We still have some of Blackwell's clients to speak to.' They made their way down the stairs to where several police officers were gathered in the foyer.

At reception Sally saw a tall man in his forties talking to one of the women. As she knew there was only one man in this area, apart from the security officer, she presumed him to be Winston. As he turned she recognised him but was unsure as to where from. The man caught her eye and came through the door to meet her.

'You must be police,' he said with a disarming smile, 'but I hadn't realised they allowed such attractive women on the force.'

'Sergeant Pringle and DC Pancholi,' said Sally, 'and I presume you are the manager.'

'Yes, Conrad Winston at your service. Dreadful business this murder of Blackwell but what can I do to help?'

'Tell us anything you know about people Blackwell dealt with and who openly showed dissent towards him.' said Narinder.

'Hmm, well, there were plenty of those I'm afraid. He wasn't the most popular man but of course he didn't deserve to be shot.'

'Can you tell us how it was that he had three offices when the regulations say each person was allowed only one?' asked Sally.

'Ah, yes, that did bother me,' replied Winston, 'but all the lettings are done by the council, not me, and although I did query it I didn't get a satisfactory answer.'

'So, what did you do about it?' asked Narinder sharply.

'I was still looking into it.'

'Don't I know you from somewhere?' asked Sally.

'I don't think so, and I know I'd remember you had we met

before. I never forget attractive women.' Winston's blue eyes sparkled, and he flicked back his fair hair with a flourish.

'You weren't here on Friday,' said Narinder, 'may we ask where you were?'

'Over in Market Harborough. I had a meeting at the Innovation Centre, a business complex like Pegasus House, it's the place that this building is modelled on.'

'That's where I've seen you,' said Sally, 'I was there with my boyfriend a couple of months ago and you were in reception.'

Winston smiled. 'What a pity we weren't introduced,' he said, 'but yes, I go there reasonably often, it's quite a place and I'd like Pegasus House to be more like it.'

'Good luck with that,' said Narinder, 'but if you think of anything or anyone who might have information regarding this murder please ring the station.'

'If I do I shall ask for you two.' Winston stuck out his hand. 'Great meeting you both and I hope we meet again.'

They shook his hand and walked away.

'He's pretty dishy,' said Narinder.

'And pretty smooth,' replied Sally, 'rather full-on and over the top.'

Going over to Duncan they told him they had spoken to the people on the floor where Blackwell had his rooms and also the manger and was there anyone else he wanted them to interview.

'I think we're all done here,' said Duncan. 'Have you discovered anything that might be helpful?'

Sally shook her head. 'Only that no one seems to have liked Blackwell, and no one is very upset or surprised that he's been killed.'

'That's what everyone else has reported,' replied Duncan, 'we'll get back to the station and report to the boss.'

Harriet and Charlie arrived back at headquarters to be greeted by Jack waving a large white envelope. 'The forensic report on the bullet, ma'am,' he said.

'Excellent.' Harriet took the envelope and quickly opened it. 'The bullet is a nine millimetre,' she announced.

'All we need now is the gun that fired it,' said Charlie.

Duncan entered the room at that moment and heard what Charlie said. 'Does that mean we know the type of bullet, ma'am?' he asked.

Harriet nodded and handed Duncan the report. He read what was written there. 'Could have been fired from a Glock or a Beretta,' he said, 'both common weapons particularly favoured by thugs.'

'Do you know of any gangsters who handle either weapon?' asked Charlie.

'One name springs to mind,' replied Duncan, 'but I think he's still inside. I'll look into it and let you know of any others who use a Glock or a Beretta. I'm down at the firing range this evening so I'll ask around.'

'Thank you, Duncan,' said Harriet, 'it's alarming to think there's a gunman out there.'

'If it is a hitman,' said Duncan, 'and the killing of Blackwell was a paid hit, then the shooter could have been brought in, say from London, Manchester or some other city, I honestly don't know of any such guys on our patch.'

'That's reassuring, I suppose,' replied Harriet. 'Get back to us as soon as you learn anything, Duncan.'

As Duncan left Harriet's office two stocky young men wearing navy overalls appeared in the doorway. Charlie jumped to his feet and went over to them inviting them in. To Harriet he said; 'Sergeants Crisp and Rogers, ma'am from the Technology department. Hopefully with good news about Blackwell's safe.'

'Ma'am,' said one of the men stepping forward. He placed a

cardboard box on the desk in front of Harriet. 'It was a small safe and we had no problem opening it. This is everything we found in it.'

'Excellent,' said Harriet.

'Well done, Crisp,' said Charlie, 'I knew if anyone could open the safe it would be you and Rogers.'

Sergeant Crisp smiled. 'I've often thought perhaps we were in the wrong line of work and should be working together at night opening safes.'

Sergeant Rogers chuckled. 'Knowing my luck, we'd get caught on our first venture.' Harriet opened the lid of the box and looked inside. 'Phew,' she gasped, 'Am I seeing what I think I'm seeing?'

'You are, ma'am,' said Crisp, 'over fifty thousand pounds in fifties and twenties; we couldn't believe our eyes either.'

'Anything else of interest in there?' asked Charlie.

'Some letters and papers, and a photograph of good-looking young woman who we doubt is the guy's wife,' replied Rogers with a grin.'

Charlie felt under the money and pulled out the letters and papers and a framed photo of a dark-haired, dark-eyed woman her late twenties. He held it for Harriet to see.

'Not the same woman as he has on his desk in his office,' said Charlie, 'and we know that was his wife, but his one! Hmm.'

'Thank you for this, gentlemen,' said Harriet to Crisp and Rogers, as she tapped the box. 'We'll have the money checked out for forgeries and let you know the outcome.'

'Thank you, ma'am,' said Sergeant Crisp, 'and any time you need our help, just call.' The two men left the room and Harriet sat looking at the things in front of her. 'Blackwell certainly had secrets,' she said, 'where on earth did he get all this money from, Charlie?'

'He'll be in the money-laundering business,' said Charlie

dourly, 'more searching into his goings on is needed.'

'He must have upset someone,' said Harriet.

'Probably double-crossed them,' agreed Charlie. As he sat talking he took the photograph of the young woman out of its frame. 'Here we are,' he said reading the inscription on the back. 'My Darling Rosetta'

'So, he had a mistress on the side,' mused Harriet, 'but that wouldn't have got him killed surely?'

'You never know,' replied Charlie, 'she's quite a beauty though and with a name like Rosetta and her dark looks she could be Italian. Well, we'll carry on delving into his past and eventually we'll uncover what was happening.'

'Let's hope so,' said Harriet. 'She picked up the bundle of letters. 'You're correct about the woman, Charlie, the stamps on these letters are Italian.' She handed them to him. 'And of course, they were not sent to his home, they are all addressed to Pegasus House. Give them to Narinder and let her go through them, it does look as if they're from our mystery woman.'

'We had another Italian on our list didn't we,' said Charlie, 'Antonio Romano, the guy who threatened to kill Blackwell.'

'But his alibi checked out, he was in Milan at the time of Blackwell's murder and Jack checked that he and his wife were definitely on the plane.'

'That's true,' agreed Charlie, 'but I reckon I'll keep an eye on him just the same.'

Chapter Nine

Freddie "Fingers" Maloney read about the murder of George Blackwell, but he was more interested in the fact that Mrs Blackwell was staying with her sister leaving the big house unoccupied. Freddie had never done an honest day's work in his life, living on benefits and his sharp brain. He was doing very nicely at the moment helping himself from houses where the owners were either in hospital or who had died, and he saw no reason why this shouldn't continue. He had no scruples; the dead were dead and the ill just unlucky. He needed money to survive and he had simply discovered an ingenious and profitable method of doing just that. He had a reliable fence for the objects he acquired and there didn't seem to be any problem moving the 'goods' on. Tonight, he would investigate the big house in Newham Drive; all being well there would be no one at the house and he could take his time in ransacking the place. He knew all about Blackwell, a crook if ever there was one, so really this was payback time. Freddie was a thin, wiry character, forty-five years of age with light brown hair with a reddish tint and sunken, shifty grey eyes. He grinned showing his uneven, yellow teeth and taking a packet of cigarettes from the side table he lit up, carefully replacing the packet on his table and making sure it was in line with the grain of the wood. As he blew smoke rings into the air he began planning the night's operation.

Leaving headquarters at seven, Duncan headed for the police firing range. As a member of the Swift Response Armed Team, he was obliged to keep up the training and this he did regularly. The small firearms range was in the basement of the old police station on Barrow Road, no longer used as a headquarters but busy as a training centre for many things, especially the firearms officers. Duncan swiped his card at the door and made his way down the stairs to the basement. There was an ante-room where the officers could change and where there were rows of secure cabinets where the guns were kept. A sergeant sat at a desk just inside the room where the officers had to sign in before being given a key to a gun case. Duncan acknowledged the sergeant, signed in and was handed a key. Before collecting a weapon, Duncan spoke to the sergeant, a large man in his late fifties with thick white hair and huge hands. Sergeant Jock Morgan had been a firearms officer for over thirty years and was considered one of the best shots in the force. Now nearing retirement, he was taking on more office work at the firearm base, and his love of guns and shooting made him happy to look after the department and to train the younger men, and some women, in the art of shooting.

'Jock, you'll have read about the shooting of George Blackwell,' said Duncan, 'Forensics have checked the bullet, a nine millimetre, and put it on file. I wondered if you had the names of any known crooks in the area who could have a weapon such as a Glock or Beretta that could have fired it.'

Sergeant Morgan pulled a face. 'Bert Coughlan used a Beretta in that post office hold up last year, but he's still serving time, so you can rule him out. Then there's Jamal Rodriguez who we're pretty sure has a Glock, but again I reckon he's back in Jamaica, you'll have to check that one out.'

'Anyone else?' asked Duncan.

'Oh, there'll be others but catching the blighters is a different kettle of fish.'

'What happened to the Beretta Coughlan used in the post office holdup?' asked Duncan.

'Good point, it was never found when we arrested him.'

'So how did you know he used one?'

'Because the tech department blew up the CCTV image of the hold up and the weapon was clearly identified as a Beretta.'

'And Coughlan? How was he identified?'

'He was stopped at a road block and still had the hoodie and balaclava in the car boot together with the money he'd stolen. He could hardly deny being involved.'

'But the gun was missing.'

'That's a sore point,' replied Jock scowling. 'The gun wasn't in the car and he denied ever having it. We think he had an accomplice, someone in the car waiting for him, but he denied that too and we never managed to prove otherwise.'

Duncan thought about what he had just been told. 'So the Beretta could be out there somewhere,' he said.

'Oh, it's definitely out there.'

'Did he fire the gun in the post office?' asked Duncan.

'One shot,' replied Jock, 'just to scare we reckon, and before you ask, yes, the bullet was retrieved and it's on file.'

Duncan grinned. 'So we can match it with the bullet that killed Blackwell.'

'You can indeed.'

Duncan thanked the sergeant and made his way to the range to start his training.

Harriet and Ed arrived at the Red Lion to discover Charlie and Liz already at their table. There were hugs and handshakes all round followed by consultation of the menu.

'It's a long time since we all met here,' said Liz, who was a sister at the local hospital.

'Too long,' agreed Harriet, 'we're all working too hard.'

'And certainly, too long a day,' added Charlie, 'the nurses at the hospital are now working these long days, as they're called, sixteen hours plus, and that can't be right. Liz gets home shattered goes to bed exhausted and has to leap out of bed at the crack of dawn to do another shift.'

'Something will be done when an over worked nurse makes a

mistake,' said Ed.

'But no one wants that,' said Liz, 'we just need more staff. But enough shop talk, let's get down to ordering dinner.'

Inevitably whilst eating, the conversation drifted back to work and the shooting of George Blackwell.

'No leads then?' asked Ed.

'Not a sausage,' replied Charlie, 'other than we now know the bullet was a nine millimetre.'

'And you think it might have been an organised hit?' asked Ed.

'Looks as if it might be,' agreed Harriet, 'but we don't have any knowledge of such people on our patch.' She had told Ed of the find in the safe and they had agreed it would be inappropriate to discuss it in public. Charlie too had told Liz but for the moment at least it was not being disclosed.

Ed frowned. 'We're not exactly London or one of the other big cities where this sort of crime happens. I'll put some feelers out tomorrow to see if any of our informants knows anything about a shooter being in the area.'

'We're doing the same,' said Charlie, 'but it's amazing how even they clam up when murder is involved.'

'They're scared of the consequences,' said Ed, 'but someone will squeal if the payment is right.'

'I think it's shocking that you pay crooks for speaking out,' said Liz.

'Sadly sometimes it's the only way to get information,' said Harriet. 'No one wants to reward criminals, but this is the way of the world.'

Liz pulled a face. 'How many nurses would that money pay for?'

Charlie put his arm around his wife's shoulders. 'Okay, Liz we all secretly agree with you, but catching criminals also costs. Now, no more talking shop, puddings are in order I think.'

Chapter Ten

Freddie Fingers put on his black anorak and pulled his black, woolly hat well down over his ears. Leaving his house by the back door he crossed the waste ground at the back to where his battered old Polo was parked. His house didn't have a garage and there was never a space outside the place, so he found it easier to park on the waste ground; it was only a stone's throw away and out of sight of neighbours prying eyes. No one was likely to steal his old waggon, but it served its purpose and had never let him down. He drove off the grass and headed for the town, it was midnight. He never did his house visits too late as he would be liable to being stopped if spotted out and about in the early hours, but around twelve there were always people about and the police took little notice of cars as they moved along. Freddie pulled into Newham Drive and drove slowly past the large houses where most were still brightly lit up. He couldn't see any beech trees and reaching the end of the road he cursed under his breath, did a three-point turn and retraced his steps, slower his time. He was feeling a bit anxious in case someone spotting him cruising and reported him. Ah, Copper Beeches at last, and only a light on over the front door. Freddie stopped and pulled on his latex gloves before slipping from his car and opening the gates. Quickly jumping back into the Polo, he drove through, stopped again and hastily closed the gates behind him. He drove half way up the drive before parking under a tree continuing the remainder of the way to the house on foot with his backpack on his back.

Freddie heard the church clock strike the half hour as he crept around the big house peering in the windows. He was sure the place was empty and taking a bunch of skeleton keys from his pocket he began the task of opening the front door. Strange but front doors were always the easiest to open and certainly better than breaking a window or forcing an entry through a back door or window. There was a click as the lock turned and Freddie opened the door and entered. He waited for the alarm to go off, but to his amazement nothing happened. That was a bit of luck; the silly cow must have left in a hurry and forgotten to switch it on. He took out his torch and flashed it around marvelling at the luxury facing him. Swiftly he went through the downstairs rooms. He didn't want anything too big and cumbersome and he picked up a silver cigarette lighter and a rather elegant cigarette box pushing the objects into his backpack. The pictures on the wall looked expensive but he knew nothing about art and so dismissed the idea of taking one. Anyway they were far too big for him to carry. He climbed the stairs and entered the main bedroom. Again, he was faced with pure luxury, but he wasn't here to admire the décor. Where would a creep like Blackwell keep a safe? He took the pictures from the wall but there was nothing. He carefully replaced them making sure they were quite straight before opening the cupboards and drawers but again there was no sign of a safe. There had to be a safe! Freddie opened the large built-in wardrobe and went over the back wall pushing and tapping with no success. He turned to leave the room and hesitated. Pulling the rug away from the side of the bed he observed the wooden floor and smiled. Kneeling down he gently lifted the square board that looked so out of place and Bingo there it was, a neat, but a piece of cake to Freddie, safe. He wasn't called Fingers for nothing and within five minutes the safe was open. Freddie gasped at the stacks of fifty-pound notes in front of him and without hesitation he stuffed them into his backpack. There were several documents, but he didn't bother with these, it was only the money he was interested in. Shutting the safe and dropping the board back into the space he pulled the rug back into place and left the room. He was about to go downstairs when he thought he would just look for Mrs Blackwell's jewellery. These women seemed to favour a "dressing room" a fancy name for somewhere to keep their clothes and private things. He opened the door of the room next to the master bedroom and was rewarded with seeing what had to be Mrs Blackwell's private room. He went over to the dressing table and shuffled through the objects in a glass tray on the top. Nothing very exciting, so where did the lady of the house keep her jewellery? Did she have a safe like her husband?

Freddie pulled the rug up but he was disappointed. Just bare floorboards. He replaced the rug carefully smoothing it out to remove any bumps. He then opened her wardrobe and was faced with a huge assortment of gowns and jackets hanging there and dozens and dozens of shoes in racks. How the other half lived. It was right that they be made to share their wealth. Freddie swept the rail of clothes to one side and grinned when he spotted the small wall safe at the back. He cracked his knuckles and went to work. The safe contained what he had hoped it would. A leather jewellery box, about 150 centimetres by 250, and several other cases that contained pearls, diamonds and stones that he wasn't sure what they were. He picked up the jewellery box which he didn't bother to open and put it in his backpack together with the other jewellery cases. He pushed the safe door to and then began opening drawers and rummaging through expensive underwear and cashmere sweaters. Nothing more to find, but it had been a very profitable night's work. He made sure all the clothing he had disturbed were left neat and tidy and with his backpack very full Freddie left the room. Half an hour later he was back in his house and opening a bottle of beer. He sat in his armchair to look at his night's haul and lit a cigarette. He liked what he saw! There was nothing he couldn't dispose of, especially the jewellery, his fence was always willing to take diamonds as they were easily broken down and re-set so they became untraceable. The box contained several glittering brooches and rings, and again he was well satisfied. Freddie took another gulp of beer from the bottle and had a spluttering fit causing him to drop the jewellery box. Cursing he picked it up and then caught his breath as he notice an envelope taped to the bottom of it. Carefully he peeled it off and then opened it. He wasn't sure what he was looking at. A jumble of letters and numbers on a piece of paper and key. He scratched his head. This had to be important or it wouldn't be stashed away like this. Freddie replaced the paper and key in the envelope and slipped it into his pocked. He would deal with this later, but he would certainly investigate the letters and numbers, they had to be of some significance. He finished his cigarette, carefully stubbing it out in an ashtray before going outside and emptying the ash into his wheelie bin. Freddie hated any kind of mess in his house and secretly wished he didn't smoke but smoking and drinking was a pleasure of his and he had no wish to stop.

Chapter Eleven

Ursula Blackwell and her sister sat at the kitchen table eating toast and marmalade on Tuesday morning neither of them speaking. Suddenly Ursula jumped to her feet.

'I must go home to day, Sis, there are things I have to do, a funeral to organise for example, and I don't like leaving the house empty for too long. Don't know what I'd do if I had my stuff stolen.'

'You have a safe,' retorted Connie, 'your things are well hidden and secure.'

'I don't think I switched the burglar alarm on when I left,' persisted Ursula, 'so I want to go back to the house to make sure.'

'If you must,' replied Connie with an exaggerated sigh.

'Anyway,' continued Ursula, 'when I've spoken to the undertaker I have to collect some things if I'm to stay here for a while.'

'I think it's a good idea that you remain here,' replied Connie, 'the longer you stay out of the limelight the better.'

'I shall have to pay a visit to the insurers and our lawyer as well,' said Ursula, 'there will be a great deal to sort out.'

'Plenty of time for that, now, we'll go as soon as we're done here. More coffee?'

Ursula shook her head. 'No thanks, I've suddenly got this urge to get back to Copper Beeches.'

Connie Hemmingway cleared the table and put the plates in the sink. 'Come on then, we can wash up when we get back; my car or yours?'

'You can drive,' answered Ursula, 'I still feel a bit shaky.' She gave a weak smile and left the room to get her coat.

At police headquarters Duncan had arrived early so that he could check on the bullet from the bank raid and compare it with the one that they were interested in today. Opening up the police website he punched in his request for information on the bank raid twelve months ago and the Forensic result on the bullet. With the bullet on the screen Duncan pulled up the picture of the bullet that had killed Blackwell. Disappointment showed on his face when he realised that the two bullets did not match. The Beretta used by Bert Coughlan in the bank raid was not the weapon used to kill Blackwell.

At briefing he explained this to Harriet and she thanked him for his effort and told everyone to stick with the questioning of everyone who had had dealings with the dead businessman. She told them of the opening of Blackwell's safe and explained that there was very little in it apart from a black notebook, some documents and fifty-five thousand pounds. There were gasps when the sum of money was mentioned and Harried stressed that this was not to be talked about outside the building. The documents and the notebook were left with Jack, and Charlie handed Narinder the bundle of letters. Harriet guessed that Jack would also co-opt her and Sally to help with the notebook and documents. Charlie had taken the money down to the duty sergeant to have it counted and locked in the safe.

With briefing over Harriet went to her office to catch up on some paperwork, the job she liked least in her new position as head of the station. She was a field operator, a hands-on police officer, and had only accepted the post of superintendent on condition that she was able to remain active. She picked up another sheet of paper and pulled a face as she read about cuts in police funding and because of this, overtime was to be curtailed. Overtime, what a laugh! They all worked overtime and rarely got home at any reliable hour. She put the paper on one of the piles and took another. The sooner she cleared her desk of all this trash the sooner she could join the rest of CID investigating Blackwell's murder.

Ursula climbed from her sister's car and opened the gates to Copper Beeches to allow her to drive through. Closing the gates behind Connie she followed on foot up to the house where she took a bunch of keys from her handbag and opened the front door. With her sister behind her she entered the house and picked up a handful of letters from the mat.

'I suppose I shall have to sort all this rubbish out now,' she moaned dumping the pile of paperwork on the hallstand.

'Let your solicitor do it,' replied Connie, 'you must be paying him enough so make sure he earns it.'

Ursula shivered. 'I've only been away a few days and the house feels cold and empty.'

'Well it's certainly empty, but why is the heating off in November?'

'George has it on a timer, he was always grumbling at my extravagance. What a cheek when he was rolling in dosh.'

'Hmm, well he won't be grumbling anymore. Come on, Ursula call the undertaker and then get the things you want and let's get out of here.'

Ursula went up the stairs closely followed by her sister. She went straight to her dressing room and froze in the doorway. A strange choking cry escaped from her lips as she opened her wardrobe door and saw that the safe door was unlocked. She pulled it open and a scream escaped from her mouth as she saw that the cavity was completely empty. 'Oh, my God!' she squealed, 'Connie, Connie I've been robbed.'

Connie rushed to her side and gasped. 'Has everything been taken?' she asked.

Ursula gazed into the safe and burst into tears. 'All gone,' she wailed, 'they've taken the lot. My beautiful diamond necklace, my emeralds, my gold earrings, everything, everything. All gone.' She sat down on the side of the bed suddenly remembering the envelope taped to the bottom of one of the jewellery case. No burglar would be bothered with what he found in the envelope surely, and they'd never discover what the key fitted so would most probably throw it away. She mustn't panic! The key she could have replaced, and as for the note, well, no thief had brain enough to know what that was all about. She stood deciding not to worry too much about the loss, but she would have to make a phone call straight away.

'What about George's safe?' asked Connie.

Ursula went next door to the master bedroom and flung back the rug. She lifted the wooden panel in the floor and without any problem opened the unlocked safe. 'Empty,' she announced, 'and I know there was always stacks of money in here.'

'I'll call the police,' said Connie taking out her mobile.

Ursula placed a hand on her sister's arm. 'Don't mention what has been taken,' she said, 'I'll do the talking when the coppers get here. While you're doing that, I have some calls to make as well so I'll use my mobile.'

Connie nodded and punched three nines into her mobile as Ursula hurried downstairs to make her calls.

Sergeant Pete Yates took the emergency call from Connie Hemmingway and having taken down the details of the robbery he called Jack in CID. Jack went to Harriet and told her of the break in at Copper Beeches.

'I'll grab someone and get over there, ma'am,' he said. 'Interesting that another property has been broken into as soon as the owner was mentioned in the newspaper as being away.'

'Give me five minutes, Jack and I'll come with you, but will you contact Inspector Cassels and ask him to meet us at Copper Beeches. I put him in charge of the house burglaries so if it is the same person who's been targeting the old and dying he needs to be involved.'

'Right, ma'am I'll do that and then wait for you in the Incident Room.'

Harriet's little red Lotus pulled up outside the big house and she slipped form the car. Jack struggled to climb out of the small two-seater and puffing and panting he finally extracted himself from the vehicle. 'Phew!' He muttered as he stood up and stretched, 'don't think I'll be investing in a car like this, ma'am, I'm not as fit as you.'

Harriet smiled. 'Sorry about that, Jack, but are you all right?'

'Fine now, thank you, ma'am, but I think I'll return to headquarters with the inspector if you don't mind.' He followed her up the steps to the front door which was ajar. On entering they were met by Inspector Cassells.

'Mrs Blackwell and her sister are in the sitting room,' he said, 'I've spoken to them and Mrs Blackwell is writing a list of things that have been stolen.'

'Good, I'll have a word with Mrs Blackwell later,' said Harriet.

'The break-in seems to have been done by an expert,' said Cassells, 'no damage to the front door which seems to have been the way he entered, and two safes opened without any problem and everything appears to have been left neat and tidy. SOCO are going over the place at the moment.'

Jack snorted. 'Let me have a look at the door and then show me the safes, I have a feeling about these break-ins.' He inspected the lock on the front door and nodded knowingly.

'And the safes?' he asked.

'Follow me, Sergeant,' said Cassells.

Jack scrutinised both safes. 'I'd bet a million that this is the handiwork of Freddie Fingers,' he said.

'What makes you so sure?' asked Harriet.

'Freddie can open any door without very much trouble and he never leaves any scratches or other marks; seems to hate leaving a trail of damage. He's known to suffer from OCD and that's why he never leaves anything out of place. As for the safes, well! A piece of cake for someone like Freddie he could open them in his sleep.'

'Do you know where he lives?' asked Cassells.

'I do indeed, Inspector, shall we pay him a visit?' He looked across at Harriet. 'All right if I go with the inspector, ma'am?' he asked, 'SOCO are going over the house so there's not much we can do here.'

'Yes, of course, you get going and I'll have a few words with Mrs Blackwell before I leave.'

Inspector Cassells and Jack left the house, Jack secretly relieved that he wouldn't have to squeeze himself into the boss's little car. Harriet watched as the two officers vanished down the drive and then made her way to the sitting room to speak to the women. She entered the room where she found the two, well rounded, heavily made-up, blonde women, sitting side by side on the sofa. She recognised Mrs Blackwell and spoke to her. 'We met at your sister's house,' she said, 'sorry we are meeting again is rather disturbing circumstances.'

'It never rains but it pours,' replied Ursula.

'I take it you have given a list of stolen items to the inspector,' said Harriet.

'Yes, all my jewellery.'

'Anything else of importance?'

'Some silver, but I've written it all down and given it to the other officer.'

'Good,' said Harriet. 'We shall need to go over the house looking for fingerprints and anything else that might help us catch this perpetrator, so if you can stay with your sister for the time being it would be a great help.'

'That's no problem,' replied Connie, 'my sister was going to stay with me for a bit longer anyway.'

'That's very good of you,' said Harriet, 'and we'll do our best to retrieve your stolen property, Mrs Blackwell. Do you have a spare key for this house?'

'Yes, I'll get you one.' She left the room to return seconds later handing Harriet a key.

'As if I haven't enough on my plate,' she wailed, 'I have a funeral to organise and people to contact.'

'When is the funeral?' asked Harriet.

'Wednesday at eleven.'

'We will be attending,' said Harriet, 'and thank you for the key, we'll make sure the property is secured before we leave.'

The sisters left the room and the throaty sound of the Audi was heard starting up. As Harriet came into the hallway Charlie arrived.

'I've just heard about the break-in,' he said. 'Much taken?'

'Mostly Mrs Blackwell's jewellery,' replied Harriet, 'but some silver items as well.'

'Have SOCO finished?' asked Charlie.

'Just about,' replied Harriet. 'I'll give this key to Sergeant Hewitt so he can lock up and then we can leave.'

Chapter Twelve

Freddie was up early that morning and assessing the spoils of the night before. The jewellery looked expensive, his fence would be more than pleased to get his hands on this little lot. He looked at the key and piece of paper he had taken from the envelope taped to the bottom of the jewellery box and frowned. Must be important to be hidden like this. Placing the paper on the table he went to the sideboard and took a ballpoint pen and a piece of paper from the drawer. Sitting down he carefully copied the letters and numbers onto the paper. He wasn't sure why he was doing this but felt there was something very significant about them. He went back to the drawer and rummaged about until he found an envelope. Freddie never wrote letters so had no need of such things. What remained here was once used by his wife, and thankfully she had left five years ago. Living with Mildred had been nothing less than torture her constant nagging being one of the reasons he had tried his hand at burglary. Mildred had never been satisfied with what he brought home every week in his pay packet and to supplement his earnings and mainly to shut her up, he had tried helping himself to other people's belongings. He had met Reggie Rawlings in prison while serving two years for breaking and entering and the two soon struck up a friendship. Reg was a fence, a very reliable fence and he advised Freddie to seek him out once he was released and found himself in possession of items that needed to vanish.

This Freddie had done and with Mildred gone he began to find life much more interesting, even exciting, and as the months went by his bank balance began to grow very nicely. He slipped the paper into the envelope and wrote an address on it. He would post it tomorrow as he would need to buy a stamp. He stuffed the envelope into his trouser pocket and decided he would hide the original envelope containing the paper and key in his special hiding place with the jewellery and other items. The jewellery boxes he thought he had better destroy. He would chop them up and burn the pieces. He had just deposited his spoils in his hiding place together with his precious bunch of special keys when a loud knocking on the front door made him jump. Hastily he shoved the jewellery boxes into a cupboard before opening the door. He looked at the two men standing there. Coppers! He knew immediately that's what they were, somehow you couldn't mistake the filth, and he recognised the older of the two men. His heart began to race, thank goodness, he had locked the stuff away and surely, he hadn't left any evidence behind at that woman's house last night? He was always so careful. Freddie stayed calm.

'What d'yer want?' he asked.

'Freddie Maloney?' asked Inspector Cassells.

'Yes, what's the problem?'

'Could we come in? We need to ask you a few questions.' Cassells held up his warrant card and Jack did the same.

Freddie hesitated but didn't want to appear anxious, so he forced a smile and held the door open standing to one side to allow the officers to enter. 'Long time no see, Sergeant Fuller', he said to Jack, 'and that's good news isn't it?'

'It is,' agreed Jack, 'so long as you haven't been up to your old tricks.'

'No need to worry, Mr Fuller, I'm on the straight and narrow now.'

'Glad to hear that,' said Jack.

Sitting in the amazingly neat and tidy front room Inspector Cassells opened the questioning. 'Could you tell us where you were last night?' he asked.

'Why should I tell you that?' demanded Freddie, 'What am I supposed to have done?'

'No one is accusing you of anything,' said Jack, 'we simply need to eliminate you from our enquiries.'

'Enquiries into what?'

'A break in at Copper Beeches on Newham Drive,' replied Jack watching Freddie's face closely.

'Nothing to do with me,' snapped Freddie. 'You can't go around accusing folk without real cause or evidence.'

'As Sergeant Fuller said,' chipped in Cassells, 'no one is accusing you, we just need to know where you were last night.'

'I was here, on me own, so now what do you do?'

'And you didn't go out at all?' asked Jack, 'because this break in has your name written all over it.'

'There you go,' snapped Freddie, 'you are accusing me.'

'Not at all,' answered Cassells, 'but is there anyone else as skilful as you in opening safes?'

Freddie felt a surge of pride. Of course there was no one else like him, well certainly not around these parts; no one could open safes as easily as he could. He scowled. 'Don't know what you're talking about, this is police harassment. Just because I've served time in the past you want to pin everything on me when you can't nab someone else for it.'

'Where's your brother these days?' asked Jack.

Freddie wrinkled his nose. 'Not sure. He moved to Birmingham and I don't hear from him that often. Why d'yer ask?'

'You two were close at one time,' said Jack, 'and I just wondered if you and he still worked together. You know, like you did not so long ago.'

'I live a quiet life these days, Mr Fuller, I've served me time and I now toe the line like a respectable citizen.' Freddie smirked and Jack shook his head.

'I'm pleased to hear that, Freddie,' said Jack.

Cassells stood. 'Thank you for your time,' he said, 'we may

need to speak to you again, but for now that will do.' He and Jack left the house and outside the inspector turned to Jack.

'What do you think?'

'I'd put money on it being him, he never leaves mess, cleans up behind himself and everything has to be in order. He has this OCD, you saw how neat and tidy his house is, and if you looked in his cupboards everything will be in straight lines.'

Earl Cassells smiled. 'I've never met anyone with Obsessive Compulsive Disorder, this is a first for me.'

'I'll find out what car Freddie drives,' said Jack. 'There are CCTV cameras at the top of Newham Drive, it'll be interesting to see if Freddie's car turns up on them.'

'Good thinking, Jack if it does we might have grounds for a search warrant.'

'I might just check up on his brother as well,' said Jack, 'they always worked together in the old days, one breaking in and the other acting as look-out.'

Freddie watched as the two officers climbed back into their car and drove off. Damn, he could do without the filth keeping an eye on him. The sooner he got rid of the loot the safer it would be for him. He picked up the telephone and dialled the number he knew by heart.

Sally and Narinder had had another busy morning checking and re-checking the statements given to them by the staff at Pegasus House. All the businesses had been called on and the people running them questioned. The only conclusion was that no one had liked Blackwell, and no one was sorry he would no longer be around. They had promised Sergeant Fuller they would help in going through the documents and note book found in Blackwell's safe and returning to headquarters they told him they would be helping him once they had gone through the pile of letters. 'Before we do anything, Jack,' said Sally, 'we need to have a word with the boss, but we won't be long.' They went to Harriet's office and asked her if they might have a word.

'Is it about the Blackwell case?' she asked.

'Indirectly,' replied Sally.

'Go on,' answered Harriet.

Sally explained about Blackwell being the only person in Pegasus House with more than one office. 'The place is supposed to help new businesses getting started and each is allotted one office, Blackwell had three, which according to the other people is out of order.'

'It all spells corruption,' said Narinder, 'and if he was paying backhanders to someone on the council, what other crooked operation was he involved in?'

'Do we know the name of the councillor who deals with these office lettings?' asked Harriet.

'Yes, ma'am,' replied Sally, 'his name is Frank Abbott.'

'Can we have permission to investigate him, ma'am?' asked Narinder eagerly.

Harriet suppressed a smile. 'Yes, go ahead, it may just turn up something that helps solve Blackwell's murder.'

'Thank you, ma'am,' said Sally and she and Narinder hurried from the room. Outside the office Narinder held clenched fists up in the air.

'Great!' she hissed, 'sorting out this creep Abbott could prove very interesting.'

'Don't get carried away, Narinder,' said Sally, 'there might be some legitimate reason for Blackwell having three offices. We need to visit the council offices and do a bit of delving before we come to a conclusion.'

Narinder chortled. 'You know very well, Sal it will be a case of corruption.'

Sally smiled. 'Well let's go and read those letters from the safe and find out what secret life this Blackwell was leading. When we've done that and had a look at the documents Jack has, we'll pay the council offices a visit.'

Returning to the Incident Room the two women sat side by side at a table and split the pile of letters between them. They began opening the envelopes. Narinder was in her element and soon began chortling over what she was reading.

'Wow! these are pretty steamy', she said. 'They're all from a woman called Rosetta and talk about passionate, but they're not recent, they're dated some time ago.'

'Well, from the stamps on these envelopes, she's Italian,' said Sally, 'and I bet Mrs Blackwell doesn't know anything about her.'

'Ah,' muttered Narinder, 'and I wonder if this Rosetta's husband knew about Blackwell?'

'What have you found?' asked Sally.

'She mentions her husband in this letter, states she is finding it very difficult to put up with his behaviour and asking him, Blackwell, to take her away.'

'Really? It's all very clandestine. What's the date on that?

'Nineteen ninety.'

Sally picked up another of the envelopes. 'How long do you think the Blackwell's have been married?' she asked.

'Heaven knows. He's fifty-three and his wife is a bit younger, so I should think they've been married twenty-three or five years. Why?'

'According to the postmarks on most of these envelopes,' said Sally, 'they were sent a good twenty-seven or eight years ago.'

'So, you reckon that perhaps he wasn't married at the time.'

'Well he possibly wasn't, but we now know this Rosetta was.' Sally put down the envelope she was holding. 'I wonder what happened to her?'

'What's the latest date on any envelope?' asked Narinder.

Sally went through the pile she had looking at the stamps.

'Nineteen ninety-three,' she said.

'Not that long ago then,' said Narinder. 'I wonder what happened to end the relationship.'

'He married, Ursula?' suggested Sally. 'We'll check on the date Blackwell was married and see where that leads us.'

Narinder held up a letter from her pile. 'This is in a different hand,' she said, 'but it's still from Italy.'

'What's the date on it?'

'Twenty seventeen.' Narinder took out the letter and began reading. 'Oh my God,' she gasped.

'What is it?' asked Sally.

'It's from someone calling herself his daughter, thanking him for the gift he sent her.

The letter starts, Cher Papa and signed. Rosalind. The letter is written in English.'

'This is equal to any TV soap,' said Sally.

'There's a newspaper cutting here,' announced Narinder, 'but it's in Italian. There's a photo of a beautiful woman and included in the text, there's the word morto, and we can guess that means dead. The name of the woman is Rosetta Bianchi. This must be a report of the woman's death, Sal, Blackwell's mistress.'

'And sent to Blackwell by the daughter do you think?'

'It gets more and more like a soap,' said Narinder.

'We'll do as we said,' said Sally, 'check on the date of Blackwell's marriage and perhaps see where Mr Bianchi is at the moment. He could be our killer if he has only just found out about Blackwell and the daughter. 'We'll lock this stuff away and come back to it later. We still have a great deal to do.'

Chapter Thirteen

Earl Cassells and Jack returned to headquarters and back in the Incident Room Jack suggested that if it had been Freddie Fingers who had broken into Copper Beeches, it was probably because the fact that Ursula Blackwell was staying at her sisters after the death of her husband had been on the front page of the evening paper.

'And if that's the case,' said Jack, 'then I reckon Freddie is our house breaker in the cases of those old folk in hospital or notifications of their death being in the paper.'

'Could be,' agree Cassells. 'I have spoken to a couple of relatives of people who have suffered a house robbery and in both cases the house was not damaged or even trashed, which we know burglars often do. So it does sound a bit like Freddie.'

'More than a bit,' growled Jack. 'I think we keep an eye on the obituaries and the next death reported that looks like a target we keep an eye on Mr Fingers.'

'Can I ask you to do that?' asked Cassells, 'and let me know when such a death turns up and we'll visit Freddie's house and keep him under surveillance.'

'My pleasure,' said Jack, 'and in the meantime I'll get onto the DVLA and run a check on his car. When I have that I'll get Ben and Luke to go and check the CCTV cameras at the top of Newham Drive. I also have those documents from Blackwell's safe to go through but Sally and Narinder have promised to help with that.'

'Excellent, perhaps we are making progress after all.'

'Talk of the devil,' said Jack as Sally and Narinder came over to his desk. 'Are you ready to go through those papers?'

'Yes, Sarge,' replied Narinder, 'we've read some of the letters found in Blackwell's safe and they make very interesting reading, we'll tell you all about it later. We'll lend a hand with these documents and then we're going over to the council offices to speak to Frank Abbott.'

'What's that about then?'

'Blackwell and a touch of corruption,' replied Narinder with a grin.

'Better get cracking on these then,' said Jack handing the papers to her. 'And here's the notebook as well.'

Narinder took the papers and the book and she and Sally went to a table and sat down. Huffs and puffs and large snorts, particularly from Narinder, came from the two women over the next hour. 'All these initials in the book are obviously customers,' said Narinder, 'and as you can see, FA turns up regularly. Has to be Frank Abbott, doesn't it?'

'You bet,' agreed Sally, 'and reading these documents you can see why Abbott was being paid large sums of money on a regular basis.'

'What have you found?' asked Narinder.

'Blackwell was buying up council property for peanuts,' said Sally, 'closed schools, old swimming pools and such like but all with prime town positions. And the councillor who organised these deals was Frank Abbott?'

'What a crook.'

'Got it in one,' said Sally, 'a crook. Let's give all this to Jack and get over to the council offices. I can't wait to hear Abbott's explanation for this.'

Sally and Narinder arrived at the council building and asked to see Frank Abbott. The receptionist looked anxious when she saw Sally's warrant card.

'Nothing wrong I hope?' she said.

'Would you show us to his office please,' said Sally not answering the young woman's query.

'Of course, of course,' said the receptionist jumping to her feet. 'Please follow me.' She led Sally and Narinder across the foyer to a staircase and pointed. 'First floor second door on the right. His name is on the door, so you won't miss it.'

'Thank you,' said Sally starting up the stairs almost at a run.

Narinder caught her up. 'Hey, slow down you're not at the gym you know.'

'I use every opportunity to train,' said Sally with a grin, 'you don't have to copy me.'

'If I don't you'll just call me a wimp. Phew, that's made me puff.'

'You need to do more exercise, Narinder, ah, here we are.' She stopped outside the door with the name Frank Abbott on it and knocked. A gruff voice called out "enter" and opening the door the two officers went in.

'Mr Abbott?' asked Sally showing her warrant card, 'could you spare us a few minutes please.'

Abbott was an overweight man in his fifties with a ruddy complexion and thinning grey hair. His small grey eyes narrowed even further and he clasped his podgy fingers together in front of him on the desk. 'What's this about?' he snapped.

'Pegasus House offices,' replied Narinder also showing her warrant card.

Abbott's face went even redder. 'What about them?' His fat fingers gripped each other even tighter.

'We understand you are the letting agent on behalf of the County Council,' said Sally, 'could you explain to us the criteria for business people obtaining an office.'

Abbott began to fidget. 'Why do you need to know this?' he

demanded.

'Could you just explain,' said Narinder sharply, 'this is a police matter.'

The councillor began to cough and Sally and Narinder waited patiently, not taking their eyes off him. 'Well?' said Sally.

Abbott took a gulp of water from the glass on his desk before replying. 'Anyone setting up in business can apply for an office in Pegasus House,' he said, 'there's no secret in how it works.'

'And is it no secret,' said Sally, 'that someone like George Blackwell not only has three offices but is already an established business.'

'He hardly fits the pattern, does he,' said Narinder.

'Ah, well that was a mistake,' stuttered Abbott, 'I was in the process of rectifying that error.'

'It was an error was it?' asked Narinder, 'and how did this error occur?'

'He applied in the name of three different businesses and I didn't spot the fact until quite recently.'

'Don't you carry out a check on these people when applying?' asked Sally, 'surely they have to submit a business plan.'

'Yes, yes they do, but George, er Mr Blackwell was very clever and his applications slipped through the net.'

'I bet they did,' muttered Narinder.

'We will need to see all of Blackwell's application forms' said Sally.

'What now?'

'Yes please,' replied Sally, 'we can wait.' She went over to a chair and sat down.

Narinder followed suit.

Abbott rose to his feet and went over to a filing cabinet. With a great deal of huffing and puffing he began fumbling through the drawers. Finally he pulled out a fat folder and dumped it on his desk. 'This is George Blackwell's folder,' he said in a strained voice.

Sally went over to the desk and picked it up. 'We'll borrow this' she said, 'I'll sign for it if you have such a document.'

'These folders aren't allowed out of the office,' snarled Abbott.

'Oh, this one is,' replied Sally sweetly, 'where do I sign?'

'We don't have such documents.'

Sally leaned over the desk and took a sheet of paper and a ballpoint pen. She wrote on the piece of paper and signed it before pushing it towards Abbott. 'Please sign,' she said.

With shaking hands Abbott signed. Sally took the paper. 'One other thing, Mr Abbott, how was George Blackwell able to purchase council property at such low prices?'

Abbott was visibly shaken. 'I don't know anything about such dealings,' he said in a choked voice.

'Strange,' said Narinder, 'as you were the officer in charge of the sales.'

'And even stranger', said Sally, 'that the properties were bought as such low prices with no other offers made by anyone else.'

'Or perhaps the buildings in question never actually went on the open market?' suggested Narinder sweetly.

By now Abbott was perspiring profusely and frantically mopping his brow. 'You've the file you asked for,' he stammered, 'now I'd appreciate you leaving.'

'Thank you, that will be all for the time being,' said Sally, 'but we may need to speak to you again.'

The two women left the office and went downstairs. At reception Sally asked the receptionist to photocopy the signed paper telling her to keep one in a safe place for the council records and the other would be kept by the police. This the woman did without a murmur and when done she handed Sally one of the papers.

'Now I expect the copy you have to be locked away safely,' said Sally, 'as we are taking a folder off the premises and you need to know that it's safe.'

'Yes officer.'

'And your name is?' asked Sally.

'Amanda Pemberton.'

'Thank you, Amanda, now please do as I say and lock that paper away.'

The young woman nodded and turned away to comply and Sally and Narinder left the building and returned to their car.

Jack had contacted the DVLA and now had the make and number plate of Freddie Maloney's car. An old VW Polo. He took these details to Luke and asked him to take Ben with him and check the CCTV camera at the end of Newham Drive. 'You can collect the film from the road traffic division at the council offices,' he told Luke, 'and when you spot this car make sure you write down the exact dates and times it was caught on camera and which way it was going and so on. You know the drill.'

'Yes, Sarge,' said Luke taking the piece of paper from Jack. He went over to Ben and explained what they had to do and together the two young DCs left the room.

Chapter Fourteen

Sally and Narinder returned to headquarters and having made themselves coffee they sat at a table in the Incident Room. They began the process of going through the folder containing all the details of George Blackwell's dealings with Frank Abbott.

'As far as I can see,' said Narinder shuffling papers, 'there's absolutely no mention of the sales of council property made to Blackwell. And the man only ever made an application for one office at Pegasus House, so how come he has three?'

'You're right,' agreed Sally, 'his business is down here as Property Development, and of course named as a new business. What a joke! And no wonder he was making millions if he was snatching up cheap properties in prime positions.'

'And in a company name rather than his own,' said Narinder, 'all thanks to that other crook, Abbott. Here are the details of payments to the council for one office,' she added, 'so if he pays for only one does he get the other two for nothing?'

'Or as I suspect does someone else collect the rent for the other two.'

'And I wonder who that other person might be?' mused Narinder. 'We need to look at Blackwell's bank statement.'

'And Frank Abbotts, I think.' said Sally. 'We'll have to ask the boss about that. Come on she's in her office.'

Luke and Ben had obtained the film from the CCTV camera at the end of Newham Drive and were sitting in Doctor Chong's laboratory watching closely for the VW Polo belonging to Freddie Fingers. 'An old Polo would stand out like a sore thumb in this road,' said Luke, 'look, a brand-new BMW, a top of the range Audi and crikey, look at that Bentley, Ben, you don't see many of those in Torreston.'

'How the other half live,' replied Ben. 'We really only need to look at the night-time shots, the house was burgled in the night after all.'

'Yep, let's skip through these tapes a bit. Right here we are eleven o'clock on the night the house was done. Now keep your eyes peeled, Ben.'

'Don't think we'll miss an old Polo,' replied Ben.

'That's midnight,' said Luke, 'ten past, half past, wow! Hang on.' He stopped the tape and rewound it. 'That was an old banger,' he said. 'Watch, Ben.' He started the tape again and there it was an old Polo.' He called to Doctor Chong. 'We've found what we want, Doctor, could you blow it up so that we can see the number plate please.'

'And it would help if we could see clearly who the driver is,' added Ben.

'No problem,' said Henry Chong coming across. 'I can do that. If you leave the disc with me I'll do as you ask and bring the pictures up to CID.'

'Thanks, Doctor Chong,' said Luke, 'that'd be great.' They left the IT department and returned to the Incident Room where they told Jack about the spotting of the Polo in Newham Drive.

'Well done, lads,' said Jack, 'that's great news, and I bet Chong will blow up the number plate and show us that the blighter driving it is Freddie Fingers.'

Sally and Narinder sat at Harriet's desk and explained to her about Frank Abbott and the letting of offices at Pegasus House and the selling of cheap properties to Blackwell.

'How much does it cost to rent one of these offices?' asked Harriet.

'Between four hundred and six hundred,' replied Sally,

'depending on whether it's a single office or shared.'

'And depending on how many people share the office,' added Narinder. 'Some of the offices have the computer wiring for three or four desks.'

'And Blackwell's offices were all singles?' suggested Harriet.

'Absolutely,' agreed Sally.

'And surprise, surprise,' said Narinder, 'Blackwell paid the lowest rate of four hundred pounds.'

'We'd like to see Blackwell's bank statements to see where the money for three offices went,' said Sally.

'That's no problem,' replied Harriet, 'this is a murder case, so we have access to all his accounts and bank statement, Chief Inspector Marlow has them. I have cast my eye over them and there were several large payments going out on a regular basis which obviously needs checking, but I am no expert in this field so will leave it to someone who is. It looks as if a great deal of his money was kept in his safe as cash but now that we have his computer we are looking for off-shore accounts.'

'And what about Frank Abbot's accounts?' asked Narinder, 'if he's the one taking the handouts then the money will surely show up there.'

'I agree, so you'd better look sharp as Abbott now knows you're on to him. You will be asked for official documents to see his accounts so I will make sure that we get one, but see what you can do without it. I'll set the ball rolling while you're away.'

'Thank you, ma'am,' said Sally, 'we're onto it. There's just one other thing, we've looked through most of the letters found in Blackwell's safe and discovered that they are all from an Italian woman called Rosetta.'

'Apart from one,' chipped in Narinder, 'and that's from her daughter, Rosalind.'

'So, what are you saying?' asked Harriet.

'That George Blackwell had a mistress and they have a daughter,' said Sally.

'Really?' Harriet wrinkled her nose. 'That is interesting.'

'We think this all happened before he married Ursula though,' said Narinder, 'so we're going to check just when the marriage took place.'

'We're wondering if the husband of Rosetta has only recently discovered the affair and it was he who shot Blackwell?'

'He is Italian after all,' added Narinder brightly.

'I'll leave it to you,' said Harriet, 'but keep me informed of any developments.'

'Yes, ma'am.'

They left Harriet's office and returned to the Incident Room. 'Blackwell's bank statement will wait,' said Sally, 'they're in our possession already, but Abbott might try something devious. Find out where he banks Narinder and we'll get over there.'

'No probs, I'll have a word with Amanda. Now she knows what we're doing, she'll come clean.'

Henry Chong came up to the Incident Room and handed Luke some photographs. 'Clear as a bell,' he said, 'this guy couldn't possible deny it was him.'

'Great, thanks, Doctor Chong,' said Luke taking the pile of photographs. He flicked through them and nodded to Ben. They went over to Jack and Luke put them in front of the sergeant.

Jack picked them up and spread then out on his desk. He grinned. 'Oh, yes! Goodnight Freddie, we have you.'

'I take it it's who you expected it to be?' asked Ben.

'It is indeed.'

'Do we arrest him?' asked Luke.

'Not yet,' replied Jack, 'catching him on camera in Newham Drive isn't evidence enough and knowing his brief, who's as bent as a banana, would get him off on some stupid count. No, we'll catch him in the act and with the stolen goods on him.'

'How do we do that?' asked Ben.

'I shall let you know as soon as I've had a word with the DI and we've organised a little surprise for Fingers. I shall make sure you two are involved.'

'Thanks, Sarge,'said Luke.

Jack took the photographs and went over to Inspector Cassells to explain what he had in mind.

Narinder obtained the information she required from Amanda Pemberton at the council offices and joined Sally at her desk. 'Right, Sal, I have what we need, Abbott banks at RBS, are we off?'

Sally jumped to her feet. 'Yes, let's get going.' They hurried from the building and with Sally driving they reached the bank in fifteen minutes. At reception they asked to see the manager.

'I'm sorry,' said the young woman at the desk, 'but Mr Frobisher is very busy, can I ask what it is about?'

'Police business,' replied Sally producing her warrant card, 'and we do need to speak to the manager now,'

The woman hesitated for a few seconds but seeing the look in Sally's eyes she nodded,

'I'll see what I can do,' she said and hurried away to vanish through a door at the back of the building. Sally and Narinder waited and were relieved when the door opened and the receptionist re-appeared.

'Mr Frobisher will see you,' she said, 'if you'll follow me.'

Entering the manager's office the two officers were surprised to see a young man sitting behind a large desk. Somehow one always imagined bank managers to be old or at least well into middle age but here they were faced by a good looking, fresh-faced individual. The young man stood and invited them to sit in the two chairs that had been placed in front of his desk.

'I'm Jacob Frobisher,' he said with a disarming smile, 'how can I help the police?'

'We are investigating the renting of offices at Pegasus House,' said Sally, 'and with the death of George Blackwell we have discovered some anomalies in his payments for the offices he used.'

'Ah, yes, I read of his murder,' replied Frobisher, 'so what exactly do you want from me?'

'We need to see the accounts of Frank Abbott,' said Narinder, 'he's the councillor in charge of lettings for the offices at Pegasus House.'

'I know who Frank Abbott is,' replied the manager somewhat dourly. 'Do you have authorisation to see these documents?'

'Not at the moment,' said Sally, 'but our boss is in the process of obtaining it. We were hoping to save time by coming directly to you.'

'This is a murder investigation,' said Narinder, 'and I'm sure you will want to cooperate.'

Frobisher supressed a smile. 'I'll give you the accounts you ask for,' he said, 'on condition you do nothing with them until I have the correct authorisation. So I would be grateful if you would drop it into me as soon as possible.' He looked at Narinder and smiled. 'You wouldn't want me to lose my job would you, officer?'

Narinder grinned. 'Absolutely not.'

'Thank you for your help,' said Sally, 'and we promise we won't use the statements until they are officially allowed to be seen by the police. We'll drop the document in to you the minute we have it.'

Frobisher turned to his computer and his fingers danced over the keys. Two minutes later he printed off several papers which he handed to Sally. 'Here you are, Sergeant,' he said, 'and I shall expect a document from you tomorrow at the latest if you don't mind.'

'You shall have it,' replied Sally rising, 'and again thank you.'

Jacob Frobisher showed the two officers to the door and

returned to his chair. He'd always wondered about Abbott. Greasy little fellow and getting huge amounts of money from somewhere and not from his work as a councillor he was sure. He disliked the man. Good! Perhaps these officers would sort him out once and for all.

Chapter Fifteen

U rsula Blackwell was still staying with her sister in Leicester and had been extremely agitated since the discovery of the break in at her house. She had been busy on the telephone all morning and to date had made six calls. She was not happy with the response she had received with two of the conversations she had had, and now feeling very hot and bothered she sat with a large glass of wine in her hand wondering what she should do next.

At police headquarters Jack explained his idea to catch Freddie Fingers to Earl Cassells and the inspector smiled. 'Do you think it will work?' he asked.

'I have a very good feeling about this,' replied Jack, 'and I think it's worth a try.'

'Right, we'll do it,' said Cassells, 'I take the evening paper so I'll keep an eye on the obituaries.'

'I'll do the same,' agreed Jack. 'I've promised young Stockwell and Granger they could be in at the kill, so I'll warn them to be on standby and join us as soon as I give them a ring.'

'We'd need to be at the property before Freddie,' suggested Cassells, 'so that we catch him in the act.'

'Oh, yes,' agreed Jack, 'we'll be sitting there waiting for him, but we'll see that our two DCs are watching his house and can direct us when they see him leave. I've put the operation down as Hide and Seek, I hope that' all right, sir?'

Cassells smiled. 'Sounds okay to me, and a good idea about using the DCs, I was wondering what we should do if there was more than one notice in the paper.' He went over to his desk and dialled the number of Central Police Station where he asked to speak to DCI Harrington. Ed came on the line and Earl introduced himself. He explained what he and Jack were going to do if they spotted an obituary in the paper that sounded a likely hit for Freddie and asked what Ed thought of the idea.

'Sounds great,' replied Ed, 'and if Jack is involved I'm sure it will be a success. Do you need any help from us?'

'No thank you, sir, but I thought it only right that I explained our plan to you as your station is dealing with the same case.'

'Thanks for that,' said Ed, 'and good luck.'

Jack felt quite excited. This little operation was his idea and he wanted it to be successful. He and Freddie were old adversaries, in fact Jack thought he was the last person to arrest the man. He went over to Luke and Ben to tell them what they needed to do in the next few days. They would have to be ready to join him and the DI as soon as an obituary appeared in the evening paper reporting that an elderly individual was dead and their house now empty, or as in the case of Mrs Blackwell, for some reason they were away from the property. His plan would work, he was sure of it.

Sally and Narinder reported back to Harriet telling her that the bank manager would appreciate having a letter of authority for allowing them having Abbotts bank statements. Harriet told them they would hopefully have the document by the end of the day, but she would know more within the hour. The two officers made their way to the Incident Room to scrutinise Abbott's accounts. Going to her desk Sally found a note with her name on it. 'It's from Jack,' she said opening the paper. 'Good old Jack, he's tracked down the marriage date of the Blackwell's and we were right, they've been married twenty-three years, so the affair happened before he was married, just.'

'But did Ursula know about it and did the husband of Rosetta find out recently?'

'We'll put that on hold for the moment,' said Sally, 'and go over these statements first.'

Sitting side by side they began sifting through the pages.

'What crooks,' gasped Sally, 'look at this! Abbott receives two thousand pounds every month, and you can bet your bottom dollar it's from Blackwell for services rendered.'

'Well, it's definitely not his salary,' agreed Narinder, 'that's clearly shown.'

'Well the money certainly isn't just for the use of three offices', said Sally, 'we now know he was being paid for insider information giving Blackwell the opportunity to buy council properties on the sly. Quite a nice little operation.'

'If we can match these payments to outgoing sums in Blackwell's accounts Abbott will have a great deal to explain.'

'I'll get Blackwell's accounts,' said Narinder, 'hang on a mo.' She went over to Jack and collected the key to the secure cabinet which she opened and took out Blackwell's folder. Returning to the table she plonked it down in front of Sally.

Sally took out the bank statements and pushed them across to Narinder. 'He doesn't appear to have masses in his account,' she said, 'but then he'll have another secret account somewhere won't he. I'll read out the dates the two thousands went into Abbotts account and you check the outgoing payments from Blackwell.'

They began the process and it soon became obvious that the two thousand pounds entering Abbotts account matched exactly the date the same amount was paid out by Blackwell.

'Yippee!' cried Narinder, 'I wonder how that nasty piece of work is going to explain this away.'

'He'll try,' replied Sally, 'but luckily this evidence is too good,'

'You don't suppose Abbot had anything to do with Blackwell's death?'

'Why would he kill the golden goose,' said Sally, 'and another thing he'd never leave all this evidence behind,'

'You're right, he's a greedy little turd and must have taken thousands and thousands over the months.'

'We can check the amount,' said Sally, 'let's add up all the thousands from Blackwell and then we'll report to the boss.' They began the process of totting up the sums paid to Abbott.

'There's another regular payment here,' said Sally picking up the bank statement, 'and again it's for two thousand pounds a month.'

'And who's that to?' asked Narinder.

'A scum-bag we all know very well.'

'Go on.'

Sally held the paper up for Narinder to see. 'Our friend Bardwell-Fox,' she said.

'Surprise, surprise,' said Narinder, 'you might know Blackwell had that creep in his pocket.'

Sally gathered up the papers. 'Come on we'll show this to the boss.'

Harriet was still shuffling papers in her office and was quite relieved when there was a knock on the door. Anything was better than all this paper work. She called out "come in" and Sally and Narinder appeared.

'What have you discovered?' asked Harriet.

'Just what we thought we might, ma'am,' replied Sally, 'Councillor Abbott has been taking handouts from Blackwell for about two years.'

'Two thousand pounds a month, to be exact,' said Narinder, 'which adds up to forty- eight thousand in total; no wonder he was happy to arrange the purchases of council properties to Blackwell.'

'That's a great deal of money,' said Harriet. 'Well done both of you, did you have much difficulty getting the bank statements without the authorisation?'

'Mr Frobisher was a very understanding bank manager,' said

Sally with a smile, 'but we can't use them until he has the document of authorisation in his hand. Have you any news of that, ma'am?'

'We promise to deliver it,' added Narinder.

'Of course,' replied Harriet, 'well as it happens I have heard, and we won't have the authorisation until tomorrow, so we'll sit on the bank information for the moment. This Abbott is obviously bent but I don't think this will have anything to do with Blackwell's murder, do you?'

'No, ma'am,' replied Sally, 'we both agree that Abbott wouldn't get rid of someone paying him such sums of money. Another regular payment is to the solicitor Bardwell-Fox, and we presume this is for services rendered.'

'No surprise there,' said Harriet, 'Bardwell-Fox is in the pay of practically all the criminals in the area. But we'll hand the Abbott case over to Fraud as soon as the bank statement are legally ours to see, and let them deal with him, we have a murder on our hands and plenty to do. I'll warn the Fraud Squad about the connection of Abbott and Blackwell and ask them to let us know if anything turns up that might involve Abbott in the murder.'

'Thank you, ma'am,' said Sally handing over the bank statement to the boss, 'and we'll deliver the authorisation to the bank tomorrow.'

'At which point I shall contact the Fraud Squad,' said Harriet. 'Any news on the Blackwell marital affair?'

'We've discovered that it happened before he married Ursula,' said Sally, 'but that doesn't mean Rosetta's husband hasn't only just found out about it, and the fact that the daughter isn't his, and come over and shot his wife's lover.'

'Get someone to check on the husband,' said Harriet, 'you two are very busy at the moment.'

'Sergeant Fuller is helping us,' said Narinder.

Sally handed Harriet the news papercutting. 'It's in Italian,' she said, 'but one word, morto, we think is dead, and wonder if it's referring to Rosetta.'

Harriet took the cutting and read aloud. 'It is with great sadness that the death has been announced of the lovely ex-model, Rosetta Bianchi who last night was killed in a car crash in Settimo Milanese. Her daughter, Rosalind who was in the car with her, was thrown out and sustained only minor injuries.' Harriet stopped there and looked up. 'No need to read any more, but you were correct in thinking the woman is dead, she was killed just outside Milan. You say the daughter still writes to her father?'

'Yes, ma'am, the last postmark was a few months ago. She writes in English, as did her mother.'

'Let me know what turns up about Mr Bianchi,' said Harriet, 'and if he was in England when Blackwell was shot, then he most certainly is a suspect. Well done, both of you; keep at it.'

Sally and Narinder left Harriet's office and headed for the Incident Room. 'You might have known the boss could speak Italian,' hissed Narinder. 'Is there nothing she can't do?'

'She read Law with languages at Cambridge,' said Sally, 'and I know one language was French.'

'And now we know another was Italian,' said Narinder. 'Pity the case with Abbott is going to Fraud,' she added, 'I would have enjoyed arresting that creep.'

'So long as he gets what he deserves,' said Sally. 'That's all that matters.'

'It looks as if we might be able to get away before seven tonight,' said Narinder, 'Dave and Gerry said they'd be round at eight, I think we're eating at Murano's.'

'Great, I love Italian food, and I'm already starving. I'll leave a note for Jack asking him to do a check on Bianchi for us. He'll be able to find out if he was in the country at the time of Blackwell's murder.' She scribbled a note and placed it on Jack's desk. 'Come on,' she said to her friend, 'let's get our notes written up and we can get off.'

There were only two deaths reported in the evening paper. One of an elderly man who had died in a nursing home where he had been resident for six months and the other a woman leaving behind a husband and teenage children. Neither fitted the bill as far as Freddie Fingers was concerned and Jack, sitting in his armchair at home felt quite disappointed as he scanned the paper. He folded it to the crossword page and tried to put Freddie out of his thoughts. Earl Cassells too read the obituaries and came to the same conclusion as Jack. Operation Hide and Seek would not take place tonight.

At the time Jack was casting his eyes over the obituaries in the evening paper, Freddie Fingers was doing the same thing. He screwed his nose up as he folded the paper. Nothing of any use here. But he could wait! He had met with his fence earlier showing him only the jewellery as he had decided he would keep the cigarette lighter and case which he liked. He had stashed these away in his hiding place at home before leaving to meet Reg. The deal over the jewellery had been quite profitable. Reggie Rawlings had known immediately where it had come from and been pretty sniffy about the price he wanted to pay for it. Freddie had argued the toss that he knew the necklaces would be broken down and moved on in which case no one could possibly recognise them for what they had been. Eventually he and Reg had come to an agreement and now Freddie was counting the cash he had been given. He would hide it away in the usual place as he had to be careful about using the bank. Too many nosey parkers who might ask questions as to where large sums of cash came from. He couldn't be doing with that. He went to the kitchen and opened the door to the old oven in the "never used" range and lifted out the ash tray at the bottom. He placed the money and the envelope in the space below with the silver from the Blackwell house and replaced the tray. Hopefully it wouldn't be too long before a new "customer" announced him or herself as being open for business. Freddie laughed to himself. Life had never been better.

Chapter Sixteen

At briefing Wednesday morning Harriet went over the happenings of the last few days.

'It seems there are several people happy to see George Blackwell dead,' she said, 'but so far we are unable to pin his murder on any of them. The bullet used does not match any records we have of weapons on file although the experts tell us the gun used was probably a Beretta or a Glock. Sergeant McAllister has ruled out the weapon used by Bert Coughlan in the post office hold up a years ago, as we do have the bullet from that gun used, on file.' She turned to Duncan, 'Do you have anything further to add?' she asked.

Duncan stood. 'There's another known crook by the name of Jamal Rodrigues who is known to use a Glock,' he said, 'but so far we have been unable to trace him. It's thought he has returned to Jamaica and we're looking into this.'

'Let us know if you have success in tracing him,' said Harriet, 'we need to know where he is.'

Duncan nodded, 'Sergeant Fuller is going to do that, ma'am,' he said and sat down.

Harriet continued. 'Sergeant Pringle and DC Pancholi have been going through the letters found in Blackwell's safe,' she said, 'and there have been revelations. I'll let you go on from here'. She nodded to Sally and Sally stood.

'We discovered that George Blackwell had an affair with a married Italian woman over twenty years ago, which resulted in a daughter,' she began. 'There were many letters from the woman, a

Mrs Rosetta Bianchi, and a recent one from the daughter, Rosalind with a newspaper cutting telling of her mother's death. It looks as if Blackwell had been communicating with them for all the time he was marred to Ursula Blackwell, but so far, we are not sure if the husband came to England at the time of George Blackwell's murder. We are still looking into this.'

'Some Casanova,' said someone at the back of the room.

Charlie rose and stood beside Harriet. 'Anything on the house burglaries, Inspector Cassells,' he asked.

'We're pretty sure the culprit is Freddie Fingers,' replied Earl, 'and Sergeant Fuller has organised a plan to catch him. Sergeant,' he said looking at Jack.

Jack coughed and gave a little smile. 'We're keeping an eye on the obituaries,' he said. 'As this is what our burglar must be doing, we thought we'd play the same game. The next time there's an obvious obituary of an old person in the evening paper and it looks as if the house has been left empty, we aim to get there first and wait for the break in.'

'What makes you so sure its Freddie?' asked Harriet.

'I'd stake my reputation on it,' said Jack, 'it has all the hallmarks of Freddie Fingers, and we will get him, ma'am.'

Harriet smiled. 'I believe you, Jack,' she said, 'keep us posted.'

'I will, ma'am.'

'Anything on the hair cutter?' asked Charlie turning to Sally and Narinder.

'There have been no further incidents,' said Sally, 'and with no CCTV coverage anywhere on the bus routes, or at the bus station, we haven't been able to do much about it.'

'Well let's hope it was just a spate of stupidity,' said Harriet, 'and we won't hear anything more about it.'

'I've given the list of jewellery stolen from Mrs Blackwell to Crime Watch and it will be on television tonight,' said Charlie, 'the list has also been sent to local dealers and shops where second-hand stuff is bought.'

'Ah, well,' said Jack, 'Freddie has a regular fence, so the jewellery won't turn up in the usual places.'

'Do we know the name of this fence?' asked Harriet.

'Oh, yes,' replied Jack, 'a real little entrepreneur. Freddie met him in prison, a guy by the name of Reggie Rawlings, he'll buy anything and move it on before you can blink.'

'We're keeping an eye on Rawlings,' said Earl Cassells.

'Good, we'll leave you and Sergeant Fuller to sort the burglaries out. Sergeant Pringle,' continued Harriet, 'perhaps you would tell us about Councillor Abbott.'

Sally explained to the team about the discovery of the payments made to Abbott from Blackwell. 'We don't think Abbott is involved with Blackwell's murder,' she said, 'but the guy's certainly bent and we're now pretty sure what Blackwell was paying him two thousand pounds a month for.' She went on to explain about the purchasing of council properties at rock- bottom prices.

'Crickey,' said Luke, 'that was a lot of dosh he was getting from Blackwell, no wonder he was helping the guy out with insider information.'

'Exactly,' agreed Narinder, 'but we've put an end to all that.'

'We are handing this case over to Fraud,' said Harriet, 'we have so much to deal with at the moment and it does come into the fraud domain. Sally, you can collect the authorisation for the bank statement from the magistrate this morning, I'm sure your bank manager will be anxious to receive it.'

'Thank you, ma'am,' replied Sally.

'I've given the Fraud Squad all the details of the case, including those bank statements,' said Harriet, 'and they will take it from there as soon as I tell them the bank manager has been given the authorisation letter. We don't want some sharp barrister saying we obtained the information illegally. With Fraud taking over the Abbott case it will take a bit of pressure off us. We're giving a press conference this morning, mainly about Blackwell's murder but no doubt the robbery will be brought up. So far the Abbott involvement hasn't been released.'

'Am I needed for the press conference?' asked Charlie.

'You are indeed,' replied Harriet.

'Right everyone,' said Charlie, 'let's get to it.'

Officers filed from the room but Jack turned to his computer. He was still trying to trace Jamal Rodrigues, and if he was unable to do this by using the police links he would telephone the authorities in Jamaica. He had asked the West Midlands police to trace Freddie's brother, Paddy Maloney for him and they had promised to call back with an address.

Harriet and Charlie faced the press at ten thirty. They sat side by side at a table in front of twenty-five to thirty journalists. The questions came hard and fast and Harriet and Charlie took it in turns to reply. Harriet recognised many of the people in front of them and was not surprised to see the smirking face of Tom Cavendish known to everyone as Beefy sitting at the front of the room. He always managed to get as close as possible and made a point of shouting unhelpful questions at the officers.

'So no progress with Blackwell's murder then?' he shouted.

Charlie jumped in with the reply. 'That's not what we're saying, we have several clues including the bullet that killed him and this is on file so that it can be matched when we discover the weapon used.'

'What weapon do you think that was?' asked Michael Dellaware of *The Herald*.

'Possibly a Glock or a Beretta,' said Charlie.

'And how many crooks use those around here,' said Beefy with a throaty laugh.

'We know the users of these guns,' said Harriet, 'not that we can disclose that to you, Mr Cavendish, but we are keeping an eye on the situation. We will keep you informed with any progress.'

Colin Bragg of *The Mail* asked about the break in at the Blackwell house.

'Several small items were stolen,' said Charlie, 'and some expensive jewellery, and these will be going on Crime Watch this evening.'

'And I don't suppose you have any idea who might have done this,' snarled Beefy.

'We have several clues,' replied Charlie ignoring the scruffy reporter's rudeness, 'but glad you asked that, Mr Cavendish, and again, we will keep you informed of the outcome of our investigation.'

Rosemary Ware of *The Independent* held up a hand and Harriet smiled at her. The reporter rose to her feet. 'Has there been any development in the hair cutting saga?' she asked.

'There have been no more incidents reported since the one last Sunday,' replied Harriet, 'so we are hoping that it's over and it was just some silly prank, although quite distressing for the victims.' Harriet brought the meeting to an end and thanked the journalists for coming and promising to keep them up to date with all the investigations.

Back in the Incident Room Charlie chuckled. 'I'm getting the hang of these press conferences,' he said. 'I used to be terrified standing in front of all those journalists, but I don't feel like that anymore, in fact I quite enjoy it. Certainly do if I can put down Beefy Cavendish, nasty little Herbert.'

'He's pretty objectionable,' agreed Harriet, 'but luckily his colleagues have very little time for him and never back him up when he's trying to be clever.'

'Just as well,' replied Charlie.

'Don't forget it's Blackwell's funeral this afternoon,' said Harriet, 'we'll be there and keeping our eyes open.'

Jack called out from behind his computer. 'I have conformation from the police in Jamaica that Jamal Rodrigues is over there and not only that, but he's been in jail for the past two months.'

'So we can rule him out as being the killer of Blackwell,' said Harriet.

'Absolutely, ma'am,' said Jack.

'Well done, Jack,' said Charlie, 'but we seem to be running out of suspects.'

'We'll track him down,' said Harriet. 'If he's a professional, which it looks as if he is, perhaps we should be casting our net further afield.'

'I'll get onto it, ma'am,' said Jack. 'I'll sort out the names of all shooters for hire and we can start eliminating them.'

'There can't be that many in this part of the world, can there?' asked Charlie.

'They don't have to actually live here,' said Jack, 'if someone has hired a killer to get rid of Blackwell then we need to look closer into all his business dealings for someone with a grudge against him.'

'That would have to be some grudge,' replied Harriet.

'It happens,' said Jack, 'I'll get onto it straight away.'

Harriet and Charlie arrived at the St. Peter's Church for the funeral of George Blackwell. They stood together at the top of the path and watched as people arrived. There were several that Charlie recognised as dubious characters, but only two that he thought were from Pegasus House. 'That's the manager of Pegasus House, Conrad Winston,' he whispered to Harriet as the man strode up the path.

'And the woman with him is the receptionist?' replied Harriet.

'Yes, Ann Peters. Neither of them look too distressed.'

Harriet wrinkled her nose. 'Here's the hearse, let's see what the widow looks like.'

The coffin was removed from the hearse and carried up the church driveway with Ursula and her sister Connie following. A tall, well-built man in his fifties walked between the two women and Harriet decided he must be Connie's husband. The widow was dress all in black with a large brimmed black hat and veil which totally covered her face. She was hanging on to her brother-in-law's arm and on several occasions stumbled having to be held up by him. They passed Harriet and Charlie and followed the coffin into the church.

Sitting at the back of the building the two officers cast their eyes over the congregation. The church was packed which wasn't surprising; people were ghoulish and many of those present had turned up simply out of curiosity to see the burial of a man such as Blackwell. Harriet wondered how many of the congregation were clients of Blackwell and delighted to see his demise. Charlie didn't know half the people present but could see no one who made him suspicious. He did spot one or two faces of people he had had dealings with in the past and they did their best to avoid his gaze. At the graveside Harriet and Charlie stood back and as the coffin was lowered into the deep hole, Ursula could be heard wailing and her sister was doing her best to comfort her.

'She's either genuinely distressed,' said Charlie, 'or a damn good actress.'

'At this moment in time we have to give her the benefit of the doubt,' replied Harriet, 'we have no evidence that the two of them weren't happily married and had no problems.'

'True, but knowing what a ghastly bully of a man he was and the fact he had a secret daughter, I have my doubts.'

'I wonder if the daughter has been informed of his death?' said Harriet.

'I'll ring the Italian police in the town where she lives, I think Narinder mentioned Milan, and ask them to look into it,' said Charlie.

Leaving the graveside, they made their way back to Charlie's car still hearing the now much louder crying coming from Blackwell's widow.

Chapter Seventeen

West Midlands police got back to Jack with the address of Paddy Maloney and Jack wrote it down in his note book for future reference. Sally and Narinder returned to the bank and gave Jacob Frobisher the letter of authorisation for him to hand over Frank Abbott's bank details. The bank manager smiled as he accepted the letter, and Sally noted a certain look of relief on his face.

'I hope you didn't doubt that we would get the letter to you,' she said.

'No, I didn't doubt you,' replied Frobisher, 'but I have to admit I'm happy to have it in my possession. Are you able to tell me what's happening?'

Narinder chuckled. 'Well Mr Abbott is about to have a big shock. The minute we tell our boss that this letter has been delivered to you, she will hand the case over to the Fraud Squad and they will deal with a very bent councillor.'

'I thought it must be serous,' replied Frobisher, 'and I'm sure I will be reading all about it in the paper.'

'I'm sure you will,' agreed Sally, 'and thank you for your help.'

'And we're glad you won't be losing your job' said Narinder with a grin.

They left the bank and retuned to Sally's car. 'Great meal last night,' said Narinder, as they climbed in, 'I could quite easily eat there every night so that we don't have to cook.'

'Me too, and luckily you're on kitchen duty tonight so I won't be cooking. What are we having?'

'Hmm, I reckon it will be risotto.'

'That's fine,' replied Sally, 'I like your risotto.'

'Just as well, I do it often enough.'

That evening Crime Watch made an appeal to the public to keep an eye out for the stolen jewellery taken from Copper Beeches. Pictures of the most valuable pieces were shown on screen and sitting in her sister's house watching the programme Ursula Blackwell began to cry. The one thing she really loved was her jewellery and now it had been stolen. There was her prize possession, she thought as she saw the photograph of her emerald and diamond necklace It had cost all of thirty thousand pounds and she only hoped George had kept the insurance payments up to date; she would have to check that out. Jack, watching the programme had little doubt that none of the jewellery would ever show up in local shops; Freddie would already have passed it on to Reggie Rawlings; that he was sure of, and Reggie never held onto stuff too long, he always had a buyer standing by. Only half watching the television, Jack ran his eye over the obituary page in the evening paper stopping at the notice of an Adrienne Dubois. The address was Waverley Court, a secluded compound of large houses on the eastern side of Torreston. The notice stated that the woman's husband had died three years previously and she had lived alone since then. Jack put down the paper. This was it. Just the sort of property that would attract Freddie Fingers. Picking up the telephone receiver Jack called Earl Cassells and told him what he had spotted in the obituaries. It was agreed that they met near the address at eleven, but Jack would contact DCs Stockwell and Granger to tell them to get over to Freddie's house at around the same time and watch to see if he left. If he did they were to call Jack immediately and let him know in which direction the man was going. Jack felt quite excited as he replaced the receiver. He explained to his wife what was happening and then sat down to enjoy a cup of coffee before he had to kick-start Operation Hide and Seek.

Freddie Fingers folded the evening paper with a grin. This old lady, Adrienne Dubois, sounded French, and would surely have a very nice collection of antique jewellery. Those houses in Waverley

Court were large and imposing; you had to have money to afford to live there. This was just what he'd been waiting for. He looked at the clock. He would do as he usually did, wait until after eleven, and then get to work.

Jack called Luke and told him to contact Ben and the pair of them were to get over to Freddie Finger's address before eleven and keep an eye on the palace to see if he left. An excited Luke did as the sergeant had asked and Ben suggested he came over to his place to wait. Ben still lived with his parents and Mrs Granger was particularly proud of her son. Now that he had been given this special surveillance assignment, even though she could not be told what it was, she was convinced that he was going places. She offered to make sandwiches for Ben and his friend in case they were out there in the night for some time and hungry, and Ben readily agreed. Luke arrived at ten and the two young men sat whispering together eager to get on with the case. Mrs Granger handed over the package of sandwiches and a flask of coffee; she was as excited as her son, and wished them both good luck. Mr Granger appeared from his study and told the young men to be careful.

'Whatever it is you're doing, 'he said quietly, 'remember there are some dangerous people about, people who don't like coppers, so watch your backs.'

'It's not a dangerous assignment, dad,' said Ben, 'just some surveillance and we're not in any danger, I promise.'

'All the same, take care.'

Ben and Luke left the house and with Ben driving they set off for Freddie's address.

Freddie watched the clock wishing the time would go faster. At eleven thirty he packed his backpack put on his black coat and woolly hat and left the house by the back door. Ben and Luke had the registration number of the car they were interested in and had found the vehicle parked on the waste ground at the back of Freddie's house. Now sitting in Ben's car some metres away they waited, watching the house munching chicken sandwiches and drinking hot coffee. 'Do we get overtime for this?' asked Ben with his mouth full.

'It wasn't mentioned,' replied Luke, 'but we can hope.'

'I've never done surveillance,' said Ben, 'have you?'

'Just once with Sergeant Pringle but it turned out to be a waste of time.'

'The lights have gone out in the house,' said Ben, 'keep your eyes peeled.'

They saw the back door open and a shadowy figure immerge. 'Here he comes,' hissed Luke, 'and he's making for his car. I'd better contact Sergeant Fuller and we'll follow Fingers at a safe distance,'

They watched as Freddie got into his car and drive slowly off the waste ground. Ben started the engine of his car and waited until the old Polo had reached the road before he began to follow with his lights off. Sitting beside Ben, his heart racing, Luke called Jack on his mobile and hastily explained what was going on. Jack asked in which direction Freddie was travelling and having been told, he was confident that he and Inspector Cassells were waiting at the correct address. He told Luke to follow Fingers at a safe distance but on no account were they to be spotted or the whole operation would be ruined. They were to wait outside the house once the suspect was inside. Luke passed this on to Ben who now had his lights on but was keeping a safe distance from the Polo.

Jack and Inspector Cassells had been in Waverley Court since ten to eleven. There was no way Jack was going to let Freddie Fingers slip through his hands. They had been sitting in Earl's car close to the Dubois house when Luke had called and now all they needed was to see the old Polo arrive on the scene.

Chapter Eighteen

Freddie Fingers drove slowly through Torreston. He didn't want to draw attention to himself by speeding or doing anything else that might attract the eye of the law. Turning into Waverley Court he was a little concerned that so many of the houses had lights on in nearly every room. But he was an experienced house burglar and had always done his work earlier rather than in the small hours when the police were on the lookout for anyone loitering, and suspicious vehicles that didn't belong in certain areas. His old Polo definitely didn't belong in somewhere like Waverley Court. Freddie drove to the end of the cul-de-sac, noting the house he was interested in as he passed it, turned around and drove out of the road. He pulled into a lane twenty metres or so from the end of Waverley Court and sat for a moment. You had to be confident in situations like this, no good creeping around looking guilty, you had to be brazen, look as if you belonged. Freddie climbed from his car and slung his backpack over his shoulder. With an air of purpose he walked back and approached The Vines, the house of the deceased. The big house was in darkness and within seconds he had opened the front door and entered. There was a definite smell of "age" about the place but this convinced Freddie that there would be antiques to hand and the obvious place to start would be the old lady's bedroom. With his torch lighting the way he went up the stairs and began opening doors. The bedroom at the back was large and elegantly decorated with a huge four-poster bed draped in what appeared to be satin. This had to be the room! He began opening drawers and cupboards. Where would the old girl hide her valuables?

A noise made him hesitate, and he stood stock still listening. Nothing! He must be imagining it. He fell on his knees and lifted the satin bedspread so that he could looked under the bed. Suddenly as he crouched there he heard a definite creak of a floorboard and looking to his left his heart missed a beat when he saw a pair of legs standing beside him. Scrambling to his feet he found himself facing Sergeant bloody Jack Fuller of Torreston CID. There was a tall black guy standing beside him and he too could only be a copper.

'Shit!' exclaimed Freddie, 'Shit, shit!'

'You could say that,' said Jack, 'and thank you for unlocking the front door it made our entry so much easier.' He indicated Earl. 'May I introduce Detective Inspector Cassells.'

'You don't have to tell me he's the filth,' snarled Freddie, 'I can smell you lot a mile away.'

'Pity your sense of smell let you down in this case then,' replied Earls Cassells with a smile, 'you're nicked, Mr Maloney.'

Freddie shrugged. 'Okay let's get going.' He turned back to the bed and smoothed down the counterpane patting it to make sure there were no creases before walking to the bedroom door. Like lightning he went through slammed the door behind him and raced down the stairs. Flinging open the front door he charged into the night falling flat on his face as Luke stuck out a leg. He and Ben had been told by Jack to wait outside in case they were needed and standing by the front door they had been dying to know what was going on inside. Jack and Earl walked slowly down the stairs and out of the front door where they found the two DCs standing with their prisoner who was now in handcuffs.

'Have you read the prisoner his rights?' asked Earl.

'No, sir,' said Luke, 'but can I?'

'Please do, constable. And well done both of you, you've done an excellent job tonight.'

The church clock was striking twelve fifteen as Jack ushered Freddie into the back of the inspector's car and got in beside him. With Earl driving they made their way back to headquarters where Freddie Fingers Maloney was handed over to the custody sergeant and locked up for the night. He could stew there until being charged in the morning. Earl decided it was too late to contact the boss to tell her of their success but he told Jack he would arrive at the station early in the morning to put her in the picture.

'One case solved,' said Jack, 'that'll please her.'

'All credit to you, Sergeant,' said Cassells as they left the station and walked to their cars, 'it was your idea and you never doubted for a moment that it wouldn't work.'

Jack chuckled. 'I know Freddie all too well,' he said, 'and he won't be helping himself to other people's belongings for some time after this. All in all, Operation Hide and Seek has been very successful. See you in the morning, sir.' Jack climbed into his car and with a wave of his hand he drove off.

Luke and Ben were feeling very satisfied with the night's work and Luke quite chuffed that he had been allowed to read the prisoner his rights. They walked back to the car knowing that they had played a small part in arresting a burglar. Ben pulled up outside his parent's house and saw that the lights were still on. He grinned at Luke. 'Parents', he said, 'they've stayed up for me, they forget I'm twenty-one.'

'They'll want to know what we got up to, my parents would be the same, they never realised I had grown up and had my own life to lead. That's partly why I got myself a flat in Torreston; best thing I ever did.'

'I think I'll do the same,' said Ben, 'next time we have time off together will you come with me to look for a flat.'

'Course I will.'

'Thanks, Luke.'

Luke got out of the car and made for his own vehicle. 'Night, Ben,' he called, 'see you in the morning.'

Earl Cassells arrived at the police station early the next morning eager to inform Harriet of the success of the night before. In the Incident Room he began writing up his notes and had barely written a dozen words before the boss came into the room.

'Good morning, Inspector,' said Harriet, 'you're early this morning.'

'Yes, ma'am,' replied Earl looking pleased with himself. 'We had great success last night when we caught Freddie Fingers in the act of a burglary. We can close the case of the people who had obituaries in the paper and had their homes burgled.'

'That's wonderful news,' said Harriet, 'well done.'

'All credit to Sergeant Fuller,' said Earl, 'it was his insistence that the culprit was Freddie, and his idea to set the trap last night.'

Harriet smiled. 'Jack's a wise old dog,' she said, 'and if he's sure of something he won't let go. Tell me exactly what happened last night'.

Earl went over the story, explaining about the obituary Jack thought was just the one Freddie Fingers would be interested in and how Luke and Ben had helped in catching the perpetrator.

'We will need a search warrant for Freddie's house,' said Earl, 'just in case he still has the stolen jewellery from the Bardwell's house, but Jack thinks he will have moved it on by now.'

'The house will still need to be searched,' agreed Harriet, 'apply for the warrant this morning and with luck we'll have it by the end of the day, we don't want Freddie released before we have it.'

'We're interviewing him his morning, ma'am, as soon as briefing's over.'

'Good, then get him in front of the magistrate when you can; he'll get bail of course but when he gets to court he'll go down for sure.'

Officers began arriving and briefing began. Harriet asked Earl to explain about the catching of Freddie Fingers and this was received by clapping and various comments. Harriet congratulated Earl and Jack and made a point of telling Luke and Ben how valuable their part in the arrest had been. She asked Charlie to ring the Press Office after briefing to give them the news of the arrest as she had promised the journalists she would do this. She reminded the team that they still had a murder to solve and they were to continue speaking to all clients of George Blackwell. 'Someone must know something,' she insisted, 'so keep digging.'

'We do have one bit of news,' said Charlie. 'I've spoken to the Milan police and they tell me that Bernard Bianchi, Rosetta's husband, has been dead for four years so we can cross him of the suspect list. I also traced the daughter who is now Rosalind De Luca and the police are going to have a word with her regarding the death of her father. If anything further turns up from Italy we'll let you know.'

Briefing over, Earl telephoned Central and told Ed of the success in catching Freddie and then made a call to apply for a warrant to search Freddie's house. Having done this, he and Jack left to interview the prisoner. Harriet went to her office where her telephone was ringing. It was Sergeant Pete Yates to inform her that the deputy chief constable was on his way up to see her. Harriet dreaded these meetings and braced herself for the arrival of Liam Fenshaw who had not been in the job for very long, replacing Martin Cotton who had been relieved of his duties because of unacceptable behaviour. She had heard that the new ACC was not overly in favour of women in high office in the police force but so far had not come into conflict with him. A loud knock on the door announce the arrival of Fenshaw and Harriet braced herself. She was relieved to see that he was smiling as he entered albeit a thin smile and she wondered if he had already heard of the arrest of Freddie Fingers.

'Good morning, sir,' said Harriet, and Liam Fenshaw nodded in return. He sat in the chair facing Harriet and placed his folded hands on the desk in front of him.

'Any news on the Blackwell murder?' he asked sharply.

'Nothing concrete,' replied Harriet, 'but we are still probing. However, last night we did catch the burglar who has been targeting people named in the obituaries, including the robbing of George Blackwell's house.'

'Good, good, but we do need progress on this murder,

Superintendent.'

'We'll get there,' replied Harriet, 'but it is quite complicated as Blackwell appears to have had many enemies.'

'So I hear, and what's this about Councillor Abbott being involved?'

'Blackwell was paying him for extra space at Pegasus House and also for underhand dealings in purchasing council property.'

'I see, and how is that progressing?'

'Fraud Squad is now dealing with Abbott,' said Harriet, 'which leaves CID to concentrate on Blackwell's murder.'

'Hmm, I wonder if you need help from another division,' said Fenshaw frowning.

'Absolutely not,' replied Harriet rising to her feet and facing the ACC across the desk. 'We are making excellent headway and will most certainly catch the person who did this.'

Liam Fenshaw stood and nodded. He knew who the superintendent's father was and how highly regarded she was in the force and felt that perhaps he shouldn't rock the boat. 'Very well,' he said, 'but I insist you ask for help should you need it.'

'Thank you,' said Harriet stiffly.

Satisfied that things were moving along in CID, and he couldn't say anything further without causing problms, Liam Fenshaw finally left.

Chapter Nineteen

Charlie contacted the Press Office and informed them of the arrest of Freddie Fingers explaining that the prisoner would be in court the following morning. Jack and Earl Cassells interviewed Freddie, this being pretty brief as the prisoner was unable to deny his attempted burglary of the Dubois house having been caught red-handed. He was adamant, however that he had done nothing like this before and had most certainly not broken into any other deceased person's house. His solicitor, Humphry Bardwell-Fox, used by many of the underworld and well known to the police, arrived and insisted Freddie should be allowed to go home but Earl had stood his ground and said the court could decide on that in the morning. Freddie was remanded in custody to appear in court the next day and leaving the interrogation room Jack was praying that they would find incriminating evidence at his house or this slimy solicitor would get Freddie a very minor prison sentence or even worse a mere fine. A telephone call from the magistrate's office informed them that the warrant to search the prisoner's house was ready and could be collected whenever they needed it.

'Now, I reckon,' said Jack, 'we need to find something to pin these other burglaries on him before he gets out on bail.'

'Let's go then,' said Earl.

'Right, sir, but let's do this by the book. I'll inform Freddie as to what we're doing and ask for his door key. He won't be able to throw this back at us when he's in court.'

'You go and do that then, Sergeant, and I'll inform the super where we're going.'

Jack went down to the cells and asked the custody sergeant to take him to Freddie's cell. Freddie was still furious at being locked up and insisted he be allowed to go home promising to appear at the courthouse in the morning.

'Tomorrow, Freddie,' said Jack, 'I'm sure they'll allow you home tomorrow but at the moment we wish to have a look in your house, so I would appreciate having your key.'

'You can't do that,' stormed Freddie, 'you can't go into my house just like that.'

'I'm afraid we can,' replied Jack, 'we have a search warrant, so if you would rather we broke the front door down that's fine, but I think you would be wise to give me your key.'

Freddie scowled. 'You won't find nothing,' he sneered taking a bunch of keys from his pocket.

'Then you have nothing to worry about,' replied Jack holding out his hand.

Freddie pushed the keys into Jack's hand and then slumped down on the small bed his heart racing at the thought of the filth going through his belongings. He hoped fervently that the money and other things secreted in the grate were well hidden and anything else that might incriminate him wasn't discovered.

Jack left the cells and re-joined Earl in the Incident Room. 'All set,' he said, 'I have Freddie's keys.'

'I bet he wasn't too happy in giving you those,' said Earl.

Jack grinned. 'Let's hope we find something that will help in putting him away.' They left the room and made for the carpark.

Commander Walter Fielding, head of the Fraud Squad arrived at Torreston police station and asked to see Harriet. Pete Yates contacted the superintendent and was asked to bring the officer to her office. Walter Fielding was a big man in his fifties with a shock of black hair and a bushy moustache. He was ex-army and still carried the bearing of the military. He shook Harriet's hand vigorously and she half expected him to salute.

'I've heard a great deal about you, ma'am,' he said in a loud voice sitting in the chair Harriet offered him, 'and I'm delighted to be working with you.'

'That's very kind of you,' replied Harriet. 'Do you have news on the Frank Abbott case?'

'I do indeed,' boomed the commander, 'we picked him up this morning and thanks to all the work your team has done it appears to be a cut and dried case.'

'Excellent,' said Harriet, 'and has he owned up to his corrupt behaviour with George Blackwell?'

'He has indeed, he could hardly deny it really with all the evidence we put in front of him. If Blackwell hadn't been murdered their little business would be continuing, I'm sure. How's the investigation coming along?'

'Slowly, I'm afraid. There are so many people he's made enemies of that we're having to search them all out and it takes time.'

'You'll get there,' said Fielding, 'if there's anything we can do to help, don't hesitate to ask.'

'Thank you,' said Harriet quite overwhelmed by the big man's loud voice and speed in talking. They chatted on for a little while longer before the commander suddenly rose to his feet.

'I wish you good luck in your murder investigation,' he said, 'and again my thanks for your help in this case of ours.' He thrust out his hand which Harriet took and all but crushing her fingers, he shook her hand.

When Fielding had gone Harriet felt as if she had been in a fight she felt so exhausted. The meeting had taken all of fifteen minutes, but it felt like hours. She leaned back in her chair and smiled. Well one satisfied customer at least.

Jack and Earl Cassells took Luke and Ben with them to Freddie's house. As the DCs had been involved in his capture Jack felt it only fair they be involved in the search, and also because two more bodies searching the house could only be beneficial. They arrived at the address and Jack took out the bunch of keys finding the one that opened the front door. The four men entered and standing in the narrow hallway Jack turned to Luke and Ben.

'Now, lads,' he said, 'a few words of advice on doing a house search. You work methodically, you remove nothing, you wear latex gloves, and you call the inspector or me if you spot anything that looks out of place or perhaps doesn't belong to Freddie.'

'What are we actually looking for, Sarge?' asked Luke.

'Stolen property, jewellery for starters, you wouldn't expect someone like Freddie Fingers to own women's jewellery, now would you?'

'No, Sarge,' agreed Luke.

'Where do you want us to start?' asked Ben pulling on his latex gloves. Jack looked at Earl. 'Sir?' he said.

'Er…carry on, Sergeant Fuller, I'll leave this search to you.'

'Right,' said Jack, 'you two upstairs, and remember what I've told you.'

Luke and Ben hurried off and Jack turned to Earl. 'We'll do down here if that's alright with you, sir.'

'That's fine with me. Let's get going.'

Jack led the way into the front room and pulling on his latex gloves began opening drawers and cupboards. Earl followed him and moving to the other side of the room followed suit. Upstairs Luke and Ben were doing the same. Opening the dressing table drawers Luke called over his shoulder to Ben. 'Have you ever seen such a tidy place? These drawers look as if they've been arranged by a professional designer of some kind, it's almost weird cos it's a bloke.'

'Same with this wardrobe,' said Ben, 'everything hung up and shoes in straight lines beneath.'

'The sergeant said this guy was OCD,' said Luke, 'but I've never actually come across someone with it.'

'Nor me. Found anything?'

110

'Nope!'

Downstairs Jack and Earl had completed the search of the front room and were now going through the kitchen. Jack laughed as he opened a cupboard door and looked at all the neatly lined up tins. 'I said he'd have everything in lines,' he said, 'just have a look at this, sir.'

Earl came over and looked in the cupboard. Everywhere's the same,' he said, 'even the pots and pans are in lines.'

'But we haven't found anything incriminating,' muttered Jack sounding disappointed.

Luke and Ben appeared and reported a negative search. 'Go out the back and check the shed,' instructed Jack, 'you never know.' He stood and looked around the neat kitchen. They had searched the whole house and found nothing. He looked at the old-fashioned stove with its built in ovens and noted how shiny and clean it was. Obviously never used, thought Jack. He opened one of the oven doors and looked inside. Nothing; too much to hope for. He opened the other one with the same result. Determined not to miss anything Jack opened the grate part and pulled out the tray where the ash would have collected. It was unbelievably clean. The tray had a second plate beneath it and taking out the top tray Jack let out a whoop. Here, there was a nice compartment and he picked up a silver cigarette lighter and then a cigarette case beneath which was a stack of fifty-pound notes. On top of the money was an envelope and a bunch of strange looking keys. 'Bingo!' shouted Jack.

Earl rushed to his side. 'Brilliant, Jack, well done,' he said.

Jack heaved a sigh of relief. 'I thought he'd been too clever for us,' he said, 'but thank goodness we've got the evidence we need, these silver items are on the list Mrs Blackwell gave us and these keys, well! We can see what they're used for.'

'And the money?' asked Earl.

'No idea,' replied Jack, 'maybe it from selling his stolen goods.'

'Or was the money taken from Blackwell's house as well.'

Luke and Ben returned with the news that a fire had recently been alight in the back yard and they had collected the remnants of items that had been burned. Luke put the charred remains on the kitchen table and Earl ran his gloved hands through the blackened pieces. He held up a piece of leather.

'This could be the jewellery case Mrs Blackwell said had been taken,' he announced, 'and this bit looks like the case handle. Well done men I think we've done well here today. We'll pack all this up and get back to headquarters.'

Chapter Twenty

Ed telephoned Harriet to inform her of the result of his chasing up information on any hit-men known to be in the area. 'The word on the street, Harry, is that there is a hitman in the area,' he said. 'There was a killing in Birmingham a couple of weeks ago when a local gangster was shot and a mate of mine in the West Midlands force is convinced there's a gang from London now working up here.'

'Good heavens,' gasped Harriet, 'that's all we need. Any names, Ed?'

'Not as yet but I've let them know we're interested in any news they might have about contract killings. Details of the Birmingham shooting with the image of the bullet are on the police web, so you can compare it with your bullet.'

'Thanks, Ed,' said Harriet, 'keep me posted and anything we uncover here, I'll let you have.'

'Great, see you tonight, Harry, love you.'

Harriet replaced the receiver and sat thinking. There was a great deal to think about and the days seemed to go by so quickly. She was delighted with the news that some of the stolen property of the Blackwell's had been discovered in Freddie's house and amazed at the wad of fifty-pound notes. Jack and Earl came to her office and she asked Jack to check on the numbers of the notes and match them against any stolen money and forgeries they had on file.

'How much is there Jack?' she asked.

'I've only flicked through the notes, ma'am,' he replied, 'but I reckon there's about fifteen thousand.'

'Amazing, and where do you think the money came from?'

'I'm wondering if he didn't take it from Blackwell's house when he stole these other things,' said Earl. 'If as Jack says he shifts stolen property quickly then some of this money could be from those sales, but it's a huge amount to have in cash, so was it Blackwell's? We must have been too quick for Freddie to have time to stash the money away.'

'Interesting,' said Harriet. 'I wonder where he keeps his money usually, other than in the grate. Can you check his accounts and look for any sign of overseas banking?' She picked up the envelope and took out the sheet of paper and the key. 'And what do you think these letters and number are with this key?' she asked. 'You say it was in his hiding place with the money and silver.'

'Yes, ma'am,' said Earl, 'he obviously wanted the envelope and its contents hidden. We tried the key in all Freddie's locks but it didn't fit any.'

'Leave the envelope with me,' said Harriet, 'and I'll see what I can come up with regarding these letters and numbers.'

'Wonder if it came from the Blackwell house as well,' said Jack.

'There's a great deal more we still have to find out about our murder victim,' replied Harriet, 'I think he had several clandestine arrangements with powerful people and we need to track them down, Sally and Narinder are working on it. Have we got Freddie in court tomorrow?'

'Yes, ma'am,' replied Earl, 'first thing.'

'Good. I'm sure Bardwell-Fox will get him bail, but when he's tried he'll certainly go down. Well done both of you, and good luck for tomorrow.'

Jack and Earl left Harriet's office and returned to the Incident Room. 'We've earned a coffee,' said Jack, 'it's already one o'clock. I'll go and do the honours before I return the keys to Freddie.'

'Thanks, Jack.' Earl sat at his desk to write up the mornings happenings on his computer. He felt really at home at the Torreston station and decided that moving here was the best thing he had done in his police career.

Sally and Narinder were still wading through the names of Blackwell's contacts that had been found in his notebook and this morning they were calling on a man called John Smith whose name turned up frequently in Blackwell's book.

'The name sound pretty dodgy for starters,' said Narinder as she sat beside Sally in her car, 'heaven knows why so many crooks use the name John Smith, it's laughable. Quite frankly I think they're taking the piss, pardon the language. There's probably no such person in this case.'

'Perhaps the address is phoney as well,' suggested Sally, 'but we'll soon find out.'

'Stadium Road,' said Narinder, 'next on the left, Sal.'

'You wouldn't want to live here when there's a football match on,' said Sally, 'must be hell to have all those supporters milling down your road.'

'I've heard that some of the residents here rent out their front gardens for supporters who want to park near the stadium.'

'Good heavens, really?' Sally pulled up outside number forty-four and she and Narinder made for the door of the terrace house where Sally knocked loudly. There was no reply and she banged on the door again. An upstairs window of the house next door opened and an elderly woman looked out.

'What you want?' she demanded.

'We're looking for John Smith,' called back Narinder.

'No John Smith lives there,' replied the woman, 'you've got the wrong house.'

'Who does live here?' asked Sally.

'Why do you want to know?'

Sally held up her warrant card. 'Police,' she said.

'Hmm.' The elderly woman pulled a face and the two officers waited.

'Well?' demanded Sally, 'who does live here?'

'Don Underwood.'

'Does he live alone?' asked Narinder.

'Yes, I don't see much of him, keeps himself to himself.'

'Thank you,' replied Sally, 'and where might we find Mr Underwood at this time?'

'At work of course.'

Narinder was getting fed up with the woman being uncooperative and spoke sharply.

'You do realise that obstructing the police is an offense, don't you?' she snapped. 'Please answer the questions or we may well have to take you down to the police station to be interviewed formally.'

'No need to be like that,' replied the woman, 'I'm trying to help.'

'So tell us where Don Underwood works,' said Sally.

'Somewhere down by the canal near a scrap yard, he has garage there. That's all I know.'

Narinder turned to Sally. 'I know the scrap yard,' she said, 'I've actually been there with Dave when he wants bits for his car.'

'That sounds like Dave,' said Sally, 'come on then let's pay this Don a visit.' She looked up at the window of the house next door to thank the woman, but she had gone and the window was firmly closed.

Sally drove to the scrap yard and parked her car in the pull-in by the entrance and well away from the piles of old vehicles and other heaps of scrap metal that spilled out of the gateway. A hundred metres or so past the yard they saw the sign The Yard Garage and leaving the car they walked to the premises. A young man with a greasy face and hands crawled from under a car when he saw their feet appear.

'Yes?' he asked as he stood up and faced them, 'can I help you?'

'We're looking for Don Underwood,' said Sally, 'is he here?'

'He's at the scrap yard.'

'Does he work there?' asked Narinder.

'Well, he owns it,' replied the young man, 'and he's often there. What do you want him for?'

'A private matter,' said Sally, 'thank you for your help, we'll see him at the scrap yard.'

The two officers walked back to the scrap yard and in through the gates. The made their way through the lanes of old cars and other junk spotting two men throwing car parts onto a trailer. They went up to them and Sally showed her warrant card.

'We're looking for Don Underwood,' she said.

'And what's our Don done?' asked one of the men.

'Nothing that we're aware of,' replied Sally, 'we just need to have a word with him.'

The second man pointed. 'He's over at the collection bay, you can't miss him, he's pretty tall and has flaming red hair. He answers to the name Red, would you believe?' Both men roared with laughter.

Sally and Narinder headed off in the direction they had been shown and rounding a pile of crushed vehicles they saw the man they were looking for. Going up to him Sally asked him if he was indeed Don Underwood.

'I am, whose asking?'

'Police,' said Narinder holding up her warrant card.

'So what do you want?'

'Do you know George Blackwell?' asked Sally.

Don hesitated momentarily. 'No,' he said, 'who is he?'

'You must have read about his death in the papers,' said Narinder, 'his murder has been in all the tabloids and on the television news.'

'Oh, him.' Don nodded. 'Yes, I did read about him, but I've never met him.'

'And you've never done business with him?' asked Sally.

'I told you, I never met him so I couldn't have done business with him.'

'Do you know a John Smith?' asked Sally.

'No.'

'His address is apparently the same as yours.'

'You've made a mistake,' said Don, 'I've lived at forty-four for thirty-five years and no John Smith has ever lived there during that time.'

'Strange,' said Narinder, 'because this John Smith did business with George Blackwell and his address was definitely number forty-four.'

'Well it isn't,' snapped Don, 'someone's lying.'

'Thank you for your time,' said Sally, 'but we may need to speak to you again.' She and Narinder walked away.

'He's the one lying of course,' said Narinder as they made their way back through the piles of scrap.

'He certainly is,' agreed Sally, 'Do you reckon he's John Smith?'

'Probably, we need to check him out. I'll go through Blackwell's book again and see if Don Underwood, or at least a DU, is in there as well as JS.'

'You'd like to see inside his house,' said Sally, 'but we wouldn't get a search warrant on such flimsy evidence. We'll dig into his past when we're back at the station.'

'It's getting late,' said Narinder, 'can we do that in the morning?'

'Yes, then we can get Jack to help us.'

Chapter Twenty-One

On Friday morning Jack and Earl attended court for Freddie Fingers Maloney's hearing. Bardwell-Fox arrived and sat smirking at the side of the room. Freddie was brought in and made to stand at the front while the case against him was read out. He was asked only to confirm his name and address. Freddie looked across at his solicitor who simply smiled and nodded. As thought, Freddie was given bail and told he would appear in court in a few weeks' time, when his case would be put before a jury. Freddie was feeling pleased with himself. With someone like Bardwell-Fox backing you there was little chance of going down. He grinned at Jack and Earl as he left the court and he was still grinning when he walked out of the court house into a barrage of flashing cameras. Many of the reporters knew Freddie and they shouted questions at him.

'Don't you feel guilty robbing the homes of dead people, Freddie?'

'How would you feel if you came out of hospital and found your house ransacked.'

'Don't you have a conscience, Freddie?'

Freddie waved a hand with the suspicion of one raised finger and climbed into Bardwell-Fox's car. Using this solicitor would, he knew, cost a princely sum, but he could afford it and every pound would be well spent if it meant he would not be going to prison. Bardwell-Fox told Freddie to stay low until the court case and he would contact him as soon as the date of the hearing was decided on. He dropped Freddie off at the end of his road and roared off into the distance. Freddie walked slowly to his house anxious as to what he might find knowing the police had been in his property. Sergeant Fuller and the other copper had said nothing to him about the visit and when Fuller had handed back his keys his face had given nothing away. Certainly, there had been no look of pleasure on the sergeant's face so Freddie had concluded that the search had revealed nothing. He unlocked the front door. Nothing looked as if it had been disturbed and he let out his breathe in relief. He hurried to the kitchen and looked at the stove. Just as he had left it! Again, Freddie felt relief flow over him but just to be on the safe side he opened the oven and took out the trays. His heart sank when he discovered the bottom compartment to be empty. He flopped to the floor dismay gripping him. All that money, gone! He wasn't so concerned about the silver, but the money, damn and blast, he needed that. Suddenly he remembered the envelope and ran his hand around the inner tray. Nothing, the filth had taken that as well. He would have to ring his solicitor and give him the bad news somehow, he would have to find a way of getting round this problem.

At headquarters Sally and Narinder had given their report regarding John Smith, at briefing and explained that they were pretty sure Don Underwood was using that name during his dealings with Blackwell.

'He lied to us of course,' explained Sally, 'said he didn't know Blackwell, and this morning we went back to the notebook and although John Smith is there with various meetings with Blackwell and JS crops up on other dates in the diary, there's no mention of a Don Underwood or a DU anywhere.'

'Perhaps Blackwell only knew him as John Smith,' suggested Duncan.

'Perhaps,' agreed Narinder, 'but the guy was certainly lying.'

'We're going to check Don Underwood after briefing,' said Sally, 'you can bet he has form.'

'Good,' said Harriet, 'keep me informed as to what you uncover.' She continued talking to the group. 'On the board, I have written a series of letters CERBERUS and the numbers that were discovered in an envelope in Freddie Finger's house. If anyone has any bright ideas as to what they might mean I should like to hear from you. The long number at the top we think is a mobile phone number but the rest is open to suggestions, especially whatever Cerberus could mean.'

Luke put up his hand.

'Yes, Luke,' said Harriet.

'Cerberus was a Victorian warship, ma'am built in 1870 and went to Port Phillip in 1871. It became part of the Australian Navy. I don't know if this is significant.'

'Thank you, Luke,' said Harriet smiling. 'I only know Cerberus as a three-headed dog from Greek mythology. What happened to the ship?'

'It was sunk as a breakwater off Half Moon Bay in September 1926 and is a popular site for scuba diving in Australia.'

Officers began to clap, and Luke blushed furiously. 'Sorry! I just happen to be an enthusiast of old ships, especially First World War and Second World War vessels.'

'No need to apologise, Luke,' said Charlie, 'it's nice to know someone is interested in things other than football and reality shows. I wonder if any of this lot have ever read a book.'

Harriet continued with briefing. 'We do have one concern,' she said, 'and that is that the killing if Blackwell might have been done by a hitman.'

There were gasps around the room. 'We're not totally sure about this,' she said, 'but the signs are definitely there and according to information we have there is such a killer in the area.'

'We will keep you up to date on this subject,' said Charlie, 'but for now, not a word about this to anyone. We still have plenty to do, so let's get going.'

Jack and Earl returned to the station and told Harriet what had happened in court. 'As we expected,' said Earl, 'Freddie got bail, but he won't do so well when he gets to the hearing. We didn't disclose the fact that we had discovered some of the stolen goods at his house; we decided to save that for the jury.'

'Good idea,' said Harriet, 'you can imagine what Bardwell-Fox will say when that bit of news comes out.'

Jack pulled a face. 'That creep will conjure up some excuse as to why the stolen items were found in Freddie's house. He'll no doubt try and make out we planted the stuff.'

'He'll struggle with that one,' replied Harriet, 'considering the fact that Freddie was actually caught on the premises of a house he had broken into and his car is on camera near Copper Beeches. Don't worry about it,' she added, 'just see that you both have your story straight before the actual court case.'

Jack and Earl went to the Incident Room where Jack was pounced on by Narinder who asked him to do a check on Don Underwood. 'We're going through Blackwell's notebook for the third time,' she said, 'and we still have several people to track down, so if you could suss out this Don Underwood for us, Sarge, it would be a great help.'

'No problem,' said Jack, 'the name vaguely rings a bell so he's no doubt done time.'

Narinder returned to where Sally was at her desk scouring the pages of Blackwell's notebook and sat down beside her to assist. Earl began a search for off-shore banking accounts that Freddie might have.

Freddie was still feeling agitated at the thought of the police having the money and that envelope. Not that he knew what the numbers and letters meant or where the key fitted, but that was beside the point. He picked up the telephone receiver and reluctantly dialled the number of Bardwell-Fox; he dreaded the thought of what the solicitor would say to him.

The solicitor wasn't too happy to be called by Freddie Maloney. He considered the man an idiot but knew that he had money to throw around so was happy to represent him. He was even less impressed to hear that the police had searched his client's house and found stolen goods.

'How stupid of you to leave the stuff in your house,' berated Bardwell-Fox, 'you might have known the police would ask for a search warrant when you'd been caught in the act.'

'It all happened so quickly,' wailed Freddie, 'I didn't have time to remove the stuff.'

Bardwell-Fox sniffed. 'Just sit tight,' he said, 'and I'll see what I can do, but this will cost you extra, you know, it puts me in a difficult position.'

Freddie would have liked to tell the man what he really thought of him. Money grabbing bastard, he'd had thousands of pounds off him and still wanted more. But Freddie could ill afford to fall out with the one man who could keep him out of prison, so he answered in a civil manner.

'Right, thank you, Mr Bardwell-Fox, I'll do as you say and wait to hear from you.' He replaced the receiver and leaned back in his chair. Freddie suddenly remembered the envelope in his pocket, the one he had intended to post but hadn't yet bought a stamp for. He took it out and opened it re-reading what was written there. This had to mean something; perhaps he could decipher the letters and numbers and find himself in the money again. He would still post the paper as he had planned, all as insurance, and collecting another piece of paper and a new envelope he copied down the cryptic message and put it in the envelope sealing it and writing the address.

In her office Harriet too was looking at the paper with the letters and numbers written on it. Charlie sat at her side frowning. 'This number has to be a mobile number,' he said. 'There are the right number of digits but having dialled it I only get a dead tone.'

'We'll give the numbers to Henry Chong and see if he can trace it,' said Harriet, 'but what do you think the other numbers are and these letters, all in capitals.' She looked at the paper in front of her. 'It's all hand written so do you think it was written by Blackwell himself?'

She read out what was on the paper. CERBERUS-12 – Cd. 2

07818277431 'must be a telephone number'.

10000

1011.4/430

'The CERBERUS-12-Cd.2 is in a different writing to the rest of it,' said Harriet, 'so I wonder who the two-people involved in this actually are?'

'Haven't the foggiest what any of it is,' said Charlie. 'Luke has heard of Cerberus as an old warship, and you think of it as a creature from Greek mythology.'

'Yes. According to Greek mythology, Cerberus was a massive hound with three heads,' said Harriet, 'the guard dog of Hades, ruler of the underworld.'

'Good lord how do you know that?' said Charlie.

Harriet smiled sheepishly. 'I used to be very interested in Greek mythology when I was younger, it always fascinated me.'

'So what else can you tell me about this monster?'

'It was said that the creature only had an appetite for living flesh so allowed the deceased to pass to the underworld. Any living creatures trying to reach there, he killed. The three heads represented the past, the present and the future.'

'Thanks for the lesson,' said Charlie smiling, 'so what do you think Cerberus represents here? A warship or a three headed dog?'

Harriet frowned. 'It must mean something,' she said, 'but at the moment I really don't know what.'

'All very weird,' said Charlie, 'but I reckon this is a door key.' He held up the key which Harriet took.

'Yes, you're right,' she said, 'this is a door key. Have we checked it with any locks?'

'Only Freddie's doors,' said Charlie, 'and Jack said it didn't fit any of them.'

'How about the Blackwell front door?'

'We could ask Mrs Blackwell,' suggested Charlie. 'Are we thinking this envelope was stolen from Copper Beeches when the silver was taken?'

'Again, we don't know,' replied Harriet, 'but for now we don't mention it to anyone, and that includes Mrs Blackwell.'

'If no one is back at the Blackwell house we could sneak up and try the key ourselves,' said Charlie.'

'Of course we can, we are after all investigating a robbery there.' Harriet handed the key to Charlie. 'I'll leave that to you, and if Mrs Blackwell is back there tell her what we're doing, that we found this key at Freddie's property and are wondering if that's how he got into her house.'

Charlie put the key in his pocket. 'Consider it done,' he said getting to his feet, 'I'll take Luke and Ben as they seem to be involved in this bit of the investigation.'

'Its good experience for them,' said Harriet, 'while you're away I'll take the number we think is a mobile to Dr Chong and I'll think about the other numbers and Cerberus.'

'Good luck with that,' said Charlie grinning, ''praps you should get Jack to help you, he's into crosswords and such like.'

'I might just do that,' replied Harriet.

Chapter Twenty-Two

Charlie collected Luke and Ben and headed off for Copper Beeches. Neither of the young men had been to the house before and as Charlie drove up the drive they gazed at the big house.

'Blimey,' said Ben, 'some pad, must cost a fortune to even run the place.'

'Well we're beginning to realise that George Blackwell was wallowing in large sums of money,' said Charlie, 'not that any of it appears to have come from legal businesses.'

'So crime does pay,' said Luke bitterly.

'They get their comeuppance in the end,' said Charlie, 'and Blackwell certainly got his.' He pulled up in front of the house and the three of them got out. Charlie rang the doorbell and they waited. He rang again and was about to try the key in the lock when the sound of bolts being pulled back was heard. The door opened and Ursula Blackwell stood there.

'Ah, Chief Inspector,' she said recognising Charlie, 'what can I do for you?'

Charlie held up the key. 'We found this in the possession of the man charged with breaking into your house,' he said, 'and we're wondering if this key fits your front door and that's how he made his entry.'

Ursula went pale and gripped the door post. 'Good heavens surely not,' she gasped, 'I don't think I'll ever feel safe here again. I might put the place on the market when I've sorted out everything and buy a smaller, cosy little place.'

'Could I try the key in the door?' asked Charlie and as Ursula nodded he tried the key in the lock. It didn't fit. Charlie held the key up. 'Have you ever seen this key before, Mrs Blackwell?' he asked.

Ursula shook her head. 'Where did you say you found it?'

'It doesn't really matter now,' replied Charlie, 'thank you for your time and I'm sorry you don't feel safe here. Is there someone who could come and stay with you for a spell.'

'My sister,' said Ursula, 'I've been staying with her since George died and I might go back there.'

'Good idea,' agreed Charlie.

Luke and Ben had been standing back listening to all that was being said and as Charlie moved away from the front door they followed him back to the car.

'Don't reckon I'd trust her any more than her husband,' growled Luke, 'there's something real shifty about her.'

Charlie laughed. 'You're a good judge of character then, are you, Luke?' he said.

'You can laugh, sir, but she's no innocent bystander.'

'I bet she'll make a killing, excuse the pun, with insurance and the like,' said Ben.

'We're not here to judge Mrs Blackwell,' said Charlie getting into his car, 'we trying to discover who killed her husband.'

'According to the book, isn't it nearly always the spouse,' said Luke.

Charlie started the engine. 'You watch too many crime programmes on television,' he said, 'don't you think we haven't checked her alibi? She was with her sister the whole day and the neighbours on both sides of the house confirm that.'

'It was just a thought,' muttered Luke.

'You're right to have such thoughts,' said Charlie, 'stick with it, we need all the good ideas you can come up with.'

Ursula Blackwell watched the car vanish down the drive standing at the window shaking. The key, the damn key, and those numbers, they could really throw a spanner in the works. She grabbed the telephone and frantically dialled letting out a scream as she received the dead tone. She was unhappy as to the way things were turning out, this was not how she had planned it, and thinking for a moment she dialled another number. This time she received a reply and speaking quickly she explained the situation with the key.

Dr Henry Chong came up from his basement laboratory to tell Harriet that the number she had given him was indeed a mobile telephone number but was no longer in use.

'It was the number of a pay-as-you-go mobile,' he said, 'no longer in use and most probably disposed of.'

'I don't suppose that's surprising,' said Harriet, 'as the people we are dealing with are crooks.'

'Anything I can do to help?'

'We have another number, or rather a row of numbers and letters,' said Harriet, 'if you would like to look at them for us.'

'With pleasure, ma'am.'

Harriet wrote them down and handed the paper to Henry. 'I'll see what I can come up with, ma'am,' he said as he left the room.

Freddie drove into Torreston and parked his Polo in the supermarket car park. He needed a few items from the store and also a stamp. He was annoyed that he had to buy a full book of six stamps, the woman, quite rudely, he thought, telling him he would have to visit the post office if he wanted only one. Slamming the money on the counter Freddie stormed away to the "baskets only" queue to pay for his groceries. Walking back to his car with his carrier bag, another rip-off having to pay five pence for it, he had the feeling someone was watching him. He stopped beside his car and looked around but couldn't see anything suspicious. He was just on edge, he decided, all this trouble with the police and now being told off by his solicitor, was getting to him. He slipped behind the wheel and started the car. It was already one o'clock and he hadn't eaten anything today. He would return home and make himself something tasty from all the things he had just purchased. Before starting the engine, Freddie fixed a stamp to his letter, he would post it on the way home.

Freddie parked on the waste ground behind his house and took his groceries from the boot. Locking the Polo he noticed a large flashy car driving slowly by. He thought it was a BMW. His heart missed a beat. Something wasn't right, was he being watched? And if so by whom? He hurried to his house and scurried round to the front opening the front door and locking it firmly behind him once he was inside. He went to the back window and looked out across the waste ground but there was no sign of the big car. Was he being foolish and simply imagining all this. After all who would want to spy on him? He took out one of his ready meals and put it in the micro wave, he would have is meal and try not to think about being watched.

Jack came over to Sally and Narinder who were sitting side by side at a table in the Incident Room. 'Here's the low-down on Don Underwood,' he said putting a sheet of paper in front of them. 'Just as I thought, the man has form.'

'Thanks, Sarge,' said Sally picking up the paper. 'Oh, Yes,' she said reading what was printed there. 'Theft, violence and several drunk and disorderly convictions.'

Looking over Sally's shoulder Narinder said; 'Theft of cars, of course, and two spells in jail for violence when stealing them.'

'We knew he was a nice guy, didn't we,' replied Sally, 'but there's no mention of him using aliases.'

'I've spoken to Duncan about him,' said Jack, 'and he's going to check out his alibi for the time of Blackwell's murder.'

'Shouldn't we do that?' asked Sally.

'No, you two stick with the diary and book, if there's anything in them you'll find it.'

'Back to the file with Blackwell's business dealings, then,' said

Narinder, 'and we'll find out what it is this John Smith, whoever he is, actually sold him.'

'Cars of course,' said Sally, 'bet your bottom dollar, its cars, and if we can trace one stolen vehicle back to Don Underwood he might just have to change his story.'

Jack chuckled. 'Go get him, ladies.'

Sally and Narinder returned to their desk and the job of going through Blackwell's notebook, diary and files.

'We can check out the car he was in when he was shot,' suggested Narinder.

'It was a BMW,' said Sally, 'but Forensics are still working on it. We have the registration, and if we're lucky we might discover that it had been stolen. Trouble is the plates will have been changed.'

'But sold to him by John Smith.'

'Well, if we dig really deep,' said Sally, 'we might be able to trace the car back to Don Underwood who will then have a job denying that he's both men.'

'All wishful thinking of course,' muttered Narinder, 'but let's give it a go.'

The Milan police got back in touch with Charlie and informed him that they had contacted Rosalind De Luca and told her of her father's death. She was very upset to hear that her father's funeral had taken place as she would have liked to attend. The senior office who called said Mrs De Luca, who was a widow, understood the situation when told that her existence had not been known in Britain until recently, but she would be visiting England to see her father's grave. Charlie asked that he be informed as to when Rosalind would be visiting England and if given her arrival time he would see that she was met at the airport. Having concluded his conversation with the Italian police Charlie went to see Harriet to tell her of the telephone call.

'I wonder if Ursula Blackwell does know of her existence?' said Harriet having been told that Rosalind would be coming to

England.

'Do we mention it to her?' asked Charlie.

'I don't think it's our job,' replied Harriet, 'but find out who her solicitor is and advise him. It will then be up to him what he does with the information.'

'I know exactly who Blackwell's solicitor was, so he must also be his wife's,' said Charlie.

'Not Bardwell-Fox?'

'The same,' said Charlie.

'Then speak to him,' said Harriet. 'You'll probably discover he knew all the time about the daughter and was being paid to keep it quiet.'

'I'll let you know what he says.' Charlie left Harriet's office and returned to his own where he picked up the telephone receiver and dialled the solicitor's number.'

Chapter Twenty-Three

Having handed over the information on Don Underwood to Sally and Narinder, Jack returned to the police web on his computer. He began checking the fifty-pound notes that had been discovered at Freddie's house against the list of stolen and counterfeit notes on record. Freddie hadn't said a word about the money vanishing which only proved the point that he had obtained it illegally. It took only ten minutes for Jack to realise that none of the notes came up as stolen or counterfeit which made him pretty sure the money had come from the Blackwell house, and most probably from his illegal dealings. He still wondered about visiting Freddie's brother, Patrick, but decided to put that on hold. Although in the past the two of them had often worked together, Paddy, as he was known, had not surfaced in the criminal world for several years so perhaps he wasn't involved in his brother's latest capers.

Having spoken to Bardwell-Fox, Charlie was not surprised to learn that the solicitor did in fact know about Rosalind De Luca. 'I can only presume that Mrs Blackwell also knows about the daughter,' he said, 'it's not something one talks about.'

'Well that's between you and your client,' replied Charlie, 'but you might like to know that this daughter is coming to England to visit her father's grave.'

'I too need to speak to Mrs De Luca,' said Bardwell-Fox, 'but thank you, Inspector for letting me know. If you could tell me when she is arriving I will arrange a meeting with her.'

'I'll do that,' said Charlie. He hung up and went to Harriet's office to tell her about the conversation with the Blackwell's solicitor.

The early edition of the local paper had a photograph of Freddie leaving the court on the front page. Pete Yates brought a copy up to Harriet's office and put it on her desk.

'Thought you might like to read the comments about Freddie Fingers, ma'am,' he said with a smile. 'Nothing very complimentary.'

'I should hope not,' replied Harriet, picking up the paper. 'Thank you, Pete. I take it we've had no further incidents of hair cutting on the X7.'

'Nothing's been reported, ma'am.'

'Good, it's as we thought an isolated incident by some lunatic.'

'Let's hope so,' said Pete as he left the room.

Harriet read the article on Freddie Fingers Maloney with the heading; CALLOUS BURGLAR WHO ROBS THE DEAD. As Sergeant Yates had said it wasn't very complimentary naming the victims who had been robbed and mentioning the break-in at the Blackwell house. It stated that Freddie had been apprehended on the premises of Adrienne Dubois and that he had been released on bail to appear in court at a later date. Harriet folded the paper and stretched her arms above her head trying to stimulate an enthusiasm for the load of documents on her desk. How she disliked the paper work she had to contend with; perhaps she shouldn't have accepted this promotion. At least she had permission to work in the field, so tomorrow she was determined to do just that.

Ed was already home when Harriet pulled up outside Magnolia Cottage. He hugged her as she came into the house.

'Busy day?' he asked.

'Too much paper work, but tomorrow I'm jolly well joining the team out of the building.'

Ed grinned. 'Good for you. George Hollyoak did tell you to make the job what you wanted it to be.'

'Easier said than done,' replied Harriet. 'Someone has to read the letters and emails, reply to them, send out memos, take note of all the bumph from government, most of which is near impossible to adhere to, and so on.'

'Poor old you,' said Ed putting his arm around her. 'Well the good news is that I've done dinner. Hope you'll like my chicken chasseur.'

'Oh, Ed you are wonderful, what would I do without you.'

'Survive, I'm sure.'

Freddie sat in his front room looking at the photograph of himself on the front page of the paper. Those reporters were bastards, any chance to have a go at him they'd be sure to take it. Well they wouldn't be laughing when they had to report he'd got off scot free. He was quite sure that Bardwell-Fox would get his case thrown out on some small indiscretion on the part of the filth, or something; he'd be the one laughing then. He'd eaten another of his ready meals and consumed several bottles of beer and was feeling quite weary. He leaned back in his armchair and closed his eyes. Freddie was suddenly awoken by a knocking on his back door. He looked at the clock. Ten o'clock! Who on earth would be calling on him at this hour. It must be his solicitor or was it his brother, he hadn't heard from him since sending him the letter. He rose to his feet and feeling somewhat shaky after his rather heavy drinking he stumbled to the door. Someone was knocking again, louder this time.

'All right, all right, I'm coming,' shouted Freddie fumbling with the bolt and then turning the key. He opened the door. 'What do you want,' he demanded.

'Not a lot.'

Freddie's mouth fell open as he looked into the long barrel of a gun. No words came out of his mouth and he barely heard the phut as the trigger was pulled. A clear round hole appeared in the centre of his forehead and he slumped to the floor. The killer pushed his body away from the door and entered. Wearing latex gloves, he began methodically searching the house rummaging through the cupboards and drawers. Going upstairs he continued the search, again without success. Slamming shut a cupboard he returned to where Freddie was lying and went through his pockets. He gave a grunt as he withdrew the envelope and opening it he took out the piece of paper and read it. A smirk crossed his face and stuffing his find in his pocket he left the house.

Sally was playing hockey for the county on Saturday morning and was grateful that the boss had agreed to some of the team having the weekend off. Dave and Gerry were collecting her and Narinder later that morning and the men were going to watch the match before taking them out to lunch. Sally was a special athlete and was a sprint champion in the summer athletics as well as her prowess on the hockey field. The two women had a lazy morning doing their washing and other household tasks and were ready and waiting when Gerry, with Dave beside him, pulled his car up outside the house.

Northants beat Warwickshire three one, Sally on the left wing scoring two of their goals. Having showered and changed out of her track suit Sally joined Narinder and the men and they headed for the restaurant where Dave had booked a table. At lunch Sally mentioned to Gerry that she had met Conrad Winston at Pegasus House.

'I recognised him from the time I was with you at the Innovation Centre,' she said, 'he's running the business premises here in Torreston.'

Gerry though for a moment. 'Oh, yes I remember him, according to Ramesh he's been pinching ideas for the new place at Pegasus House and often turns up there.'

'Do they mind him doing that?' asked Narinder.

'Not at all, it's all council run and won't affect Harborough.'

'This Conrad is a pretty smooth guy,' said Sally smiling, 'we had quite a chat up line from him.'

'Did you now?' said Dave, 'but I'm sure he didn't get very far with you two.'

Narinder laughed. 'Don't be so sure, he's rather gorgeous.'

Dave poked her. 'Watch it, Narinder or you'll be walking home.'

Sally's mobile rang, and her face fell as she saw who it was calling. She answered the call and spoke briefly. Closing down she looked at the group. 'Duty calls, I'm so sorry.'

'What is it?' asked Narinder, 'we're supposed to be off duty today.'

'The hair-cutter's at it again. A very distressed mother is at the station with her twelve- year-old daughter who has just got off the X7 minus one pigtail.'

'Blast!' said Narinder, 'surely we deserve some time off.'

'That's a bummer,' said Dave.

'Look,' said Sally, 'it won't take all day and we'll still have this evening to go to the cinema as planned.'

'It can't be helped,' said Gerry, 'come on I'll drop you off at the station.'

'Thanks, Gerry,' said Sally. 'I did warn you about dating a police officer.'

'You did indeed, but it doesn't appear to have put me off.'

Driving back to the police station Gerry told Sally to ring him when their investigation was completed and he would come and collect them. 'Depending on the time, we can go straight to the cinema,' he said.

'Bless you, Gerry,' called Sally as she and Narinder jumped from the car. 'See you later.'

Entering the station the two officers were confronted by a howling girl and an agitated mother who was trying to comfort her. Pete Yates came forward and introduced them.

'This is Sergeant Pringle and DC Pancholi,' he said, 'they are dealing with this person who is cutting hair on the bus.'

'There have been other cases?' squealed the woman.

'There have, I'm afraid,' said Sally going up to the woman and her daughter. 'Come with us and tell us the whole story. Thank you, Sergeant Yates we'll take care of things.'

Narinder went to the girl and took her arm. 'It'll grow again,' she said gently, 'try not to cry and we'll do our best to catch the person who did this.'

In the interview room the woman gave her name as Samantha Robinson and her daughter Silvie. They had been to Market Harborough that morning and on getting off the bus in Torreston on their return Mrs Robinson had noticed the loss of one of her daughter's pigtails.

'And you were travelling on the X7?' asked Narinder.

'Yes. We often go to Market Harborough on a Saturday morning.'

'What time did the bus leave Harborough?' asked Sally.

'Eleven thirty.'

'Did you know anyone else on the bus?' asked Narinder.

'No.'

'Can you remember who was sitting behind you?' asked Sally.

The woman shook her head. 'No. The bus was quite full and most of the seats were occupied.'

Narinder spoke to Silvie who had stopped crying but still looked very upset. 'And can you remember who was sitting behind you, Silvie?' she asked.

The girl sniffed and wiped her hand across her eyes. 'No,' she whispered, 'but there was definitely someone in the seat behind us.'

'Man or woman? Can you remember?' Narinder placed a hand on the girl's arm. 'Don't worry if you can't.'

'I think it was a woman because I remember the strong smell of perfume.'

'You've been very helpful,' said Sally, 'and we're so sorry about your hair, but we'll do our best to catch this person.'

'I think you will look wonderful with short hair, Silvie,' said Narinder, 'and if you don't like it you can grow it again.'

'You've been very brave,' added Sally, 'and we'll be in touch with any developments.'

They showed mother and daughter out of the building and went up the stairs to CID to write their report as quickly as they could.

Chapter Twenty-Four

At three o'clock Sally and Narinder left headquarters having written all they could about the reported hair cutting incident.

'We'd better visit the bus station,' said Sally, 'but you can guarantee nobody saw anything. '

'With luck we'll still make it to the cinema in good time,' said Narinder.

They had to request a pool car as Gerry had dropped them off and collecting it from the police garage they set off for Northampton. At the X7 stand at the bus station they approached a group of drivers and asked if any of them had driven the eleven o'clock back from Market Harborough that morning. A middle-aged man stepped forward.

'That was my run,' he said, 'anything wrong? I take it you're coppers.'

Sally showed her card. 'There has been a spate of young women having their hair cut on the X7,' she explained, 'and it happened again this morning. Can you remember anything out of the ordinary happening on that trip?'

One of the other men spoke. 'I've heard about this,' he said. 'You questioned my mate a few days ago and quite honestly I didn't believe the story.'

'Well it's true,' said Narinder, 'and as you can imagine it's pretty upsetting for these women to get off the bus and find they've lost some hair.'

'I've got a teenage daughter with long hair,' said another of the drivers, 'and you're right, she'd be bloody devastated if she lost it.'

'So have any of you spotted anything that might help us?' asked Sally.

Narinder turned to the driver who had been on today's bus. 'Did you notice any woman on your bus who smelled particularly strongly of perfume?'

The man frowned. 'Now that you mention it, there was a woman who got on the bus in Harborough, and I thought at the time how strong her perfume was.'

'Can you describe her?' asked Sally.

The man wrinkled his brow. 'I'm not very good with ages,' he said, 'but she wasn't young, and she wasn't old; you know, she was somewhere in the middle. She wore a headscarf and dark glasses.'

'Well that's a start,' said Narinder,' and where did this woman get off?'

'Here at the bus station.'

Sally handed him her card. 'If you ever see her on your bus again would you give me a call,' she said.

'Of course, I may not recognise her face, but I would recognise the perfume.'

'Brilliant,' said Narinder, 'how come you'd know the perfume so well?'

'My wife wears it and it costs me a fortune, it's called Obsession.' He grinned looking a bit sheepish.

'Good for you,' said Narinder, 'keep it up.'

'Could we have your name and address,' asked Sally, 'you could well be the link we need in catching this person.'

'Of course, I'm Kevin Mathews.' He gave them his address and thanking him Sally and Narinder left to return to the car. As they walked from the bus station Sally patted her friend on the back.

'Well done asking about the perfume,' she said, 'it might just be

140

the thing that exposes our hair cutter.'

'It suddenly came to me,' replied Narinder, 'smells can be very noticeable, and as we were talking I could smell the guy standing near me, he stank of cigarettes, and the smell of perfume was one of the things today's victim mentioned.'

'Well let's hope Mr Mathews smells this woman again,' said Sally. 'It might be a good idea if we speak to one of the other women who had their hair cut to see if they smelled heavy perfume behind them on the bus.'

'We don't have to do that today do we?' asked Narinder anxiously.

'No, we've been noble enough on our day off. Come on, back to the station and I'll call Gerry and ask him to come and pick us up.'

'Great,' said Narinder, 'we won't miss the cinema after all.' As they walked towards the car she began giggling.

'What's tickling you?' asked Sally.

'You know who wears Obsession perfume, don't you?'

'Oh crikey, yes, the Boss,' answered Sally with a grin.

Narinder chuckled. 'How often have you heard people say at the station, you can always tell where the boss is because of the smell of her perfume left behind.'

'True,' said Sally, 'but I don't think the superintendent is our hair cutter, do you?'

Harriet and Ed had a quiet morning at home on Sunday although they did spend some time together going over the possibility of there being a hit-man in the area. West Midlands police had promised to keep in touch with Ed if they heard anything but so far there had been no information forth coming.

'Who was the person shot in Birmingham?' asked Harriet.

'A small-time gangster,' replied Ed, 'and well known to the police.'

'And do they have any suspects?'

'Nothing so far, but they're digging. Now no more talking shop, Harry, you need a break from work and I insist I do lunch. This afternoon we'll curl up and read. And not police files.'

Harriet smiled. 'Thanks, Ed but you need a break too.'

'We're not half as busy at Central as you are, but when we're run off our feet I'll let you wait on me hand and foot.'

'That's a promise,' agreed Harriet.

At Tumbledown cottage in Wicken where the two officers shared a house, Sally and Narinder had only just got up. Sally was busily scrambling eggs and there were sausages sizzling in the frying pan. Narinder was making a large pot of coffee and she looked up as she heard the men coming downstairs. Gerry and Dave were both yawning after the late night they had had. After returning from the cinema they had opened a couple of bottles of wine and spent hours laughing and talking well into the small hours.

'You can lay the table for whatever meal this is,' called Narinder from the kitchen.

'Brunch, I think.' replied Gerry, 'do you realise its eleven.'

'Who cares,' said Narinder, 'we've earned a lie in.'

'Let's hope none of us get called in today,' said Dave.

'It can't possibly happen twice,' replied Narinder.

'Is that table laid?' called Sally, 'this is ready.'

Harriet and Charlie stood at the front of the Incident Room on Monday morning and Charlie began briefing. 'We're still no nearer catching George Blackwell's killer,' he began, 'and we really do need the remainder of the people from his book to be sussed out and spoken to.'

'We haven't fully interviewed Conrad Winston, the Pegasus House manager,' said Sally, 'he told us he was over at the Innovation Centre in Harborough on the day Blackwell was murdered.'

'Why hasn't he been interviewed?' asked Harriet with a slight frown.

Duncan answered. 'We've been up to our eyes with people to speak to at Pegasus House who were actually there at the time of the murder, ma'am and they have all been accounted for now. We spoke briefly to Winston who said he was over at Market Harborough on the day of the shooting and he is down to be interviewed in more depth. We've also started on the people named in Blackwell's book.'

Harriet nodded. 'Could you see that this manager is spoken to today,' she said.

'It was me who spoke to him at Pegasus House, ma'am,' said Sally, 'but we have to visit Innovation in Harborough to confirm that that's where he was on Friday and who he spoke to.'

'We did ring them to ask if Winston had been there,' said Narinder, 'and the receptionist confirmed he had signed in, but she was unable to tell us anything else.'

'Very well,' said Harriet, 'but can we have Winston's visit checked out with the time of his arrival and exit confirmed.'

'Yes, ma'am,' said Sally, 'I'll go to Harborough as I have actually been to the Innovation Centre and know some people there.'

'Good,' said Harriet, 'and I see from the information board that you were called in on Saturday to deal with another hair cutting incident.'

'Yes, ma'am, it now looks as if these incidents occur mostly at the weekend with just the one on a Friday.' Sally went on to explain about the girl who was the latest victim and how they now had a slight clue having been told how she thought it was a woman sitting behind her on the bus with her perfume being very strong.'

'Not only that,' said Narinder grinning, 'but the driver of the bus also remembers a woman who got on at Harborough and smelled strongly of a perfume he recognised.'

Harriet smiled. 'Sniffer dogs eat your hearts out,' she said.

Inspector Cassells's informed Harriet that he had asked

Duncan to call on jewellers and dealers in the area to see if any of the stolen jewellery had been offered to them. 'So far nothing has been reported since the stuff was shown on Crime Watch,' he said.

'Perhaps that's why,' suggested Jack, 'now that the stolen jewellery has gone public, fences in the area will be cautious about buying it.'

'Check out the fences we know, Duncan,' said Charlie, 'you never know, one of them might be prepared to squeal as a murder is involved.'

Harriet explained to the group about the revelation that George Blackwell had a daughter in Italy. 'We are not sure if his wife knows of this daughter and we only found out when Sally and Narinder read the letters found in his safe. Blackwell appears to have had an affair with a married woman before he married Ursula, so it may be that she was told, and it had no effect on their marriage.'

'Whether Mrs Blackwell knows or not,' said Charlie, 'her solicitor Bardwell-Fox...' this was greeted by groans from the officers in the room...'certainly did.'

'That could produce fireworks if she didn't know and Bardwell-Fox has to tell her,' said Duncan.

'We'll have to see,' said Harriet, 'because the daughter, Rosalind De Luca, is coming to England to visit her father's grave, as soon as she can get away.'

'Does this mean Mrs Blackwell won't inherit everything?' asked Jack.

'Again, we'll have to wait and see what the will says,' replied Harriet.

It was agreed that Sally and Narinder would go to Market Harborough to check on Conrad Winston's visit and once briefing was over they left the station and headed for the car park.

Bardwell-Fox sat in his office still feeling annoyed with Freddie Maloney for being so stupid at leaving stolen property in his house knowing the police were onto him. The solicitor was a rotund man in his fifties barely five feet ten, with a shock of light brown hair and a substantial, bushy moustache which at this moment he fiddled nervously with. He wasn't sure what to do about the stolen property and how he might be able to explain it in court and decided he would go over to Freddie house to speak to him. He disliked the petty crook but the money he was paid to represent him was substantial and he wasn't going to let that go easily. He also now had to deal with Blackwell's daughter in Italy and he was beginning to think he was earning his money. There was going to be trouble, he knew this, as Ursula Blackwell had no knowledge of her late husband's off-spring, and he was going to have to inform her. Taking his briefcase from the side of his desk he lifted his overweight body from the chair and left his office.

Chapter Twenty-Five

Sally drove to Market Harborough with Narinder sitting beside her chatting on about the great evening they had had the previous day. At the Innovation Centre they parked and walked across the carpark where the smell of roasting coffee hung in the air. They entered the building through the automatic doors and made for the reception. The main foyer was bigger than the one at Pegasus House and in front of them was the café area with four or five tables and a counter with a cabinet displaying cakes and lunches.

'The cakes are all homemade,' said Sally. 'Karen, whose business it is, is an amazing baker and in my opinion, you won't find anything better in Harborough. Her friend Donna helps her run the place with Rebecca, and they're all very popular at the centre.'

'This is where you came with Gerry?' asked Narinder.

'Yes, his mate, Ramesh, who used to be an IT teacher decided to try his hand in business so he set up here and is doing very well.'

'It's all very light and airy,' said Narinder,

'We have to sign in,' said Sally moving over to the reception desk where a fair haired young woman of about twenty-five stood watching them.

'Write your name and the name of the person you are visiting?' instructed the receptionist pushing the signing-in book towards them.

Sally signed and added the name of Ramesh Chowdhury, Gerry's friend whom they were going to see at the end of the day. As Narinder signed the book Sally showed her warrant card. 'We'd like to ask a few questions before we call on Mr Chowdhury,' she said.

'Of course, how can I help?'

'We'd like to know the time Conrad Winston arrived here on Friday the tenth and at what time he left.'

The receptionist pulled the book towards her and flicked through the pages.

'Here it is,' she said pointing to an entry. 'He arrived at exactly nine o'clock and signed out at five. That's the time we lock up, although members do have their own key so that the can come in at the weekend should they need to.'

'And who did he visit?' asked Narinder.

'Initially, Steven Capstan who has been here the longest.'

'And what's his business?' asked Sally.

'Something to do with property development. Mr Winston had requested visiting several people who had just started up their businesses here and as Steven had been here the longest was going to do the tour of the premises with him before he spoke to the others with companies in the building. Mr Winston wrote to Harborough Council some weeks ago asking if he could do this and his request had been granted. We put out a memo to our members asking if anyone would be prepared to meet him and we had numerous offers.'

'Do you have the names of these people?' asked Sally.

'Somewhere. If you can give me a few minutes.'

'We'll go and have a coffee while you look,' said Sally. They went over to the café area where the smell of freshly roasted coffee was strong. 'It's Carrara coffee,' said Sally, 'all roasted over on the other side of the campus, hence that wonderful smell as you arrive. The boss would love it, you know how she hates the instant stuff.'

'It certainly smells the part,' said Narinder, 'and I'm not going to resist one of those amazing looking flapjacks.'

As they sat drinking coffee and munching flapjacks they watched the coming and going of the men and women who had offices in the centre.

'It's a thriving place,' said Sally, 'about sixty-one rooms but more office spaces as most of the rooms are shared.'

'It looks busy,' agreed Narinder, 'so what does Gerry's friend actually do.'

'IT programming and advising companies on how to set up their websites., Gerry thinks Ramesh is very talented.'

The receptionist came over to them and handed Sally a sheet of paper. 'These are the names of the people who agreed to see Mr Winston on that Friday,' she said. 'Our manager Liza Menzies says she's free at the moment if you would like to speak to her.'

'Great, thanks,' replied Sally getting to her feet. As they followed the receptionist, Sally called over to Karen at the café counter. 'Thank you, Karen excellent flapjacks as usual.'

'The best,' added Narinder.

The receptionist showed them through to an office where the manager sat behind her desk. She rose as the two women entered and offered a hand which Sally shook. 'Liza Menzies,' she said. The woman who was slight and about five feet four or five and, as Sally thought, young to be the manager, had fair hair and a bright alert face.

'Sergeant Pringle, and DC Pancholi,' said Sally.

'Now, how can I help the police?' asked the manager sitting down again and indicating two chairs in front of her desk for them.

Sally and Narinder sat and Sally opened the questioning. 'We're making enquiries about Conrad Winston who visited you on Friday November the tenth. We need it confirmed that he was here all day.'

'According to the book he signed in at nine and out at five,' said Narinder.

'Then I'm sure that's correct. I have the times of his visits to the various companies throughout the day and the last one was with Bernardo Rossi of Business Security, so I'm sure he will be able to confirm the time Winston's visit ended. He's not in any trouble, is he?'

'We are simply eliminating everyone from Pegasus House from our enquiries,' said Sally, 'and we have that list of names, thank you.'

'Ah, yes the murder of George Blackwell at Pegasus House,' said Liza.

'Did you know him?' asked Narinder.

'Not personally, but I'd heard of him. I have to say though, I can't think of anyone less likely to kill someone than Conrad Winston, he's such a nice guy and pops over here quite often, eager to get Pegasus House up and running like this place.'

'Then we're sure we will be able to cross him off our list,' said Sally rising to her feet.

Narinder followed suit. 'We have the names of the people we need to speak to,' she said, 'and the office numbers so we'll be fine,'

Sally thanked Liza Menzies and the two officers left her office.

'Right,' said Sally, 'let's get started with these interviews.' Going up the stairs they made their way to first floor offices.'

Bardwell-Fox parked in front of Freddie Maloney's house and climbed out taking his large leather briefcase with him. He locked his car door, not at all happy about leaving his precious car in this seedy looking street and walked up the over-grown path to the brown front door with its peeling paintwork. He knocked loudly and waited tapping his foot impatiently. There was no movement from inside the house and he knocked again. Still nothing, Blast! muttered the solicitor. Bending down he pushed open the letterbox and peered into the hallway. He caught his breath as he saw the figure of Freddie lying in the hall. Was he dead? Nothing would surprise him; Freddie was such a nasty piece of work. Thank goodness he had paid him for his services in advance.

Bardwell-Fox took his mobile phone from his pocket and dialled three nines. As he waited for the police response he walked round to the back of the house and tried the back door. It opened to his touch and as it swung inwards he observed Freddie lying on his back in the hallway a puddle of blood surrounding his head. Having a keen understanding of the law the solicitor remained outside not wishing to contaminate a crime scene, if that's what it was.

Harriet's little red Lotus pulled up outside Freddie Maloney's house and she climbed out. Charlie took longer to unravel his long legs from the car and joined her seconds later. Bardwell- Fox was standing at the gate and he hurried towards them.

'I haven't been into the house,' he said, 'but the back door is open and Freddie is lying in the hall. I think he's dead.'

Harriet and Charlie followed him to the back of the house and they peered into the building through the open door. A voice behind them announced the arrival of the pathologist.

'Is it another murder?' asked Stacey coming towards them dressed in her white overalls ready for work.

'We'll let you decide that,' replied Harriet standing to one side to allow Doctor Boston through.

Stacey entered the house and bent down beside the body. 'Same as the Blackwell killing,' she called over her shoulder. 'One shot through the head.'

'Any idea when that happened?' asked Charlie.

'Give me a few minutes.'

Harriet turned to Bardwell-Fox. 'Did you have an appointment with Mr Maloney?' she asked.

'Not exactly, but I needed a word with my client and decided to come to his house to speak face to face.'

'You can leave now,' said Harriet to the solicitor, 'and we'll be in touch if we need to ask you anything further.'

Bardwell-Fox nodded. He was happy to be leaving the crime

scene, and not all that disappointed that he would no longer be representing Freddie Maloney in court.

Stacey called out. 'He was shot sometime after ten last night,' she said. 'He must have come to open the door and was confronted by his killer.'

'SOCO are on their way,' said Charlie, 'but if as you think he was shot as he opened the door I doubt they will find anything inside the house.'

'Well on this occasion the bullet appears to have exited the head,' said Stacey, 'so SOCO will be able to find it somewhere in this hall. I'll leave that to Sergeant Hewitt and his men.'

'If it's here, Phillip will find it,' said Harriet, 'we need to compare it to the one that killed Blackwell.'

Stacey came out of the house just as a car was heard pulling up at the front of the building. Scene of Crime Officers had arrived. Sergeant Phillip Hewitt and his team of officers dressed in their white apparel came over to Harriet.

'Morning, ma'am, Charlie.' he said. 'Morning, doctor, anything you can tell us that will help?'

'The victim was shot where he is in the passage,' replied Stacey, 'and the bullet has exited the body so will be somewhere in the hallway.'

'Thanks, we'll see what we can do.' The sergeant turned to the officers. 'Right, take your photographs, Jim and then we'll get started.' They moved into the house and Harriet and Charlie stood to one side.

'As soon as the photographs have been taken, I'll remove the body,' said Stacey.

'And the post-mortem?' asked Harriet.

'Tomorrow, say nine thirty.'

'We'll see you there.'

Phillip Hewitt appeared from the front room. 'Whoever shot

Freddie turned the house over, ma'am,' he said, 'the whole place has been searched.'

'So, the killer did come into the house,' said Harriet, 'I wonder what he was looking for?'

'The cryptic message do you think?' suggested Charlie.

'Possibly. Let's get back, Charlie. Phillip will you leave the house as a crime scene please and tape the door. And we'll see you tomorrow, Stacey.'

They left Freddie Maloney's house and the pathologist set about organising the removal of the body.

Chapter Twenty-Six

Sally and Narinder knocked on the door of the first person who had agreed to see Conrad Winston on Friday the tenth. Two companies shared this room. Accurate Accounting was one of the businesses and the other was Policy Programming and both were run by young men in their late twenties. The first young man held out his hand and introduced himself as Simon Pettigrew. The second man was Roger Phelps.

'We understand you spoke with Conrad Winston on Monday,' began Sally, 'what exactly did you talk about?'

'How satisfied we were with the facilities here and was there anything else we might need to help our business,' replied Simon.

'And were you able to give him all the information he required?' asked Narinder.

'I think so,' answered Roger, 'our only gripe really, is that mobile reception isn't too hot and if we need to talk in private we go outside and find a spot with reasonable reception.'

'But you have landlines?' said Sally.

'Oh, yes,' agreed Simon, 'but as Roger said if we have a call that needs privacy we go outside.'

'I see,' said Sally, 'and how long did Winston spend with you both?'

'Ten, fifteen minutes,' answered Roger.

'Nice guy?' asked Narinder.

'Very,' the two men replied together.

A few more questions were asked before Sally thanked them and she and Narinder left.

The next call was to a Naomi Camp on the second floor who ran a business called Extreme Examples. 'Heaven knows what this business could be about?' said Narinder as they climbed the stairs, 'some of the names are so obscure they could mean anything.'

'We'll soon find out,' said Sally knocking on the door of the office they were interested in.

A young woman of about thirty opened the door. She was plump, no more than five feet five and solidly built. She had a mass of fair hair and sparkling brown eyes. 'You must be the police,' she said brightly. 'We were told you'd be calling. Come in, come in.'

Sally and Narinder entered the office which was quite large and set out for four businesses.

'I share with another guy,' said Naomi, 'the other two places are vacant at the moment. The guy I share with is away, so I have the place to myself. Now how can I help you? I've been told you are speaking to all of us who saw Conrad Winston when he visited, is that correct?'

'Yes,' agreed Sally, 'what can you tell us about his visit?'

'Not a lot, really,' replied Naomi, 'we chatted on about Innovation and the facilities we have here, and I showed him the conference room which he said they didn't have in Torreston and he would be looking into that. He was quite a charmer and we got on really well.' She gave a little laugh and Narinder smiled.

'Yes, he's certainly a charmer,' she agreed. 'Can you tell us what your business is?'

'I help people get their own businesses started by using extreme methods, like bold advertising, posters and leafletting in the street and so on.'

'I see,' said Narinder, 'and I take it you have plenty of enquiries?'

'Dozens, I'm kept working flat out.'

'Good for you,' said Sally, 'thank you for your help, we have to move on.'

They left Extreme Examples with Narinder chuckling. 'Wonder what I'd call my business if I ever decided to set one up. Let's think. How about Perfect Protection and I'd advise people on home security.'

'Let me know when you decide to do that,' said Sally, 'and I might join you, but for now you're a copper so let's see the next person on our list.'

Gary Lunt of Customer Attuned, was next to call on and he was another eager entrepreneur who shared an office set out for four businesses. Standing a good six feet, he rose and shook the officer's hands. He was less complimentary about Conrad Winston and didn't mince his words. 'I found the guy pretty condescending,' said the big man. 'He was what I'd call a know-it-all, didn't really want to hear what I had to say about starting a business but eager to tell me what I should be doing.'

Narinder smiled. 'There are people like that,' she said, 'I know a few.'

'And how long was he with you?' asked Sally

'Ten minutes max, I couldn't get rid of him quick enough.'

Sally handed him her card. 'If you think of anything that you might consider strange or odd about his behaviour during his visit or if you remember him leaving the building during the day, could you give me a call.'

'I can answer that question now,' replied Gary Lunt taking the card, 'I saw the guy sneaking out just after two thirty, I presumed he was off home but now you ask me about "odd things", I saw him back in the building at five; he was just signing out.'

'How did you manage to see him leaving the building from up here?' asked Narinder.

'I went out to use my mobile phone, the reception in this building is poor but you can get lucky in places in the car park.'

'What about using the landline?' asked Sally.

'As you can see,' replied Lunt, 'this is a shared office and I wasn't alone that Friday and as my call was with a client and private, I went outside.'

'And you saw Winston leaving,' said Sally, 'that is interesting. Did he get in his car?'

'Yes. I watched him drive off.'

'You can get to Torreston in less than an hour,' said Narinder turning to Sally.

'What's he accused of doing?' asked Lunt.

'I'm afraid we can't discuss that,' said Sally, 'but you've been a great help.' They thanked him and left his office.

'We need to delve into Conrad Winston's past,' said Sally, 'and see if he has anything to hide. Charmer he might be, or at least that's what the ladies think, but perhaps he's too good to be true.'

'He wasn't a favourite of Mr Lunt,' said Narinder, 'but yes, the women seemed to like him.'

'We found him pretty slimy,' said Sally.

'Ah, but we are so discerning!'

'Come on, let's go and eat,' said Sally, 'and then we'll do out last visit before calling on Ramesh.'

By now the two officers had spoken to all but one of the people who had met with Conrad Winston on Friday November the tenth. They snatched a coffee and sandwich at the cafe and at one o'clock they climbed the stairs once again. Bernado Rossi was a swarthy, dark skinned, dark haired man of about forty and looked every bit the Italian he was. He greeted Sally and Narinder with great gusto and kissed their hands as he welcomed them into his office. This room was smaller than the ones they had already visited but it was arranged for only two which explained the reason for this.

'How can I help you, ladies?' he asked having invited them to sit down in a voice that was deep and heavily accented.

Sally explained that they were speaking to everyone who had entertained Conrad Winston when he visited the Innovation Centre.

'Yes, I remember Mr Winston,' replied Rossi, 'but he was only here about ten minutes asking questions about my business and how I liked it here.'

'And what is your business, Mr Rossi?' asked Narinder.

'Security,' replied Rossi, 'and please call me Bernado.' He smiled and gave a slight bow. 'It is not often I entertain such lovely ladies.'

Narinder gave a slight giggle and Sally hastily asked the next question.

'Was Conrad Winston interested in security?' she asked.

'Only for Pegasus House, not for personal use. He was very interested in the Innovation Centre and how it was run.'

'Did you like him?' asked Narinder.

'He was okay.'

'You were the last person he called on,' said Sally, 'what time did he leave here?'

'Just before five.'

'Thank you,' said Sally, 'and we appreciate you speaking to us.'

'Any time, any time,' replied Rossi going to the door and opening it. 'It is my pleasure.' Sally and Narinder left the office and Narinder chuckled. 'Talk about charming,' she said, 'he's another.'

'Take it all with a pinch of salt, Narinder,' said Sally. 'Now I'd like to call on Ramesh, and he's a genuine charmer.' They made their way to the office Ramesh shared with another young entrepreneur and as Sally knoced on the door, the door of the office next to Ramesh opened, and a solidly built man dashed out nearly colliding with Narinder who was following Sally.

'Sorry, so sorry,' gasped the man.'

'No problem,' replied Narinder with a smile.

The man smiled back. 'Just very busy,' he said, adding, 'Hi, Ramesh,' as the man in question come out of his office.

'Morning, John,' called Ramesh as the burly young man dashed down the stairs.

'He nearly flattened Narinder,' said Sally with a smile, 'he was in such a hurry.'

'He's always in a rush,' said Ramesh, 'but he's an okay guy, name of John Patterson runs a business called Confidential Communications. Come on in,' he added.' He kissed Sally on the cheek and she and Narinder followed him into the room.

'Great to see you, Sally,' he said, 'and this must be Narinder.' He shook Narinder's hand. 'I've heard a great deal about you,' he said grinning.

'All bad I presume,' replied Narinder.

'Hardly, Gerry thinks you're unique.'

'You can say that again,' said Sally, 'there's only one Narinder Pancholi.'

'Can I get you a coffee?' asked Ramesh.

'Thanks,' said Sally, 'but we've just had one.'

'Did you see Conrad Winston when he called here on Friday the tenth?' asked Narinder.

'No, I didn't. I read the memo about him wanting to speak to people with businesses here, but I had a very busy day planned so felt I couldn't spare the time. I was told he was interested in security and I believe he visited Bernado Rossi about that.'

'Yes, he did,' replied Narinder, 'and looking at the board downstairs in the foyer there seems to be several security businesses here.'

'Well, two or three, in fact the guy next door to me, John Patterson who you just met, is Security, he has a single office and works alone.'

'But he didn't see Winston?' said Sally.

'No, I don't think so.'

'He's not on our list,' said Narinder.'

'I've seen Winston in the building on other occasions,' said Ramesh, 'and I did see him on that Friday as well, he was talking to Guy Chambers.'

'Yes, I saw him here once myself when I was with Gerry,' said Sally, 'that's how I recognised him from Pegasus House. I think Gerry told you about our investigation, so perhaps we could ask you to keep an eye on things and let us know if Winston returns at any time.'

'Ah, you want me to be a spy.' Ramesh held up his hands in mock horror.

'You could say that,' said Narinder smiling, 'and we have to add that it's unpaid.'

Ramesh grinned. 'Of course, I'll keep an eye open, it'll liven up my working day. Give me your card, Sally and I'll call you if I see this Winston back in the building at any time.'

'Thanks, Ramesh,' said Sally handing him her card, 'and you must join us some time when we all go out.'

'That'd be great, I'll be in touch with Gerry and we'll arrange something.'

Sally and Narinder left Ramesh's office almost bumping into a tall, youngish man coming along the passage in a hurry. 'Sorry about that,' he said with a slight bow, 'I'm always in a rush.' He went into the room on the other side of Ramesh.

Sally turned and knocked on Ramesh's door which he opened immediately. 'What have you forgotten?' he asked.

'We just bumped into the guy from the office on the other side of you,' said Sally, 'What does he do?'

'That's Martin Meadows, nice guy, keeps himself to himself and always busy, he's an accountant.'

159

'There are plenty of attractive young men in this place,' said Narinder 'and most of them appear to be in a rush.'

Sally poked her friend. 'Come on you flirt time to go.' She thanked Ramesh again and the two officers returned to the foyer to sign out. 'Do you realise we've been here practically all day,' said Sally as she signed the book.

'Let's hope it proves useful,' replied Narinder. 'Mind you it was nice to meet Gerry's mate, and he really is delicious.'

'None of that, Narinder,' said Sally, 'let's get back.'

Chapter Twenty-Seven

Returning to the station Harriet told Jack and DI Cassells what had happened to Freddie. 'He was shot in the same manner as Blackwell,' she told them. 'through the head at close range.'

'And whoever did it searched his house,' said Charlie, 'and we're thinking they were looking for the paper with the numbers and letters.'

'Ma'am,' said Earl, 'Jack has this idea that it might be worth us speaking to Freddie Finger's brother, so it might be a good idea now that Freddie has been killed. Paddy Maloney might just be able to throw some light on his murder.'

Jack had a bee in his bonnet about the brothers always working together in the past and was eager to discover if maybe this was still the case. 'I just wondered, ma'am,' he said, 'if Paddy might know something of what Freddie was up to, and now, if he knows of anyone who might want to kill him. I think it's worth a shot.'

'Good idea, Jack,' agreed Harriet, 'and good luck with that, do you know where the brother lives?'

'Yes, ma'am,' replied Jack, 'I've been in touch with the West Midland guys and they gave me the information I asked for.'

'Excellent,' said Harriet, 'you'd better get going then.'

With Earl driving the two men set off for Birmingham. Jack was warming to the new inspector finding him friendly, intelligent and a good team member. He wasn't the slightest bit bossy, never pulled rank and was always willing to listen to suggestions from other officers. All in all, thought Jack, a decent guy.

They arrived in Birmingham and with Jack negotiating the satnav they found the address they were looking for without much trouble. It was nearly mid-day when Earl knocked on the door of Paddy Maloney's house and Jack was not surprised when it was opened by Paddy himself. As far as Jack could remember neither brother had ever had regular jobs and how they made their money was no real mystery as they were well known in police circles as always being on the fiddle or having fingers in illegal goings on. Both had spent time in prison, although the word on the street was that Paddy was now going straight.

Paddy stood on the doorstep in pyjama bottoms and a grubby T shirt bearing the slogan; Those Who Can, Do!

Earl held out his warrant card. 'Torreston police,' he said.

'No need to tell me who you are,' replied Paddy scowling, 'what do you want with me?'

'Can we come in?' asked Jack, 'I'm afraid we need to give you some bad news.'

Still scowling Paddy held the door open for them to enter. He was not as tall as his brother, but his skinny body was identical to Freddie's. He had the same long nose and sallow complexion, and like Freddie, his grey eyes lacked lustre. He led the two officers into the front room and turned to face them.

'Well?' he asked.

'I'm afraid we have to tell you that your brother is dead,' said Earl, 'we're very sorry.'

'I bet you are.' Paddy sat down heavily in an armchair and shook his head. 'What happened?'

'He's been murdered,' said Jack, 'shot at close range, and we wondered if you might know who would want to kill him.'

Paddy looked genuinely upset and he shook his head. 'I don't work with Fred any more, I decided to go straight after my last time inside and I tried to get him to do the same. I told him we were getting too old for thieving and being inside is no joke anymore.'

'But you knew Freddie was still involved with burglary?' said Jack.

'Well, I guessed as much. A couple of years ago he asked me to help him in a job and I flatly refused, so I gather he went ahead on his own.'

'Do you have any idea what he was involved in recently?' asked Earl.

Paddy shook his head. 'I'd tell you if I knew, but I don't know what he was up to.'

'Well thank you for speaking to us,' said Earl, 'and we're sorry for your loss.'

Paddy rose and walked them to the front door. 'If you think of anything that might help us catch the person who killed your brother,' said Jack, 'ring us.' He handed Paddy a card and they left the house. As they walked down the path Paddy called out to them.

'Hang on minute,' he shouted.

Jack and Earl returned to the house where Paddy was standing on the doorstep. He held out a piece of paper to them. 'This came in the post from Fred the other day,' he said. 'It's all mumbo jumbo to me, but it might be something.'

Earl took the paper and held it so that Jack could read it too. They both recognised the letters and numbers they had found hidden in Freddie's house.

'Did this have a message with it?' asked Earl.

'All the note said was; Keep this safe, it might be important. And it was signed Fred.'

'Thank you,' said Earl, 'we do know about this, and yes, it might be important.'

'Let me know if you find out anything,' said Paddy gruffly, 'and I'd better see about organising the funeral.' He turned abruptly and closed the front door.

In the car on the return journey Earl asked Jack what he made of Freddie posting the letters and numbers to Paddy.

'Freddie obviously thought them important,' replied Jack, 'and if he was killed for that bit of paper then what we need to find out is where it came from.'

'And you think he took it when he burgled Blackwell's house?'

'I do, sir. He had it with the silver he stole from Copper Beeches so I have no doubt that's where he found the paper.'

'And of course, there was all that money,' added Earl.

'Blackwell must have had dozens of scams going,' said Jack, 'is it any wonder someone was out to get him.'

'We'll give the superintendent this piece of paper and see what she thinks about it.'

'Do you think it might be worth asking Mrs Blackwell if she knows what the letters and numbers mean?' asked Jack.

'Hmm. We'd better ask the boss about that when we get back.' Earl drove up the slip road onto the M6 and headed for home.

Ursula Blackwell had no desire to eat the breakfast her sister had made but accepted a cup of coffee. 'I must get to my insurers,' she wailed, 'I have no idea what insurance is current and if my jewellery is covered. As for George's will, again I have no idea what it says.'

'Of course, you do,' replied Connie rather sharply, 'you know very well he's left everything to you, there isn't anybody else.'

'I need it confirmed,' snapped Ursula, 'I've made an appointment to see the solicitor this afternoon.'

'And your insurance company?'

'This morning. I shall go home first to look for the policies and then go on to his office.'

'I'll come with you,' said Connie.

'I'd rather you didn't,' replied Ursula gravely, 'I shan't be coming back. I've decided to return home, it's where I should be after all.'

'Oh, so you don't need me any longer,' said Connie, 'and that's all the thanks I get, is it?'

'I'm grateful for your support,' said Ursula, 'but I need to cope on my own now.'

'Suit yourself,' replied Connie, 'but I suppose you'll call me if and when you need me.' She turned to leave the room. 'Shut the front door behind you as you leave,' she called over her shoulder.

Ursula shrugged, picked up her handbag and left the house. Climbing into her red Audi TTRS coupe she set off for Copper Beeches suddenly feeling excited. She had things planned and now she was able to do them.

Jack and Earl found Harriet and Charlie in the Incident Room when they returned, and they explained to them what had transpired on their visit to Freddie Finger's brother.

'We don't think Paddy Maloney was involve with Freddie in the burglaries,' said Earl, 'but interestingly Freddie sent him this just before he was killed.' He handed Harriet the piece of paper.

'Ah,' said Harriet showing it to Charlie.

'The cryptic letters and numbers,' said Charlie.

'Freddie obviously thought they meant something,' said Jack. 'and wanted them kept safe.'

'So, we're back to a three-headed dog or a Victorian warship,' replied Harriet with a slight smile.

'And most probably it refers to neither,' said Charlie.

'Do you think we should ask Mrs Blackwell if she knows what they mean?' asked Earl.

'No,' replied Harriet firmly, 'if the letters and numbers refer to something illegal she may well know exactly what it is and we don't want to alert her.'

'I agree,' said Charlie, 'we're not absolutely sure how involved with her husband's goings on she was, so we're right to keep a low profile on what we're doing.'

'We do have one bit of news,' said Harriet, 'Sergeant Hewitt found the bullet that killed Freddie and it has gone to Forensics to be compared with the one that killed Blackwell.'

'And if it matches,' added Charlie, 'we need to consider the fact that his killing does have something to do with him breaking into Copper Beeches.'

'Poor old Fingers bit off more than he could chew this time,' said Jack, 'but I'm convinced the paper came from the Blackwell house.'

'Did he take something else of great importance that caused his death?' asked Harriet pensively, 'or was it the paper with these number and figures that hold the key.'

'But Blackwell's dead,' said Earl, 'so who could be that concerned about what was taken?'

'Mrs Blackwell?' suggested Charlie.

'She was with her sister when her husband was killed and still there when her house was burgled,' said Jack.

'Do a background check on her, Charlie,' said Harriet, and turning to Jack and Earl asked; 'was she very upset about the burglary?'

'No more so than anyone else who's been broken in to, ma'am,' replied Jack.

'Right,' said Harriet, 'we'll keep delving and see what turns up.'

Duncan and Ben came into the room to announce that they had visited all the local dealers in second hand objects and particularly jewellery and come up with only blanks.

'We spoke to three known fences,' said Duncan, 'and quite honestly I felt the first two were both telling the truth when they said they wouldn't touch anything Freddie offered them. Reggie Rawlings was a different matter, as shifty as hell, sorry ma'am, and very fidgety when we mentioned Freddie.'

'We told him Freddie had been murdered because of what he'd

stolen,' said Ben, 'and Rawlings definitely turned white.'

'You need to visit the antique dealer in Troverton,' said Jack, 'that's who Reggie sells to. It's owned and run by a creep called Jarrod Jefferies, and I'm pretty sure he's was as thick as thieves with Freddie and Reggie Rawlins.'

'Call on him tomorrow,' suggested Harriet, 'and apply a little pressure by saying you could get a search warrant for his premises if he didn't cooperate. I'm sure he wouldn't want the publicity, especially if somehow the Press got wind of what was happening.' She gave a sly smile.

'Right, ma'am,' replied Duncan, 'we'll do that first thing in the morning.'

Other officers began filtering into the room, returning to their desks to write up their notes of the day's investigations. As they typed they listened to what the boss was saying.

'We're at Freddie's post-mortem tomorrow morning,' said Charlie.

'Well go straight there after briefing,' replied Harriet. 'Have we heard from Sally and Narinder?'

'No,' said Charlie, 'but I'm sure they'll be back soon.'

The door opened at that moment and the two officers in question entered.

'Talk of the Devil,' said Charlie with a grin. 'Welcome back, you two.'

'Where has the day gone?' said Sally flopping onto a chair.

'How did you get on at the Innovation Centre?' asked Harriet.

'We spoke to everyone who saw Conrad Winston on the day Blackwell was killed,' said Sally, 'and apart from one man who thought he was condescending, everyone else seemed to like him.'

'Winston did leave the building during the day though,' said Narinder, 'and at a time that allowed him to drive back here to Torreston, kill Blackwell and return to Market Harborough to sign out at Innovation at five.'

'Ah, did he,' said Harriet. 'Can we have CCTV cameras checked to see if his car is spotted anywhere near Pegasus House that afternoon.'

'I'll get someone to do that in the morning,' said Charlie.

'Good, anything else?' asked Harriet.

'Nothing more we can do today,' replied Charlie.

'In which case, we'll call it a day,' said Harriet, 'and I'll see you all in the morning.'

Chapter Twenty-Eight

Tuesday morning was cold and Sally and Narinder wrapped up warmly before leaving the cottage for work. They discussed their visit to Market Harborough as Sally drove to Torreston but were unable to come to a conclusion as to what they thought about Conrad Winston.

'If his car turns up on CCTV near Pegasus House on Friday the tenth then he's in real trouble,' said Narinder. 'I can't say I got the feeling he was a killer though,' she added.

'We all know killers don't have a hunch back and one eye,' replied Sally smiling, 'in fact some vicious murderers have been tall, good-looking guys.'

'I know,' agreed Narinder, 'but I just didn't get the feeling he's a murderer, even though he's a real smooth talker and you wouldn't believe a word of flattery he said to you.'

Sally laughed. 'No one would fool you, Narinder, now look at the town, it already feels like Christmas with the shops full of cards and gifts and decorations already everywhere.'

'I can't think of Christmas,' replied Narinder, 'for heaven's sake it's only the twenty-first of November.'

'Not that many shopping days left to the big day,' replied Sally. She drove through the town to where Police Headquarters was situated and pulled into the staff car park at the front of the building. Entering the station, they were met by sergeant Pete Yates.

'Mrs Robinson has rung in to see if any progress has been made with catching the person who cut off her daughter's hair,' he said.

'I'll call her back,' replied Sally, 'we have a slim lead, Pete but as this person only seems to strike at the weekend we're having to wait to put our plan into operation.'

'Well good luck,' said Pete, 'I hope you get him.'

'Or her,' said Narinder

Sally and Narinder hurried up the stairs to the CID block. 'So, what's this plan we have to catch the hair cutter?' asked Narinder.

'I thought we'd go to the bus station to sniff out the passengers,' said Sally with a grin.

'You are joking?' said Narinder.

'Not at all. We both know the smell of Obsession, we smell it all the time around the station, so we'll have a go at spotting it on someone on the X7 at the weekend. '

'Both days?'

'Well, let's wait and see how Saturday goes, I'll give Mrs Robinson a call and tell her things are progressing and we will contact her as soon as there is any development.' They entered the Incident Room and made for their desks where they fired up their computers.

Harriet kept briefing as short as possible as she and Charlie were due at Freddie Fingers post mortem that morning. She explained to the team that sergeant Fuller and DI Cassells had been to see Freddie's brother and he had given them the paper that had been sent him in the post.

'It's the same numbers and lettes that we have here,' said Harriet, 'Freddie obviously considers them important or he wouldn't have sent them to his brother for safe keeping. So far we have no idea what they are, and as I said to DCI Marlow, we're back to a dog with three heads and a Victorian ship.' There were titters of amusement around the room and Harriet smiled.

'But if Freddie was killed for it,' said Charlie, 'then it definitely is significant.'

'The trouble is,' said Harriet, 'the death of George Blackwell is very sinister and the powers that be will soon be breathing heavily down my neck if we don't come up with something positive soon.'

'We are wondering where Freddie got the paper,' said Charlie, 'and Jack is pretty convinced that he took it from the Blackwell house when he stole the other things that we discovered at his property, but so far we haven't come up with anything. The money found at his house has been put through the system and none of the notes are forgeries and none have turned up on the stolen register. Again, we have a mystery.'

Harriet held up the paper she was holding. 'We do have the forensic report on the bullet that killed Freddie, and it is a match with the one that killed Blackwell, so we now know the killings are linked.'

'If anyone has a bright idea as to what the letters and numbers might be,' said Charlie, 'please speak up even if you think it stupid.'

'And of course, there's the key found at Freddie's with the letters and numbers,' said Harriet. 'It looks like a door key but fits nothing at his house or at Copper Beeches so, again we're open to suggestions.'

'Could we have a photo of the key up on the board?' asked Duncan, 'it might help us spot a lock it could fit.'

'Good idea,' said Charlie, 'Inspector Cassells, would you see to that please.'

'Yes, sir, straight away.'

'We have a busy day ahead of us,' said Harriet. 'The antique dealer at Troverton is to be interviewed, that's you, Duncan, and we need a deeper check on Mrs Blackwell that so far we haven't done. We did check her alibi for the day her husband was killed, and that was sound, however we need to make sure she has no involvement in her husband's underhand dealings. DCI Marlow and I will be at Freddie Maloney's post-mortem after this briefing and I understand there is still plenty for the rest of you to do.'

'Anything on the hair cutter?' asked Charlie looking at Sally and

Narinder.

'We have a plan,' replied Sally, 'but apart from that one Friday, this person appears to only strike at the weekend, so we will have to put it on hold for the time being.'

'Keep us informed,' said Charlie, 'but first thing would you check CCTV cameras near Pegasus House to see if Winston's car turns up. You only need to look at the time between four thirty and five thirty, so it shouldn't take long. Do you have his car reg?'

'Yes, sir,' said Sally.

'Good! Let's get going, and good luck everyone.'

Sally and Narinder collected a car and headed for Pegasus House to check on CCTV images and Harriet and Charlie left for the mortuary where Stacey was waiting for them.

'How's the investigation going?' she asked.

'Not terribly well,' replied Harriet. 'Clues are pretty thin on the ground.'

'But you think this killing is linked to the Blackwell murder?'

'We do,' replied Harriet.

'Freddie stole stuff from Blackwell's house,' said Charlie, 'and we think he took something important, something that someone wants back.'

'So, did they get it when they killed him?' asked Stacey.

'We're not sure,' said Harriet, 'but if they think they did, and it's what we think they were after, well, we actually have a copy of it.'

'All very intriguing,' said Stacey. 'Well let's get started and we'll see what turns up.'

It was confirmed that Freddie "Fingers" Maloney died from a single gun-shot wound to the head. His stomach contents showed that he had just eaten some sort of chicken pie, and his lungs proved that he had been a very heavy smoker. His liver too was in a poor state and Stacey put this down to heavy drinking. There was

172

nothing in the post-mortem that could help with the investigation but at least the bullet found by Sergeant Phillip Hewitt and his men now linked the killings of Freddie and Blackwell. With the post-mortem over, Harriet and Charlie left the mortuary and with Charlie driving, they returned to headquarters. Back in the Incident Room they sat together at a table with a mug of coffee each and with the paper containing the cryptic numbers and letters in front of them. Sally came over to report that there was no sign of Conrad Winston's car returning to Torreston on the day Blackwell was killed.

'We checked all the camera's in the vicinity of Pegasus House during that hour,' she said, 'and his car definitely did not appear, nor did he, on foot.'

'Right,' said Harriet, 'perhaps he simply left Innovations to do some shopping in Harborough.'

'Next time we see him I might just ask,' said Narinder.

'If we could puzzle this out,' said Harriet returning her attention to the paper, 'it might help solve the question as to who killed Blackwell.'

'Jack's convinced Freddie took it when he robbed the Blackwell's,' said Charlie.

Harriet placed her elbows on the table and held her head in her hands, gazing at the paper; thinking. Suddenly she looked up. 'Charlie,' she said excitedly. 'Supposing we break up these numbers.' She picked up a pencil and began writing beneath the letters on the paper.

'If we write it like this, she said; '10.11.4-430, we have November the tenth four o'clock to four thirty, the date and time of Blackwell's murder.'

Sally and Narinder and other officers in the room lifted their heads to listen.

'Crickey, Harry,' gasped Charlie, 'that could be it.'

'In which case, the paper wouldn't have been found at Copper

173

Beeches, Blackwell would hardly be given the date and time of his own murder.'

'What about his wife?' suggested Charlie.

Narinder nudged Sally on hearing this. 'I said it's usually the spouse,' she whispered.

'Good point,' agreed Harriet. 'Although she and her husband didn't appear to be having any problems, you never can tell.'

'You've asked me to check her out,' said Charlie, 'so I'll do that straight away and see if I can uncover anything.' He finished his coffee and left the room for his office where he heard his telephone ringing. Opening the door quickly Charlie took the call. It was from the Milan police telling him that Rosalind De Luca would be coming to England on Friday arriving at Heathrow at four fifteen. Charlie thanked the officer and made a note of the woman's arrival in his diary.

Sitting at their desks, Narinder nudged Sally again. 'How about the boss cracking some of the code then?'

Sally grinned. 'And without the help of the Enigma machine.'

Harriet remained sitting at the table pondering over the rest of the writing on the paper determined to solve the puzzle.

Ursula Blackwell drove into Torreston and her first call was at Copper Beeches. Parking at the front steps she hurried into the house. On entering the building, she hastily made a phone call and having done this she went to the sideboard and pulled out a box which she opened and took out various documents. She found what she was looking for; the insurance policy for her jewellery. Checking the date of expiry, she relaxed. The policy was current which meant that she would be able to claim for her stolen jewellery. Putting the document into her large Gadino handbag designed by Hilde Palladino, one of Norway's leading fashion figures, which she was so proud of, she went upstairs to have a shower and put on clean clothes before leaving for her appointments.

Precise Insurance was situated on Torreston High Street and parking at the back of the building Ursula entered the premises and approached reception. Informing the young lady at the desk that she had an appointment she was asked to wait while Mr Cavendish was advised of her arrival. Allan Cavendish was a middle-aged man, tall and distinguished looking with salt and pepper hair and sharp grey eyes. He appeared in the foyer and invited Ursula to his office where he pulled out a chair for her.

'Do sit down, Mrs Blackwell,' he said, 'and may I offer my condolences on the death of your husband.'

'Thank you,' said Ursula eager to get on with the business in hand. She produced the insurance document and placed it on the desk in front of Cavendish. 'I'm sure you will realise what I have come to see you about.'

Allan Cavendish understood all too well what this visit was about, he was only surprised it had taken this long for the woman to contact him. He had never liked George Blackwell and his wife even less. Both were money grabbing creatures happy to spend money on the most expensive items possible, regardless of taste. He did his best to hide his feelings when dealing with either of them, but having read of the burglary at Copper Beeches knew that his company would just have to pay up. He picked up the document.

'Yes, I have this policy,' he said, 'and I will have to obtain the police report and get a list of the stolen items.'

'Well I can give you that,' said Ursula, 'together with the cost of my jewellery.'

'The price of your jewellery is on the policy that I have,' replied Cavendish, 'so there won't be any problem with that.'

'The jewellery has gone up in value,' snapped Ursula, 'I need its current price if I'm to replace it.'

'I'm afraid we will be paying you the price listed in the policy,' said Cavendish calmly.

'That can't be right!'

'It's what's in the policy.'

'Robbery, it's robbery,' squealed Ursula rising to her feet. 'I'm not happy with this and I shall be taking my business somewhere else in the future.'

'As you wish.' Allan Cavendish rose and walked to the door opening it and standing to one side to allow Ursula to leave.

Red in the face and huffing and puffing she stormed out of the room. Cavendish returned to his desk and sat down. One client he was not in the least sorry to lose.

Chapter Twenty-Nine

Duncan took Ben with him to Troverton where they called at the large showroom called The Artifax Centre. It stated that all items were genuine antiques and Duncan opened the door which set off a peel of bells situated somewhere at the back of the room. The two officers walked around the many shelves containing an assortment of bowls, plates and exotic looking chargers. Many, in Duncan's eyes, appeared to have been made yesterday and probably in China. A rotund man in his fifties wearing mettle-rimmed, old fashioned glasses, hurried towards them openly rubbing his hands together.

'Can I help you, can I help you?' he gushed stopping in front of them.

'I hope so,' replied Duncan holding up his warrant card. 'Sergeant McAllister and this is DC Granger.'

The smile vanished from the man's face. 'And what do you want from me?' he asked.

'You are Jarrod Jeffries?' asked Duncan and as the man nodded said; 'We're interested in the jewellery Reggie Rawlins brought to you.'

Jeffries face changed colour. 'Who told you he brought me any jewellery?'

'We searched the house of Freddie Fingers,' said Duncan, 'and found a great deal of stuff to help us in our enquiry into the burglary at the home of the Blackwell's.' As the antique dealer fidgeted Duncan continued. 'You must have read in the paper that Freddie has been murdered and his death is being linked to the robbery.'

'Linked? How?'

Duncan noticed that the man didn't deny being offered the jewellery and he pressed home his accusations. 'Freddie sold Rawlings the jewellery,' he said firmly, 'and Rawlings brought it to you to move along. If you don't want to be the next victim you would be wise to hand it over because someone definitely wants it back and doesn't care how he does it.'

'I didn't know the stuff was stolen,' spluttered Jeffries, 'Reggie sometimes brings me items and if I sell them I give him a share of the money.'

'So, you're not his regular fence?' asked Duncan.

'I object to that word,' muttered the man in front of them, 'I'm no fence although I admit I sometimes buy stuff. We all make mistakes and getting mixed up with Reggie Rawlings and Fingers was one of mine.'

'We can be back in minutes with a search warrant,' said Duncan, 'but I'm sure you wouldn't want everyone to see your premises turned upside down by the police. But then, that might not be such a bad idea, who knows what we might uncover.'

'Now come on,' wailed Jeffries, 'there's no need for that.'

'Just get the jewellery then,' snapped Duncan.'

Now sweating profusely, Jeffries told them to wait a moment and he vanished into the back of the showroom,

'That was impressive, Sarge,' said Ben, 'you really had him on the ropes.'

'Most small crooks crumble in the end,' replied Duncan, 'and I should think Jarrod Jeffries is feeling pretty nervous at the moment knowing Freddie was murdered.'

'Will he produce the stolen jewellery?' asked Ben.

Duncan grinned. 'He will.'

Charlie sat in his office doing research into Ursula Blackwell. It seemed she had her own bank account which had a considerable amount of money in it. It appeared she was in the habit of taking out large amounts and only recently she had withdrawn ten thousand pounds. Charlie whistled. What on earth had the woman wanted with such a large amount of money in cash. A new car perhaps? She drove a very up-market Audi, but ten thousand pounds wouldn't have been enough to buy it. Clothes? Far too much. What then? Charlie sat pondering the question for some minutes before continuing with his searching. He soon discovered that Ursula owned a cottage in Norfolk, but Copper Beeches was in the name of both the Blackwell's. Charlie decided he ought to obtain a copy of the will to establish the new ownership of everything George Blackwell had owned. If everything had been left to his wife did this also mean she now owned all the businesses, and if this were the case, then she would be a very rich woman. But what about the newly discovered daughter?

In the Incident Room Jack too was at his computer. He was looking into the provenance of Blackwell's BMW which was still in the police garage. He soon discovered that the car had been bought at The Yard garage and, yes! no surprise here, the owner of the garage was Don Underwood and in Jack's mind, the car had most probably been stolen. He checked his notes seeing that Underwood had been visited by Sally and Narinder both of whom were convinced that the man was in fact John Smith an associate of Blackwell. He would have a word with them and see if there was a way they could determine Underwood's real connection to the Blackwell's.

Jarrod Jeffries returned from the back room and without ceremony dumped a small cloth bag on the counter. 'Here's the rotten stuff,' he growled, 'and I'll tell you now, I've been done! the stuff is all fake, not a genuine stone among any of it.'

Duncan suppressed a smile. 'Is that so?' he said, 'no wonder you're so happy to give it to us.'

'You can't charge me for taking stuff that's not genuine,' snapped Jeffries.

'Stealing is stealing,' replied Duncan, 'no matter what it is.'

'I didn't steal it, I just accepted it in a sale in good faith.'

'Well, we'll let you know what our boss says on the matter,' said Duncan, 'so you might be hearing from us again.' Leaving the anxious antique dealer fidgeting with some small glass figures on his counter, Duncan and Ben left the show room.

Ursula Blackwell arrived at the solicitors in plenty of time. Her appointment with Humphrey Bardwell-Fox was at eleven so she had about ten minutes to wait. Sitting in the waiting room she flicked through one of the elaborate glossy magazines stopping at the property page. Gazing at the magnificent houses she decided that once her husband's affairs had been settled she would buy a beautiful home like these. Somewhere in the country away from the traffic and prying eyes, somewhere where she could do as she liked with whoever she liked. Hearing her name called she looked up to see the solicitor standing in the doorway.

'Mrs Blackwell,' he said, 'do come in.'

Feeling a little nervous Ursula rose and followed Bardwell-Fox into his office where he invited her to sit down. The solicitor looked at the woman in front of him with a feeling of distain. Another client he disliked and her dead husband even more so. But the money he received from them could not be sneezed at, so he forced a smile and offered Ursula his condolences on the loss of her husband.

'Such a loss, such a loss,' he said shaking his head, 'if there's anything I can do to help you, Mrs Blackwell don't hesitate to ask.'

'Thank you, Mr Fox...'

'Bardwell -Fox,' interrupted the solicitor.

'As you wish, but I need to know the contents of my husband's will?'

'Of course, but surely you have a copy of the document.'

'No, I haven't,' replied Ursula.

'But I'm sure you know what is in it?' Bardwell-Fox raised an eyebrow.

'Could you just read it to me,' snapped Ursula now getting agitated at the casual attitude of the solicitor.

'I have the will here,' said Barwell-Fox holding up a document. 'I collected it immediately you telephoned to say you were coming.'

'I presume George left everything to me,' said Ursula, 'there shouldn't be any problems.'

'Ah, well, I'm afraid that's not the case,' said Bardwell-Fox, 'although your late husband does say that the holiday cottage is yours and half the proceeds from the sale of Copper Beeches.'

Ursula jumped to her feet. 'What do you mean half the proceeds from the sale of the house, I'm not selling Copper Beeches until I've found another property I like. Copper Beeches is my home and if I sell it all the money comes to me.'

'I'm afraid the house will have to be sold as soon as possible,' said Bardwell-Fox, 'as half of the proceeds has been left to Rosalind De Luca.'

'Who the hell is Rosalind De Luca?' shrieked Ursula.

'Mr Blackwell's daughter, I thought you would have known all about her.' He said this slyly knowing full well George Blackwell had kept this an absolute secret from his wife. He had after all been paying him handsomely to keep several things secret, and the daughter was one of them he had never divulged, although telling Ursula Blackwell about Rosalind De Luca at this moment, gave him great pleasure.

Ursula sat down heavily. 'Since when has my husband had a daughter?' she spluttered.

Bardwell-Fox looked at the paper in front of him. 'Well, Mrs De Luca is twenty-seven.'

Ursula took a large handkerchief from her handbag and mopped her perspiring face.

'This can't be happening,' she wailed, 'the bastard had a secret child before we were married and never told me.'

'I'm sorry, I had no idea he had kept it from you.'

'It won't be true of course, someone is trying to get money from me based on a lie.'

The solicitor took out another paper and pushed it across the table. 'A copy of the birth certificate of Rosalind Blackwell,' he said, 'she was given her father's name; De Luca is her married name. She lives in Milan and your husband has kept in contact with her. There is also this sealed letter that he left for you in the event of his death.' He handed Ursula an envelope.

'Perhaps you would like to open it at home to read it in private,' he said, 'I expect it is an apology for keeping such a secret from you.'

Ursula snatched the envelope and stuffed it in her handbag. 'What about the businesses and all his money?' she demanded.

Bardwell-Fox was now feeling quite jubilant. 'All the businesses are to be sold,' he said working hard to keep the delight out of his voice, 'and the money to go to his daughter.'

'No,' screamed Ursula, 'this is not going to happen, I won't let it. I'm his wife and I deserve to have everything; no illegitimate daughter is going to get in the way of my inheritance. Do something about it, Mr Fox...'

'Bardwell-Fox,'

'Just do something about it, what do I pay you for?'

'Well, actually it was your husband who always paid me and therefore I am obliged to carry out his wishes. If you choose to contest the will you will have to apply for a court hearing, but I have to warn you, Mrs Blackwell, Mrs De Luca is the legitimate daughter of your late husband and I doubt his requests will be over-ruled.'

'The bastard, how could he do this to me, who was the woman, and where did this happen?'

'As I said, Mrs De Luca is twenty-seven, and according to your husband he was in Milan at that time he met Rosetta Bianchi, her mother, who was already married at the time,' said Bardwell-Fox, 'so as you stated she was born before you were married to him.'

'And where is this Rosetta now?' demanded Ursula.

'Apparently, she died a couple of years ago, in a car crash, but your late husband has always provided for the daughter, so she is being taken care of.'

'Well, it's time all that stopped,' snapped Ursula, 'I am the legal widow and I shall see to it that no illegitimate creature gets a penny of my rightful inheritance.' She stormed from the room slamming the door behind her.

Humphrey Bardwell-Fox leaned back in his chair with a definite smirk on his face. He didn't like Ursula Blackwell, such a vulgar woman, not that he had had any great regard for her husband who was equally as crude. But money was money and with George gone and now Freddie, he would be down on his monthly income. He folded the documents in his hand and rose to lock them in his safe. He would wait to see what Mrs Blackwell did regarding the contesting of the will, but he didn't see there would be any problem with him carrying out the wishes of his late client.

Chapter Thirty

Duncan and Ben returned to headquarters and hurried up to the Incident Room where Duncan dumped the small bag of jewellery on the desk in front of Jack.

'All present and correct,' he said.

'Well done, lad,' said Jack, 'so Jefferies decided to cough up, did he?'

'Quite happy to,' replied Duncan, 'especially as the stuff is fake.'

'Is it now? Oh dear, Mrs Blackwell is going to have a shock.'

'Unless she knew,' suggested Duncan, 'and it's all a fraudulent insurance claim, if she's making one that is.'

'I'm sure she'll be making one,' replied Jack.

Harriet came into the room and Duncan eagerly told her about the recovery of Ursula's jewellery and the fact that it was all fake.

'Do we know who her insurers are?' she asked.

'No, ma'am,' said Jack, 'but I'll find out.'

'When we know who they are,' said Harriet, 'get over to them, Duncan and hand over the jewellery and let them explain the situation to Mrs Blackwell, it's not really our business unless the insurance company thinks the claim is fraudulent, but ring her to tell her we have recovered them.'

'Right, ma'am.'

'Make sure you check the jewellery and record each item in the book.'

'We'll do that straight away, ma'am,' said Duncan picking up the bag. 'What do you want us to do about Jeffries?'

'A caution I think,' replied Harriet, 'but make him aware that we will be keeping a close eye on him.'

'And Reggie Rawlins, the fence?'

'The same,' replied Harriet, 'with Freddie dead we're rather short of evidence against him, but make sure they both know we are aware of what they're up to.'

'Yes, ma'am. I'll just ring Mrs Blackwell, Jack and then we'll go and put the stuff in the book. We'll be back as soon as possible and hopefully by then you'll have the name of the insurers. With me, Ben,' he said, and the two men left the room.

'Is there anything else, Jack?' asked Harriet.

'I've tracked down Blackwell's BMW, and it was sold to him by Don Underwood of The Yard Garage. We're still waiting for Forensics to complete their search of the vehicle as we need to have confirmation that it was stolen. Sally and Narinder suspect the Yard Garage of being bent and this Don is in fact John Smith one of Blackwell's cronies. With luck, once we know for certain the car was stolen we can close in on him.'

'Good,' said Harriet, 'things are moving along but we're still none the wiser as to who the killer could be. Blackwell's daughter is arriving on Friday, so Charlie will be meeting her at Heathrow in the afternoon.'

'That should be interesting,' replied Jack.

'We just need to find out who our killer is,' said Harriet, 'the days are slipping by.'

'We'll get him, ma'am, don't you worry.'

Harriet smiled. 'Thank you, Jack. I'll be in my office if I'm needed.'

Harriet was at her desk when Commander Walter Fielding, head of the Fraud Squad called her.

He told her that they had discovered an account of George Blackwell's in the Cayman Isles.

'A very lucrative account,' said Fielding. 'He was sending money there at regular intervals and there's over three million stashed away.'

'Heaven's,' said Harriet, 'and did Abbott have a hidden account as well.'

'No, he didn't, he appears to be a small-time crook and stupidly was keeping all his money in his own bank here in Torreston. He doesn't come across as very bright either. He's appearing in court next week and may well get a prison sentence or at the least a hefty fine and will certainly lose his job at the Council Office.'

'That's punishment in itself,' said Harriet, 'he'll struggle to get another job with that against his name.' She thanked Commander Fielding for the information about Abbott and Blackwell and hung up. She picked up the piece of paper with the cryptic letters and numbers and once again poured over it.

Duncan recorded the jewellery in the book that Pete Yates produced for him and the duty sergeant signed as a witness. Returning to the Incident Room he and Ben were met by Jack waving a piece of paper at them. 'The name of the Blackwell insurers,' called Jack. 'You can hand over the stuff to them but make sure you get each item signed for.'

'Will do,' answered Duncan, 'pity we won't see Mrs Blackwell's face when she's given the news that the stuff is fake.'

'As you said earlier, perhaps she knew.'

'Bet she didn't,' said Ben with a grin, 'George Blackwell was a real creep, you wouldn't trust him with anything.'

'Well let's do it,' said Duncan. 'See you later, Jack.' He took the paper from the sergeant and with Ben on his heels hurried from the room.

In the police garage a team of Forensic experts was going over the Blackwell's BMW with a fine-tooth comb. The men knew that these cars were a prime target for car thieves and in most cases the crooks had clients for the stolen vehicle already lined up and the car was stolen to order. It didn't take long to discover the erased numbers on the chassis and soon after that they traced the original owner of the BMW. It had been stolen nearly six months ago from Milton Keynes and telephoning Harriet, Fraser Overton gave her the news. Harriet thanked him and ending the call, she hurried to the Incident Room where she found Sally and Narinder at their desks. Jack was busy at his computer and looked up when Harriet entered.

'Some good news for you all,' she said, 'Forensics have discovered that the BMW was stolen six months ago from Milton Keynes, so this will give us the excuse we need to obtain a search warrant for the Yard Garage.'

'As we expected,' grunted Jack.

'Brilliant,' said Sally jumping to her feet, 'perhaps we'll find the information we need that tells us Underwood really is the John Smith in Blackwell's book.'

'I'll leave that in your capable hands,' said Harriet leaving the room with a smile on her face.

'I'll set the ball rolling for the search warrant,' said Jack, 'and when we have it I'm sure you two will get a kick in organising the search of the garage.'

'We certainly will,' agreed Narinder.

Harriet sat at her desk her eyes once again glued to the cryptic letters and numbers. She picked up the telephone receiver and called Charlie asking him to come and see her and to bring Ursula's bank statements with him. Charlie arrived in minutes.

'Charlie,' said Harriet once he was seated, 'read out the dates of any ten thousand pounds going out of Mrs Blackwell's account.'

Charlie ran his eyes over the sheets of paper and looked up. 'There are several large sums withdrawn but only one of ten thousand.'

'And the date of that withdrawal?'

'Tuesday November seventh.'

Harriet pushed the paper with the numbers and letters across to Charlie. 'Under CERRBERUS-12 there's 10000. Just supposing that represents ten thousand pounds. We think the other numbers could be the tenth of November four o'clock to four thirty so is this figure a payment for the killing. I can't imagine what Cd, 2 is.'

'Crickey,' said Charlie,' you reckon Ursula did away with her husband?'

'I'm, only guessing,' replied Harriet, 'but some of these things are surely more than a coincidence. If Ursula withdrew ten thousand the week of the murder it is rather suspicious.'

'We need to know if the Blackwell's had any marital problems,' said Charlie.

'If they did have, Ursula did well in keeping them a secret. No one has made any suggestion they had problems.'

'We need to bring her in and ask some questions,' said Charlie.

'We'll do that, and we'll interview her together,' said Harriet. 'It will be interesting to know what she needed ten thousand pounds for.'

Jack told Sally and Narinder that a warrant to search the Yard Garage would be available the following morning. 'Collect it first thing,' he advised them, 'and with luck you'll surprise this Don Underwood.'

'We'll certainly do that,' said Sally, 'he thinks we're only interested in someone called John Smith.'

'Take several guys from uniform with you,' said Jack, 'we don't want you two putting yourselves in harm's way. Not that you can't handle yourselves,' he added hastily.

Narinder smiled. She knew Jack of old and how he secretly kept an eye on the young officers and especially the females. 'We'll take care, Sarge,' she said, 'don't you worry.'

'And you wear stab-vest,' added Jack, 'I'm not being over protective of you two, I'd say it to any officers, we don't have to be heroes so protecting ourselves against these violent people, is just common sense.'

'You're right, Jack,' said Sally, 'and we'll do as you say, I promise.'

Duncan and Ben called on the Precise Insurance Company and asked to speak to the person dealing with the Blackwell robbery claim. They were shown into the office of Allan Cavendish where Duncan handed over the jewellery.

'Excellent news,' said Cavendish, 'you've saved us a great deal of money as we were going to be obliged to pay out on Mrs Blackwell's claim.'

'There is one thing you might like to know,' said Duncan, 'all the jewellery is fake. We've had it examined by an expert and he agrees that it's all paste. None of the diamonds are genuine.'

'Good heavens!' Cavendish was astounded but within seconds of the news, Duncan and Ben were convinced he suppressed a smile. 'I shall inform Mrs Blackwell immediately. I'm sure she had no idea this was the case. Or at least I hope she didn't know or she would be facing a case of fraud.' He had his elbows on his desk and he pressed his hands together. 'Dear me,' he muttered, 'what a situation.'

'We'll leave you to sort it out,' said Duncan, 'if you would just check the jewellery and give us a receipt for it.'

'Of course, of course.' Cavendish tipped the contents of the bag onto his desk and shuffled through it. 'Strange,' he said, 'when you know the jewels are fake you can see they're not at all beautiful.' He checked them against the list Ben handed him and then wrote out a receipt which he handed over.

'Thank you,' said Ben putting the paper in his pocket.

Duncan too thanked Cavendish and the offices left. Outside the building Ben spoke.

'The guy smiled when he heard the stuff was fake,' he said.

'I noticed that as well,' agreed Duncan, 'I'm beginning to think the Blackwell's were a bit short on friends and admirers.' Grinning the two men climbed into their car.

Allan Cavendish picked up the telephone receiver and dialled the number of Copper Beeches. Ursula picked up almost immediately.

'Mrs Blackwell?'

'Yes,' replied Ursula, who is this?'

'Allan Cavendish, Precise Insurance, I have some good news for you.'

'Well that makes a change. Are you going to tell me you're prepared to up the pay-out money?'

'Better than that,' answered Cavendish, 'the police have found your jewellery and given it to me return to you.' He had decided not to inform her over the telephone that the jewels were fake but would wait until she was in his office to collect them.

'Is it all there?' asked Ursula disbelief in her voice.

'Everything on your list. Are you able to call in tomorrow to collect it?'

'Absolutely, I'll be in after lunch as I have an appointment in the morning.'

'At your convenience, Mrs Blackwell,' said Cavendish. 'I'll see you tomorrow.' He replaced the receiver and leaned back in his chair. There would be tantrums tomorrow, he was sure of that, but he would cope with those when they happened, nevertheless, he thought he might make sure his secretary was in the office when he broke the news that the jewels were fake. The good thing was, his company would not be paying out thousands of pounds in compensation.

Chapter Thirty-One

First thing the following morning Sally and Narinder called at the magistrates and collected the search warrants for the Yard Garage, and Don Underwood's house. They had been excused morning briefing as it had been agreed they should arrive at the garage early and unannounced. They collected their stab-vests from stores and pulled them on with Narinder complaining that they made her feel fat.

'Better fat than dead,' replied Sally, 'and we won't be wearing them for long.'

Sally drove her car with Narinder beside her and following them was the unmarked blue van carrying six uniform officers. Stopping at the gates of the garage, Sally went to the van and handed one of the warrants to the officer in the driving seat together with a paper with the registration numbers of recently stolen cars.

'You start on the garage,' she said, 'we're going to Underwood's house before someone tips him off that we're here.'

'Right, Sarge. Is it just stolen cars were looking for?'

'Primarily, but anything that looks the least bit suspicious pick up. You know, documents, false number plates and the like; anything that might be connected to dealing in stolen vehicles.'

'Names of clients might be a help,' said Narinder, 'he must have a book stashed away somewhere listing all the crooks he deals with.'

'We'll do our best,' said the officer and climbing from the van he went to the back of it and opened the doors. 'Right, guys,' he said, 'we're on!'

'Before you dash off,' said Sally, 'could we borrow one strong guy, we promised Sergeant Fuller we wouldn't face this Don Underwood on our own. He's a big brute of a man and known to be violent.'

'Not that we couldn't handle him,' insisted Narinder, 'but Jack Fuller likes to keep an eye out for us.'

'I know Fuller,' said the officer, 'great guy, I remember when I was a probationer how he looked after me and my mates. Jason!' he called out, 'you're with Sergeant Pringle, the rest of you with me.'

'Thanks,' said Sally as a tall, young man jumped from the van and came over to her, 'we'll return him in good order.'

The constable who looked rather like a rugby player grinned and introduced himself as Jason Richards before climbing into the car with them. Starting the engine, Sally headed for Don Underwood's house in Stadium Road. She parked a few doors away from number forty- four and she, Narinder and Jason walked the rest of the way.

'We don't want him spotting us,' said Sally, 'it would give him time to burn any paperwork he might want hidden from our eyes.'

Narinder chuckled. 'He's going to have quite a surprise. I wonder if we'll find anything that identifies him as John Smith?'

'We can hope,' replied Sally.

'Is there anything in particular you want me to do?' asked Jason.

'No,' replied Sally, 'just follow our lead.'

'Yes, Sarge.'

Sally knocked on the door and they waited. Narinder cast her eyes up and saw a bedroom curtain move and a face look down on them; a face she thought she recognised. 'He's got a woman with him,' she hissed.

'I thought he lived alone,' said Sally, 'at least that's what that helpful neighbour told us.' She knocked again much louder this time and noises could be heard inside the house. More scuffling was heard and somewhere in the house a door slammed.

'I think we've caught him on the hop,' said Narinder, 'I have a thought, Sal, I won't be a tick.' She hurried back down the path and onto the street.

Sally knocked for the third time and a voice called out. 'Hang on I'm coming.'

Another two minutes passed and as Narinder came back up the path, they heard bolts being withdrawn followed by a key turning in the door. A dishevelled Don Underwood stood in the doorway. 'What do you want now?' he demanded scowling.

'Sorry to disturb you,' said Sally sweetly, 'but we have a warrant to search your house.'

'Like hell you do,' snapped Underwood, 'you're not searching my house.'

Sally held up the warrant. 'I'm afraid you get no say in the matter,' she said, 'this warrant gives us the authority we need.' She stepped forward and Underwood did the same blocking her path. Jason thrust himself into the doorway past Sally, and Narinder moved as if to intervein but Sally quickly put out a hand and stopped her.

'If you'd rather be taken down to the station, sir,' said Jason firmly, 'I'll call for a car to transport you.' The young constable was taller than Underwood and quite a bit broader and he faced the man confidently. Underwood hesitated before taking a pace back.

'Thank you, sir,' said Jason as he moved into the hallway. Sally and Narinder followed.

'Please sit in the front room,' said Sally, 'we shouldn't take long.'

'I'll bloody watch what you lot are up to. I'll be right behind.'

'Where's your lady friend?' asked Narinder, 'we're sorry we disturbed her.'

'There's no lady friend,' snapped Underwood, 'I live on my own.'

'Right,' said Narinder.

Sally sent Jason upstairs and she and Narinder began their search in the downstairs sitting room. 'We could have handled Underwood,' hissed Narinder not wanting the man in question to hear, 'we don't need protecting.'

'Of course we don't, and yes, we could have coped,' replied Sally in a whisper, 'but you should never knock someone down when they think they're doing the right thing, especially a young guy like Jason.'

Narinder grinned. 'Point taken.'

Methodically the two went through the cupboards and drawers finding nothing incriminating. Sally's phone ran and opening up she heard the voice of the officer in charge of the search of the Yard Garage. She hurried outside to take the call where she was told that the men at the garage had found several cars that were on the stolen list, a box of number plates and a pile of documents relating to the vehicles. 'And a book with names and addresses, Sarge' he added, 'something your colleague wanted us to find.'

'That's great news, bring everything in,' said Sally, 'and when we're done here I shall arrest Underwood, so would you send a squad car to forty-four Stadium Road to pick up the prisoner.'

'My pleasure, Sarge.'

Sally re-joined Narinder who held up a book. 'A very interesting diary,' she said.

'Bag it,' said Sally. She didn't disclose what she had just been told as Underwood stayed very close behind them at all times.

'You won't find anything in that,' sneered Underwood, 'just a few business appointments.'

'Then you have nothing to worry about,' replied Sally.

Constable Richards came down the stairs holding a box. 'There's this, Sarge,' he said, 'found it under the bed.' He placed the box on the table and opened it disclosing bundles of fifty-pound notes each secured with an elastic band.

'Keep your hands off that,' stormed Underwood, 'it's all hard-earned money and none of your bloody business.'

'Rather a lot of money to be kept in the house,' said Narinder picking up a bundle and flicking through the notes. 'A thousand in each pack, would you say?' She riffled through the box. 'That makes a total of about twenty thousand pounds I should think, all accounted for to the tax man I'm sure.'

'Bloody cops!' Underwood kicked a chair across the room.

A car was heard pulling up outside and Sally looked through the window and saw the police car she had requested. 'Mr Underwood,' she said, 'I'm arresting you for being in the possession of stolen vehicles'…she read him his rights and as two uniform officers entered the house she asked them to take the prisoner to the station.

'What about my money,' shouted Underwood.

'I'll give you a receipt for it,' said Sally, and taking a notepad from her pocket wrote a receipt for twenty thousand pounds. 'Are you happy that that's the correct amount,' she asked him.

The prisoner muttered 'Yes' as he was led away.

Once on their own Narinder took out her mobile and called headquarters where she spoke to Jack. She told him of the arrest of Don Underwood and then asked him to check three car registration numbers for her. 'Could you call me back when you have the owners, Sarge?' she asked.

'Give me five minutes,' said Jack.

'What are you up to?' asked Sally.

'I definitely saw a woman at the bedroom window,' replied Narinder, 'so I'm checking the owners of the cars I saw tucked away in the side lane.'

'Ah,' said Sally, 'very shrewd. You'll be pleased to hear that they've found stolen cars and several number plates at the garage and especially for you, a book containing names and addresses.'

Narinder smiled. 'Great, it's all falling into place.'

They continued the search of the downstairs rooms bagging the diary and some documents. Delving into the back of the side board cupboard, Sally let out a yelp. She held up a bundle of letters 'All addressed to Mr John Smith,' she announced.

'Great,' said Narinder, 'I wonder how Don Underwood is going to explain those.'

'With difficulty.' Sally picked up the laptop, 'let's go,' she said, 'we have everything we need.'

Narinder's phone rang and eagerly she answered it. 'Is there any name there that you recognise?' she asked hearing Jack's voice.

'There is indeed,' replied the sergeant, 'Mrs Ursula Blackwell's Audi is one of the cars.'

'Thanks, Sarge, I thought it was her I spotted. I'll explain when we get back,' she added. Jack chuckled. 'I bet you will,' and he hung up.

'So, who was it?' asked Sally.

'I thought it was Ursula Blackwell I saw at the bedroom window, so I took the numbers of the cars in the lane and Jack confirms that one of them belongs to her.'

'No wonder it took so long for Underwood to open the door,' said Sally, 'she must have been bolting through the back door.'

'And getting dressed in a hurry,' added Narinder with a grin.

'We'll see what Underwood has to say when we get back to the station,' said Sally,

'Come on.' She turned to Jason. 'Thank you for your help,' she said, 'we'll drop you off at headquarters.'

'It was good fun,' replied the young constable, 'hope I didn't interfere, Sarge when I spoke to Underwood.'

Sally smiled. 'We'll give you that one,' she said, 'let's get back to the station.'

Back at headquarters the duty sergeant signed the prisoner in and he was taken to a cell swearing and cursing at the top of his voice. Sally and Narinder arrived and Sergeant Carl Fisher told them where they could find Underwood. 'He's not very happy,' said Carl, 'he's swearing like a trooper and throwing out all kinds of threats.'

'I think we'll leave him there for a bit, then,' said Sally, 'and let him cool down.'

They made their way back up the stairs to the CID block, Sally doing her usual by running to the top without even breathing heavily. She always told Narinder that this was an ideal way for her to train as she wasn't always able to get to the gym as often as she liked.

Narinder caught her up at the top of the stairs. 'You just like to show me up,' she grumbled.

'Not at all,' said Sally with a grin, 'but one of us has to be able to chase the bad guys and catch them.'

'We can't all be champion sprinters.' Narinder punched her friend on the arm, 'but I'm always happy to let you do the leg work when I'm with you.'

'We'll tell the boss about Underwood before we do anything else,' said Sally.

'I'm getting out of this stab-vest before I do anything,' said Narinder, 'I feel as fat as a pig.'

'Okay, we'll dump them in the Incident Room and return them later,' said Sally entering the room.

Taking off the vests they dropped them on a chair and then headed down the corridor to knock on Harriet's door.

Harriet was very interested in the finding of the stolen cars, the letters and various number plates and the subsequent arrest of Underwood, but more especially in learning that the visitor at his house had been Ursula Blackwell. Opening her desk drawer, she took out a key and handed it to Sally. 'This is the key found with the stolen goods at Freddie's house,' she said, 'go back to Underwood's house and see if it fits his door.'

'Right, ma'am.' Sally took the key and she and Narinder hurried off.

When they had gone Harriet called Charlie and asked him to come to her office. He arrived seconds later and she told him of the development over at the Yard Garage and at forty-four Stadium Road. 'We said we needed to speak to Mrs Blackwell,' she said, 'and I think now is the time, Charlie.'

Travelling in Charlie's car they drove to Copper Beaches where they saw a red Audi parked at the steps. As they climbed from the car Charlie went across to it and placed his hand on the bonnet. Ursula opened the door to Harriet's knock.

'Superintendent,' she gushed, 'and Chief Inspector Marlow, how nice, how can I help you.'

'May we come in?' asked Harriet.

'Of course, of course.' Ursula opened the door wide and stood to one side. They followed her into the sitting room where they were invited to sit down. 'Now what is it you want?' she asked.

'We're interested in your relationship with Don Underwood,' said Harriet.

'Who?'

'Don Underwood,' repeated Charlie, 'the person your husband bought his BMW from.'

'I can't say I know him personally,' said Ursula, 'but then I suppose I meet lots of people involved with my husband and I can't possibly remember them all.'

'I understand you were at his house this morning,' said Harriet.

'I beg your pardon!' Ursula was most indignant. 'I most certainly was not at anyone's house this morning, I'm still grieving for my dear husband and am not yet up to visiting anybody.'

'Your car was in the lane outside Underwood's house,' said Charlie.

'Oh, I don't think so! You must be mistaken.'

'So, are you saying you haven't been out in your car today?' asked Harriet.

'Correct, I'm really not up to doing anything just yet.'

'Funny,' said Charlie, 'the car has definitely been driven recently, the engine is still hot.'

Ursula became flustered. 'What is it you're up to?' she demanded. 'You can see I'm suffering, I've just lost my husband and here you are harassing me.'

'We're investigating a murder,' said Harriet. 'Two murders in fact, and we should like you to come to the station in the morning to answer a few questions.'

'This is outrageous,' stormed Ursula, 'I was nowhere near Pegasus House when my husband was killed, how could anyone think that I would harm George.'

'Please be at the station at ten tomorrow,' insisted Charlie, 'and you can tell us all you know about your husband and his business then.' He and Harriet left the room leaving Ursula weeping loudly behind them.

Chapter Thirty-Two

Arriving back at Stadium Road the two officers approached number forty-four. Sally put the key in the lock and turned it. 'Bingo!' she said as the door opened.

'Blow me,' said Narinder, 'all the dramatics we've seen from that woman and she's been having it off with Underwood all the time. Do you think she killed her husband to get him out of the way?'

'She has an alibi for the time of the murder, but perhaps Underwood did it.'

'Did he have an alibi?' asked Narinder.

'We'll check that out when we get back,' replied Sally, 'it was Duncan who questioned him. Mind you we certainly didn't find a gun when we searched his house.'

'He wouldn't keep it at home surely, perhaps we need to search the garage again.'

'We'll see what the boss has to say,' said Sally.

Harriet was interested to learn that the key found at Freddie's house fitted the door of Don Underwood's house. 'So, Mrs Blackwell was having an affair with this man,' she said.

'Still is,' said Narinder, 'she was in his bedroom when we arrived at his house and they didn't want us to see her; she nipped out of the back door before Underwood let us in.'

'And you don't give someone your door key unless the relationship is serious, do you?' added Sally.

'Have you checked Underwood's alibi?' asked Harriet.

'Yes, ma'am,' replied Sally. 'Sergeant McAllister questioned him and was told that he was at the scrap yard until six o'clock and the men who work there confirmed this.'

'So, he's off the hook for the killing,' said Harriet.

'More's the pity,' muttered Narinder, 'he's a nasty piece of work.'

'It doesn't make him a killer thought, Narinder,' said Harriet.

'No, ma'am.'

'We've instructed Mrs Blackwell to come to the station tomorrow morning,' said Harriet, 'Chief Inspector Marlow and I will question her under caution; we're not at all happy about her part in this crime. If, as we now know the key, which obviously belonged to her, was found in Freddie's possession, then I'm beginning to think Sergeant Fuller is right and the cryptic message came from Copper Beeches too.'

'So, do you think that belongs to Mrs Blackwell as well?' asked Narinder.

'I do wonder, not that we have deciphered it yet.'

'If you're thinking in terms of a hitman, ma'am,' said Sally, 'how on earth does someone like Ursula Blackwell know where to find one.'

'She must have contacts.'

'Like Don Underwood,' suggested Narinder.

'Exactly. Anyway,' said Harriet, 'we'll see how the interview goes tomorrow; I might even show her the paper with the letters and numbers on it and see how she reacts.'

Narinder smiled. 'That could be interesting,' she said.

Jack received a call from Bardwell-Fox to ask if he knew of the whereabout of Freddie's brother. 'Someone has to be responsible for Mr Maloney's funeral,' he said, 'and I have the name of Patrick

Maloney as next of kin but am unable to contact him.'

Jack told him that Paddy had agreed to organise the funeral of his brother but gave the solicitor the address he required. Jack decided to contact Paddy Maloney himself, he had after all, been quite upset at the news that Freddie had been killed. He picked up the receiver and dialled the number of Paddy Maloney.

Ursula made herself a salmon sandwich and poured a glass of Chardonnay. She was still quite shaken by the close call over at Stadium Road this morning and felt the wine might steady her nerves. She couldn't do with the cops knowing about her relationship with Don, although knowing about it shouldn't put her in the frame for murder. Her alibi for the time of George's murder was sound as was Don's. Hang the coppers, she wouldn't go to the police station tomorrow as she had been instructed, if they needed to speak to her again they could jolly well come to her. They couldn't pin anything on her; she had nothing to worry about. Ursula was feeling calmer already and she decided that when she had finished lunch she would go to the insurance company and collect her jewels. Things were looking up after all.

Finishing her lunch, Ursula put her plate and glass in the sink, washed her hands, picked up her handbag and left the house. Sitting in Allan Cavendish's office twenty minutes later she smiled at the man opposite her.

'Such good news, Mr Cavendish,' she said, 'and how clever of the police to find my jewellery.'

'It's very good news, Mrs Blackwell, especially for us, and I'm delighted to be able to hand everything back to you. Please check it all carefully and then I'd like you to sign for each item.'

'No problem. The police did notify me that they had been recovered and that I had to check them as being all there when you returned them to me.'

Cavendish took the bag from a drawer in his desk and placed it in front of Ursula. She grasped it eagerly and tipped the contents onto the desk. Checking through them carefully she looked up and nodded. 'Everything's here,' she said. 'Where do I sign?'

The insurance manager gave her a sheet of paper. 'Each item is down there,' he said, 'if you would just initial each piece and then sign at the bottom.'

This was done with a flourish and Ursula rose to leave. 'There is just one thing,' said Cavendish, 'I think you might want to reassess your valuation of these items.'

'What do you mean?' demanded Ursula sitting down again.

'I feel you are paying a very high premium for paste jewellery, and in the circumstance, in the case of theft or loss, we would be unable to pay out the sum we originally quoted.'

'Paste?' shrieked Ursula, 'what do you mean paste? These jewels cost a fortune.'

'The originals may have done,' replied Cavendish calmly, 'but these baubles here are paste.'

'Baubles?' again the shriek was almost deafening and even Cavendish winced. 'Who says they are fake?'

'The police had them checked as have we, and I have to tell you that they are all paste. I'm sorry, Mrs Blackwell but that is the case so I'm sure you will want to stop payments immediately, so I shall tear up the contract I made with your husband.'

Ursula leaped to her feet. 'The bastard, the utter bastard, I'm bloody glad he's dead. He's a cheating, bullying, bastard. Firstly, I have to contend with a secret daughter who wants to get her hands on my money and property and now you tell me my jewels are worthless. What's the world coming to,' she shrieked. Tossing her head Ursula grabbed the bag containing her jewellery and stormed from the room slamming the door behind her.

Allan Cavendish leaned back in his chair and mopped his brow with a large white handkerchief. Nice language he thought, the woman is certainly no lady. Good riddance to her as a client. He picked up the agreement document on his desk and put it into his shredder where it was gobbled up.

At Torreston Police Station Don Underwood was brought to an

interview room where Inspector Earl Cassels was to speak to him. Sally sat at the inspector's side and a uniformed officer waited at the door. A scowling Underwood slammed himself down in the chair at the table and Earl switched on the recording machine and announce the time and who was in the room.

'Please state your name for the tape,' said Earl.

'Don Underwood.'

'Are you known by any other name?'

'Only Red, my nickname.'

'How about John Smith?' asked Sally.

'Rubbish, never heard of him, we've been over this before.'

Sally held up the bundle of letters addressed to John Smith. 'How about these?' she asked, 'all to a John Smith and all with the address forty-four Stadium Road.'

'No comment.'

'Right,' said Inspector Cassells, 'we should like to know about your relationship with George Blackwell. We have discovered that the BMW you sold him was stolen and now, having searched your premises we have discovered several other stolen vehicles and various number plates, obviously being lined up for further use.'

Underwood sneered. 'Okay, so you've caught me out in nicking a few cars, but if you think I had anything to do with Blackwell's murder you're up a tree. Why would I kill someone who was paying me good money?'

'You are having an affair with his wife,' said Sally. Underwood's eyes flickered at this. 'Who says I am?'

'I do for one,' replied Sally, 'my colleague and I saw Mrs Blackwell at your house when we called this morning and now we find that she has a key to your front door. I'm sure you don't give your front door key to any-old-body, Mr Underwood. Also, some of these letters are letters from her, would you like me to read some of them out?'

'My relationship with Ursula is nobody's business but ours. George Blackwell was a bully and frequently beat her up, so she turned to me for comfort.'

'Did her husband know about your relationship?' asked Earl.

'No.'

'Do you own a gun?' asked Sally.

'No.' He slammed a fist on the table. 'This has gone far enough, I want a solicitor.'

'Certainly,' replied Earl, 'do you have one?'

'No. Never needed one.'

'We'll see that you get a solicitor,' said Earl. 'Officer,' he turned to the constable, 'take the prisoner back to his cell.'

'Hey,' shouted Underwood, 'I want to go home.'

'All in good time,' said Earl, 'as soon as our interview is concluded in the presence of a solicitor. Take him down, constable,'

Ursula returned home to Copper Beeches, sat down on the sofa and called Don Underwood on her mobile. It went straight to voicemail. She tried again several times calling his home, the garage and even the scrap yard. Without success. She held her head in her hands and burst into tears. Everything was collapsing around her. Her late husband's will was a calamity, with him leaving practically everything to this secret daughter and now her jewels turn out to be fake so she would be unable to cash in on them if she needed to. The thought of selling Copper Beeches made her feel sick, even though she had though she might do this at a later date. Surely, she couldn't be made to do this before she was ready? It was her home and she couldn't envisage sharing the profits with someone else. She suddenly remembered the letter she had been given by the solicitor and groping in her handbag she pulled it out. She tore the envelope open and saw the letter written in her husband's handwriting. She began reading.

If you are reading this letter it means I'm dead. Hope you are not too upset at discovering I have a daughter, Ursula, a beautiful daughter something you never wanted to give me, but then you always were selfish. I have left strict instructions as to how my business and money is to be distributed, Rosalind is my main concern, so don't have any bright ideas about changing my bequests. I know all about you and Don Underwood, so I hope he can provide for you as I have done in the past. Ha Ha! I hope you will be very happy, Ursula, not that you deserve it. Oh, and by the way, sorry about your jewellery but fake stuff is all you deserve, and Fake suits you.

Good bye, From your loving husband, George.

Ursula was shaking, and tears were streaming down her face. How she hated the man she had been married to, and how glad she was that he was dead. Her sobs became louder and she flung herself onto her face on the sofa and buried her head in a cushion. Life would never be the same again.

Sally joined Narinder in the Incident Room and told her that the interview with Don Underwood had been put on hold until he had a solicitor.

'I suppose that will be Bardwell-Fox,' said Narinder.

'Actually, no, he doesn't appear to have a solicitor,' replied Sally, 'DI Cassells is contacting the duty solicitor for him.'

'You'd have thought a creep like him would have had a solicitor,' said Narinder.

'Well it means he has to stay in custody until one arrives,' said Sally. 'He wouldn't say anything about the name John Smith but it's obvious he used the name as a cover for his shady dealings. He didn't deny his affair with Ursula Blackwell, but then that's not a crime is it, he'll just get done for pinching cars.'

'We're none the wiser then as to who shot George Blackwell, are we?' said Narinder.

'Or Freddie Fingers,' said Sally. 'Let's get our notes written up and then perhaps we might get away at a reasonable time. We'll go through the stuff taken from Underwood's place in the morning.'

'What time are the guys coming around this evening?' asked Narinder.

'They're picking us up at seven thirty, they've booked a table at Pierre's for eight and Gerry has invited Ramesh to join us.'

'Does Ramesh have a girlfriend?' asked Narinder.

'I really don't know, but we'll find out this evening.'

In her office Harriet yawned. Another long day. Ed had telephoned to ask what time she would be home and hearing she was still in her office working told her he would collect take-aways and have them ready for eight thirty. 'You've done another sixteen-hour day, Harry,' he said, 'you'll make yourself ill if you don't have a break.'

'You know what it's like when you have a murder to solve, Ed. As soon as we crack this case I'll have a couple of days off, I promise.'

'Is there anything our station can do to help?' asked Ed.

'Find this hit-man,' replied Harriet.

'Maybe he's returned to London or wherever he came from. But I'll keep my ears open. Now pack up there, Harry and come home, I'm off to collect the take-aways.'

Chapter Thirty-Three

Sitting at a corner table at Pierre's, the five friends were in a light-hearted mood enjoying a splendid meal. Ramesh was good company and had several funny stories to tell them about things that went on in his work-place.

'Oh, and I meant to tell you, Sally,' he said, 'the guy you asked me about was at the Innovation Centre yesterday. I didn't ring you because I knew I was seeing you this evening.'

'You mean Conrad Winston from Pegasus House?' said Narinder.

'Yes, that's him.'

'Who did he visit?' asked Sally.

Ramesh fished in his pocket and pulled out a piece of paper. 'I knew you'd want to know everything,' he said with a grin, 'so I wrote it all down.' He pushed the paper across to Sally.

'Bernado Rossi,' she read out, 'the Italian guy, and you say he was there all afternoon.'

'Can we do this after dinner?' interrupted Dave, 'it'd be really nice to get away from work for a while.'

'Dave, you're one of us,' said Narinder, 'and sometimes you have to go with it when something important crops up.'

'Yes, I know but there's nothing you can do tonight so let's have a nice meal and evening together and you can deal with this guy tomorrow.'

'Yes, sorry,' said Sally, 'but sometimes it's jolly hard to shake work off, you know that, Dave. But, thanks, Ramesh, can I call you in the morning?'

'Yes of course, I'll be in my office by eight thirty.'

Harriet arrived home soon after eight-thirty and could smell food the moment she opened the front door. She hadn't realised until this moment that she hadn't eaten since breakfast that morning and now she could feel her stomach rumbling. Ed had laid the table and he greeted her with a hug and a glass of claret. 'Now come and sit down,' he insisted, 'and I'll call you when dinner is on the table. Hope you're up for Chinese?'

'Oh, anything, Ed I'm starving and whatever it is you have in the kitchen smells wonderful.' Ed took her arm and guided her into the sitting room where she flopped down in an armchair suddenly feeling very tired. She sipped the wine beginning to feel more alive and minutes later Ed called to say dinner was ready.

Sitting together later Harriet thanked Ed for dinner and told him she felt human once again. She handed him the paper with the cryptic letters and numbers. 'This is the paper we found at Freddie Finger's house and we now think it was stolen from Copper Beeches with the other stuff we found there.'

'So, you think Blackwell's wife had something to do with his murder?'

'We can't rule that out,' replied Harriet, 'we've told her to come to the station tomorrow morning and we're going to interview her under caution.'

'That makes sense, but she has a sound alibi for the time of the shooting I take it?'

'Yes, she does, but we've just discovered she was having an affair with Don Underwood the owner of the Yard Garage and we're wondering if they wanted Blackwell out of the way.'

'Pretty drastic measures,' said Ed, 'couldn't she just divorce him? She'd have come off pretty well if he's as rich as everyone seems to think he was.'

'I just don't know, Ed, but we do think this paper is significant if Freddie Fingers was then killed for it.'

'If that is why he was killed, he was a pretty shady character.' Ed took the paper and read it. 'Double Dutch to me,' he said. 'But enough shop, Harry, time to switch off. Let me fill your glass, this is a particularly excellent claret.'

Harriet slept well that night and arrived at the station early to finish off the paperwork she still had to complete. She found Sally and Narinder already in the Incident Room.

'You're in bright and early,' she said with a smile.

'We need to ring a friend of mine at the Innovation Centre,' said Sally, 'he gave us some news last night about Conrad Winston turning up there again yesterday.'

'Really?' said Harriet, 'and do we know who he was visiting.'

'Bernardo Rossi,' replied Sally.

'There was another Italian on our list,' said Harriet, 'DCI Marlow and I interviewed him.'

'Yes,' answered Narinder, flicking through her notes., 'that was Antonio Romano, the client of Blackwell who threatened him.'

'We checked his alibi,' said Harriet, 'and confirmed he and his wife were out of the country at the time of Blackwell's murder.'

'Thinking in terms of hitmen,' said Sally, 'and the fact that Italian names keep turning up, does make you wonder.'

'Blackwell's daughter is Italian,' said Harriet, 'Mrs De Luca will be arriving tomorrow so it will be interesting to hear what she has to tell us. Have you spoken to this friend in Market Harborough yet, Sally?'

'No, ma'am I was about to make the call.'

'Carry on, I shall be in my office if you need me.' Harriet left the room and Sally picked up the telephone receiver and dialled the direct line of Ramesh. He answered immediately.

'Hi, Sally,' he said, 'great evening last night, thanks for inviting me and I hope we can do it again.'

'We most certainly will. Now what can you tell me about this visit of Conrad Winston?'

'He arrived about one thirty and I saw him go into Rossi's room. I have no idea how long he stayed but the next time I saw him it was after three thirty, and he was with Rossi having tea in the café.'

'Do you know what time he left the Centre?' asked Sally.

'Because you'd asked me to keep an eye on things, I did just that, and kept finding excuses to pass through the foyer. I saw Conrad leave at four.'

'Stupid question,' said Sally, 'but I don't suppose you have any idea what they were talking about?'

'Sally, I'm not MI5, or James Bond, so the answer is no, I have no idea what they were talking about.'

'Sorry, Ramesh, that was just a shot in the dark. Thank you for the info you've just given me and we'll meet up soon.'

There was a chuckle from Ramesh at the end of the phone. 'Okay, Sally and I'll keep my ear to the ground. Bye.'

Sally replaced the receiver and faced Narinder telling her what she had been told about Conrad Winston.

'Sounds fishy mind,' said Narinder, ''praps we should ask Winston what he was doing at Innovations this time.'

'We can't push our luck,' replied Sally, 'he has every right to visit another work place, and we've been told Pegasus House is using the Harborough set up as a model for themselves.'

'Hmm, I'm beginning to wonder about the Mafia being in the area.'

Sally got up. 'I'll just go and tell the boss what we've been told by Ramesh and see what she has to say.'

Harriet agreed with Sally that it would be a good idea to keep an eye on Conrad Winston and if possible the Italian working at the Innovation Centre in Harborough. 'Having a friend acting as a spy is very helpful,' she said with a smile, 'I hope we don't get him into trouble.'

'Ramesh is very discrete, ma'am,' replied Sally, 'he'll call me if

Winston turns up there again.'

'Good, well done, Sally. Now let's get briefing over.'

The duty solicitor arrived at nine and Pete Yates rang CID to tell them he was there. Inspector Cassels called across to Sally. 'Ready to interview Don Underwood, Sergeant?'

'Absolutely, sir.'

They left the Incident Room and went down to reception where sergeant Yates introduced the duty solicitor. 'The prisoner is being taken to room three,' he said.

Don Underwood was brought to the interview room still shouting and cursing. 'You had no right to keep me locked up over-night,' he stormed.

'We had every right,' replied Cassells. 'This is your solicitor, Mr Braithwaite.' Underwood glared at the solicitor. 'I hope you're going to get me out of here,' he snarled.

'I'll do my best,' replied the solicitor.

Cassells began the questioning. 'We'd like to know exactly what your relationship with George Blackwell was?'

'Okay, so you know he had me in his pocket, and I was obliged to do favours for him.'

'Like producing stolen cars to order?' suggested Sally.

'Yeah. But that's all. I never did anything vicious, just a bit of car dealing.'

'What did Blackwell have on you?' asked Cassells.

'Documents on the cars I'd pinched, said he'd ruin me if I didn't help him from time to time.'

'And how did you help him?' asked Cassells.

Underwood pulled a face.

'By supplying him with the cars he asked for, I suppose,' said Sally.

'Yes, that's all I did for him, but I never killed the guy.'

'What other favours did you do for him?' asked Cassells.

'I didn't do anything else for him.'

'Did Blackwell find out about your affair with his wife?' asked Cassells.

'Don't think so.'

They learned very little more and the solicitor told Underwood that he would be released on bail and be obliged to turn up to court when given the date of his hearing.

At ten o'clock Harriet and Charlie were in Harriet's office awaiting the arrival of Ursula Blackwell. Ten fifteen came and went and at ten thirty Harriet rang down to Inspector Baldwin, head of uniform division, and asked him to send a patrol car to Copper Beeches and bring in Mrs Blackwell. 'If your officers have any trouble, Vic, tell them to arrest her. She was told to be here at ten and I'm not prepared to wait any longer.'

'I'll do that straight away, ma'am,' replied the Inspector, and hanging up he radioed in to Sergeant Mirams, who was out on patrol, and instructed him to go to Newham Drive to Collect Ursula Blackwell.

Ursula sat in an armchair drinking coffee. She would have preferred a gin and tonic but as she wanted to meet Don later she felt she couldn't afford to get done for drink-driving. A loud knocking on the front door made her jump and leaping to her feet she hurried to open it. Standing on the step she was confronted by a burly police sergeant with a younger constable at his side.

'What do you want?' she demanded in a surly voice.

'We've been instructed to take you to headquarters,' said Sergeant Mirams, 'you were told to report there at ten o'clock and it's now ten forty-five.'

'I decided I didn't want to go to the station,' snapped Ursula, 'I have nothing more to say on the matter.'

'I shall be obliged to arrest you, madam, if you refuse to cooperate,' replied Mirams.

'Arrest me?' yelped Ursula, 'I've done nothing wrong, you have no right to arrest me.'

'If you've done nothing wrong, you have nothing to fear,' said the sergeant, 'but I would advise you to come with us of your own free will rather than under arrest.'

'This is ridiculous, I shall be making a complaint you can be sure of that. I take it I'm allowed to get my coat?'

'Of course, we'll wait here for you.'

Ursula stamped her way down the passageway and grabbed a coat, picked up her handbag and appeared back at the front door which she locked behind her as she left. As Sergeant Mirams guided her down the steps to his car a flash of light made them all look up. Beefy Cavendish had appeared from the bushes and was gleefully taking photographs.

'Clear off, Cavendish,' shouted Mirams, 'there's nothing here for you.'

'Oh, I think there is,' replied Beefy grinning, 'anything that involves you lot is news for me.'

The sergeant hustled Ursula into the car and the constable got in beside her. Jumping into the driver's seat Mirams started the engine and drove off down the drive with the reporter still taking pictures.

When Harriet received the call that Ursula was in the building she asked the duty sergeant to take her to one of the interview rooms. She and Charlie went down to the foyer where Pete Yates told them that Mrs Blackwell was in Interview Room two. Entering the room, they found Ursula striding up and down and openly fuming.

'You haven't heard the last of this,' she shouted, 'I shall be contacting my solicitor when I leave here.'

'You were asked, in a civilised manner, to come to the station

214

at ten this morning,' said Harriet, 'you failed to this, so we had no option but to collect you. You will be read your rights and then I should appreciate you answering our questions.'

Ursula scowled and muttered something under her breath.

'Please sit down,' said Charlie pulling out a chair at the table and then switching on the recording machine.

Ursula sat, and Harriet announced the time and who was present in the room and Charlie read Ursula her rights. They were ready to begin.

'How long has your relationship been going on with Don Underwood?' asked Charlie.

'That's no one's business but ours,' snapped Ursula.

'We are investigating your husband's murder,' said Harriet quietly, 'I should have thought you would want to know who killed him.'

'Of course, I do, but what has this got to do with Don and me?'

'Don Underwood is at this moment in custody,' said Harriet, 'charged with the theft of cars among other things.'

'And he did sell the BMW to your husband,' added Charlie, 'and as you were having an affair with this man behind his back you both automatically come under suspicion.'

'This is just rubbish,' stormed Ursula getting to her feet.

'Sit down,' said Harriet firmly.

The woman did as she was told but was now quite flustered. 'You can't keep Don locked up,' she wailed, 'he's done nothing wrong.'

'Is that apart from stealing vehicles?' asked Charlie.

'I don't know what he does apart from selling cars, his business is nothing to do with me.'

Harriet produced the paper with the cryptic message and pushed it across the table in front of Ursula. 'Can you tell us what this means?' she asked.

Ursula glanced at it and shook her head vigorously. 'I've no idea, where did it come from?'

'Your house we think,' replied Harriet.

'What nonsense, I never mentioned any paperwork being stolen, what makes you think it came from my place?'

'It was found with the stolen silver that we discovered at Freddie Maloney's house,' said Charlie, 'the silver that was stolen from you and that you identified.'

'That means nothing, this message obviously belongs to this Maloney person, because it most certainly isn't mine.'

'It was in an envelope with Underwood's front door key,' said Charlie.

'So, this crook keeps things hidden, nothing to do with me, apart from the door key of course which I admit is mine. He must have just put my key in the same envelope as this paper, which I have to say I have never seen before.'

'You're treading on very dangerous ground here,' said Harriet, 'and you would be wise to cooperate.'

'Cooperate, cooperate?' shouted Ursula, 'that's all anyone wants from me. I've now been confronted by my husband's secret daughter and my solicitor tell me she is to have half of everything he owned. How am I expected to live?' She suddenly burst into tears and began to howl in a very theatrical manner. Charlie pushed a box of tissues towards her and she grabbed a handful and vigorously wiped her eyes.

'Very well,' said Harriet, 'we can see you're upset so we'll leave it at that for the moment. You may go, Mrs Blackwell, but we might need to speak to you again.'

'Harassment, this is just harassment,' snarled Ursula rising to her feet, the tears having miraculously subsided, 'I'm going straight to my solicitor to lodge a complaint about the way a grieving widow like me has been treated.' She stormed from the room and Harriet looked at Charlie.

'What do you think?' she asked.

'Did you see her face change colour when you showed her the paper?' asked Charlie, 'she definitely knows more about that than she's letting on.'

'Keep an eye on her, Charlie, she might slip up.'

Chapter Thirty-Four

Sally and Narinder sat side by side going through the books and diary that had been removed from Don Underwood's house and garage. The book contained lists of car registrations and Sally wrote these down to check, at a later date, for being from stolen vehicles. There was also a page full of various cars with initials at the side of them.

'I'm thinking these cars are on order to be found for customers whose initials are beside them,' said Sally.

'So, Underwood steals to order?' Narinder turned another page of the book she was checking. 'Read out the initials you have, Sally.'

'They go back years,' replied Sally, 'I'll start with this year.' She began reading the list.

Narinder gave a whoop. 'This is easy, the guy's not very bright, the initials beside the cars all match up in this book with a name and address.'

'No!' Sally was amazed. 'Try the GB,' she said.

'Yep, here it is, George Blackwell Pegasus House. And I take it the car is a BMW.'

'It certainly is,' agreed Sally, 'he'll have trouble denying his little racket.'

'Is UB in the list?' asked Narinder, 'Mrs Blackwell has a red Audi.'

'No, there's no Ursula Blackwell,' replied Sally, 'but surprise, surprise, there is an FA.'

Narinder flicked through the pages again and chuckled as she read out the name Frank Abbott. 'He had a Saab from Underwood last year,' she said, 'and you can bet anything it will have been stolen.'

'These letters addressed to John Smith confirms the deals,' said Sally, 'there are the names and addresses of the people who bought the cars from him, some of them requesting a further car if he can find it for them.'

Narinder laughed. 'He thought he was playing safe using the name John Smith, he was trying to keep his real name out of it. Bad luck Mr Smith!'

'His customers won't be too happy finding out Don has dumped them in it by disclosing who they are,' said Sally.

'They'll get such a surprise when the police turn up on their doorstep,' agreed Narinder.

'I'll get onto the guy's downstairs to check out all these cars,' said Sally, 'Inspector Baldwin has a team investigating a stolen car racket, so he'll be pretty grateful for this little list. A lot of people with nice big cars are going to get a shock.'

'They won't all be stolen of course,' said Narinder, 'and those that were, the customer might not have known it. Mind you I'm hoping Frank Abbott's Saab was stolen.'

'You're right,' agreed Sally, 'there's always the possibility the purchasers didn't know the cars were stolen.'

'Oh Yeah!' Narinder let out a whoop. 'Not according to some of these letters.' She held out a letter from one of Underwood's customers It clearly hinted that the owner of the Yard Garage had told him it wouldn't take long in acquiring someone else's car as he knew someone who had the very Audi that this person desired.

Duncan and Ben returned to Troverton Antiques and Duncan explained to Jarrod Jeffries that on this occasion he was receiving a caution regarding his accepting property from suspect characters without checking first that the items being offered were not stolen. 'Count yourself lucky,' said the sergeant, 'this little episode could have landed you in jail and that would have been an end to your business.'

'I told you,' stuttered Jefferies, 'I didn't know the stuff was stolen.'

'A description of the stolen jewellery was circulated to all dealers,' said Duncan, 'so don't go spinning us a yarn. Now, if you know what's good for you, you'll shut up and just accept the caution and count your blessings.'

'Yes, officer of course, and it won't happen again.'

'We'll be keeping an eye on you,' said Duncan as he and Ben left the showroom.

Harriet stacked a pile of papers and put them in a desk drawer. She sighed and leaned back in her chair relieved that for the moment at least she had completed the necessary reading and signing of the documents that had begun to grow on her desk. Charlie bounded into the room carrying a tray of coffee and Harriet beamed. 'What a life safer, Charlie, I was beginning to wilt.' She took two china mugs from the desk cupboard and placed them on the desk.

'I thought you could do with an infusion of caffeine,' said Charlie putting down the tray. 'How's the paper work going?'

'All done for the moment.'

'Brilliant, what do you want us to do after coffee?' Charlie poured and handed Harriet a mug.

'I'd like to return to Pegasus House, Charlie, perhaps have a word with the manager, Conrad Winston, and some of the other staff who were in the building the day Blackwell was shot.'

'Okay,' agreed Charlie, 'might be useful, it is Friday tomorrow, the day the murder took place, so people might just be a bit apprehensive and remember things.'

'Well we'll see. This is wonderful coffee, Charlie. It's the one thing that keeps me going.'

Entering Pegasus House an hour later, Harriet and Charlie went to the reception window to report their presence. Ann Peters pushed the signing-in book across and asked them both to sign. Having done this Harriet explained that they would be visiting George Blackwell's rooms and speaking to one or two other people in the building.

'Of course, of course, Superintendent,' said Ann, 'and anything else that I can do to help don't hesitate to ask.'

'How long have you worked here?' asked Harriet.

'Oh, not that long, only six months. But I love it here and hopefully will be staying for some time.'

'How well did you know George Blackwell?' asked Charlie.

'As well as the other people with offices here. I spoke to him when he arrived and when he left; not that he always replied.'

'He didn't appear very popular,' said Harriet.

'He wasn't very likeable,' agreed Ann, 'but even so he didn't deserve to be killed.'

'That's true,' agreed Harriet. 'What can you tell us about Conrad Winston, the manager.'

'Now, he's a very nice man. Always ready to help any of the clients and very busy about the place trying to improve things.'

'He seems to go to Market Harborough quite often,' said Charlie, 'is that really necessary now that this place is up and running?'

'He does bring back some good ideas,' replied the receptionist.

'Is he here today?' asked Charlie.

'Yes, he is, he's in his office. Would you like me to buzz him for you?'

'No, don't bother,' said Harriet, 'just show us where his office is.'

Ann pointed down the corridor. 'Second door on the right, his name is on the door.'

Thanking the receptionist Harriet and Charlie made their way down the corridor to Conrad Winston's office. The manager opened the door to Harriet's knock. 'Ah, the police,' he said, 'come in, how can I help?'

Harriet and Charlie were given seats at Winston's desk and Harriet opened the questions. 'You go to the Innovation Centre in Market Harborough quite often, Mr Winston, is there anyone in particular you like to speak to when you're there.'

Conrad Winston appeared flustered but quickly recovered and smiled. 'I try to speak to as many people as possible, and I have to say I have learned quite a lot. It all helps to make Pegasus House a flourishing establishment.'

'On the Friday Blackwell was killed,' said Charlie, 'you left Innovations and vanished for an hour or so. Can you tell us where you went?'

'I don't think that is anyone's business but mine,' replied Winston, 'I do have a life outside work.'

'But you were at work on that day,' insisted Harriet, 'and as this is a murder enquiry we do need to ask you where you were that afternoon.'

Winston fidgeted and then stood. He walked across the room and stood at the window before answering. 'I visited a friend.'

'Could we have the name of this friend?' asked Charlie.

Winston returned to his desk and sat down again. 'This is all very embarrassing,' he muttered, 'can't we keep my friend out of this.'

'We'll do our best,' replied Harriet, 'if we could have her name and address please.'

Winston wrote on a piece of paper and handed it across. 'It's a he actually,' he muttered. 'He lives in Harborough and going to the Innovation Centre give us the excuse to meet up.'

'Can't you do that after work?' asked Harriet.

Winston looked sheepish and ducked his head. 'I have a wife,' he said.

'I see,' replied Harriet, 'well, we'll speak to your friend and that will probably be the end of it.'

Winston looked up. 'Thank you,' he muttered.

Harriet and Charlie left the room and went up the stairs. 'So, Winston has clandestine meetings with a male friend in Harborough,' said Charlie, 'and uses the Innovation visits as an excuse to visit him.'

'His personal life is none of our business, Charlie so we'll check his alibi when we've done here and leave it at that.'

Arriving at Blackwell's rooms they found Sophie Gilbert at a desk outside his main office and she smiled when she saw them. 'Have you come to remove the blue tape?' she asked.

'There are things in his office that I need to have as I'm still continuing with some of the work I had started before Mr Blackwell was killed.'

'I'll have it removed very soon,' replied Harriet. 'We'll just have a last look around before we do that.' She unlocked the office door and she and Charlie ducked under the tape and entered.

'Nothing's been removed,' said Charlie, 'in fact he had very little here.'

'Yes, it's pretty sparse,' agreed Harriet. 'Nothing was found on his computer and his diary revealed very little.'

'We didn't find anything incriminating at his house either,' said Charlie.

'Did he have a workplace somewhere else?' asked Harriet.

'That's a thought,' answered Charlie. 'He was hand-in-glove with that councillor, Abbott, I wonder if he was renting him another property?'

'Get that looked into, Charlie. There's nothing here to help us, let's get Winston's alibi checked and then get back to the station. And will you see that the police tape is removed.'

Returning to the main foyer they signed the book to say they were leaving. Ann Peters smiled and asked them if they had seen everyone they needed to.

'We'll just have a word with security on the way out,' replied Harriet. 'I can see him outside.'

'Having a quick siggy,' said Ann.

Harriet and Charlie left the building and went over to Alf Brooks holding out their warrant cards. Brooks quickly stubbed out the cigarette he was smoking. 'Worst thing that ever happened,' he said facing them, 'this smoking ban, I think it's a violation of people's rights.'

'And what about the rights of the people who don't wish to breathe in the smoke?' asked Harriet.

'Ah, well, they can go somewhere else.'

'And that's what the smokers are now doing,' replied Harriet. 'But we're not here to discuss social issues, we'd like to ask you a few questions about George Blackwell.'

Alf Brooks was a big man with a substantial beer belly, sallow complexion and small eyes that appeared to be too close together. He scowled at the two officers. 'I've told the police everything I know,' he said sullenly.

'Perhaps you could tell us,' said Charlie taking an instant dislike to this man.

'What do you want to know?' His unpleasant expression didn't change. He couldn't get his head around female police officers, it shouldn't be permitted, so he directed his questions to Charlie.

'You were in the foyer the night George Blackwell left,' said Charlie, 'did he say anything to you as he went?'

'No, he rarely said anything, he was a rude bastard and no one's the slightest bit surprise he's been knocked off. Someone's done us all a favour.' He grinned exposing set of crooked, discoloured teeth.

'Murder is never a favour to anyone,' said Harriet sharply.

Brooks didn't look at Harriet but again spoke to Charlie. 'He did have a visitor that afternoon, shifty looking character. This bloke asked about Blackwell and I told him to go to reception and

224

sign in.'

'And did he?' asked Charlie.

'I suppose so, he went over to the reception desk.'

'Thank you,' said Charlie, 'why didn't you mention this to the officer who spoke to you the day Blackwell was killed?'

'I didn't think it important.'

'Everything and anything is important in a murder,' said Harriet, 'it's up to us to decide what information is relevant and which isn't.'

Brooks kept his eyes averted and Harriet turned on her heels and walked away. Charlie caught up with her as she returned to the reception window. She asked to see the signing-in book and quickly turned to the day Blackwell was shot. Running her finger down the list of visitors she stopped at the name where George Blackwell was in the "company visited" column.

'John Smith,' she read out, 'how original.'

'Sally and Narinder have been looking into a John Smith,' said Charlie, 'they now know he's Don Underwood and at the moment he's being charged with car theft. DI Cassells is dealing with it.'

'I'll have a word with him when we get back and see if we can push that investigation along.' They left the building, seeing no sign of Alf Brooks as they went.

Chapter Thirty-Five

Sally and Narinder were in the Incident Room when Harriet and Charlie returned, and Harriet told them about the visitor Blackwell had received the afternoon he was killed.

'I was always convinced Don Underwood was John Smith,' said Sally, 'and, I was with DI Cassells when he interviewed him. I was almost relieved when we found those letters sent to Underwood's address even though he's not exactly admitting he is Smith. We didn't learn very much, but you get the feeling Underwood is something of a pawn in this game.'

'We're wondering if Blackwell was renting another property somewhere,' said Harriet.

'From his good pal Frank Abbott,' added Charlie.

'He had so little paperwork at his office at Pegasus House,' said Harriet, 'it does make you wonder.'

'We'll get onto it, ma'am,' said Sally, 'I wouldn't put anything past that creep Abbott.'

'Good,' replied Harriet,' I'll leave that little job to you two.'

'I think another visit to the council offices is in order,' said Narinder when Harriet and Charlie had gone. 'There must be books showing rental property and such like.'

'Absolutely,' agreed Sally, 'let's get going.'

At the council offices Sally and Narinder showed their warrant cards to Amanda Pemberton who remembered them both. 'What can I do to help you now?' she asked.

'We need to visit Frank Abbotts's office,' said Sally.

'It's locked at the moment,' said the young receptionist, 'I think an officer from your force told us we had to do this.'

'That'll be Fraud Squad,' said Narinder.

'Could we have the key please,' asked Sally, 'it will be all right,

I can assure you.'

'Of course,' said Amanda, 'give me a minute.' She went through a door at the back of reception and returned seconds later and handed Sally a key. 'Could you sign for it please,' she said. 'Everything in this pace has to be signed for.' She wrote in a small blue book and then pushed it across to Sally.

Sally signed beside the entry, "key to Frank Abbotts office."

Once in Abbotts office Sally and Narinder began opening the drawers in the filing cabinet. 'There has to be a property rental book somewhere,' said Narinder.

'If Fraud haven't taken it,' replied Sally.

'They're only interested in money deals,' said Narinder, 'they might not be interested in rental stuff.' She pulled out a folder and dumped it on the desk. 'This looks promising.'

Sally came over and looked at the fat folder with the title RENTALS on the cover. 'we need the name Blackwell somewhere,' said Sally, 'start turning the pages, Narinder.'

'How far back do we start?' asked Narinder.

'Hang on a mo,' replied Sally, and taking her notebook from her pocket she flicked through her notes. 'Here we are,' she said. 'Blackwell had been at Pegasus House for ten months, so go back to January of this year.'

Narinder began checking clients from January and within seconds she let out a whoop.

'Guess what name turns up in February?' she asked.

'Go on.'

Narinder chuckled. 'John Smith,' she said.

'No! Really. And where is the property?'

'Abbington Street,' said Narinder.

'I know it,' said Sally, 'there are several blocks of offices there, so which one is rented by our friend John Smith?'

'Corporation House number four,' read Narinder.

'There must be spare keys somewhere,' said Sally, 'we need to find them, Narinder.'

'The obvious place is the key cupboard,' replied Narinder with a grin, 'after all he wouldn't have been hiding anything then, would he?'

'I suppose not.' Sally went to a box on the wall and opened the door. There were dozens of keys on hooks in neat rows. She took out the first key and read the label attached to it. 'At least they're all labelled,' she said running her fingers along the various bunches. 'Here we are, Corporation House.'

'Brilliant,' said Narinder, 'I take it there's a number four?'

'Absolutely, let's get going.'

Bardwell-Fox telephoned the police station and Jack took the call. The solicitor informed the sergeant that having spoken to Patrick Maloney, the funeral of his brother, Freddie was being organised by him and was to be at the Crematorium the following Monday. Jack thanked Bardwell-Fox and then went to Harriet's office to give her the news.

'Would you mind if I attended the funeral, ma'am?' he asked. 'I've had dealings with Freddie for many years and somehow I feel I should be there.'

'Of course, Jack,' replied Harriet, 'take Inspector Cassells with you and keep your eyes open.'

'Yes, ma'am, and thank you.' Jack returned to the Incident Room and told Earl Cassells of his talk with Harriet. 'Hope you don't mind, sir,' he said,' but I've lumbered you with attending Freddie Finger's funeral next Monday.'

'That's all right, Jack,' replied the inspector, 'I'll be happy to accompany you and you never know we might spot something that throws a light on this murder.'

Jack went to his desk with a feeling of satisfaction. Freddie might have been a crook but somehow, having had contact with

228

him for many years, he felt it in order for him to pay his respects to this man.

Sally and Narinder arrived at Corporation House and entered the large brick building. The place was divided up into offices and checking the board in the hallway discovered number four was on the second floor and the name John Smith was beside the office they were interested in.

'The mysterious John Smith,' said Sally. 'Let's go and see what this place has to offer.'

They climbed the stairs, Sally taking the steps two at a time, and found number four immediately in front of them. Putting the key in the lock Sally opened the door and the two officers entered. They were faced with a pretty ordinary office with a large desk by the window, filing cabinets a shredding machine, a computer and all the things you would expect to find in a working office.

'Nice little hideaway,' said Narinder casting her eyes around the room. 'If there's anything to hide here I'm surprised that John Smith, or Don Underwood or whoever the person is, hasn't been here to clear things out.'

'Well, Blackwell's dead and Underwood has been in custody,' said Sally, 'so if its Underwood, then we've probably beaten him to it.'

'Let's get searching this place then,' said Narinder.

'I'll call headquarters and ask for a van to come over to help take some of this stuff away,' said Sally. 'The computer for starters, and then some of the documents and papers from the filing cabinets.' She took out her mobile and called the station.

Narinder went to the desk and picked up a photograph in a silver frame. 'Look at this, Sal,' she called.

Sally came over and looked at the picture of a dark haired young woman. 'Quite a beauty,' she said, 'Blackwell's daughter, do you think? she looks Italian.'

'Could be, she's not that old.'

'He wouldn't be able to have this on display at his other office,' said Sally, 'as everyone knows what his wife looks like.' She turned the frame over and unclipped the back. Taking the photograph out she read the inscription on the back. With much love, Rosalind. XX 'Yes, it's the daughter.'

Narinder opened a large book on the desk and flicked through the pages. 'I reckon this was definitely Blackwell's hideaway,' she said, 'and he probably used the name John Smith for everything he did, making sure it would be Don who took the rap if it all blew up.'

'So, Underwood rented this property for Blackwell, keeping Blackwell's name out of it,' said Sally, 'crafty devil.'

'Well, this is definitely Blackwell's little hideaway,' said, Narinder, 'all these things are his. It makes you wonder how many other addresses he used.'

'It shows that he and Underwood were as thick as thieves,' said Sally busily going through one of the filing cabinets. 'There are dozens of business files here, Narinder, and definitely all Blackwell's dealings, his signature is on the documents in the files. Heaven only knows how many shady deals the man was conducting from here. We'll stack the paperwork we need to take away over by the door with the computer and any books we think ought to go back to the station.'

A loud knock on the door announced the arrival of two uniformed officers. 'Hi, Sarge,' said the first man coming into the room. 'We've been told you have things that need taking back to headquarters,'

The second officer entered and Narinder pointed to the pile of papers and books that they were accumulating by the door. 'All that so far,' she said, 'and there will probably be more before we've finished.'

'No problem,' said the constable, 'we brought a small van.' The two men began carrying the things downstairs and Sally and Narinder continued opening cupboards and drawers.

'When we've been through this stuff back at headquarters,' said Sally 'we'd better inform Fraud about it.'

'Yes, we're only looking for something that might give us a clue as to who killed Blackwell,' said Narinder, 'the rest of his dirty business can be dealt with by them, with pleasure.'

'I think we have enough,' said Sally. 'Thanks, guys,' she said to the two constables.

'We'll follow you back to the station.'

Sally locked the office door and pocketed the key. 'I'll give this to the Fraud Squad,' she said, 'I won't bother to return it to the council offices. Right, let's get back.'

Jack was at his desk when Sally and Narinder returned. He smiled as he saw the two constables follow them into the Incident Room carrying the computer and piles of folders and documents.

'Got you working have they, lads?' he said to the young men.

'You can say that again, Sarge,' said one of them, 'but it's quite an eye opener as to how CID work.'

'And this is quite a set-up,' said the second man. 'Could quite fancy working here.'

'No vacancies at the moment,' said Narinder, 'but would you mind taking the computer down to Doctor Chong in the tech department.'

'Will do.'

'And thank you for your help,' said Sally.

The two constables left to take the computer down to Henry Chong and Sally went to Harriet's office. She explained what had happened and handed her the key to Corporation House. 'I expect the Fraud Squad will need to know about this office Blackwell had hidden away,' she said, 'I hope they won't think we've trodden on their toes by going there.'

'Don't worry about it,' replied Harriet, 'I'll explain to Commander Fielding that you're only interested in trying to discover who might want Blackwell dead. He can have all the paperwork as soon as you have been through it.'

'Thank you, ma'am.'

Harriet smiled. 'You were the ones who discovered this second office, after all,' she said, 'Fraud could have done it if they'd been on the ball.'

Sally grinned. 'Yes, ma'am, but don't tell them that.'

'Would I?'

'Oh, and, ma'am,' said Sally as she went to leave, 'look, this photograph was on the desk and the writing on the back tells us it's Blackwell's daughter.' She handed Harriet the photograph.

'Good looking young woman,' said Harriet. 'I'll give this to Chief Inspector Marlow as he will be meeting her at Heathrow tomorrow and this will help him identify her.'

That evening Harriet was annoyed to see that Ursula Blackwell was on the front page of the evening paper. This had to be the work of Beefy Cavendish, he turned up everywhere he wasn't wanted. The headline read, MURDER VICTIM'S WIFE TAKEN INTO CUSTODY and there was Ursula being guided into a police car by Sergeant Mirams.

'Look at this, Ed,' said Harriet, 'Mrs Blackwell will be at her solicitor's in the morning and we'll be receiving a complaint.'

'It's not your fault some reporter snatches a photo,' replied Ed, 'I can guess who the reporter was and you're not his responsibility. Has Mrs Blackwell been charged with anything?'

'No, but we interviewed her under caution as she is one of our prime suspects.'

'Fair enough,' said Ed, 'don't worry about it, Harry, you've done everything by the book.'

Harriet got up and made her way to the kitchen. 'Dinner in fifteen minutes, Ed,' she called.

Ed picked up the paper and read the story under the photograph of Ursula Blackwell. It certainly hinted that she knew something about the death of her husband but avoided making an outright accusation. He guessed the article was the hand of Beefy Cavendish; the journalist was no fool and knew just how to sensationalise something at the same time avoiding going over the top and putting himself in the firing line. Ed folded the paper and leaned back. He wished there was something he could do to help his wife, she was so stressed at the moment. Tomorrow he would make a greater effort to track down any hit-men in the area. Harriet's voice calling him to dinner broke into his thoughts and jumping to his feet he hurried to the dining room.

Chapter Thirty-Six

Vadim Kuznetsov sat in his armchair in front of an electric fire looking at the photograph of Ursula Blackwell on the front page of the evening paper. He was red in the face and tapping his foot irritably as he read the article. The woman was a menace, a dangerous menace. He folded the paper and threw it across the room. Jumping to his feet he went to the sideboard and poured himself a large glass of vodka. Vadim was a big man with a sallow complexion, a bushy moustache, a mass of unruly grey hair and pale eyes which appeared to be sunk deep in his head. He sat down again to drink his vodka and pondered over the situation and what he would have to do about it. Enough was enough, and quite frankly he'd had his fill of blunders and mistakes; far too many for his liking. It was time he thought of himself, he couldn't afford to put himself in danger so orders or no orders he would take the situation into his own hands unless he was advised otherwise by the powers that be.

Ursula Blackwell was also reading the evening paper and was fuming. How dare they! The article made her out to be a criminal. She would be contacting her solicitor in the morning; something had to be done about this. She poured herself another gin and tonic and lay back on the sofa. Stupid of her to worry, she had no cause to, her alibi at the time of her husband's murder was sound, nothing could connect her to his death. She had waited all evening for a call from Don and was becoming anxious in case he had not been released from the police station. She needed to speak to him. Don would know what to do about the article in the paper, she would ask him to accompany her to see the solicitor tomorrow. Now that their relationship was out in the open there was no need to be secretive. She rang his mobile again and it went immediately to voicemail. Ursula left a message asking him to call her. She drained her glass and poured another; at least she was beginning to feel a little more relaxed. She closed her eyes and within minutes was fast asleep.

On being released form the police station Don Underwood had returned home feeling fed up. He had no idea what was actually going on. He knew he was in big trouble having been caught with the evidence of car theft, but to be accused of murder was another thing. He was beginning to wish he had never met George Blackwell and his wife, and he certainly wasn't going to contact Ursula. He had made sure his mobile was turned off and hoped she would think he was still in custody. He drove to the breakers yard where his men were anxious to know what had been happening. He explained the situation and told them they had no need to worry as he had kept their names out of it. 'We put the car business on hold,' he said, 'but we still have plenty of work from crushing and selling car spares.'

The men were relieved to hear this and thanked Don for his support. 'Pity the cops got all the paper work, Red,' said one of them, 'they caught us by surprise with that search warrant and there was nothing we could do about it.'

Don Underwood shook his head. 'Forget it, I was already in the shit, so I'll be the one to carry the can. Carry on with the legit stuff and I'll see what I can do to cover my back.' He left the yard and went to the garage when he said the same to the two mechanics who worked there. Having done this, he returned home to Stadium Road.

Friday morning was foggy, and Harriet drove slowly to the police station. Ed had left for Central earlier as he was meeting a colleague from another force who was carrying out a follow- up on a prisoner at his station, who was also wanted by the Lincolnshire police.

Arriving at headquarters Harriet discovered that Charlie was already in the Incident Room. 'Couldn't sleep, Charlie?' she quipped as she came into the room.

'Slept like a log,' replied Charlie, 'that's why I awoke so early. As I was up I decided to come in and go over the stuff we have on this case.'

'Find anything that might help us?'

'Not really, but I am wondering how Blackwell used Don Underwood to secure a second office, he obviously had the guy under his thumb and was able to make him do as he asked.'

'I'm sure Blackwell didn't want his name turning up as a tenant of a second office,' replied Harriet, 'felt safer getting Underwood, ie Smith to rent the place for him.'

'I'm sure that's right,' agreed Charlie, 'and he certainly had a hold over Underwood.'

'That was a good job done by Sally and Narinder finding this second office of Blackwell's', said Harriet.

'Certainly was,' agreed Charlie, 'although it was you who suggested it. Blackwell was pretty devious having these secrets from everyone, including his wife. Underwood insists he used to beat her up, you know.'

'Yes, I saw in the statement he gave to DI Cassells, and I can't say I'm surprised.'

Charlie picked up the photograph of Rosalind De Luca. 'I'll take this with me when I meet her at Heathrow this afternoon,' he said, 'it will help me identify her.'

'Good idea, and take Sally with you, Charlie, it might be appropriate to have a female officer with you as she's in a strange country.'

'Right. I've booked her into the Glebe Hotel but didn't say how long she would be staying. The hotel doesn't appear to be very busy at the moment, so I don't think they were bothered.'

'When you take her to the hotel,' said Harriet, 'see that she's settled in, and tell her we'll speak to her tomorrow. She's bound to be tired, so we won't press her with questions today. Tell her we'll send a car to pick her up in the morning.'

'She's seeing Bardwell-Fox in the morning,' said Charlie, 'so if we take her to see him first thing she can come here afterwards.'

'I'll leave you to organise that then, Charlie.'

At briefing Harriet explained that she and DCI Marlow had checked the alibi of Conrad Winston during his absence from Innovation, and he was in the clear; she did not mention the fact that the manager was in the habit of clandestine meetings with another man. She told them about Blackwell's secret office and that the computer they had removed from there was now with Henry Chong. 'We'll keep our fingers crossed that something might be found in it that can help us find his killer,' she said.

'Underwood has been released on bail,' said Charlie, 'and will appear in court next week charged with car theft and at the moment nothing else.'

'Blackwell's daughter, Rosalind De Luca arrives from Italy today,' said Harriet, 'and DCI Marlow will be meeting her at Heathrow. Sally you are to go too as we felt she might feel happier with a female officer present.'

'Yes, ma'am.' Sally nodded.

Harriet cast her eyes around the room noting how tired some of the officers looked and decided they needed time off. She would speak to Charlie about this and ask him to arrange a rota so that they could be away from the station for a break.

Briefing over, Harriet and Charlie sat in Harriet's office discussing the case. 'I'm expecting the ACC to visit me any day,' said Harriet, 'he wanted this case closed days ago.'

'Bad luck,' growled Charlie, 'let him see what clues he can dig out of all this. We've spoken to dozens of people, most of who hated Blackwell's guts, and all the people we consider to be in the frame have solid alibis.'

'It hasn't been easy, but somewhere out there, there is a killer and we have to track him down.'

'Oh, I'm not giving up,' said Charlie puffing out his cheeks, 'but just let Mr Fenshaw start throwing his weight about and telling us we're not getting anywhere, and I think I might just tell him where to go'

'Don't you dare, Charlie, that's all I need, you being suspended.'

Charlie grinned. 'I'll just keep out of his way then.'

'The team is looking tired, Charlie,' said Harriet, 'some of them were yawning at briefing and they need a break. Could you arrange something so that they have time off.'

'Yes, I can do that, but you need a break too, Harry.'

'We both do. We'll try and get Sunday off if we can clear our decks a bit.'

Detective Chief Inspector Ed Harrington sat in his office talking to DCI Alex Barker from the Lincolnshire Police Force. Ed and Alex had been at Hendon together and had kept in touch albeit infrequently, over the years.

'I hear you're married, Ed,' said Alex, 'I thought you were a confirmed bachelor.' Ed grinned. 'I might have been if I hadn't met Harry.'

'Harry?'

'Harriet,' said Ed, 'an amazing person who just took my breath away the first time I saw her.'

'Good for you, she must be special for you to say something like that.'

'You must meet her, Alex perhaps you and Jennie could come down and have dinner with us some time.'

Alex's eyes clouded. 'We split up a year ago,' he said, 'I'm afraid she met someone else who didn't spend hours at work and didn't come home hours after the time he said he would. Coppers don't have it easy if their wives can't cope with the job. I hope Harry can handle it.'

'I'm sorry to hear about you and Jennie,' said Ed, 'but I have it made, as Harry is also in the force. She's the super over at Torreston Station.'

'No, really, and she outranks you. How do you feel about that?'

'Doesn't bother me at all,' replied Ed, 'give me time and I'll catch up. Now about this scum-bag you want to interview, I've had him brought up to one of the interview rooms if you'd like to follow me.'

'Thanks, Ed and afterwards we'll talk about this hit-man you are interested in. Word on the street is that there's a Russian in the area touting for business.'

'Russian, eh, that's interesting as I think it was thought that the hit-man Torreston are after might have been Italian Mafia.'

'No,' said Alex, 'the guy being talked about is definitely Russian.'

'Anything to do with the poisoning of Segei Skripal and his daughter earlier this year?'

'Shouldn't think so, poisoning is the favoured political assassination method, shooting is paid gangster stuff.'

'Right,' replied Ed, 'when you've spoken to Sammy Goldsmith we'll meet back in my office for coffee and talk about your suspected Russian hit-man.'

Ursula Blackwell was up early Friday morning and at nine o'clock on the dot she telephoned her solicitor. Bardwell-Fox answered, and his heart sank when he heard the hysterical voice on the line.

'Yes, Mrs Blackwell,' he said desperately trying to keep his voice calm, 'what can I do for you?'

'I'm being put in an impossible position. My photograph appeared on the front of the evening paper making me out to be a criminal and I want something done about it immediately.'

'What exactly do you expect me to do?' asked Bardwell-Fox.'

'Sue someone,' screeched Ursula.

'And who might that be?'

'The police, the paper, oh, I don't know, that's why I pay you.'

'Are you paying me? Mrs Blackwell, I hadn't realised that was the case.'

'Of course, I'm paying you, nothing has changed, you're still my solicitor.'

'Even so,' replied Bardwell-Fox, 'no one has done anything wrong. The reporter took a photograph of you getting into a police car and the police were well within their rights to take you in for questioning. I take it you weren't arrested?'

'No, I wasn't arrested, but that's not the point, my good name is now tarnished.'

The solicitor wondered about the good name but kept his voice on the level. 'I'm afraid there's nothing I can do, Mrs Blackwell, you have no chance at all of suing anyone. I was going to contact you today to inform you that your husband's daughter is arriving in England this afternoon and will be visiting me tomorrow when I will read her the will and discuss how to proceed. I'll see that you hear of her decision on the matter. I'm afraid I'm very busy this morning and will have to leave it at that. Good morning.' He replaced the receiver and then took it off the hook to ensure he couldn't receive any further calls.

Ursula was beside herself with anger. To think of all the money her husband had paid him in the past and now he was dumping her; he didn't care one iota what happened to her, she could tell. Well he wouldn't be getting any more money from her unless he came up with the goods and that meant sorting out that bastard of a daughter of her husband. What a cheek, she, Ursula Blackwell, was to wait until this creature, this illegitimate creature, decided what to do with her house and her money. She picked up a vase from the table and threw it across the room where it smashed in the grate, as she did so, she let out a scream. She sat thinking for a few moments holding her head in her hand. There was something she could do. Of course, there was. Why hadn't she thought of it before. She took her laptop from the sideboard drawer and fired it up. Punching in the word she knew only too well, she entered the password and scrolled down the page. She copied down the number she required and submitted her request. She closed down the laptop feeling satisfied.

Chapter Thirty-Seven

Charlie and Sally arrived at Heathrow in plenty of time for the flight arriving from Milan. Standing at the arrivals gate Sally was holding up a large poster with the name Rosalind De Luca on it in large black letters. People began exiting from the arrivals doorway and the two officers scrutinised the passengers coming through. Rosalind De Luca was unmistakeable as she came towards them. She was exactly as the photograph Charlie was holding and as soon as he spotted her he slipped it into his coat pocket. Sally held up her poster and the woman hurried over to them.

'Mrs De Luca?' asked Charlie thinking how amazingly beautiful she was.

'Yes,' replied Rosalind, 'thank you for meeting me.'

Her English was almost perfect with only the slightest trace of an accent. Her dark eyes held a sadness which Charlie put down to the fact that she was here to pay her respects to her dead father. Charlie gave her his name and introduced Sally. He then explained that she had been booked into a hotel for two nights and would be collected the following day to be taken to the solicitor before being brought to the police station.

'Thank you,' said Rosalind, 'everyone is being so kind.'

'We're very sorry for your loss,' said Sally, 'and the fact that you missed your father's funeral.'

'No one knew of your existence,' said Charlie as they walked towards the car park.

'I am sorry that my father kept me hidden, I did not want secrets.'

Sally wondered how such a lovely woman with an obvious gentleness could possibly be the offspring of the bully George Blackwell.

'We'll discuss all that tomorrow,' said Charlie, 'when you will meet our boss Superintendent Love.'

'Thank you, I look forward to that.'

They reached Charlie's car and he opened the door for Rosalind who slipped gracefully into the vehicle. Sally climbed in beside her and minutes later they were on their way back to Torreston.

Having delivered Rosalind De Luca to the Glebe Hotel Charlie and Sally returned to headquarters where they reported to Harriet.

'How is she?' asked Harriet.

'Pretty solemn,' replied Charlie, 'but I can't see her making any fuss over the will and demanding half Blackwell's property.'

'It is her right,' replied Harriet, 'but it's none of our concern, Bardwell-Fox can sort that out.'

'He's meeting Mrs De Luca in his office at ten tomorrow.' said Charlie.'

'I've never known that creep work on a Saturday before,' said Sally, 'he must think there's money in it for him.'

'He'll be charging her double I'm sure,' said Harriet. 'Now, Sally can you take the day off tomorrow, you do need a break.'

'Narinder and I have a plan to catch the hair cutter tomorrow,' replied Sally, 'but if we can clear the case quickly we'll take the afternoon off, ma'am, if that's in order.'

'I'm insisting,' said Harriet, 'and I don't want to see either of you back here until Monday.'

'Thank you, ma'am.' Sally left Harriet's office and Charlie looked at Harriet.

'Here you are insisting officers have time off because they're working hard,' he said, 'and yet when did you have a break?'

'I'll get one as soon as this case is over, Charlie. Now I know you are busy tomorrow, but I'd like you to have Sunday off as well.'

'Only if you do too.'

'That's agreed,' said Harriet, 'but I shall be on call and probably do some work from home.'

Charlie shook his head. 'I'll have Ed on my back,' he said with a slight smile, 'but I shall be on call as well, and no arguing,' he added as Harriet went to speak.'

Ursula called Don again, once again the call going straight to voice mail. She telephoned the police station and asked if he was still in custody.

'Who's enquiring?' asked Sergeant Yates.

'His girlfriend,' replied Ursula with confidence.

'Just a moment, madam,' said Pete and put the call on hold. He rang through to CID and asked for Charlie who came on the line immediately.

'Yes, Pete, what is it?'

'I have a woman on the line claiming to be Don Underwood's girlfriend asking if we still have him in custody. What am I to tell her?'

Charlie thought for a moment realising the woman had to be Ursula Blackwell. 'Tell her he was released on bail yesterday.'

'Yes, sir.' Pete replaced the receiver and picked up the other telephone. 'Mr Underwood was released on bail yesterday, madam,' he said.

Ursula clenched her hands together and her stomach churned. Don had gone home and not contacted her; what was happening now? Without replying she replaced the receiver feeling sick and dejected. She sat thinking for a few moments before leaping to her feet, grabbing her handbag and coat and rushing from the house. She would visit him at his house and find out exactly what was going on. Jumping into her car she started the engine and drove down the drive at high speed.

Vadim Kuznetsov had received a call from his boss that morning, and the conversation that ensued had not surprised him. He agreed that he too was thinking along the same lines and he was convinced that what they were now discussing was the answer to their problems and as soon as he had carried out the first assignment he would see to the next. Having ended the call, the big Russian began to outline his next move. The first project was no problem and the second he didn't consider the plan to be difficult at all. In a strange way he felt this one he would enjoy. He couldn't do with trouble makers or situations where he felt he was losing control. No, what they had decided was the right way to go. His time in England was coming to an end and he would be happy to be back in his own country where there were always demands for his talents. The payments here were due to end at the end of the month and then he would be off.

Ursula arrived at forty-four Stadium Road and hammered on the front door. She had not replaced the key that had been stolen and was now in the hands of the police, and she began to realise that Don had not been exactly eager to have another one cut for her. She banged on the door again with no success. Returning to her car she set off for the Yard Garage. Screeching to a halt in front of the building she strode into the garage and confronted one of the mechanics.

'Where's Don?' she demanded.

The man shook his head. 'Not here, perhaps he's at the yard.'

Ursula left her car where she had abandoned it and walked the few metres to the breakers yard. She saw two of the men she vaguely knew and went up too them.

'Is Don here?' she asked.

'Haven't seen him since the coppers took him,' said one of the men.

'Hasn't he been in touch?' asked Ursula.

Both men shook their heads. Ursula let out an expletive and turned on her heels leaving the yard to return to her car. The two men grinned and made their way to the office where Don Underwood was standing behind the door.

'That was close, Red,' said one of the men.

'Too bloody close,' replied Don, 'but thanks, guys, and please do the same if she returns.'

'No problem,' said one of the men, 'but it's time you sorted your love-life out, mate or you really will be in hot water.'

'I have it in hand,' replied Don, 'but of course I might not be around after the court hearing.' He gave a forced laugh and made his way outside careful to check that Ursula was nowhere around.

A miserable Ursula returned to her car and made her way home. It was getting dark and she was cold as she had rushed from the house without being properly dressed for the November weather. Arriving home, she flopped into an armchair and burst into tears. Everything was going wrong; her life was in tatters and she didn't know what to do next. She hoped her latest plan would work, which would take a load off her shoulders and rid her of that parasite of a step-daughter, but before anything could happen she would have to go to the bank. She rose and poured herself a large gin and tonic to drown her sorrow. She turned up the thermostat on the central heating and sat down to enjoy her drink. Three gin and tonics later Ursula was feeling light headed but less anxious. The grandfather clock struck eleven and she decided to go to bed. As she rose to leave the room she heard a knock on the front door. Rather late for callers. She made for the front door excitement gripping her. Perhaps it was Don. As she lifted her hand to open the door Ursula hesitated. 'Who is it?' she called hoping fervently to hear Don's voce reply.

'I have a message for a Mrs Ursula Blackwell,' came the response in a strong foreign accent.

Ursula was beginning to feel concerned. Who would deliver a message at eleven o'clock at night? 'Who is it from?' she called.

'I do not know but I have been instructed to deliver it to you personally.'

Ursula was now trembling and quietly she backed away from the front door. Returning to the sitting room she picked up the telephone to call the police. The line was dead, and she dropped the receiver in panic. Fumbling in her handbag she searched for her mobile, her drunken state not helping. As her fingers closed around it she heard a loud crash from somewhere in the house and feeling sick and with shaking fingers she dialled three nines. The emergency service asked for her name and then her address with Ursula getting more and more panicky as the seconds slipped by. 'Just get the police,' she shouted, there's someone in my house.' The person at the end of the line advised her to lock herself in a room and stay calm until the police arrive and closing down her phone Ursula pulled the armchair across the room and wedged it under the door.

Sergeant Carl Fisher was on duty at Torreston Police Station when the emergency call was put through and recognising the address he immediately contacted motor patrol and told all cars in the area to get over to Copper Beeches as quickly as possible.

The first police car to arrive at the house was driven by a young, newly promoted sergeant with an even younger constable at his side. Jumping from the car the sergeant shouted to the constable to go around to the back of the house and he dashed up the steps to the front door. Sergeant Justin Delany tried the door. It was firmly locked. Suddenly he heard a scream and without hesitating he took his baton and smashed the glass in the door. Knocking the broken glass out of the frame he leaned through and unlocked the door. Entering the house he cautiously moved down the corridor feeling along the wall until he found a light switch which he flicked on. Shouting 'Police' as he continued through the house he suddenly heard the slam of a door from somewhere at the back of the building suggested to Delaney that the intruder was making good his escape. He hoped that Constable Franks would be able to detain him.

A terrified voice shouted, 'Here, I'm in here.'

Delaney went to the room where the voice had come from and called out Police. He told Ursula to stay where she was but that she was safe. He then hurried down the passage way to the back door which he found swinging open. He shouted for Franks and to his dismay he heard a groan from just outside the house. Roy Franks lay on the ground writhing in obvious pain and holding his chest. The sergeant knelt beside him.

'Where did he hit you?' he asked

The young constable struggled to talk but managed to whisper, 'shot'.

Delaney froze and opened his colleague's jacket to discover his shirt soaked in blood.

'Oh God,' he muttered and taking his mobile from his pocket he called for an ambulance. He then phoned the station where he told Sergeant Fisher what had happened. 'We need the firearms guys here,' he said, 'we have a shooter, and send Forensics.'

Carl Fisher dialled the emergency number for the Swift Armed Response Team and then sent another message to motor patrol asking them to attend the scene at Copper Beeches. Having done this, he picked up the telephone and called Harriet.

Chapter Thirty-Eight

Harriet was in a deep sleep when the call came from headquarters and within minutes she was dressed. She put on trousers and a shirt under a thick sweater and prepared to leave. Ed was also dressed and insisted he went with her.

'It's after midnight, Harry,' he said, 'and if as you say an officer has been shot, no way are you going on your own.'

'Thank you, Ed, but I doubt if the gunman has hung around knowing backup had been called. It sounds as if it was Ursula Blackwell he was after.'

'Is she okay?'

'Carl didn't say what had happened to her, just that we have an officer down.'

They left the house and with Ed driving set off for Newham Drive.

The ambulance had arrived at Copper Beeches followed by a car containing reporters who were eagerly taking pictures. The ambulance had been directed to the back of the house where Sergeant Delaney was nursing his colleagues head in his lap. Delaney felt frightened and sick and was relieved when the paramedics arrived. Roy Franks was now unconscious, and the sergeant stood watching as the paramedics attended to the injured officer. He hoped fervently he had done everything correctly. Delaney was silently praying that the constable would be alright, and he wouldn't die. He had only been a sergeant for two months and this was his first encounter with anything serious. The three stripes on his sleeve, at that moment felt very heavy.

Standing at the back door was Ursula Blackwell who was sobbing hysterically. 'It was me they were after,' she squealed, 'I was going to be shot. Oh, God they want me dead, it must be someone with a vendetta against my husband and now they're after me.' The flash of a camera made her look up and she quickly brushed her hair back and tilted her head.

Delaney looked at her with distain. 'You're quite safe, madam,' he said rather sharply, 'this young officer who came to take care of you is the one who has been shot.'

'It was me they wanted,' she insisted, 'I've never been so terrified in all my life.'

The sergeant turned to one of the constables who had arrived after the incident and told him to take the woman inside and sit her in the front room until she could be interviewed. This he did, but Ursula could still be heard sobbing as she was led away. The paramedics carefully transferred Franks to the ambulance and with one of them inside with him the other closed the doors and went to get into the driver's seat.

The sergeant went up to him. 'How is he?' he asked.

'It's serious,' replied the paramedic, 'but they're on standby at the hospital for a gunshot wound so he'll be in good hands.'

'Which hospital is he going to?' asked Delaney.

'Torreston General,' replied the paramedic. He climbed into the ambulance and with the blue light flashing set off down the drive.

Ed arrived at Copper Beeches just as the ambulance came through the gates. Harriet clenched her hands together dreading what she was going to find at the house. A Forensic van stood at the front steps and there were two police cars nearby. Two constables stood guard at the front door. Officers in bullet-proof vests were visible and Harriet winced when she saw the weapons they were carrying. She and Ed got out of the car and walked towards them. The officers recognised them immediately.

'The armed-response team is here, ma'am,' said one of the men, 'the house has been checked and it's clear. Forensics are at work at the back where the intruder broke in.'

'Thank you,' said Harriet, 'who's in charge?'

'Sergeant Delaney,' said one of the men, 'he's in the house.'

Harriet and Ed entered the building and could hear someone crying close by. Following the sound, they found Ursula and the sergeant in the front room. Justin Delaney jumped to his feet as they came into the room a feeling of relief sweeping over him. It was stupid, but he felt he wanted to cry, his colleague had been shot, might even die, and he had had to carry the can all by himself. He pulled himself together. This was after all why he had joined the police force, and this was an opportunity to show just what he was made of.

'Ma'am,' he said.

'Sergeant Delaney,' said Harriet, 'are you all right?'

Delaney nodded. 'Yes, thank you, ma'am, a bit shaken, Constable Franks has been shot and he's on his way to hospital.'

'Do you know how he is?'

'It's not good, ma'am, he took the bullet in the chest. They've taken him to Torreston General.'

Harriet's heart sank. 'You know DCI Harrington,' she said indicating Ed, and Delaney nodded. 'What family does Constable Franks have?'

'He lives with his parents, ma'am.'

'In Torreston?'

'Just outside, in a village called Camberwich.'

'I'll contact them,' said Harriet, 'now, can you tell us exactly what happened, Sergeant, did you hear the shot?'

'No, ma'am so I presume he used a silencer.'

Ursula let out as wail. 'What about me, I'm the one he was after. Banged on my door and I had the sense not to open it, but he broke in any way and I'm lucky to be alive.'

Harriet looked at the woman her dislike for her intensifying. 'Perhaps you could tell us how all this began then, Mrs Blackwell,' she said, 'and then Sergeant Delaney can fill us in as to what happened after he arrived.'

Throwing herself around, sobbing and mopping her eyes, Ursula told them she had no idea why anyone would want to harm her, but thought it must have something to do with the activities of her late husband. 'I've never done anything dreadful in my whole life,' she wailed, 'and only now am I learning that perhaps dear George might have done some illegal things, which has triggered all this nasty stuff off.'

'I see,' said Harriet, and turning to Sergeant Delaney asked for his story. This he related calmly and accurately, happy that now there were senior officers present to take over.

'I hope I did the right thing, ma'am,' he said, 'calling out the armed-response guys and Forensics. I didn't hear the shot, but I could see Roy was bleeding and he said to me "shot" so I knew what had happened. I've never had anything to do with firearms and seeing Roy bleeding like that was a sickening experience as I had sent him round to the back of the house.'

'You did everything correctly, Sergeant,' replied Harriet, 'and I'm so sorry your colleague has been injured. We must pray he recovers.'

Delaney nodded but found suddenly he had a lump in his throat and couldn't speak. He just nodded again and left the room.

'Ma'am.' A voice from the doorway made them turn around to see a bleary-eyed Duncan McAllister standing behind them holding a weapon on his hip.

'Duncan,' said Harriet, 'so you got called out.'

'Yes, ma'am, about half an hour ago, but the shooter has done a bunk, the house is clear. Sir,' he said seeing Ed, 'nice to see you again.'

'And you, Duncan,' said Ed, 'pity it's under these circumstances.'

Duncan, being part of the Swift-Response Firearms Team was on call at all times and like tonight he had to be dressed, armed and out in four to five minutes. 'I'll see you in the morning, ma'am,' he said turning to leave, 'and I hope young Roy Franks is okay.' He left the room to report to the firearms officer in charge. Harriet turned to Ed. 'Would you ring headquarters,' she said, 'and ask them to find the address of Roy Franks and contact his parents. They should be notified so they can get to the hospital.'

'Of course,' replied Ed, 'only too happy to do something.'

Harriet suggested to Ursula that she go to her sister's rather than remaining at Copper Beeches.

'I suppose I shall have to,' said Ursula, 'but my sister is being rather difficult at the moment and not a great deal of help. I wouldn't dare stay here after tonight thought. I think perhaps I'll go to a hotel.'

Harriet bit her tongue but said she would wait until the woman had packed an overnight bag before she left. 'I'll have an officer board up the back window where the intruder broke in, and the gap in the front door,' she said, 'and perhaps you could arrange for replacement glass in the morning.'

'I trust I shall be getting police protection after this little episode,' snapped Ursula, 'quite honestly, I don't think the police have been very supportive of me over my husband's murder and me being on my own.'

'We did advise you to stay with your sister,' said Harriet as politely as she could muster, 'and you do have Mr Underwood who I am sure would be happy to look after you.'

Ursula was convinced the superintendent spoke with sarcasm and she tossed her head.

'Don's been very busy, but I'll speak to him in the morning; at least he cares what happens to me.' She flounced form the room.

'She's quite a piece of work,' said Ed when she had gone, 'and you say she's on your suspect list?'

'She is indeed, I'm not sure about her at all, Ed.'

'I can see why.'

Harriet waited for Ursula to return with her case and Ed went to check that someone had boarded up the back window and would do the same in the front door. Sergeant Delaney appeared looking drawn and very pale and told her he was leaving to continue his shift on patrol. Harriet felt the young man was still stressed and in no condition to work; he had after all experience a harrowing incident, so she told him to call it a night and go home.

'Are you sure, ma'am?' he said, 'I should be on patrol until the morning.'

'I'm sure, Sergeant, I'll square it with your superior officer.'

'Thank you, ma'am.' Delaney left the house suddenly realising that his legs felt like jelly and it was difficult to walk. He slid into the patrol car and placed his head on the steering wheel shaking uncontrollably. He remained like that for several minutes until he felt able to drive, and then starting the engine, he drove slowly down the drive and out onto the road heading for headquarters.

At one thirty Ursula drove away from Copper Beeches, and the Forensic team packed their van in readiness to leave. The firearms officers had already gone, and it was Harriet who dropped the catch on the front door and closed it. Fraser Overton, senior Forensic officer, came over to Harriet and Ed to say goodbye.

'The guy who broke in was a professional,' he said. 'Left no fingerprints, no bullet casing or anything else that we might be able to find clues on. Firearms were quick to get here, and frightened him off. Sergeant Delaney was pretty sharp in sending for help.'

Harriet thanked Doctor Overton and he climbed into the van and vanished down the drive. Ed took Harriet's arm. 'Home,' he said, 'or neither of us will be fit for anything tomorrow.'

'You mean today.' Harriet smiled and allowed Ed to guide her to his car, 'but I must call at the hospital on the way home, Ed, I won't sleep knowing that young man has been shot.'

'We'll do that,' agreed Ed as he opened the car door for her.

On leaving her house Ursula drove into Torreston and called at the Glebe Hotel where she booked a room. She told the night receptionist, a middle aged, experienced man, that it was an emergency as she had just had a terrifying experience and wasn't sure how long she would be staying. The man recognised her from her picture in the paper and told her she could have room one hundred and two. He pushed the signing-in book across to her and Ursula picked up the pen. She was about to sign when she read the name of the last person on the page. Rosalind De Luca. Her stomach turned over. George's brat! Her solicitor had told her she was arriving from Italy and calling to see him on Saturday. But to discover she was here, actually in the same building as herself, made her blood boil. Well what a shock dear Rosalind was going to have in the morning when she confronted her. Ursula took the key she was handed and allowed the porter, who had been summoned, to carry her bag to the lift. At her room door Ursula took her bag from him and entered, locking the door firmly behind her.

Chapter Thirty-Nine

Harriet and Ed arrived at the hospital and went straight to A and E where Harriet enquired about the injured officer. They were told he was in theatre and being operated on to remove the bullet.

'There is an officer in the waiting room,' said the sister, 'a colleague of the injured man.'

'That must be Sergeant Delaney,' said Harriet, 'poor man, he was very distressed over the incident.'

'It was his first major incident,' said Ed, 'it always hits you hard until you get used to it.'

'Some things you never get used to, Ed' said Harriet quietly remembering the death of Bob Finch a few years ago.

Ed put his arm around her shoulder. 'Let's go and have a word with Delaney,' he said.

Justin Delaney was sitting on his own in the small waiting room holding his head in his hands. He looked up as he heard someone come into the room and jumped to his feet when he saw who it was. 'Ma'am, sir,' he said.

'Sergeant, why don't you go home,' said Harriet kindly.

'No, ma'am I can't go until know how Roy is. I feel responsible, as it was me who sent him to investigate at the back of the house.'

'You only did what was your duty,' said Harriet, 'you are not to blame for what happened.'

'Thank you, ma'am, but I'll wait until he's out of surgery if you don't mind.'

Harriet nodded. She understood exactly how this young man felt. Ed offered to get them all coffee and Delaney accepted gratefully. Harriet sat down, and they waited in silence. Ed returned and handed them polystyrene mugs of hot coffee whispering an apology to Harriet. For once Harriet didn't care about the quality of the drink she had been given and barely notice how it tasted as she sipped the coffee. Ed's mobile rang, and he took the call speaking briefly. He turned to Harriet. 'That was your station,' he said, 'there's no one at the address we gave them for Frank's home but they're doing their best to track his parent's down.'

'He has an aunt and uncle in College Street, Torreston,' said Delaney,' they might know where they are.'

'Same name as him?' asked Ed taking out his mobile.

'Yes, sir.' Ed called the police station again and gave them this information.

An hour passed and then another with the three of them taking it in turns to pace the floor. At three thirty the door opened and the surgeon wearing his greens entered the room. They all stood.

'Superintendent Love?' he asked casting his eyes over Harriet and Ed.

'Yes,' answered Harriet.

'We've removed the bullet,' said the surgeon, 'and although the constable is still in a critical state at this time, I am hopeful that with intensive care he will pull through.'

There was a stifled gasp of relief from Delaney who sat down suddenly. Harriet placed a hand on his shoulder. 'Thank you,' said Harriet, 'his parents are being traced and hopefully should be here soon. We do need the bullet,' she added.

The surgeon gave a slight smile and produced a small packet from his pocket which he handed to her. 'I knew you would ask for it,' he said.

They were not allowed to visit Roy Franks and finally Sergeant Delaney was persuaded to go home. Headquarters contacted Ed to inform him that the constable's family had been contacted and were on their way to the hospital. Harriet and Ed remained in the waiting room and waited for their arrival. The couple hurried into the room twenty minute later and Harriet explained to them what had happened. She did her best to reassure them that their son would recover and told them that the surgeon would speak to them. Seeing the man himself approaching, Harriet took leave of Mr and Mrs Franks and she and Ed slipped away.

On arriving home at Magnolia Cottage Harriet rang the police station and spoke to the duty sergeant. She told him that Roy Franks was out of the operating theatre and hopefully would recover. She asked Sergeant Fisher to explain to DI Marlow what had happened when he came on duty and that she would be in later that morning and he was to carry on without her. 'Would you also tell Inspector Baldwin about constable Franks,' she added, 'and I will be down to see him when I get in.' It was now nearly five o'clock and Harriet yawned. She would snatch a few hours to ensure that she got through the day and insisted Ed rang Central to tell them he would be doing the same and going in late.

Ursula had telephoned a glazier when she arrived at the hotel and left a message on the answering machine asking him to meet her at her house the following morning to repair two broken windows. She stressed that it was important as she had been broken into and feared for her safety. She knew they would oblige, they always had done when her husband had contacted them needing a speedy job doing. She also knew it wouldn't be cheap. Crooks, they're all crooks, she thought, were there no decent people in the world? That evening she set the alarm on her mobile phone for seven thirty and climbed into bed feeling exhausted and nervous.

The following morning on hearing the buzzing of her alarm, Ursula jumped from her bed, showered and dressed. She decided she would confront Mrs De Luca at breakfast. That madam was going to get such a surprise. She left her room and went downstairs to the breakfast room where she cast her eyes over the tables. There was no woman sitting alone so she took a seat near the door where she could see who entered. Ursula ordered toast and marmalade and a pot of coffee. The minutes ticked by and she had all but finished breakfast when a young, dark- haired woman appeared. This had to be her! She watched as the woman sat at a table in the window. Wiping her fingers on her napkin Ursula rose and walked over to her and without speaking pulled out a chair and sat down.

Rosalind De Luc looked up in surprise. 'Good morning,' she said.

'Is it?' snapped Ursula. 'But then I suppose it is when you are about to take things that don't belong to you and ruin another person's life.'

Rosalind widened her eyes in amazement. 'I'm sorry?' she said, 'I think you have the wrong person.'

'You are Mrs De Luca?' asked Ursula.

'I am. And you are?'

'Mrs George Blackwell.'

'Ah, I see.'

'Do you indeed,' snarled Ursula, 'and do you see what a greedy, heartless little cow you are, coming over here to take whatever you can lay your hands on and leaving me destitute.' She jumped to her feet and slammed her fist on the table making the coffee pot leap off the table onto the floor. Rosalind squealed, and a waiter rushed over to see what was happening. Ursula was not about to back off. 'You're just the result of a fling with a whore,' she shouted, 'you're not going to get anything from my husband's estate I can assure you. Go back to Italy and leave decent people alone.'

The waiter took Ursula's arm just as the hotel manager arrived. 'Please, Mrs Blackwell,' he hissed, 'this is not the place for disagreements, people are looking at you.'

Ursula shook her arm free from the waiter's grip. 'Don't touch me,' she shouted, 'how anyone with any class would want to stay in a place like this, where foreign dregs are allowed to stay, beats me. I shall be leaving immediately.' She stormed from the room with the other guests staring in amazement. Rosalind was weeping and dabbing her eyes with her napkin.

'I'm so sorry,' she whispered. 'I only came to England to pay my respects to my father who died recently, I had no intention of causing any trouble.'

'It wasn't your fault, Mrs De Luca,' said the hotel manager, 'I'm afraid Mrs Blackwell was quite out of order. Allow me to take you to your room to avoid any further confrontation.'

Rosalind rose from her seat. 'Thank you,' she said, 'and then I shall be going out. A car is picking me up.' With the manager at her side she left the breakfast room hoping she wouldn't bump into the hateful Ursula Blackwell.

Charlie had arrived at headquarters early to be told by Sergeant Fisher what had happened the night before.

'The boss told me to tell you to carry on, sir,' said Fisher, 'and she'll be in later. It must have been well after four when she got home.'

'Who was the officer shot?' asked Charlie.

'Young Roy Franks from motor patrol. He hasn't been on the job for very long, poor sod. He was with Sergeant Delaney who the boss sent home as he was in shock.'

'Has Inspector Baldwin been told?'

'No, sir, he hasn't arrived yet. He should be in at eight thirty.'

'I'll go down and tell him,' said Charlie. 'Do we know how Franks is?'

'The super was with him until his parents arrived and she said he had come through surgery and the surgeon thought he would recover.'

'Thank, God.'

Charlie went straight to motor patrol and arrived just as Inspector Baldwin came through the door. 'Don't tell me, Charlie,' he said, 'I heard on the news an officer had been shot, who is it?'

'Roy Franks.'

'Will he live?'

'The surgeon is hopeful,' replied Charlie, 'Harry was with Franks last night and spoke to the guy who operated on him, so we'll learn more when she gets in.'

'He was on patrol with Sergeant Delaney, do we know if he's

okay?' asked Baldwin.

'He's fine, Harry sent him home after the incident as he was in shock.'

'Good,' muttered, the inspector, 'but poor Franks, what an introduction to policing.'

'He'll get used to it, I'm afraid,' replied Charlie. 'I'm sure Harry will be down to see you when she gets in, but if I hear anything before then I'll be in touch.'

Charlie returned to the CID block and went straight to the Incident Room. Jack was already at his computer and he looked up. 'I've heard,' he said, 'how is Franks?'

'The boss left a message to say the operation to remove the bullet had been successful and Franks was stable. She'll be in later and knowing her she'll call at the hospital on the way here.'

'That's a relief.'

Charlie went to his office and picked up the phone. He called the hospital and asked to be put through to A and E where he asked to speak to Sister Marlow, his wife. Liz came to the phone. 'Charlie,' she said, 'I expect you're calling to see how the constable is.'

'Yes, I am, how is he, Liz?'

'He hasn't come around yet, but the surgeon is hopeful. All we can say at this time is that he's comfortable.'

'We'll keep our fingers crossed,' said Charlie. 'I'm sure Harry will call in on her way here, she's coming in late as she was at the shooting last night and didn't get home until the early hours.'

'Yes, I heard, I'll look out for her.'

'Thank, Liz.' Charlie said goodbye and returned to the Incident Room to get ready for briefing.'

Chapter Forty

That morning Harriet and Ed left home at ten thirty and went their separate ways. They both felt tired but decided they couldn't spare any further time away from work. Harriet drove to the hospital and went to A and E where she was met by Liz who told her Roy Franks had been moved to the small ward attached to casualty.

'Charlie rang earlier,' said Liz, 'and guessed you would be in, I'll take you to see the patient.'

The ward was just down the passage off the A and E department. 'We've put him in a single room,' said the sister. 'He's still under close observation but recovering slowly. His parents were here most of the night and he did come around briefly.'

'May I see him, Liz?' asked Harriet.

'Of course you can, but only for a few moments, I'll get back to A and E, Staff Nurse Dabrowski is in charge of this ward if you'd like to speak to her, Harry.'

Harriet was shown into the small room where Roy Franks lay looking very wan. His eyes were closed, and he had a blood transfusion in one arm and oxygen tubes in his nose. She went to his side and placed a hand on the young man's as it rested on the white sheet. Roy Franks didn't move. He looked so young, thought Harriet, so helpless. She left the room and went to the nurse's station where she spoke to the staff nurse.

'Take good care of him,' she said.

'We will, he's stable,' replied the nurse, 'but we're keeping a close eye on him.'

'Sister Marlow said he came around briefly.'

'Yes, he did, but we're happy that he remains asleep as rest is what he needs at the present time. He was lucky,' added the staff nurse, 'another couple of centimetres to the left and it may well have been a different story.'

Harriet shuddered. 'Thank heavens that wasn't the case.' She left the side ward and returned to A and E.

'I'll call in again later today if I may, Liz,' she said.'

'Yes, do.' said Liz. 'Give my love to Charlie.'

'I will. I'm going on duty now to explain to everyone what happened.'

'Try not to worry about Franks,' said Liz, 'we'll take great care of him.'

'Thank you,' said Harriet and she left the department.

At the police station Harriet was met at the door by Pete Yates who had taken over from Carl Fisher as duty sergeant. 'How is he, ma'am?' he asked not needing to name the injured officer.

'Stable,' replied Harriet, 'and in good hands. Did DCI Marlow get my messages from Sergeant Fisher?'

'Yes, ma'am.'

'Thank you, Pete, I'll keep you informed as to the condition of Roy Franks.' Harriet hurried up the stairs to CID and poked her head round he door of the Incident Room. Only Jack Fuller was there.

'Good morning, Jack,' she said, 'everything running smoothly?'

'Yes, ma'am. DCI Marlow asked me to tell you that he's gone to collect Mrs De Luca from the hotel to take her to the solicitors and them he'll bring her back here as soon as she's finished there. Sally and Narinder are off on this hunt for the hair-cutter, they seem to have a plan they want to put into action.'

Harriet smiled. 'Thank you, Jack, let's hope they succeed.'

'How is the young constable, ma'am?'

'I've just come from the hospital,' replied Harriet. 'He came around briefly, and the surgeon is hopeful that he will recover.'

263

'Thank goodness,' said Jack.

Harriet held up the little bag containing the bullet. 'We do have this, Jack, would you take it to Forensics for me, they are expecting it.'

Jack took the bullet and left the room, Harriet made for her office where she hung up her coat before leaving to go down to uniform division to speak to Inspector Baldwin.

Charlie arrived at the Glebe Hotel and parked at the front door. As he entered the building he saw Rosalind De Luca standing in the foyer with a smartly dressed man. He went over to them.

'Are you ready? Mrs De Luca?' he asked.

Rosalind looked agitated and Charlie asked her if she was all right.

The man who was with her introduced himself as the hotel manager and explained to Charlie that there had been a disturbing incident in the dining room that morning. 'I'm afraid Mrs Blackwell, who is also a guest here, became very aggressive towards Mrs De Luca at breakfast,' he said, 'and I had to intervene. I promised I would remain with her until you arrived. I take it you are the Chief Inspector?'

'I am,' replied Charlie, and turning to Rosalind asked; 'What was the argument about?'

'Mrs Blackwell accused me of coming to England to rob her of her home and inheritance,' she replied, 'but I can assure you that is not the case, I do not need money, I just wish to pay my respects to my father.' A tear ran down her cheek and she took a hankie from her pocket and dabbed her eyes.

'I'm sorry about that,' said Charlie, 'but let's go and speak to the solicitor and find out exactly what the situation is with your father's affairs; my car is outside.' He thanked the manager for looking after Rosalind and left the hotel with the young woman.

Sally had asked Charlie if she and Narinder could miss briefing as they needed to be at the bus station in Northampton early. 'We intend catching the hair-cutter this morning,' she said with a grin, 'and we'll let you know how we get on once we have him.'

'And then you are to go off duty,' said Charlie, 'the boss's orders.'

'Yes, sir,' said Sally.

'Before you leave,' said Charlie, 'there is one thing that I shall be saying at briefing and that is that a young PC from motor patrol was shot last night as he attended a break in at the Blackwell house.'

'Oh, no,' Sally gasped. 'Who was it?'

'Roy Franks, a relatively new recruit.'

'How is he?'

'We won't really know until the boss gets in, she was at the scene most of the night and won't be in until later.'

'I don't know him,' said Sally, 'but I hope he'll be okay.'

'We'll let you know when you call in to tell us you've caught the hair-cutter.' Charlie grinned, and Sally went over to Narinder's desk to ask if she was ready to leave. Duncan arrived at that moment visibly yawning and Charlie told him he was to go home as soon as briefing was over. 'The boss sent word that you were to leave as you were at the Blackwell incident last night, but if you stay for briefing you can tell us what exactly happened at Copper Beeches.'

'Yes, sir and thank you,' said Duncan.

Sally and Narinder arrived at the bus station and went to the stand of the X 7. Both were dressed in jeans and anoraks and Narinder was wearing a baseball cap with her dark hair spilling out the back in a pony tail. They sat on one of the seats and waited, watching as the people climbed onto the bus, keeping an eye out for a young woman in a headscarf. They had agreed if they spotted such a woman and could definitely recognise the perfume on her then Narinder was to get on the bus ahead of her and Sally behind. The first bus left, and then another with no success. Narinder began to fidget. 'I could do with a coffee,' she moaned.

'And then you'd want a pee,' said Sally, 'Just hang on, Narinder,

I have a positive feeling about this.'

At ten thirty another X7 pulled into the stand and the waiting passengers began to board. There was no young woman. There were elderly couples brandishing their bus-passes, two young couples with small children, a man with a boy in football kit and a woman with a teenage girl with one long pigtail. The driver was standing at the side watching the hands of the large station clock tick round. Sally recognised him as the man they had spoken to when they first began their investigation into the hair-cutter. She went up to him and quietly explained what she and Narinder were up to.

'The woman I described to you hasn't been on any of my buses since I spoke you,' he said.

'We think she mainly works at the weekends,' said Sally, 'that's why we're here today If we spot her we'll just hop on the bus if that's all right with you?'

'Just hold your warrant car at my window when you get on,' said the driver, 'and people will presume you have a pass.'

'Thanks,' said Sally.

'It's nearly time to leave,' said the driver, 'I'd better get on the bus.' He moved away and at that moment Sally smelt the definite smell of the perfume she and the rest of the officers at Torreston Station knew so well. A young woman in a belted, black coat and a floral headscarf carrying a shopping bag on her arm walked by and quickly Sally held up a hand to Narinder who caught on immediately and jumped to her feet. She darted to the bus ahead of the woman who followed her onto the X7. Narinder flashed her warrant card to the driver shielding her action with her body. Sally fell in behind them and did the same. She watched as Narinder sat on a seat on her own near the back of the bus and a thrill went down her back as she saw the woman in the headscarf take the seat immediately behind her friend. Sally casually walked down the bus and sat at the back making sure she could keep an eye on the woman they were interested in. The woman in the headscarf was of medium height, quite good looking and looked to be in her thirties and Sally wondered why on earth someone like this should be committing such an offence as cutting other women's hair. The bus set off stopping at various places to pick up more passenger. The bus began to fill, and Sally became anxious that she might lose sight of the target. An opportunity arose to help the situation when an elderly lady stood in the aisle and Sally was able to offer her a seat which she gratefully took. Sally stood and moved slightly so that she was nearer the woman in the headscarf. The smell of "Obsession" was strong and Sally was convinced that they were onto the hair-cutter. The bus was now nearing Market Harborough and Narinder, who had been sitting on a pin the whole journey now felt the slight movement that she had been waiting for. This was followed by the definite sound of her hair being cut and it took great strength for her not to turn around. Sally had been watching and as the bus pulled into the stop on the square in Harborough she made sure she was right behind the woman in the headscarf as she left the bus. Once off the bus she took the woman's arm and hissed in her ear that she was a police officer and she was to remain where she was. They were joined by Narinder. Sally turned her friend around and looked for the pony tail which was missing. Sally took the woman's bag and looked inside. She produced the missing hair at which point the woman burst into tears.

'I'm sorry,' she wailed, 'so sorry.'

'No need to be sorry for me,' snapped Narinder taking off her cap and shaking down her real hair, 'I wasn't going to let you do to me what you've done to other people, so I came prepared.' She removed the rest of the false hair from her cap which she replaced on her head.

'What's your name?' asked Sally.

'Katherine Waterford.'

'Do you live in Northampton?'

The woman nodded. Sally read her her rights and Narinder phoned in for a police car to come and collect them. Sergeant Mirams was not far away and arrived ten minutes later to pick them up.

Chapter Forty-One

Charlie dropped Rosalind off at the solicitors and told her he would be back in half an hour and would wait in the car for her. Rosalind entered the building and stood in the hallway not sure of what to do next. She saw a bell-switch on the wall and pressed it. Hearing footsteps on the stairs Rosalind looked up to see the portly figure of Bardwell-Fox descending. He hurried down the stairs and with hand outstretched came over to her.

'Mrs De Luca,' he gushed, 'you can be no other. I am Humphrey Bardwell-Fox at your service.' He took her hand and shook it vigorously.

Rosalind smiled awkwardly and nodded. 'Yes,' she said, 'I am she.'

'Come up to my office, I have all the paperwork ready for you.'

Rosalind followed the solicitor up the stairs and into his office where she was asked to sit down. 'Now,' said Bardwell-Fox, 'your late father has made you a very wealthy young woman.' He rubbed his fat fingers together and continued. 'You are to have the proceeds from his businesses, which are to be sold, and half the money from the sale of his house.'

Rosalind held up a hand. 'If that means his wife will lose her home, then I don't wish for that to happen.'

'But it's what your father wants.'

'But not what I want. I encountered Mrs Blackwell at my hotel this morning and she is very distressed at the thought of losing her house, and I am not here to upset her. I only wish to see my father's grave and pay my respects.'

'I hope Mrs Blackwell is not intimidating you,' said Bardwell Fox scowling, 'I am here to carry out your father's wishes and he wants Copper Beeches sold and the money shared between you.'

'No,' said Rosalind firmly getting to her feet, 'the house is not to be sold and my stepmother must not be evicted, if the business is to be sold then I will be happy to share the money from this with Mrs Blackwell. That is all thank you, Mr Bardwell- Fox, now I am going to see my father's grave.'

'If that is really what you want, Mrs De Luca then I should be grateful if you would call in on Monday morning as there will be documents you will have to sign.'

'Of course,' replied Rosalind, 'I'm sure that will be in order, I am booked in at the Glebe Hotel for two nights, so Monday morning will be convenient. I am catching an afternoon flight home.'

She left the room leaving the solicitor quite disappointed. He so wanted to tell Mrs Blackwell to put the house on the market, she deserved to be humiliated, but now the wind had been taken out of his sails. He felt somewhat annoyed and decided he would sit on this information for a while and not tell Mrs Blackwell. Perhaps he could get Mrs De Luca to change her mind, although he would see that the legal documents were drawn up but not be too eager in presenting them to her.

Sally and Narinder were dropped off at headquarters by Sergeant Mirams, and thanking him they escorted Katherine Waterford into the station. They reported to the custody sergeant and told him they wished to speak to the prisoner before deciding what to do. In one of the interview rooms they sat her down and then Sally asked Katherine why she had been cutting hair on the X7. The woman began to cry again. She looked up and removed her headscarf disclosing a totally bald head.

'I'm having chemo,' she muttered, 'and I couldn't bear seeing all those women with lovely hair like I used to have.'

Sally and Narinder looked at each other suddenly feeling mean. Sally spoke quickly.

'We're very sorry that you're not well, Katherine,' she said, 'but you can't take it out on other people. What you have done is a criminal offence and you could be prosecuted. I'm sure you don't want that on top of everything else you're going through.'

Katherine shook her head. 'It wasn't just my loss of hair,' she said quietly, 'but my husband walked out on me when he heard I had cancer and was going bald. That was the last straw and I don't know what came over me.' She began to cry again. 'I'm not a hateful person, really I'm not, I just don't know what came over me when Gordon left, I went to pieces.' She dabbed her eyes. 'I'm so sorry, will those women forgive me?'

Narinder walked over to her and placed a hand on her shoulder. 'Your hair will grow again and be as lovely as it was before,' she said, 'it only takes time.'

'We'll speak to the superintendent tomorrow,' said Sally, 'and see how we are to proceed. If the victims agree not to press charges you could be lucky and get off with a caution.'

'Perhaps you could then apologise to those women,' suggested Narinder.

'I will any way,' replied Katherine. 'I'm glad you've caught me, I did so want to stop.'

'We'll have to keep your bag with the hair and scissors,' said Sally, 'as its evidence, but if no charges are brought against you they will be returned.'

'I don't think I want them back,' said Katherine. 'Thank you, you've both been so kind to me and I don't deserve it.'

'We'll run you home,' said Sally, 'and be in touch on Monday to tell you what the boss has decided.'

Charlie was waiting in the car outside the solicitors when Rosalind appeared from the building. He got out of the car and held the door open for her to get in. Sitting beside her Charlie asked her how it had been with Bardwell-Fox. Rosalind explained what she had been told and stressed that she wanted no part in evicting Ursula from her home.

'That's jolly good of you,' said Charlie, 'not many people would be that generous.'

'I'm not after money, but if my father's business is sold, then

I will accept a share of the proceeds. I have to return to see the solicitor on Monday morning to sign the appropriate documents.'

'No problem,' replied Charlie, 'I'll see that you get there and then I'll drive you to the airport in good time for your flight.'

'Thank you, Chief Inspector, you have been very kind.'

'You said you wanted to visit your father's grave,' said Charlie, 'shall we go there now and then continue to police headquarters.'

'Thank you that would be splendid.'

Charlie drove to the church and escorted Rosalind to the grave of her father. There were still flowers on the raised mound and a temporary wooden cross bearing the name George Blackwell at one end. Charlie hung back and allowed the young woman to move forward on her own. She stood with bowed head and crossed herself. Charlie waited. Several minutes later Rosalind turned and came over to him.

'Thank you, Chief Inspector,' she said, 'I am ready to come with you to the police station now.'

Sally arrived at the address Katherine Waterford had given them, which was on one of the new housing estates on the North side of Torreston, and pulled up. She turned to the passenger.

'Good luck with the chemo,' she said.

'Thank you, and I really am sorry for what I have done. If you give me the names and addresses of the women I've upset I shall go and apologise.'

'We'll have to check with them first,' said Sally, 'and we'll come and see you on Monday to tell you what our boss has decided.'

Katherine nodded and climbed from the car.

'Good luck,' called Narinder.

They watched as she entered the house and as the door closed behind her Narinder let out a sigh. 'Poor soul,' she said, 'to get into such a state you do something so horrid.'

'Some husband,' said Sally, 'to desert her like that.'

Narinder snorted. 'What about "in sickness and in health" I'd like to know.'

'I hope he doesn't insist the house is sold, or heaven knows what she will do.'

'Some shitty guy,' said Narinder, 'to ditch her when she needed him most.'

'We'll do our best to see that charges aren't brought against her,' said Sally, 'we'll nip back to the station now and catch the boss.'

'Then I presume we can take the rest of the day off?'

'And we still have Sunday,' added Sally.' She put the car in gear and headed for headquarters.

Charlie took Rosalind to Harriet's office when he returned to headquarters and leaving them together he made for the kitchen to make coffee. Harriet offered the young woman her sympathies in the loss of her father and asked if there was anything she could do to help. Rosalind thanked her but said she had done the main thing she had wanted to do on coming to England but would have to re-visit the solicitor on Monday. 'I have instructed Mr Bardwell-Fox as to what I wish to be done,' she said, 'and told him that my stepmother is not to be evicted from her house. Because of this I have documents to sign.'

Harriet nodded. She could see that Rosalind De Luca was no money grabber and had genuinely come to England simply to visit her father's grave.

'I shall see that your solicitor carries out your wishes,' she said, 'even though your father wanted you to be his main beneficiary.'

Charlie arrived with the coffee and Harriet gave him the message from Liz. Talk of George Blackwell ceased and the three chatted in a friendly manner until it was time for Rosalind to leave. Charlie escorted her from the police station and guided her to his car to drive her back to the hotel. Harriet had told him to go home when he had done this so at least he would have a free evening.

Sally and Narinder returned to headquarters and hurried to Harriet's office where they explained what had happened on the X7 bus.

'Good heavens, Narinder you haven't lost your hair, have you?' said Harriet.

Narinder removed the baseball cap and grinned. 'No fear, ma'am,' she said, 'I bought a false bit and pinned it inside the cap.'

Harriet smiled. 'Well done you two, and Narinder bring me the receipt for the hair and I'll see that you are refunded.'

'Thank you, ma'am.'

'Would it be in order for Katherine Waterford to be given a caution,' asked Sally, 'we feel she has been through a great deal and was driven to acting the way she did.'

'That would seem to be the obvious outcome,' agreed Harriet, 'but before doing that, check with the victims that they are happy with this. I'm afraid that if any of them insist they press charges then our hands will be tied.'

'I don't think they will want to prosecute when they hear the story,' said Narinder, 'and we'll lay it on thick.'

Harriet smiled. 'I'm sure you will. Now off you go, and I'll see you back here on Monday.'

Charlie dropped Rosalind off at the Glebe Hotel and watched as she entered the building. He hoped that Ursula Blackwell had signed out and returned to Copper Beeches as she had been told there would be a police guard on her house, and that was where she was to stay. Charlie drove through Torreston; if he was in luck he would be able to salvage the rest of Saturday. He had asked his wife to check on Roy Franks for him before she came home, but he knew Harriet would be visiting the hospital when she left the station.

Harriet left headquarters at five and drove straight to the hospital where she was met by Sister Marlow. They greeted each other warmly. 'How are you, Harry?' asked Liz, 'managing to keep your eyes open?'

'Just about.'

'You look tired, I hope you're on your way home.'

'I am,' replied Harriet, 'and hopefully Charlie will be home when you get off duty.'

'Great, I shall be off in about an hour. Charlie tells me you're having a busy time at work'

'We are, murder is not a quick or easy business,' replied Harriet, 'and this one is particular nasty, as you can see with the shooting of Roy Franks. How is he?'

'He's conscious, and the surgeon is confident he will make a full recovery.'

'That's great news, Liz,' said Harriet, 'I'll go and see him.' She hurried down the passage to the side room and knocked gently on the door before entering. Roy Franks was lying propped up in bed his eyes closed. The blood transfusion was gone as were the nasal tubes. The young man was still very pale, but he looked a great deal better than the last time Harriet had seen him. She went over to the bed and looked down at Franks. The young man opened his eyes and took a few moments to recognise the superintendent.

'Ma'am,' he said tying to sit up.

'Stay as you are, Roy,' said Harriet quickly. 'How do you feel?'

'Sort of numb, and a bit sore.'

'That's not surprising, but the surgeon is confident that you'll make a full recovery.'

'Yes, he told me.'

'I'm sorry to ask you this,' said Harriet, 'but did you get a good look at the person who shot you?'

'Not really, ma'am, I found the back door open and was just going inside when he burst out and nearly knocked me down. I grabbed his arm and that's when he opened fire, so I didn't see his face. I can tell you, ma'am I was not expecting that. Took me quite by surprise and the next thing I woke up in here.'

'Don't get yourself in a state worrying about the shooter,' said Harriet, 'but if you do remember anything that might be a help in catching him, let us know.'

'I will, ma'am, but there is one thing, there was no bang from the gun, just a sort of plop. I only realised I'd been shot when I actually saw the gun and felt this searing pain in my chest.'

'We think he used a silencer,' replied Harriet, 'did the gun have a long barrel.'

'Yes, it did ma'am.'

'The silencer,' said Harriet. 'Now just rest, Roy and get strong.' Harriet left the hospital thankful and relieved that the young constable was going to be all right.

Chapter Forty-Two

When Rosalind had left the hotel that morning Ursula packed her bags, paid her bill and stormed off. She had a plan and she needed to be at home to set it in action. That bitch needed teaching a lesson. She would be sitting in Bardwell-fox's office gloating over the news that the rightful heiress was to be evicted from her legal home and she was to take half the proceeds from the sale. That's what she thinks! Thought Ursula as she drove to Copper Beeches, what a shock she was going to have, what a shock in deed.

Rosalind De Luca sat in her room at the Glebe Hotel feeling pretty low. She had visited her biological father's grave, her Italian father, the man who had brought her up, had died some years ago, and was feeling sad. She had been upset by the hatred thrown at her by her stepmother and secretly wanted to return to Milan. She still had Sunday to get through before visiting the solicitor Monday morning to sign documents and then thankfully she would be flying home. She so wanted to be back in Italy.

On Monday Harriet was pleased to see that the team appeared to be brighter than they had been on Friday and decided it was important that they had time off when it could be arranged. She too felt more energetic having spent a quiet day at home with Ed on Sunday, but now it was back to the grindstone and the hunting down of a gunman. Harriet explained about the condition of Roy Franks and instructed all officers that they were to wear bullet-proof vests when attending any incident.

'There is a killer at large who is indiscriminate as to whom he shoots,' said Harriet. 'We could well have been looking at a dead police officer after the incident Friday night, but thankfully PC Franks was lucky, and he will recover.'

'Are we to presume the shooter was after Mrs Blackwell?' asked Inspector Cassells.

'That's what we think,' replied Harriet, 'and so we are putting an armed guard on her until further notice. Duncan, seeing that you were called to the incident at Copper Beeches, would you contact the Armed Response Unit and sort that out for us.'

'Yes, ma'am, and is it all right if I do one of the shifts?'

'Of course, just let us know what's happening.'

Charlie then told the team about the visit of Rosalind De Luca and how Blackwell's daughter had no intention of turning Ursula out of her house. 'She is a very decent human being,' said Charlie, 'and how that creep George Blackwell could be her father, heaven only knows.'

'Her mother must have been a different kettle of fish,' said Narinder.

Sally was asked to tell everyone about the success in capturing the hair-cutter, explaining about the tracking down of the woman with the recognisable perfume, and how Narinder had worn a false ponytail rather than risking losing her own hair. This was greeted by much laughter and applause. Harriet held up her hand.

'Right, we still have a great deal to do, so Duncan if you would like to get over to "Firearms", DCI Marlow will find out where Ursula Blackwell is at the moment and he'll let you know.'

'She stayed Friday night at the Glebe Hotel where Mrs De Luca stayed,' said Charlie, 'and at breakfast Saturday morning she had a right go at Blackwell's daughter. The hotel manager had to intervene. I'll give the hotel a ring to see if she's left, and I'll text you, Duncan.'

'Right, thank you, sir, I'll get going then, as I have to nip home to get into uniform.'

Duncan left the room and Harriet turned to Sally.

'If you and Narinder could speak to the hair-cutting victims this morning to see if they want to press charges,' she said, 'it would be useful if we could close the case so that we can all concentrate on this killer.'

'Yes, ma'am,' said Sally, 'we'll go straight away.' She looked across at Narinder who nodded.

Officers began dispersing, some to on-going enquiries they had planned, and others went to their desks to follow up on something they had already begun. Sally and Narinder left to chase up the women who had lost their hair to Kathrine Waterford, hopeful that they might dissuade them from pressing charges. Harriet went to her office where she rang the hospital to ask how Roy Franks was. She was relieved to hear that he was making good progress and asked the nurse to give him her regards. Charlie went to his office and called the Glebe Hotel to ask if Ursula had signed out. The hotel manager informed Charlie that Mrs Blackwell had stormed from the building telling them she was going home, adding that he was not sorry to see her leave. Charlie thanked him and then texted Duncan to give him this information.

Duncan was at the Firearms base when he received Charlies message and he passed this on to Inspector Ravenscroft, the head of the local division. 'Is it okay if I take the first shift, sir?' asked Duncan, 'I have cleared it with the superintendent.'

'Yes, you do that, sergeant, and if Mrs Blackwell leaves the building, go with her but let me know immediately. Everyone will do a four-hour turn and always in twos. Take Williams with you, McAllister and do your best to advise the woman to stay at the house until this shooter is apprehended.'

'I'll try, sir,' said Duncan, 'but she's not the easiest of people to advise.'

'So I've heard, but it's her damn life we're protecting,' growled the inspector, 'doesn't she want to live?'

'I'll get going,' said Duncan, 'and I'll let you know how things work out, sir.' He went over to constable Williams and donning their bullet-proof vests, they left the building to drive to Copper Beeches.

Ursula had left the Glebe Hotel in a real paddy. She knew that Rosalind De Luca was now with the solicitor and she was furious. How dare this foreign intruder come into her life and disrupt it. No way was this going to happen, she would put a stop to it. Arriving at her house she found the glazier already there and quickly she told him what she wanted him to do. She unlocked the front door and hurried inside, at least she wouldn't be on her own whilst the windows were being repaired, but for now she had things to do. First of all, there was something very important she needed to attend to. Ursula removed her coat poured herself a glass of red wine and took her laptop from the sideboard cupboard. She opened it and booted it up and sat at the table in front of her computer. She punched in the relevant words and waited as the website she wanted opened up. She put in the password and waited. Something appeared to be wrong, the programme wasn't responding. She tried again with no luck. She knew the password off by heart, so couldn't understand what was happening.

A loud knock on the front door made her jump and going to the window she cautiously peered out. Two tall police officers in uniform, and carrying weapons, stood on the front step and she felt a thrill of excitement go through her. This was more like it! Some attention at last. She went to the front door and opened it.

'Sergeant McAllister and Constable Williams here to keep you safe,' said Duncan.

'About time too,' snapped Ursula, 'I was nearly killed the other night and it's taken me all this time to get the police to take any notice of my predicament.'

'We're here now, madam,' said Duncan, 'and we would appreciate you staying on the premises until further notice.'

'Oh, I don't know about that, I do have things to do.'

'It's your safety we're concerned with,' said Duncan, 'but if you do have to leave the house please let us know. One of us will be at the front of the building and the other at the back. I see you are having the glass replaced in both areas.'

'Yes, yes, it's being done by someone I've used before, so I know he's all right.'

'Good,' said Duncan turning away. He asked Williams to go

to the back of the house and to call him if anything suspicious occurred. 'Not that I think a gunman would attempt anything during the day,' he added, 'especially with armed officers in sight.'

'Right, Sarge,' said Williams and vanished around the corner of the building.

It was cold, and Duncan stamped his feet. He decided there was little chance of Mrs Blackwell offering them hot drinks and the four hours ahead of them might well become a drag.

It took Sally and Narinder all morning to contact the four women who had been Katherine Waterford's victims. Millie Walters and Christine Shepherd were at work and they had to be traced through neighbours to find out where that was. Having done this, the two officers drove to the office of Millie and then the new hairdressers where Christine now worked. Neither woman wanted to press charges against Katherine when Narinder told the story of her cancer and her husband abandoning her, and both agreed to Katherine calling on them to apologise. The two teenagers, Karen Chadwick and Silvie Robinson were at school but in both cases the mothers agreed that it would not help anyone by dragging the ill Katherine into court. As Mrs Chadwick said, the woman was suffering as it was, but she gave permission for the police to hand over her address if the woman wished to apologise. Mrs Robinson too, agreed to this. Sally and Narinder then visited Katherine and gave her the good news. They handed her the addresses of the victims at which point Katherine burst into tears saying she would visit them that very evening. The two officers returned to headquarters relieved that the case was closed. They reported to Harriet who praised their effort, telling them she was grateful to have the matter over with and they could now return to the murder investigation.

The Forensic report on the bullet that struck Roy Franks was delivered to Harriet and she was not the least surprised to read that it matched the bullets that had killed both George Blackwell and Freddie Fingers. Harriet was glad she had advised all officers to wear bullet-proof vest if called to an incident and she hoped that the firearms division could keep Ursula Blackwell safe.

Ursula was restless. She couldn't understand why she couldn't access the website she wanted and on top of that she had been unable to contact Don. She dialled his mobile number for the third time and scowled when the call went straight to voice-mail. Something was definitely wrong, and she was determined to get to the bottom of it. Going to the front door she called the sergeant standing there.

'I'm going out,' she said, 'but I won't be long.'

'I shall have to come with you,' replied Duncan, 'but my colleague will remain here to keep an eye on the house.'

'Oh, very well if you must,' said Ursula, 'but please keep your distance as I have matters to attend to.'

Duncan thought what an ungrateful woman she was and, waiting until she got into her car, he slipped into the back seat.

Chapter Forty-Three

Ursula drove to Don's house where she leaped from the car and all but ran up the path. She banged furiously on the front door. There was no response, so she peered through the downstairs windows cursing under her breath. She could see no one, in fact the house looked particularly un-lived in. Where the hell was the man, and what exactly was he playing at? Returning to her car she got in and slammed the door shut forcefully. Duncan said nothing but was carefully noting all that was happening. Ursula drove off making her way to the Yard Garage. Climbing from her car she went into the garage and looked around. No sight of Don She strode up to a mechanic working on a car and demanded to know where Don was.

The man shook his head. 'Sorry, no idea, he called in first thing this morning and then went off.'

Ursula didn't believe him and returned to her car. She said nothing to Duncan but slipped behind the wheel and started the engine. She drove the few metres up the road to the scrap-yard, through the gates at some speed and down between the piles of old cars. She stopped at the row of sheds where two men were standing and slamming on the brakes she squealed to a stop. The two men looked up as Ursula got out of the car and went over to them. Duncan remains in the car watching.

'Where is he?' she demanded.

'Who, Don?' asked one of the men.

'You know bloody well who I mean,' screeched Ursula. 'Where is he, I know he's here.'

Before either of the men could reply the tall, red-haired man appeared from one of the sheds. 'I don't want a fuss, Ursula,' he said, 'but I need some time and space to understand what exactly is going on.'

'What do you mean, "going on"? shouted Ursula, 'you know exactly what's going on. We're supposed to be an item, and now that George has gone I expect us to be together all the time.'

'I don't know about that,' replied Don, 'things have change and I'm getting very nervous. I don't want to have anything to do with a murder investigation; I might be involved in car nicking but murder, that's well out of my league.'

'Nobody we know has murdered anyone,' said Ursula, 'whoever killed George did it because of some crooked business deal, that's all.'

'I'm sorry, Ursula,' said Don, 'but it's over, I'm not going to get tangled up with anything sinister like murder.'

Ursula flew at him her fists waving, battering him on the chest and head and screaming at the top of her voice. Don put up his arms to defend himself, but she continued to lash out. Duncan put his gun on the seat breaking the golden room of never leaving your weapon, and jumped from the car hurrying over to the fight. He grabbed Ursula's flaying arms and pinned them to her side.

'Calm down, Mrs Blackwell,' he said, 'you can't behave like this, I think we should return to the house.'

Ursula tried to free her arms from Duncan's grip without success. He began guiding her back to the car and looking over her shoulder she shouted at Don. 'You shit, you utter shit when I think what I've done for you. Just you wait, you'll be sorry.'

Duncan helped her into the car and got into the passenger seat beside her. He wasn't sure if he should let the woman drive she was in such a state and he mentioned this to her.

'Would you like me to drive, Mrs Blackwell?' he asked. Ursula nodded and climbed from the driving seat to come around to the other side of the car. Duncan got out and took the keys from her feeling relieved that she hadn't made another scene. He collected his gun from the back seat and pushed it into his coat pocket before getting into the driving set. He drove back to Copper Beeches and escorted Ursula up the steps and into the house. He followed her into the sitting room and watched as she flung her coat and handbag onto a chair and then poured herself a large glass of wine. She flopped into a chair.

'Help yourself to a drink, officer,' she said taking a large gulp from her glass.

'No thank you, madam, I'm on duty. I'll go and have a look round the house. Call me if you need me.' He left the room and went down the passage to the kitchen where her found the glazier finishing off the replacing of the window there.

'All done, officer,' he said, 'the place is safe and secure again.'

'You're off then?' asked Duncan.

'Yep, I've plenty of jobs still to do.' He packed his case and said goodbye. Duncan watched as he climbed into his van and drove away. Returning to the kitchen he knocked on the window to PC Williams, beckoning him to come in. As the young constable entered Duncan told him he would check with Mrs Blackwell if it would be in order for them to make a cup of tea as it was so cold outside.

Williams stamped his cold feet and rubbed his hands together. 'We can keep an eye on things from inside the house just as well as from the outside,' he said.

'I suppose so,' agreed Duncan, 'I'll just go and speak to the lady of the house about that cup of tea.' He went back up the passage to the room where Ursula was on her second glass of wine. She was busy on her laptop and hastily closed it down as Duncan entered the room.

'Just seeing if I have any messages,' she said.

Duncan asked if they could make a cup of tea and she agreed readily. Duncan got the feeling she just wanted him out of the way and thanking her he returned to the kitchen.

Ursula re-booted the laptop and once again tried to access the account she had used before. Again, she had no success. She would have to have a word with her source, but certainly didn't want the police to follow her and begin to pry. She would wait until tomorrow and try to slip away, or at least, if the officers were ones who didn't really know her she would ask them to drive her to where she wished to go. She poured herself another glass of wine planning what she would write when she finally got into the website she needed.

Charlie received a phone call from Rosalind to say that she had been unable to get a flight until Tuesday morning and so would be staying at the Glebe Hotel for another night. 'I am seeing Mr Bardwell-Fox this morning,' she said, 'and I shall be signing the papers that disclaim the part of the will that insists Copper Beeches be sold.'

'Would you like me to collect you from the hotel and drive you to the solicitors?' asked Charlie.

'That's very kind of you, Chief Inspector, but I now know the way and it isn't far, I shall enjoy the walk.'

'If you're sure,' said Charlie, 'but I'll pick you up tomorrow to take you to the airport. What time is your flight?'

'One thirty.'

'Right, I'll be at the hotel at nine thirty. Good luck at the solicitors.' Charlie hung up, thinking what a lovely person Mrs De Luca was and quite the opposite of Ursula Blackwell.

Duncan and PC Williams were relieved by colleagues at one o'clock and Duncan drove them both back to headquarters. Guarding Mrs Blackwell was not exactly exciting nor was it rewarding as the woman was decidedly uncooperative and very aggressive. Duncan was not surprised that Don Underwood no longer wanted anything to do with her and he told Harriet this when he reported to her that he was back.

'I'm convinced he had nothing to do with any killings, ma'am,' he said, 'and he's determined to break free of Mrs Blackwell. He told her he wanted nothing to do with murder and that their relationship was over. She flew at him and had a real go at hitting him, I had to intervene.'

'Thank you for that, Duncan,' said Harriet, 'that's useful to know. Where is she now?'

'At Copper Beeches, two colleagues have taken over the watch.'

'Right, carry on with whatever you were doing, but don't bother to go home to change, stay in uniform for the rest of the day.'

'Right, thank you, ma'am.' Duncan left Harriet's office and made his way back to the Incident Room.

Ursula looked at the armed officers outside her house and decided that now was the time to make her visit. She wasn't sure when Mrs De Luca was going back to Italy, but whenever it was it would be too late for her to stop her little game of robbing her of what was rightfully hers, if she didn't act now. Going to the front door she told the officer that she needed to go out but wouldn't be long. Just as Duncan had done the officer insisted he accompany her. There was nothing Ursula could do, and so she agreed to this but said she would drive her own car if that was alright. The officer agreed and so with him beside her in the Audi, they set off. On the way she stopped at the bank saying she needed money but wouldn't be long and he could wait in the car. PC Clement ignored this instruction and got out of the car with her. He stood a short distance away from the bank keeping a sharp look-out for any movement in the crowd. His Glock was in his belt and out of sight but within easy reach should he need it. All was quiet, and when Ursula returned with the money she had withdrawn they both returned to the car.

Ursula drove to Pegasus House and parked in the carpark telling the officer that she had some business of her husbands to deal with and again, she wouldn't be long.

'I shall have to come in with you ma'am,' he said.

'Must you really? I'll be as safe as houses in here I can assure you.'

'I'm sorry, ma'am but my orders are to stay with you.'

'Oh, very well, but please give me some space, I'm beginning to feel claustrophobic.'

PC Clement thought how ungrateful the woman was having been told by sergeant McAllister that it was she who had demanded police protection. He followed her into the building and stood just inside the door keeping a watchful eye. Ursula went over to reception and he saw her go into the office. He decided she would be safe in there as nobody had entered Pegasus House after them and no one had known they were going to be there. Ten minutes later Ursula re-appeared and joined him.

'I have to wait a few minutes for Ann Peters the receptionist to return,' she said, 'and then I have to go upstairs with her.'

'I'm afraid I must accompany you,' said Clements.

Ursula scowled. 'This is beginning to annoy me,' she snapped, 'I'm beginning to think I'm the suspect.'

'I thought it was you who insisted on being given police protection,' said Clements, also beginning to feel annoyed with this selfish woman.

'I hadn't realised it would be like this,' retorted Ursula, making for the stairs.

One of the women in reception slid back the glass window and informed Ursula hat Ann Peters had returned and was waiting for her. Ursula hurried to the stairs and PC Clements followed. At the top of the stairs Ursula vanished into one of the rooms where she firmly closed the door. Clements heard her talking to another woman as he stood close to the door. He waited outside wondering if he should have gone in with her. As he pondered over this the door opened and Ursula reappeared.

'All done,' she said, 'It was just a small matter relating to my husband that needed clearing up.' She made for the stairs again and PC Clements followed her down, out of the front door and back to the car where Ursula handed him the keys and asked him to drive. Sitting in the back seat on the return journey to Copper Beeches Ursula looked at the envelope in her hand and a smile spread over her face. Opening her handbag, she slipped it inside. Yes, she thought, normal services have been resumed.

Chapter Forty-Four

Rosalind De Luca arrived at the solicitor's office and went to the reception desk where she informed the young woman that she had an appointment with Bardwell-Fox. She was shown into his office and was greeted by the man himself who was his usual gushing self. He invited her to sit down and then took a sheaf of papers from his desk drawer.

'Now, you are sure this is what you want to do?' he asked pushing the papers across the desk to Rosalind.

'Quite sure,' replied Rosalind casting her eyes over the words in front of her. The paper stated that she was refusing any part of Copper Beeches but would be happy to accept a share of any money made from the sale of her father's businesses. She looked across at Bardwell- Fox.

'That's quite in order,' she said, 'do I just sign at the bottom.'

'Yes,' replied the solicitor, 'if you really are sure about it.'

'I am.' Rosalind took the pen offered her and signed the document with a flourish. 'If that is all,' she said, 'I will be leaving.'

'When are you retuning to Italy?' asked Bardwell-Fox.

'Tomorrow. I shall be at the Glebe Hotel this evening should you wish to speak to me. Have you informed my stepmother of my decision not to evict her from her home?' she added.

'Er, not yet, I had to be sure you hadn't changed your mind.'

'Please speak to her as soon as possible,' said Rosalind. 'Thank you, Mr Bardwell-Fox, I'll say goodbye.' She left the room and hurried down the stairs feeling a weight had been lifted from her shoulders. If there was any money to come to her from the sale of her father's businesses then all well and good, but if there was nothing then so be it. She left the building and set off for the hotel, suddenly having a feeling of homesickness creep over her. All she wanted was to get back to Milan as soon as possible. Only one more night and she would be off.

Ursula arrived home and immediately took out her laptop. She produced the envelop she had put in her handbag and eagerly opened it. Now she had what she needed, and she punched in the letters for the website she required. As soon as it appeared she did as she had done before and entered the password. A number came up and she jumped to her feet and went over to the book shelf where she took down a book. Flicking through the pages she found what she was looking for and jotted on her pad. Returning her attention to the screen Ursula typed in the word from her pad and waited. Yes! she was in. The telephone number she wanted appeared on the screen and taking her mobile she put it in. She waited her heart pounding with excitement. The call was answered almost immediately and staying as calm as she could she explained what she wanted.

Charlie returned to headquarters and joined Harriet in her office. He told her Rosalind was signing the final papers at the solicitor's office and had opted to walk there rather than be driven. 'I should think she'll be glad to get back home,' he said, 'having met her ghastly stepmother she must think she's well out of it living in Milan.'

'Ah, the wicked stepmother,' said Harriet, 'let's hope she doesn't offer Rosalind a juicy apple.'

'No need if Bardwell-Fox has told her Rosalind wants no part of Copper Beeches, she'll be quite happy with that bit of news.'

'Let's hope so.'

'So, for how long do we give Ursula Blackwell police protection?' asked Charlie.

'Until we have this hitman in custody.'

'Why do you think he's now after her?'

'I have no idea, Charlie,' replied Harriet, 'unless she too was mixed up in her husband's shady affairs and someone wants rid of them both. I'm now completely baffled about the whole situation as I was beginning to think Ursula had something to do with her husband's death, but we'll have to play safe and keep an eye on her.'

'We're still very short on clues,' said Charlie, 'but I have to agree with you in thinking Ursula was involved with the killing.'

'And then there's Freddie Maloney,' said Harriet.

'And we think his killing was because of something he took from the Blackwell house.'

'This piece of paper,' said Harriet taking it from a drawer in her desk.

'Has Chong come up with any ideas' asked Charlie.

'Not yet he's been very busy lately but will get back to it as soon as he can.'

'Did we remove the tape from Blackwell's office door?' asked Charlie.

'Yes, I think so. We've removed everything we need from the office, so we no longer need the room sealed off.'

'I'll get over there and check,' said Charlie.

'I'll come with you,' said Harriet, 'this paper work is driving me mad. We'll call at Copper Beeches on the way and see what's going on there, and then I'd like to visit young Franks at the hospital.'

'My car?'

Harriet smiled. 'That would be fine, thank you.'

Rosalind walked into Torreston on her way back to the hotel and began looking in shop windows. Everywhere in the town there were Christmas decorations and she felt a longing to be back home. A band in the town centre was playing Christmas carols and she stood for a moment and listened. She decided she would buy some Christmas presents to take back with her and went into a large department store. She didn't notice the tall figure in a bulky anorak with a woolly hat pulled well down over his ears who was behind her, nor did she notice that he was still behind her as she paid for her purchases and left the shop. Rosalind made her way back to the hotel pleased with the presents she had bought and stopped at a small restaurant to have some lunch. She was booked to have dinner at the hotel at seven and then she would have an early night and home tomorrow. Things weren't that bad after all.

Harriet and Charlie called at Copper Beeches on their way to Pegasus House and arrived just as Ursula Blackwell and a police officer were getting out of Ursula's car at the front steps. Ursula hurried into the house and Harriet and Charlie went up to the officer.

'Any problems?' asked Harriet.

'No, ma'am, Mrs Blackwell insisted she had to go out, so I went with her as instructed.'

'Where did she want to go?' asked Charlie.

'Pegasus House and she called at the bank on the way.'

'Any idea what she wanted at Pegasus House?' asked Harriet.

'No, ma'am but she wasn't in there for very long, said she had some business of her husbands to deal with, but I didn't ask what that was, it was dealt with by the receptionist.'

'Right thank you,' said Harriet. 'Ring in if anything out of the ordinary occurs.'

'I will, ma'am.'

Harriet and Charlie left, and their next call was at the hospital. Checking that they could visit Roy Franks they were told that he had been moved to the main ward as he was making such good progress. Liz was not on duty but the sister in charge recognised Charlie. They had a few words together before he and Harriet made their way to the main surgical ward. Roy Franks was sitting up in bed and looking decidedly better than he had done when they last saw him.

'Ma'am, sir,' he said shyly when he saw who his visitors were.

'How are you, Roy?' asked Harriet.

'Much better, thank you, ma'am.'

'Are you up to telling us what happened again, in case you've thought of something else?' asked Charlie.

'It all happened so quickly,' replied constable Franks. 'I went around to the back of the house as instructed and saw the broken window and as I went to the back door to investigate, this guy burst out. I tried to stop him but he, and I can't believe this,' the young man swallowed hard before continuing, 'he shot me.'

'You said you didn't hear a shot,' said Harriet, 'but noticed that the gun had a long barrel.'

'Franks nodded. 'Yes, ma'am you suggested the gun had a silencer fitted. That's pretty frightening.'

Harriet nodded. 'We're convinced that was the case,' she said.

'This is a stupid question,' said Charlie, 'but I don't suppose you saw his face or can remember anything about this guy.'

'No, sir, it was pretty dark at the back of the house and he had a hat pulled well down over his ears.'

'We'll leave you to rest, Roy,' said Harriet, 'and we're told that you will make a full recovery, thank goodness.'

'Thank you, ma'am, sir.'

Harriet and Charlie left the hospital and continued their journey to Pegasus House where Charlie parked in the car park. They entered the building together and went to the reception window where they were met by Ann Peters who smiled at them.

'How nice to see you again,' she said, 'how can I help?'

'Mrs Blackwell called here yesterday,' said Harriet, 'can you tell us who she visited?'

'Yes, she did pop in. She asked if there were any letters for her husband.'

'And were there?' asked Charlie.

'Just one.'

'Why did it not go up to his secretary?' asked Harriet.

'All mail comes here first,' replied Ann, 'and then we send it up to the various floors and put it in pigeon holes for people to collect. Mrs Gilbert was out of the building when the post came so I put it in Mr Blackwell's office myself.'

'I see,' said Harriet, 'and Mrs Blackwell collected it, did she visit anyone while she was here?'

'No, she went up to her husband's office, but as I said she was only here for about ten minutes in total.'

'Thank you,' said Harriet.

They left the reception window and climbed the stairs to where the Blackwell offices were situated. Sophie appeared from her room and Charlie explained that they were checking that the police tape had been removed from Blackwell's office door.

'Yes, it has,' replied Sophie, 'not that it will make any difference, the business is closing down and is going to be sold. I'm not sure what is happening next, but I'm frantically applying for jobs, as I don't think I'm going to be paid at all this month.'

'What did Mrs Blackwell want when she called?' asked Charlie.

'I didn't see here, but I was told she came up here, not that I can understand why; she's never been in the slightest interested in the business. Ann Peters looked after her, I'm told. I've done my best to keep things ticking over but quite honestly I've had enough, I'm looking for employment elsewhere, that's why I was late arriving yesterday.'

'I can't say I blame you,' said Harriet, 'good luck with that.'

On the way back to the police station Harriet asked Charlie why he thought Ursula was interested in her husband's mail. 'After all, it can only be business affairs if it goes to Pegasus House,' she said.

'And according to all and sundry, Mrs Blackwell had no dealings at all with the business,' said Charlie.

'Well it seems she collected one letter,' said Harriet, 'I wonder what it was about.'

'Do we ask her?'

'No, leave it for now,' replied Harriet, 'but we continue to keep an eye on her.' They arrived back at headquarters and Charlie offered to make the coffee.

'Thank you, Charlie, I'll be in my office,' said Harriet as she turned off at the top of the stairs and made her way to her room where she knew a pile of paper work still needed dealing with.

Rosalind returned to the Glebe Hotel and collected her key. She decided she would shower and change her clothes in readiness for dinner that evening. The hotel had a decent lounge where she could sit and read her book and the time would soon pass. She climbed the stairs preferring not to take the lift and unlocking her door she went inside. Down stairs the hotel receptionist looked up as a tall man with bushy, steel-grey hair approached the desk and asked if there was a room he could have for just one night. He explained that he was passing through on his way to Scotland and needed to break his journey. He told her he would be continuing his trip up north the following day.

'No problem, sir,' said the receptionist, handing him a key to room one hundred and six. 'If you would just sign the register, please.' She pushed the large book towards him which he grasped and quickly cast his eyes down the page. The name he was looking for was easily spotted. Mrs Rosalind De Luca! Room one hundred.' He signed as Peter Harris and pushed the book back across the counter.

'I'll go and collect my case,' he said, and turning on his heel he left the hotel.

Chapter Forty-Five

The Incident Room was a hive of industry with everyone at their desk either doing research or writing up their notes of the days investigations. Harriet and Charlie entered and went to the front of the room.

Officers stopped work and looked up as Harriet spoke. She began by telling them that Roy Franks was making good progress and thankfully would make a full recovery. This was greeted by clapping and sheer relief from the officers. They all knew that it might have been any one of them caught up in the shooting incident.

'Just to bring you all up to date on what else has been happening,' continued Harriet. 'Mrs De Luca has signed papers at the solicitors to disclaim her inheritance on Copper Beeches allowing Mrs Blackwell to remain there and she will be returning home to Milan in the morning.'

'She'll be spending another night at the Glebe Hotel,' said Charlie, 'and I should think she will be glad to get home having had a nasty confrontation with Mrs Blackwell who also, unfortunately chose to spend Friday night at the same hotel and went for her at breakfast the following morning.'

'She's a hateful character,' said Sally, 'doesn't she realise how generous Mrs De Luca has been. Not many people would be so decent in not claiming their inheritance.'

'Rosalind De Luca is certainly not after money,' said Harriet, 'but obviously Mr Bardwell-Fox hasn't got around to telling Mrs Blackwell of her decision not to want Copper Beeches sold.'

'I wouldn't be a bit surprised if he wasn't deliberately holding back on divulging that news,' said Charlie, 'you know what a scoundrel he is, and all the time he has these women at his mercy, he's charging them the earth.'

'Part of Ursula Blackwell's problems appear to be the indifference now being shown to her by Don Underwood,' said Harriet. 'We're not sure what has gone wrong there, but it seems Mr Underwood is fearful of being tied up in a murder.'

'He's happy to hold his hands up to nicking cars,' said Charlie, 'but he draws a line at murder.'

'Does this mean he's no longer a suspect?' asked Duncan.

'I don't think he had anything to do with Blackwell's death,' replied Harriet, 'but we leave him on the list to play safe.'

Jack held up a hand. 'Ma'am,' he said, 'we've had an email from the West Midlands Force to say that they are now sure that the hitman in the area is a Russian and it seems he has a female accomplice.'

'Have they got a name for this guy?' asked Inspector Cassells.

'They're working on it,' said Jack, 'and will get back to us if they have any further information.'

'Not a lot of help really,' said Charlie, 'we can't go around pouncing on anyone with a foreign accent asking if they're Russian.'

'It does make you think of the incident with Sergei Skripal and his daughter,' said Earl, 'but it was a nerve drug that was used then, not a bullet.'

'And Litvinenko was killed with polonium in twenty o six,' said Harriet, 'but those were considered to be political assassinations, the people being killed here are not Russians. No, our man is a paid hitman and using a gun.'

'With a silencer, which shows the guy is a professional,' added Charlie.

'Were there any Russians at the Innovation Centre?' asked Cassells.

'Sally?' asked Harriet looking across at the sergeant.

'Not that we discovered,' replied Sally, 'but of course we weren't checking on that at the time.'

'Do you want us to go back there and check?' asked Narinder.

'What about the insider you have there?' asked Harriet.

'I'll have a word with him,' said Sally.

'Good,' said Harriet, 'then we persevere and stick at it, something will break sooner or later. Check estate agents and letting agencies to see if anyone has rented a property in the last six months or so. These criminals have to be staying somewhere.

'West Midlands did tell us the gang appeared to arrive here about six months ago,' said Charlie, 'so if any new lettings have been taken by a foreigner then, that would be worth looking into.'

'Collect the names of all estate agents and any letting agencies in the Torreston area,' said Harriet, 'and we'll start checking them tomorrow. Good luck, we really do need some.' She left the Incident Room and officers began running off the names of estate agents. Sally picked up the phone and called Ramesh to ask him if he knew of any Russians who worked at the centre. He told her that that were one or two men with foreign accents, but he didn't know if they were Russian. He promised to do his best in finding out. Narinder came over to Sally and suggested they had a word with Don Underwood.

'If he's dumped Ursula Blackwell,' she said, 'do you think he might know something about the murder of her husband and that's why he wants out. We're told he doesn't want to get mixed up in any killings, so you have to wonder why he's left Ursula.'

'It's worth a try,' agreed Sally, 'give me ten minutes to finish here, and I'll be with you.'

Harriet sat in her office sifting through the papers on her desk trying to decide which were important and had to be dealt with immediately and which could be put to one side. There was a knock on her door and she called out "come in". Dr Chong came into the room.

'Good afternoon, ma'am,' he said. 'I've been struggling with this paper I was given and have been pretty unsuccessful until now.'

'You mean the cryptic letters and numbers?'

'Yes. We know the long number was a mobile phone number no longer in use, but I've discovered CERBERUS is a website.'

'Oh, well done, Henry, and what is this website.'

'Ah, well, that's not easy. You need a password to open it up and so far, I've been unsuccessful in that.'

'But it's a break through,' said Harriet, 'will you keep working on it, Henry, if we could just get in, that would be fantastic.'

'I'll keep trying,' replied Henry Chong, 'and get back to you if I discover anything.'

'Thank you,' said Harriet suddenly feeling more hopeful. She knew the ACC would be back to ask why more progress wasn't being made on the murders and perhaps she would have something to tell him if they could only break into this website.

When Dr Chong had gone Harriet called Charlie and Earl Cassells to her office.

'Somewhere along the line we've missed something,' she said. 'Blackwell's associates need delving into more thoroughly and all the alibis of the people we were suspicious about need re-checking. If the killings, which includes Freddie Fingers, were done by a hit-man, then the hunt becomes more difficult, because it means we not only have to find who wanted Blackwell dead, but who the hit-man is. There can't be that many Russians in Torreston and if one of them is a killer then we need to flush him out quickly.'

'We now know he has a female accomplice,' said Charlie, 'but does that make it easier or harder for us to track him down.'

'They most probably have nothing to do with each other on the surface,' said Earl, 'just contact each other by mobiles or other means.'

'So, do they each have their own accommodation, or do they live together?' said Harriet.

'Let's hope this check on letting agencies turns something up,' said Charlie, 'the team is working on it now.'

'Good, but it's all very sinister,' said Harriet, 'I've never had dealings with hit-men before, and certainly not Russians.'

'Not an everyday occurrence here in Torreston,' said Charlie with a grin.

'Thank goodness,' replied Harriet. 'Now can I leave it to you, Earl to keep an eye on the house hunting, and, Charlie will you organise the re-checking of all the alibis of the original suspects and the people Blackwell had dealings with, especially those who felt he'd cheated them. There's not a lot of today left, so we'll continue with it tomorrow.'

The two men left the room and once again Harriet turned her attention to the dreaded paper work.

Sally and Narinder drove to Station Road and were not surprised to discover Don Underwood was not at home. Back in the car they made for the breaker's yard, where Sally parked just inside the gate and the two women got out and made their way through the piles of wrecked vehicles Don Underwood was standing talking to one of his men and he frowned when he saw the two police officers approaching. 'What now?' he asked as they came up to him.

'Sorry to bother you again,' said Sally, 'but we are still investigating the murder of George Blackwell. As you are close to his wife, obviously we feel you might know something that could help us.'

'I told the other officer,' said Don, 'I don't do murder.'

'No one is accusing you of murder,' said Narinder, 'we are just wondering if you know who might have a cause to kill Blackwell?'

'Like his wife,' suggested Sally. 'We're curious to know why you no longer associate with her.'

'I'm playing safe,' replied Don.

'Are you saying you think Mrs Blackwell might be involved in her husband's death?' asked Narinder.

'I'm not saying anything,' said Don, 'but I don't want to have anything to do with murder, so I'm staying clear.'

'I see,' said Sally, 'and how does Mrs Blackwell feel about that?'

'I have no idea, I haven't spoken to her for a few days.'

Sally handed him her card. 'Thank you, Mr Underwood, and if you think of anything that might help us in this enquiry please get in touch.'

Don took the card and grunted some sort of reply. Sally and Narinder returned to the car and Sally suggested they re-visit Pegasus House. 'If Ursula was that keen on going there after the death of her husband, it makes you wonder what exactly she's up to,' she said.

'Let's go,' agreed Narinder.

At Pegasus House they reported to reception and explained they were going upstirs to speak to Sophie Gilbert.

'No problem,' said Ann Peters pushing the signing in book across to them.

Sally signed the book and they went up the stairs to the Blackwell offices. Sophie appeared from her room and asked them what she could do to help.

'What can you tell us about Ursula Blackwell and her relationship with her husband?' asked Sally. 'She insists they were very happy but other signs seem to tell a different story.'

'Like her affair with another guy,' said Narinder.

'Ah, so you've heard about that,' said Sophie. 'Mr Blackwell had his suspicions and I did hear them arguing about it in his office one day.'

'You didn't mention this in your original statement,' said Sally.

'That was given on the day of the murder and I was so shocked by everything I think there were several things I forgot to mention.'

'Such as?' said Narinder rather sharply.

'Well, I think Blackwell used to hit his wife.'

'And when were you going to tell us this?' pressed Narinder frowning. 'The man has been killed and this could be a vital piece of information.'

Sophie looked miserable. 'As I said I was in shock over the murder and couldn't think straight. I've been thinking about things since, and was going to tell you about the violent arguments the two of them had.'

'And the beatings?' asked Sally.

'That day I heard them going at each other,' said Sophie, 'I heard a definite smack, and Mrs Blackwell screamed and then began swearing. I backed into my office so as not to be seen when she came out.'

'This is very important information, Sophie,' said Sally.

'I was going to tell you, I did say in my statement that Mr Blackwell was a bully and greatly disliked by everyone.'

'Did you see Mrs Blackwell after this incident? 'asked Narinder.

'I went down to reception soon after that and she was being looked after by Ann Peters. I think she was crying, so I came away quickly.'

'What's going to happen to Blackwell's business?' asked Sally.

'The solicitor told me it's going to be sold, but I have to say I don't really care because I'm off.'

'When are you leaving?' asked Narinder.

'Today. I've had enough, and I haven't been paid for weeks although the solicitor said he'd see that I was.'

Sally handed her a card. 'We need to know where you will be,' she said, 'and if you think of anything else that you forgot to tell us about please ring me.'

Sophie took the card and nodded. 'I will,' she muttered.

Sally and Narinder left Pegasus House and returned to the car.

'What do you think about Ms Gilbert?' asked Sally as she started the engine.

'She seems genuine enough,' replied Narinder.

'She has a slight foreign accent,' said Sally, 'could she be Russian do you think?'

'Well, I don't know, the name Gilbert is pretty British.'

'She doesn't wear a wedding ring,' said Sally, 'and if she is central European, Gilbert can't be her real name.'

'Something else for us to check tomorrow,' said Narinder.

'Yep, I think we've done enough for today, let's get home.'

Chapter Forty-Six

Rosalind sat in the hotel lounge reading an English newspaper. She didn't understand all that she read and quite frankly she wasn't really interested in what was going on in Britain. She had eaten dinner, which she had quite enjoyed, but now all she wanted was to get home to Milan. Time was dragging, and she kept looking at her watch. At nine o'clock she went up to her room, showered and got into bed with the book she had brought with her from Italy. Soon she felt her eyes closing and putting the book on the bedside table she turned off the light and snuggled down.

She wasn't sure what woke her, but suddenly Rosalind was wide awake. She was no stranger to crime and sinister happenings, but hadn't expected danger here in England. Her late husband, Lorenzo De Luca had been murdered only twelve months ago and his killer never caught, so she was used to being wary. Her husband's murder had been due to his shady business dealings, which she had been aware of but never involved with, and the police had been convinced the Mafia were the perpetrators. Rosalind had been left well provided for, but she had always felt the need to keep looking over her shoulder.

Now, she sat up in bed and listened. There was a definite noise at her door, someone was trying to open it. Slipping from her bed she pushed the pillows under the covers giving the impression she was still there, then on her hands and knees Rosalind crawled into the bathroom where she closed the door behind her and sat on the floor with her back to the door. She waited in the dark straining her ears for any movement in the bedroom. She could hear nothing. Although the bathroom was warm, she began to shiver and feeling her way in the dark she found the rail with the thick towels. Pulling two free she sat on one and wrapped the other around her. She remained huddled against the door. She had no idea of the time or how long she sat on the floor of the bathroom but knew that from time to time she had nodded off.

Eventually she got to her feet and pressed her ear to the door. Not a sound. Quietly she opened the it. The room was in darkness and she could hear nothing of anyone being there. If it had been an intruder, then he had most surely gone. She went to the bed and switched on the light. She gasped when she saw the holes in the bed covers, holes she knew were gunshots, they were the same she had seen on the covers of their bed when she had discovered her husband's body. Rosalind sat down heavily on the floor, suddenly feeling weak and very frightened.

Sergeant Pete Yates was on night duty at Torreston police station when the emergency call came through. It was two o'clock, and without hesitating he dialled the number of Superintendent Love.

Harriet answered the call immediately and listening in horror to what he had to tell her she instructed the sergeant to call Charlie, SOCO and Forensics and she would meet them at the Glebe Hotel.

There were two police cars outside the hotel when Ed pulled up in front of it. He had insisted he accompany Harriet and she had made no objection to this. The blue lights on the cars were flashing ominously and there was a great deal of activity in the main entrance of the hotel. Harriet and Charlie entered the building to find a tearful Rosalind De Luca in her dressing gown sitting on a chair at reception being looked after by the manager who was also in his dressing gown. He hurried across when he saw Harriet and Ed.

'I can't believe this is happening in my hotel,' he wailed, 'what will this do to our reputation.'

'Probably give it a boost,' replied Ed dryly, 'but more to the point, how is Mrs De Luca?' He and Harriet went across to Rosalind and Harriet placed a hand on her shoulder. 'Are you all right?' she asked.

Rosalind nodded. 'Just very scared,' she whispered.

'What exactly happened?' asked Harriet.

Rosalind told her story and Harriet had a feeling of dread creep over her. The hit-man was evidently still active, but why did he want Rosalind dead? 'Did you hear the gun shots?' she asked.

'No, I heard nothing from inside the bathroom.'

'Sounds like a typical hit-man,' said Ed, 'he used a silencer.'

Charlie hurried into the hotel and came across to them. He acknowledged Ed with a slap on the back and said 'morning' to Harriet. Rosalind looked relieved to see him and managed a smile. Harriet told him what had happened, and he looked visibly shaken.

'Good God, what is going on?' he said. He crouched beside Rosalind's chair and spoke to her.

'Why would anyone want you dead?' he asked. 'Please don't hold anything back if you want us to protect you.'

Rosalind shook her head. 'The only thing I can think of, Chief Inspector, is that my husband was murdered a year ago, probably by the Mafia, and they think I had something to do with his dirty businesses. But I promise you, although I guessed he had unsavoury contacts, I knew nothing of my husband's actual dealings, and only found out about them when the police told me what he had been up to.'

Charlie was inclined to believe her, and he stood up and turned to Harriet. They moved away to be out of earshot. 'This is getting out of hand, Harry,' he said quietly.

'It certainly is,' agreed Harriet, 'and the sooner Mrs De Luca is on that plane back to Italy the better.'

'We've had no further information from the West Midlands on the hit-man,' said Ed, 'and so far, there's been no news about who or where the female associate might be.'

'I'm expecting the ACC to be on my back any day now,' said Harriet, 'we're just not making any headway on this.'

SOCO and the Forensic team came into the hotel followed by three men well known to the officers. Harriet puffed out her cheeks. How the Press knew when a story was in the offing, heaven only knew. She frowned as she saw Beefy Cavendish sucking on his pencil; she might have known he'd be at the forefront of a breaking news item. Charlie saw the reporter too, and turned away to speak to the Forensic team. He directed them up to Rosalind's room. 'At least there will be bullets to compare with the ones that killed Blackwell and Fingers,' he said, 'and we can guess they'll match.'

'Rosalind was very smart in getting out of bed and hiding,' said Harriet lowering her voice so as not to be heard by the reporters, 'it makes you think she has an understanding of the underworld.'

'Well, she explained why,' said Charlie in a defensive manner, 'and thank goodness she left her pillows in the bed to make it appear she was still there, or she could well be dead now.'

'Doing that certainly saved her life,' agreed Harriet.

Ed pulled a face. 'Having heard about her husband and her father, she sounds as if she might be a professional gangster herself.'

'It does appear her husband was something of the kind,' agreed Harriet.

'Well, yes, we know her father was a crook,' added Charlie, 'but I can't honestly believe Rosalind is involved with anything criminal.'

'I hope you're not being blinded by this woman, Charlie,' said Ed.

'Not at all, I just feel a bit sorry for her, knowing all she's been through.'

'Any chance of a quote for us?' shouted Beefy.

Harriet went across to the three men. 'I won't ask how it is you always turn up when there's been an incident,' she said, 'but of course you just happened to be passing by.'

'Can you tell us what's happened, Superintendent?' asked a young man Harriet had never seen before.

Harriet knew there was no point in covering up the fact that there had been a shooting and so she explained that an attempt had been made on the life of Rosalind De Luca and that she was unharmed. 'She will be returning to Italy this morning,' said Harriet, 'so that will be the end of the matter.'

'Isn't this woman the daughter of George Blackwell?' asked Beefy, 'and she's over here to claim her inheritance.'

'She is the daughter of Mr Blackwell,' agreed Harriet, 'but her affairs are personal and nothing to do with us.'

'Who would want her dead?' asked Colin Bragg of *The Tribunal*, 'Is it to do with her father's shady businesses?'

'That we don't know,' replied Harriet, 'but the murder of George Blackwell is an on- going investigation, so I'm afraid I am unable to say any more.' She turned away and went back to Ed and Charlie.

'We need to keep Rosalind safe until we can get her on the plane,' said Harriet. 'Now that the press has got hold of the story her still being alive might trigger a further attempt to kill her. I think we'll take her back to the police station and let her curl up in my office until morning. It's already three forty-five so there's not much of the night left.'

'I'm taking her to the airport first thing in the morning,' said Charlie, 'so I reckon that's a good idea, Harry. I'll go and tell her to dress and pack.' He moved away to speak to Rosalind.

The hotel manager appeared with a tray of coffee and biscuits and gratefully Harriet and Ed accepted the refreshments. Charlie joined them and as they were drinking the coffee Sergeant Phillip Hewitt, head of SOCO, came down the stairs to tell them that Rosalind's room was clean.

'Not a fingerprint or smudge of any kind to be seen, ma'am,' he said. 'The lock had been picked on the door and it was a professional job, very slick. I should think he fired at what he thought was the person in the bed, from the doorway.'

'Thank you, Phillip,' said Harriet, 'we expected that to be the case.'

'Is it all right if we leave, ma'am?' asked Phillip, 'there's nothing further we can do; Doctor Overton is going to cordon off the room when Mrs De Luca leaves.'

'Yes of course, do go,' replied Harriet, 'and I'm sorry we had to call you out.'

'All part of the job, ma'am.' The sergeant smiled shyly and returned to his men.

A pale and anxious looking Rosalind De Luca came down the stairs with her case and Charlie hurried towards her to help. A flash from a camera made her freeze and Charlie glared at the reporters. 'I'll drive her back to the station, Harry,' he said in a whisper, 'and I'll hand her over to Pete Yates. I'll then nip home and get a few hours kip before returning to take her to the airport.'

'Thank you, Charlie,' said Harriet, 'I'll leave you to organise that, and we'll see you when you get back.'

Charlie and Rosalind left the hotel just as Fraser Overton appeared holding up two evidence bags. 'Two bullets,' he announced, 'and you can bet your bottom dollar they're from the same weapon that killed your other two victims.' Again, a camera flashed.

'Thank you, Fraser,' said Harriet, 'we'll await your report. Is the room sealed?'

'Yes, all done, and I've instructed the hotel manager that no one must enter it as it remains a crime scene.'

'He won't be very happy about that,' said Ed.

'I'll have a word with him before we leave,' said Harriet. 'I don't think we'll need to keep the room sealed for very long.'

Having spoken to the hotel manager Harriet and Ed left, quickly followed by the three reporters. It was four thirty.

Chapter Forty-Seven

Charlie returned to the police station and explained to Sergeant Yates what was happening. He then took Rosalind up to Harriet's office telling her she would be quite safe there. There was a solid armchair in the corner of the room and Charlie suggested she curl up in it and try and get a few hours sleep. He found a car blanket in a cupboard and handed this to her. Charlie asked her if she would like a coffee or anything to eat to which she shook her head.

'No thank you, Chief Inspector,' she said, 'I just want morning to come so that I can go home.'

Charlie understood exactly how she felt. He showed her where Harriet's cloakroom was and telling her he would be back later that morning, he left. Neither of them would get much sleep, in fact Charlie decided he wouldn't bother but would have a strong cup of coffee and curl up in a chair as soon as he got home as going to bed would make it very difficult for him to get up again. He decided it was jut as well that Liz was on night duty, she did worry about him, but he would leave her a note explaining what had happened and where he was going.

Harriet and Ed arrived back at Magnolia Cottage and Ed made a pot of coffee. 'We'll get three or four hours sleep, Harry,' he said, 'and no one will blame you for going into the station late. Shall I give Pete Yates a call and tell him to get Cassells to organise things until you get in.'

'Being up all night is becoming a regular occurrence,' said Harriet, 'but I'll ring Pete, thanks, Ed, and explain things. Charlie will already have told him of the outcome of the hotel incident, so he won't be surprised if I tell him I'll be late in the morning. Or rather this morning.'

Charlie arrived at the police station at ten to six and hurried up to Harriet's office. Rosalind was up and told him she had washed and felt refreshed. Charlee offered to make coffee before they left but Rosalind declined the offer stating she would have breakfast at the airport. Charlie realised she was eager to get away from Torreston, her only wish to get home to Milan. Picking up her case Charlie led the way downstairs where he spoke briefly to Pete Yates.

'The boss rang in last night,' he told Charlie, 'and I'm to tell Inspector Cassells to carry on until she gets here. You must be pretty tired yourself, sir,' he added.

'I'm propping my eyelids up with matchsticks,' replied Charlie with a grin, 'see you later, Pete.' He and Rosalind left the station.

Inspector Earl Cassells was pounced on by Pete Yates as he came into the station and told of the happenings at the hotel the night before. 'I heard on the news there had been a shooting incident in Torreston,' said the inspector, 'and was keeping my fingers crossed that it had nothing to do with our case.'

'I'm afraid it has everything to do with the current investigation,' said Pete. 'You're to carry on, sir until the superintendent gets here, but knowing the boss she won't be that late. She told me you knew what had to be done today, and you were to tell the team about the attempt on Mrs De Luca's life last night.'

'Right, thanks, Sergeant Yates.' Earl hurried up the stairs to the CID block and went straight to the Incident Room where he went to the information boards and began reading what was written there. He felt he needed to be up to date with all that was going on if he was to be in charge. He made a few notes in readiness for briefing and confident he knew what to say to the team he went to the kitchen to make a coffee.

At eight o'clock the Incident Room was as busy as ever and moving to the front of the room Earl Cassells held up a hand. 'Good morning everyone,' he said suddenly feeling nervous.

'Some of you may well have heard about the incident at the Glebe Hotel last night, there was a brief statement on the early news.'

'I'm never awake enough to hear the early news,' said Narinder, and this was greeted by titters and agreement from the other officers.

'What happened?' asked Sally.

'An attempt was made on the life of Mrs De Luca,' said Earl. Gasps ran around the room. 'Is she all right?' asked Duncan.

'Thankfully, yes, two bullets were fired into her bed but amazingly she was not in it.'

'Firearms weren't called out,' said Duncan, 'why was that, sir?'

'When Superintendent Love and DCI Marlow arrived at the hotel, the shooter had long gone, and it was thought that he was convinced he had killed his victim. The shooter was certainly nowhere in the building.'

'I take it Forensics were called?' asked Jack.

'They were,' replied Earl, 'and two bullets were removed from the bedding and have gone for analyses.'

'We know they'll match the other bullets,' said Duncan.

'Where is Mrs De Luca now?' asked Sally.

'DCI Marlow has taken her to the airport and he will stay with her until she's on the plane.'

'She'll be glad to get back to Italy,' said Jack, 'she's had a rough time while she's been here.'

'We have to pull out all the stops now,' said the inspector, 'we need to track down this hit-man, and if possible his female accomplice. We now have a list of estate agents and letting agencies and all need visiting as soon as possible. I've divided them up so that we should be able to get to them all today. We're looking for any rentals taken up in the last six to eight months and make sure you check if any of these lettings were taken by foreigners. Do not call on any of these people just bring the name of the person and the addresses of the properties back here. This shooter is quite capable of killing any one of you so don't play the hero.'

Sally and Narinder approached the inspector and Sally asked him if it would be in order if they did a check on Sophie Gilbert from Pegasus House. 'She has a convincing British name,' said Sally, 'but has a definite foreign accent so probably needs checking now that we know our killer has a female accomplice.'

'Well spotted.' said Earl, 'give her name to Sergeant Fuller and you two start on the estate agent check.' He handed Sally a piece of paper with the names of three estate agents.

'This is your assignment,' he said, 'good luck.'

Sally gave Jack the name, Sophie Gilbert and asked him to check her background. 'She could well be Central European,' said Sally, 'but with such a British name we thought she should be looked at.'

'She's probably married to a Brit,' said Jack.

'She doesn't wear a ring,' said Narinder.'

'They don't all wear wedding rings,' replied Jack, 'but leave it with me, I'll suss her out.'

'Thanks, Jack,' said Sally, 'we're off to start the estate agent check, we'll speak when we get back.'

Charlie and Rosalind had coffee in the departure lounge where Charlie had been allowed to go having told security who he was and why he was there, and they now sat waiting for the Milan flight to move to the top of the departure board. The minutes ticked by until finally the board indicated the Milan flight as Boarding. Charlie got to his feet and handed Rosalind her case.

'Good luck, Mrs De Luca,' he said offering her his hand, 'I hope everything turns out for the best.'

'Rosalind, please, and thank you, Chief Inspector, Charlie, you have been most kind.' She shook his hand and then to Charlies amazement kissed him forcibly on the lips before turning on her heels and hurrying to the departure gate. She didn't look back and Charlie sat down in something of a daze. He was still sitting there some forty minutes later when he saw on the board that the Milan flight had left. He felt strangely flat and leaning back in his seat he closed his eyes. Seconds later he was fast asleep.

Duncan and Ben called at the first estate agents on their list and showing their warrant cards, they were ushered into the manager's office. Duncan explained what they wanted, and the manger opened his filing cabinet and took out a fat file.

'These are all our lettings in the last eight months,' he said.

'Were any of the people foreigners do you know?' asked Duncan.

The manager ran his finger down the list of names. 'This name could be of interest to you,' he said. 'A Mr and Mrs Nowakowski, renting a property in Normandy Street.'

'That's a Polish name,' said Ben.

'We'll put them on our list,' said Duncan. 'Were any of the other clients foreign?' he asked.

'There are no other foreign names,' replied the manager, 'but you will have to ask the assistant who dealt with the letting to see if any of them were. I have the names here of the people who dealt with each case.'

'That's great,' said Duncan, 'if we could have a couple of minutes with each of them that would be a help.'

The manager handed Duncan the list of lettings with the name of the agent who had done the deal with the client, at the top of the page. 'I'll send in the first assistant,' he said, 'and I would appreciate you being as quick as you can, we are very busy. Please use my desk.'

Duncan sat at the desk with the list of lettings in front of him and waited for the first person to arrive.

Charlie awoke with a start. He had a crick in his neck and a throbbing head. He was horrified to see the time. He had been asleep for nearly two hours but knowing he hadn't slept at all the previous night decided that perhaps it was a good idea that he slept now before the drive back. He jumped to his feet and made his way to the exit, showing his warrant card when confronted by a large security guard who barred his way. On reaching his car, having collected his parking ticket, Charlie fished in the glove department and took out the first-aid box that Liz always kept well stocked. He took two paracetamol tablets and drank the whole of a small bottle of water they kept in the bottle holder in the car. Feeling a bit better he started the car and drove from the airport carpark.

Harriet walked into the police station at ten o'clock to be greeted by sergeant Carl Fisher.

'Everything all right, ma'am?' he asked. 'Sounds as if you had a hectic night.'

'Pretty busy,' replied Harriet, 'but thankfully no one was killed.'

'This guy sounds like a maniac,' said Fisher.

'He probably is,' agreed Harriet, 'so let's hope we catch him soon. Any messages?'

'Just one, ma'am, the manager of the Glebe Hotel called and asked you to ring him when you arrived.'

Thank you, Carl,' said Harriet, and hurried up the stairs. She went straight to her office where she picked up the telephone and dialled the Glebe Hotel. She spoke to the manager for about ten minutes and ending the conversation, she hung up and went to the Incident Room. Earl Cassells was talking to Jack Fuller and they both looked up as the superintendent came into the room.

'Morning, ma'am,' said Cassells and Jack together.

'Good morning,' replied Harriet, 'everything running smoothly?'

'Yes, ma'am everyone is out checking on the letting agencies and Sergeant Fuller here has been checking on Blackwell's secretary Sophie Gilbert.'

'Really?' said Harriet, 'what has she done?'

'Nothing that we know of, ma'am,' replied Jack, 'but Sally and Narinder visited her the other day, as we'd been told our hit-man has a female accomplice and she does have a foreign accent.'

'And?'

'They were curious about her having a very British name, so I was asked to check her out.'

'And what have you discovered?' asked Harriet.

'Well, as we thought she is married to a Brit, a Charles Gilbert an exporter, and she's a Lithuanian by the name of Sofija Adamkute.'

'There's nothing suspicious about the couple though?' asked Harriet.

'Not that I can see,' replied Jack, 'but I'll keep looking just to be safe.'

'I'll pay them a visit with Charlie when he gets back,' said Harriet. 'Anything else to report, Earl?' she added.

'No, ma'am, but I have told everybody not to visit any of the people who have rented properties but to report back here with names and addresses. If this shooter is as vicious as he sounds, we don't want any casualties.'

'Well done, Earl. Now, I have just spoken to the manager of the Glebe Hotel and he tells me that a Peter Harris signed in at the hotel last night and took a room close to Rosalind De Luca. This morning there is no sign of this man, it seems he left during the night and has not paid his bill.'

'Pretty suspicious,' said Jack. 'Was this guy a foreigner?'

'I don't know,' replied Harriet, 'the receptionist won't be on duty until later today, so we won't be able to speak to her until then. I have asked the manager to seal the room this Harris was in and we'll get Forensics over there to see what they can find.'

'Shall I see to that, ma'am?' asked Cassells.

'Yes, please do,' replied Harriet, 'and I'll be in my office if you need me.'

Sitting at her desk later, Harriet flicked through the morning paper relieved to see that there was no mention of the shooting at the Glebe Hotel. It had obviously been too late to go to print.

There had been only a brief mention about "a shooting incident at a hotel in Torreston" on the radio that morning and no mention of any names. Hopefully Rosalind would be out of the country before anyone realised she had not been killed.

Chapter Forty-Eight

A bleary-eyed Charlie came into Harriet's office and sank into a chair. 'All done,' he said.

'She's safely on the plane and on her way back to Italy.'

'That's good news,' said Harriet, 'but you look done in, Charlie, go home and don't return until tomorrow.'

'I'm going to accept that offer,' said Charlie, 'I feel like Hell.'

'I feel guilty that I allowed you to drive to the airport knowing how little sleep you'd had.'

'I'll survive,' said Charlie, 'but I will go home, Harry, I've got a thumping headache, but nothing sleep won't put right.'

'See you tomorrow then, Charlie,' said Harriet, 'we're going to call on Sophie Gilbert, Blackwell's secretary, who turns out to be a Lithuanian by the name of Sofija Adamkute. She's married to a Brit by the name of Charles Gilbert but now that we're looking for the hit-man's accomplice we need to check all suspicious woman who had contact with George Blackwell.'

'The receptionist at Pegasus House has a foreign accent too,' said Charlie yawning, 'we'd better get Jack to check on her as well.'

'I'll give him her name,' said Harriet, 'now off you go, Charlie and get some sleep.'

Charlie held up a hand and left the room. He not only felt very tired, but he still felt totally flat and despondent, and wasn't sure why although he was concerned that he had been attracted to Rosalind De Luca. With heavy feet he left the station and went to his car and twenty minutes later he pulled up outside his house. The bedroom curtains were closed as Liz would be in bed having done a night shift at the hospital. He let himself into the house quietly and crept up the stairs. He felt shattered and was barely able to clean his teeth without falling asleep.

He undressed letting his clothes drop to the bathroom floor and leaving them where they fell, he tip-toed into the bedroom and slipped beneath the covers. Liz rolled over and wrapped an arm around him, not really awake. 'Hello, Charlie,' she said, 'love you.'

All at once Charlie knew what mattered to him most and he held his wife close. 'Love you too, Liz,' he whispered and immediately fell asleep.

Ursula got up late and made a pot of coffee. She rarely had anything to eat at breakfast and this morning was no exception. She turned on the television just as the Midlands news came on. She caught her breath as she saw the Glebe Hotel on the screen. The newscaster was speaking, and she sat upright eager to hear what had happened.

"The police were called to the Glebe Hotel in Torreston last night where there was a shooting incident involving a visitor to this country. At the moment we have no details of what occurred but have been promised a full report from the police later this morning." The newscaster moved on to a statement made in the House of Commons by a local MP about something entirely different and Ursula switched the television off. She was excited but also a little disappointed. She wanted Rosalind's name splashed all over the news, but this would probably happen later when the police named her and gave their full report on what had happened. She poured herself another coffee; she would no doubt hear from her solicitor this morning to inform her that due to the demise of the woman names in George's will there would be no need to sell Copper Beeches. She sipped her coffee suddenly feeling very pleased about life and decided that enough was enough, she would dispense with the police guard and have the officers hanging around her house removed; they so impeded her movements. She went to the front door and spoke to the office standing there.

'You can go home now,' she said, 'I don't need protection anymore.'

'We can't leave without being instructed to do so,' said the armed officer.

'Then get in touch with your boss and tell him that's what I want,' snapped Ursula.

'He'll be round soon,' said the officer brusquely, 'and you can tell him yourself, ma'am.'

Ursula scowled at the officer, turned on her heels and returned indoors slamming the door. Insolent man she thought, showing no respect for his betters. She would report his rudeness to his superior when he arrived.

Harrier asked Inspector Cassells to accompany her to the Glebe Hotel and travelling in her little car they arrived at their destination. The manager hurried towards them as they entered, and Harriet introduced Earl.

'Your officers have arrived, Superintendent,' said the manager, 'and they are in the room Mr Harris booked.'

'You say Mr Harris had gone by morning,' said Harriet, 'did no one see him leave in the night.'

'No, or something would have been said.'

'Was this Mr Harris a foreigner?' asked Earl.

'That I don't know. As I said, Mis Dawson is our evening receptionist and she won't be back on duty until six this evening.'

'We'll have to come back to speak to her, then,' said Harriet. 'We'll just go up and speak to the Forensic team. What room is it?'

'Number one oh six.'

Harriet and Earl climbed the stairs and found Fraser Overton and his men busy scouring the room that Peter Harris had booked.

'Nothing so far, Harry' said the head of the Forensic team as they appeared outside the room. 'Quite frankly I don't think this guy so much as sat down in here. He certainly never slept in the bed and nothing in the bathroom has been touched.'

'A true professional hit-man,' said Earl, 'they're experts at leaving nothing behind.'

'He'll have worn gloves the whole time' said Doctor Overton, 'there's absolutely no trace of a fingerprint anywhere.'

'Thank you for trying,' said Harriet, 'we'll leave you to finish off.'

They returned downstairs and Harriet thanked the manager for his help and told him that someone would visit the hotel later that day to speak to the evening receptionist. They left the hotel and Harriet apologised to Earl for having to squeeze into her little Lotus. Earl was enjoying his time working with the superintendent and thought what a charming woman she was. He had heard she was special but until actually arriving at Torreston Police Station and working with her, had hardly believed it.

Sally and Narinder had called on two of the estate agents they had on their list with neither establishment having rented a property to anyone with a foreign name, or as far as the assistant could remember, with a foreign accent in the last six months. Now they entered Owen Baxter's a small private business. Sally showed her warrant card and asked about any recent lettings to foreigners. They were attended to by the owner himself. Owen Baxter was a man in his forties dressed very smartly in a navy pin-striped suit, blue shirt and tie with very fair hair and sharp grey eyes. He was intrigued by the request and quickly found the book containing all the lettings they were interested in.

'We do get more foreigners renting properties these days,' he said, 'but have never had any problems with payment of rents or anything else.'

'That's not what we're looking into,' said Sally, 'it's just a particular person we're interested in.'

'If we find him we'd like to speak to him, that's all,' said Narinder.

'Oh, I see, well, all the names are in the book, so I'll leave you to it. Call me if you need me.' Owen Baxter left them at his table and Sally began turning the pages. 'I'll read out the names and addresses, Narinder, and you write them down.'

'I'm ready,' replied Narinder, 'are there any men on their own or are they all couples?'

'They appear to be couples.'

'Could be a blind of course.'

'We'll note them all to be safe,' said Sally.

Jack had been given the name of the receptionist at Pegasus House to check and was now putting Ann Peters into the police network on his computer. So far nothing had come up. She was not known to the police. He traced her address to Lambourne Road, Torreston where it stated she lived with a Victor Peters, the other occupant of the house. Jack jotted this down to give to the boss later.

Duncan and Ben were visiting their second estate agent and felt excited when given the name of a solitary man with a foreign name who had requested renting a property six month ago. The property was a terrace house on Canal Street. The estate agent, Arnold Peach, had dealt with this rental and told the police officers that the man was definitely Central European.

'He spoke reasonable English,' said Peach, 'but I think he could have been Polish.'

'Could we have his name please,' said Duncan, and as the estate agent went to his office to oblige, Duncan turned to Ben and said, 'This looks promising.'

'We're not to visit any of the properties, are we?' said Ben.

'Absolutely not. The armed-response-team will have to accompany any visits if there is the sign of this killer being in the house.'

'It's all very exciting,' replied Ben.

'You wouldn't say that if you were ever involved in a shooting incident,' said Duncan, 'it's damn scary I can tell you.'

'Weren't you involved in a shootout some years ago?' asked the young DC.

'Hardly a shootout,' replied Duncan, 'but yes I was involved in a firearms incident.'

'I heard you saved the boss's life.'

'I don't know about that, I just happened to be the officer on hand. Ah, good,' he said eager to change the subject, 'here comes Mr Peach.'

The estate agent returned and handed Duncan the name and address of the man they were interested in. Thanking him the officers left. Outside Duncan looked at the paper.

'Sergey Andruko', he read out. 'Sounds Russian to me.'

'Crikey,' gasped Ben, 'does that mean we've found the hitman?'

'Who knows,' replied Duncan, 'but we'll get back and hand in this bit of info.' They made for Duncan's car and headed back to headquarters.

By three o'clock officers were comparing notes in the Incident Room. Ben went over to Luke and reminded him that he had agreed to go flat hunting with him.

'Visiting estate agents today has given me the urge to find a flat of my own,' he said.

'The next time the boss gives us time off we'll start looking,' said Luke, have you broken the news to your parents yet?'

Ben grinned. 'Not yet, I'm waiting for the right moment.'

Harriet and Earl Cassells went to the front of the room and Harriet held up her hand.

'Going around the room,' she said, 'tell us how many lettings have been made in the last six months and how many of those were made to foreigners.' She nodded to Duncan who began.

'Eight lettings in total but only two to foreigners,' he said, 'one a single man called Sergy Andruko which we thought sounded Russian.'

'Could be Ukrainian, I think,' said Harriet, 'but even so he will need checking.'

'The other foreigner is a Mr Nowakowski,' said Ben, 'and I reckon that name's Polish.'

'I think so too,' agreed Harriet. 'There are quite a few Polish people in the area and we do have to be careful that we don't upset them.'

Sally went next. 'Only four lettings,' she said, 'but again two were foreigners one couple definitely Russian as I checked the name on Google.'

Harriet smiled. 'What was the name, Sally?'

'Igor Sokolov'.

'Yes, that is Russian,' agreed Harriet.

Other officers came up with similar numbers of lettings but among them only one couple was foreign. Harriet asked that all the names and addresses be put on the board. 'We will have to check them all out, but no one goes to any of these palaces without my say-so and without out firearm back up.'

'And as the superintendent has told us, wearing bullet proof vests,' added Earl.

'Jack has done a check on Sophie Gilbert,' said Harriet, 'and has discovered her name is Sofija Adamkute a Lithuanian married to a Brit, Charles Gilbert. She has been in this country for four years but even so, we'll dig a little deeper to play safe. I shall visit the Gilberts with DCI Marlow as soon as possible. Did you find anything on Ann Peters, Jack?'

'Nothing on the police computer, ma'am, but according to records she lives in Lambourne Road with a Victor Peters, presumably her husband, but I can't find anything on him at all.'

'Peters is one of the names on our list,' said DC Luke Stockwell. 'Not down as foreign, but the house was rented in the last six months, so we wrote it down.'

'So again, we presume Ann is married to a Brit, do we?' asked Earl.

'The estate agent didn't say the person renting the house is foreign,' said Luke, 'so if Victor Peters is a Brit, as we think he is, then it was probably him who did the talking.'

'Do a bit more checking on the husband, Jack,' said Harriet, 'where he works and so on, and where they lived before, if this renting was only taken out six months ago. But again, I'll do this visit with DCI Marlow.'

'Yes, ma'am.' Jack nodded happily.

'Good,' said Harriet, 'we've covered some ground today and tomorrow we'll do some visiting. I'll speak to firearms so that we have back up when we visit.'

'We'll start a new board with all these names and addresses,' said Earl, 'and that will make it easier for us to cross them off when checked.'

'Thank you, Earl,' said Harriet, 'I'll leave you to see that the names are written up and I'll get in touch with Firearms, we'll start these visits tomorrow, so I'd like you all in by seven thirty so that we catch people at home. Sorry about the early start, but we need to find this hitman as soon as possible. If any of these tenants turn out to be suspicious we'll apply for search warrants. Finish what you have to do regards writing up your notes and get off home.'

Harriet went to her office and called up Commander James Upton, the new boss of the firearms division, and explained what she needed as back up the following morning. 'We have several addresses we need to visit,' she said, 'and knowing somewhere there's our hitman we have to play safe.'

'Absolutely, Harriet,' replied the commander, 'we'll meet you at the front of the station at a quarter to eight.'

'Thank you, James, I'll speak to you then.' Harriet replaced the telephone receiver and leaned back in her chair. She hoped tomorrow would go smoothly and more importantly they might find the Russian they were looking for. The trouble was they had no idea what the man looked like and at this stage of the investigation all they could do was ask questions of the people they were to find in the houses they were going to visit. Harriet sighed. Was this going to be a fruitless assignment? Or might tomorrow give them the answers they needed.

Chapter Forty-Nine

It was early evening when Commander James Upton checked on the officers at Copper Beeches. He was told by one of his men that the lady of the house no longer wanted them to be there. He rang the doorbell and it was opened by Ursula.

'I understand you wish me to withdraw the police guard,' said Commander Upton.

'Yes, yes, it's now quite unnecessary.'

'I shall require a written note to that effect,' said Upton.

'Oh, really,' replied Ursula, 'is that quite necessary.'

'It is indeed,' said Upton firmly, 'if I could come inside perhaps you would be good enough to write the note before I remove the men.'

Huffing and puffing Ursula stood back and allowed the commander to enter. He followed her into the front room where she took a notepad from the sideboard drawer and began writing. She handed Upton the paper and he read what she had written.

'If you would just sign and date it please' he said handing it back to her.

'For heaven's sake,' snapped Ursula taking it and scribbling her name at the bottom of the sheet. She thrust it back at Upton and he wondered why any of them should bother about this woman.

'Thank you,' he said, 'we will leave you in peace.' Going outside he called the two officers and told them they could go home. 'Give me a couple of minutes to contact Superintendent Love to let her know what's happening, and I'll drive you back to headquarters.' He opened up his mobile and punched in Harriet's number.

Harriet was at home when the call came, and she agreed with Commander Upton that there was little they could do if Mrs Blackwell was insistent on the guard being withdrawn.

'Goodness knows what we do if someone takes a shot at her,' said Harriet.

'Hardly our fault,' replied Upton, 'but don't worry, Harriet I made her sign a statement to the affect that she insisted we remove the guard and leave her alone.'

'Well done, James, that should cover us if anything happens.' She said goodbye and then dialled Ursula Blackwell's home number. Ursula answered immediately.

'I understand you have dismissed the police guard from outside your house,' said Harriet, 'do you think that wise? You may have heard that an attempt was made on the life of Rosalind De Luca last night, thankfully unsuccessfully.'

Harriet heard a choking sound from the other end of the phone and waited. Ursula came back on the line. 'So, Mrs De Luca is still alive?'

'She is, and now she's on her way back to Italy, she was put on a plane first thing this morning.'

There was silence at the end of the line and again Harriet waited. 'Are you there, Mrs Blackwell?' asked Harriet after a few moments.

'Yes.'

'I'm sure you must feel grateful to your stepdaughter for relinquishing her claim to Copper Beeches,' said Harriet, 'I understand she refused to have you sell the property and have to move from your house and insisted she sign a document to this request.'

Harriet heard gasps from the telephone and began to wonder if Ursula was all right. She was about to ask this when the woman spoke again.

'I'm extremely happy,' she said, 'and so glad that Rosalind is safe.'

Harriet thought the voice was strained and asked her if all was well. Ursula insisted she was fine and having advised her to call if she had any concerns about her safety, Harriet hung up.

Ursula was shaking when she replaced the receiver. That bastard Bardwell-Fox, he knew the bitch wasn't going to make her sell Copper Beeches and he hadn't told her. She'd make him suffer for this, just wait and see. She suddenly had a feeling of power as she saw the police officers leave. She had dismissed them, she had taken charge of the situation and she wasn't going to be told what to do by anyone. Now she no longer had the threat of losing her house hanging over her and George's rotten daughter was no longer on the scene. All she needed now was to get Don back. He was usually putty in her hand and tomorrow she would become the temptress that so excited him. She lay on the sofa with a bottle of gin on the small table beside her feeling like her old self again. She poured a glass and sipped her drink happily. This was followed by another, and another and feeling warm and relaxed she closed her eyes.

The clock struck eleven and Ursula sat up feeling rather heavy headed. She decided her bed was calling and rose somewhat shakily to her feet, stretched and yawned. Perhaps tomorrow she would not be sleeping alone. Draining her glass, she made her way upstairs.

Ursula was dreaming. She was with Don and they were walking in the garden at Copper Beeches. Suddenly she tripped and fell on the little statuette of a mermaid beside the ornamental pond. It crashed to the round and Ursula sat up in alarm. The crash had been so real. She froze as she heard a noise again. This was no dream; the noise was in her house. She suddenly wished she had not been so hasty in insisting the police leave her and she slipped out of bed and pulled on her dressing gown. Tiptoeing to the bedroom door she turned the key in the lock and stood still listening. She could definitely hear movement downstairs and shaking from head to foot she went to her handbag and took out her mobile phone quickly pressing in three nines. The call was answered immediately and keeping her voice low she asked for the police.

Pete Yates took the emergency call at two o'clock and recognising the name Ursula Blackwell, immediately, told her to wait a moment white he activated help. Having done this, he returned to the call. 'Help is on the way, madam,' he said, 'keep your bedroom door locked and is there anywhere in the room where you can hide in case the perpetrator gets in?'

'My small dressing room.'

'That's better than nothing,' said Pete, 'it will delay things until we get to you, so go there now.'

Ursula closed down her phone and went to the dressing room where she went inside and closed the door behind her. There was no lock on this door, so she hid herself among her many dresses hanging in a large cupboard. She stood among her expensive gowns trembling and feeling sick. The minutes ticked by and then she heard it; the crash as someone forced her bedroom door open. She clutched her silk dresses around her and closed her eyes, her heart pounding in her chest like a pneumatic drill. She waited, praying under her breath that she would not be harmed. She could barely stand as her legs felt so weak and sliding to the floor of the wardrobe she covered her head with one of her gowns, shaking so hard that she feared whoever was out there could hear.

Having instructed all police cars in the area to attend the incident at Copper Beeches, Pete Yates called Harriet. Harriet was awake and dressed in minutes and with Ed beside her in her little Lotus she drove as fast as she could to the Blackwell house. Pulling into the driveway they could see the flashing blue lights of two police cars standing at the front door. Harriet came to a stop behind them and she and Ed ran into the house. A uniformed officer stood just inside the doorway and recognising Harriet and Ed, he acknowledged them and moved to one side. Voices could be heard upstairs and together they climbed the stairs. Sergeant Delaney came towards them looking drawn and anxious.

'Ma'am,' he said, 'Mrs Blackwell is dead.'

'Shot?' asked Harriet suddenly feeling sick.

'Yes, ma'am.'

'Have you called the Armed Response Team?'

'I have, ma'am, and SOCO.'

'Well done and I take it all officers are wearing flak jackets.'

'We are, ma'am.'

'Good,' replied Harriet. 'Is Mrs Blackwell in her bed.'

'No, she was obviously hiding in her dressing room, and that's where the killer found her.'

'Would you like me to call Forensics and Doctor Boston?' asked Ed.

'Thank you,' said Harriet, 'yes, please do that, and I'll call Charlie, he would hate not to be involved.'

They both took out their mobile phones as footsteps were heard on the stairs. Commander Upton appeared. 'So, he got her, did he?' he asked frowning. 'Stupid woman insisting we remove the guard. We'll check the house, Harriet but our shooter will be long gone.' He beckoned his team of armed officers and they began moving stealthily through the rooms. Sergeant Delaney stood on guard at the bedroom door hardly believing that this could happen to him twice. Thank God the killer had done the deed and left before he'd arrived, but he could only just have missed him.

Harriet thought how stressed the sergeant looked and went up to him and asked if he was all right.

'Yes, thank you, ma'am, just having a bit of déja vu.' He smiled weakly.

Harriet patted his arm. 'You'll be all right,' she said, 'what time did you get the emergency call?'

'Four minutes after two, ma'am and we were here at two fifteen exactly.'

Harriet shivered at the thought of Sergeant Dealey arriving at Copper Beeches and being confronted by the killer; it had to have been a close call. 'Well done, Justin,' she said' 'you're doing just fine.'

'Thank you, ma'am, and its good news that PC Franks is going to be okay. I've been to see him in hospital and they say he'll be home by Friday.'

'That's excellent news, and well done to you, Justin for coping so well.'

Justin Delaney pulled himself up straight; if the superintendent felt he was okay then he could certainly cope. He was always amazed at her kindness and generosity and was beginning to understand why the officers at Torreston Station regarded her as the best.

Ed told Harriet that Stacey was on her way and Harriet confirmed that Charlie too would be here very soon. 'I won't go into the room until Stacey has looked at the body,' said Harriet, 'and then we'll let Forensics go over the place to see if this time our hit-man has left any clues.'

'Which he won't have of course,' said Ed.

Charlie and Stacey Boston came up the stairs together and greeted Harriet and Ed.

'This is getting quite like the old times,' said Stacey. 'How are you, Ed?'

Ed grinned. 'Not too bad but it would be nice to have a full night's sleep some time.'

Stacey smiled. 'You should be used to this by now, Ed. Right where's the body?'

Harriet directed the pathologist to Ursula's bedroom and she vanished inside. The murdered woman lay on the floor in front of the open door of a large wardrobe with a collection of dresses on top of her. The room was obviously her dressing room, and lifting the clothes Stacey gazed at the lifeless body of Ursula Blackwell. Her hands were clutching her chest where blood had oozed through her fingers and a solitary bullet hole was in the centre of her forehead. Stacey checked that she was dead and briefly examined her before returning to where Harriet was waiting with Charlie and Ed.

'She must have hidden among her clothes in the wardrobe,' she told them, 'and that's where she was shot. The first bullet hit her in the chest, but it was the second shot to her head that killed her.'

'Poor wretch,' said Harriet, 'she certainly had problems.'

'You can say that again,' agreed Charlie, 'but why has she been killed?'

'How many does that make?' asked Ed.

'George Blackwell was the first,' said Harriet, 'followed by Freddie Maloney.'

'And we think he was killed because of something he found at the Blackwell House,' said Charlie.

'Then there was the attempt on Blackwell's daughter's life,' said Harriet, 'and we don't know why that was.'

'And now Ursula Blackwell,' added Charlie, 'so we're not really sure what the Hell is going on.'

Commander Upton came up to Harriet and told her the house was clear. 'The shooter did the deed and scarpered,' he said, 'there's certainly no sign of him now. He got in through a back window and the guys are boarding it up.'

'Thank you, James,' said Harriet, 'at least it leaves us all feeling a little safer knowing the gunman is no longer in the building.'

More officers arrived including SOCO and Forensics and after briefly greeting Harriet, they set about their work.

By three thirty the search for evidence and the dusting for fingerprints was concluded and the officers involved had left. The necessary photographs had been taken and the body had been removed and taken to the morgue. Stacey told Harriet she would do the post-mortem the following day and they agreed on two o'clock. She said her goodbyes and went to her car to follow the mortuary vehicle back to the hospital.

Harriet turned to Charlie and Ed. 'We'll have a look around the house ourselves before we leave,' she said, 'I'd like to know what secrets Mrs Blackwell is hiding, and I'm quite sure there are many.'

Leading the way Harriet went down the stairs and made her way to the front room.

Chapter Fifty

Harriet, with Charlie and Ed began searching the sitting room where Ursula spent much of her time. The side table had on it, one empty, but used glass, and two gin bottles, one empty the other half empty. Harriet looked at the objects. 'Well it looks as if she was drinking alone this evening,' she said

'She liked her drink,' said Ed, 'I'm surprised she was ever sober.'

'Half the time I don't think she was,' said Charlie.

'That might account for her sudden bursts of temper,' said Harriet.

Charlie found the laptop in the sideboard cupboard and placed it on the coffee table.

'This could prove quite interesting' he said.

'Good,' agreed Harriet, 'and any paper work you can find we'll take back with us too.' She picked up a book that was on the sofa and peered at it. She smiled as she read the title. Replacing it she called out to her husband. 'Have you found anything interesting, Ed?'

'Some letters, but that's about all. I'll put them on the table with the laptop.'

'We'll take all this with us,' said Harriet, 'and give the laptop to Doctor Chong. We'll go through the paper work tomorrow. Time to go,' she added, making her way to the front door. She removed the keys from the lock and handed them to Charlie.

'We'll lock up and hang on to these,' she said.

They left Copper Beeches and Charlee stretched the blue police tape across the front door before locking it. As they walked

336

down the steps a flash of light made them jump. A grinning Beefy Cavendish stood in front of them with another man behind him that they didn't recognise.

'I thought something was going on,' he said, 'all this police activity in the middle of the night, care to tell me what's happened, Superintendent.'

Harriet was annoyed but felt she couldn't hide the events of the night. 'Who is this with you, Mr Cavendish?' she asked.

The man stepped forward. 'Gordon Rutherford of *The Herald,* ma'am,' he said.

'Friend of Cavendish are you?' asked Charlie frowning.

'Not exactly, I was out and about and saw him suddenly dash off so decided to follow.'

'Are you going to tell us what's happened?' demanded Beefy.

'You might do better if you minded your manners,' said Ed.

'Oh, so you're in on this as well are you?' said Beefy. 'Long time no see Chief Inspector.'

Harriet decided it would be better to give the reporters a brief story or they would never give up. 'As you will have gathered,' she said, 'there has been a serious incident here tonight and Mrs Blackwell has been shot.'

'Is she dead,' demanded Beefy.

'I'm afraid so, but that's all I can give you at the moment, as soon as we have more information we will be holding a Press conference.'

Beefy moved forward and Charlie stepped in his way. 'You heard what the superintendent said, that's all we can tell you at the moment, now I think you should leave.'

Rutherford had already returned to his car and reluctantly Beefy Cavendish did the same. The three officers continued to their own vehicles and waited until the two reporters had driven away.

'I'll ring Sergeant Yates,' said Harriet, 'and tell him what happened here tonight and that we'll see him later this morning. Will you be able to manage seven thirty, Charlie?'

Charlie stifled a yawn. 'Absolutely,' he replied, 'how about you, Harry?'

Harriet smiled. 'I'll be there, we have a very busy morning planned with the firearms team and we can't possibly miss that.'

'And we have the post-mortem in the afternoon,' said Charlie. 'I might just fall asleep during that.'

'I'll ask Earl to attend the PM,' said Harriet, 'he's fitting in very well and we need to involve him as much as possible. I'll ask him to get someone to go to Leicester to inform Mrs Blackwell's sister what has happened.'

'Good idea,' agreed Charlie, 'We don't want her reading about her sister's murder in the paper before we can tell her.'

The two cars drove away and Copper Beeches was left behind. It stood empty and silent with the blue police tape across the front door fluttering slightly in the breeze ominously indicating the horrific incident that had occurred in the house.

Sometime before seven thirty officers began arriving at police headquarters. Harriet pulled up in the carpark at the same time as Charlie who looked surprisingly bright considering the few hours' sleep he'd had. Harriet's eyes were pricking through tiredness, but she put on a cheerful face as Charlie came up to her.

'How'd you feel, Harry?' he asked.

'Oh, wonderful,' replied Harriet dryly, 'and you?'

'Okay so far but I reckon it will hit me later on.'

They entered the building where Pete Yates was preparing to hand over to Sergeant Carl Fisher. 'Good morning, ma'am, sir,' said Pete, 'another hectic night.'

'We're getting used to it,' replied Harriet

'Are the troops arriving?' asked Charlie.

'Most of them are already here,' replied Pete, 'they all seem very eager for whatever it is you have planned.'

'You'll hear all about it,' said Harriet setting off up the stairs to CID. Charlie followed and as they neared the Incident Room they could hear the excited voices from inside.

On entering, Harriet went straight to Earl Cassells to explain to him what had happened the night before. 'I didn't call you, Earl,' she said, 'as I will want you to take over later this afternoon when DCI Marlow and I go home before we fall asleep on the job.'

'I understand, ma'am, but are you sure you will be all right this morning.'

'I'll cope, but I should like you and Duncan to attend the post-mortem of Ursula Blackwell at two this afternoon.'

'Of course, ma'am.'

'Thank you, Earl.' Harriet went over to Luke and gave him the laptop from Copper Beeches. 'Take this down to Doctor Chong,' she said, 'and then meet us at the front of the building. You will need a bullet proof jacket so take one with you.'

Luke took the laptop grabbed a jacket and hurried off. Harriet moved to the front of the room. 'Everyone ready?' she asked. 'Firearms are meeting us at the front of the building in a few minutes, and thank you, Duncan for agreeing to stay with us We have two vans to transport us and Firearms will follow in their own vehicle. There is to be no communication on mobile phones to or from the station landlines as we don't want to alert the press. We know they listen in on our wave length and we can do without any publicity this morning. Jack,' added Harriet, 'I, or possibly Sally, will contact you mobile to mobile to give you any names we might need tracking.'

'I'll be ready, ma'am.'

'Is everyone wearing a flak jacket?' asked Charlie.

This was greeted by a positive response and Charlie handed one to Harriet as he put on his own. 'Firearms will be on standby to support us,' said Harriet, 'but the operation is ours, so follow my lead.'

'Superintendent Love and I are wired,' said Charlie, 'and will be in constant contact with Commander Upton and the CID van. The commander will keep his men out of sight but ready to move in if there is any trouble. The rest of you will remain in our vehicles also listening to what is going on. No one moves without our hearsay.'

'We'll be playing the situation down,' said Harriet, 'stressing to the occupants of these flats that the visit is simply one of elimination. Hopefully we will just talk, but we will keep our eyes open at the same time. We will only be visiting the foreign tenants, Jack will be undertaking a search of the other people who have begun renting in the last six months.'

'Right,' called Charlie, 'let's go.'

Officers left the room, but Jack remained at his desk as Harriet had instructed him. Charlie checked his wire was in place and Harriet did the same before following them down to the waiting vans.

Harriet spoke into her concealed microphone. 'We'll start with the most Russian of the names,' she said, 'that's Igor Sokolov at fifteen Templeton Street.' Officers in the two vans listened to what she had to say on the speaker. 'If firearms would park opposite the house,' she continued, 'CID park a little further away. DCI Marlow and I will approach the house and speak to the occupant. If there is any trouble we will ask for help, but no one is to do anything unless that happens.'

Commander Upton in the lead van was not happy about this and wanted an armed officer to go with her, but Harriet had been adamant that they had no proof that the killer they were after lived at any of these addresses and their visits were simply a reconnaissance. Charlie was driving his car with Harriet beside him. He pulled up outside number fifteen Templeton Street and they got out. "Firearms" stopped opposite and the CID van moved further on before parking. All officers were listening intently to Harriet's voice.

'Approaching the front door now,'

'All pretty quiet,' came Charlie's voice.

Harriet rang the doorbell and they waited. Watching from his van Upton saw the door open and heard the voice of the occupant. 'Yes, what can I do for you?'

'We're so sorry to bother you' said Harriet, 'but we are doing a check in the area and need to ask you a few questions.' She held up her warrant card and Charlie did the same.

'Are you Igor Sokolov?' asked Charlie.

'I am.'

'Do you live alone?' asked Harriet.

'I do.'

'As you have only lived here for six months,' said Charlie, 'could we ask where you lived before.'

'What is this all about?' asked Sokolov.

'As I said,' replied Harriet, 'we are undertaking an investigation where we have to question several people who are renting property in the area.'

'So, it's about renting property, is it?'

'Yes, it is,' said Harriet, 'but you don't have anything to worry about.'

The man frowned. 'I used to have a rented room in Brixworth, I work at the Mercedes business there. I wanted something more personal and away from the place of work so managed to find this flat about six months ago.'

'Thank you,' said Harriet, 'that's all we need to know, so sorry to have troubled you.'

They returned to their car and Harriet spoke to Commander Upton. 'That's an easy one to check if he works for Mercedes, we'll get Jack onto it immediately. Sally will you do that please.'

'Yes, ma'am.' Sally opened her mobile and called Jack on his mobile. She gave the name of Sokolov to him and told him where he worked.

'Where next?' asked Upton.

'Fletton Road, the names Dabrowski,' replied Harriet

'We'll follow you,' said Upton.

Charlie drove off and the teams followed. The same procedure as before was carried out and at Fletton Road officers in the vans watched as Harriet and Charlie approached the house. Harriet knocked on the door and it was opened almost immediately. Standing there was a young woman in nurses' uniform.

'Superintendent,' said the woman, 'how nice to see you, you've just caught me as I'm going on duty.'

Harriet recognised the woman as the nurse she had spoken to in A and E when Roy Franks had been brought in. For a moment she didn't know what to say. Charlie stepped in quickly.

'Of course,' he said, 'you work with Liz my wife.'

'Yes, I recognise you Chief Inspector,' said Anna Dabrowski, 'how can I help you?'

'We're doing a routine check on rented property in the area, but I don't think there's any need to ask you any questions.'

'Anything I can do to help,' said Anna.

'How long have you lived here?' asked Harriet finding her voice.

'Only six months. I had only one room and a shared bathroom before and have been saving to buy somewhere of my own. So far, this flat is the best I can do, but it is so much better than the one room.'

'We won't hold you up any longer,' said Charlie, 'give my love to Liz when you see her.'

'I will, and I'm so pleased your colleague is almost fully

recovered.'

'Thank you, Nurse Dabrowski,' said Harriet and she and Charlie walked away.

Back in Charlie's car Harriet puffed out her cheeks. 'Phew, seeing Nurse Dabrowski caught me off guard, thank you, Charlie for taking over so swiftly.'

'I was surprised too,' replied Charlie, 'but I don't think Anna Dabrowski, who incidentally is Polish, is a hitman's mol, do you?'

Harriet smiled. 'Hardly, but we'll do everything by the book, Charlie and check the NHS files as to how long she has been at the hospital and so on. She spoke into her microphone; 'Another one for Jack, Sally.'

'I'm onto it. ma'am,' replied Sally.

Charlie started the engine and moved away. 'Next address, Harry?' he said.

Chapter Fifty-One

By twelve thirty all the properties rented by foreigners had been visited and names of the occupants relayed to Jack to undertake checks on them. The two police vans pulled into a side road and Charlie stopped behind them. He and Harriet got out and joined their colleagues.

'Anything interesting?' asked Commander Upton.

Harriet shook her head. 'Nothing. Have we heard from Jack, Sally?' she asked.

'Yes, ma'am, he reports that Sokolov has worked at the Mercedes headquarters for twelve years and is one of their most experienced engineers. They speak very highly of him and agree that he used to live in Brixworth and recently moved.'

'And of the five tenants he was the only Russian,' said Charlie.

'Jack said the nurse was easy to check up on and she's definitely in the clear, been with the NHS for five years and at Kettering General for four.'

Sally read out the results of the check Jack had made on a Polish couple, a young Lithuanian woman and a Ukrainian man. All had been in the country for some time and all were in employment. 'Jack can find nothing suspicious about any of them, ma'am,' said Sally.

Harriet felt despondent. 'It was worth a try,' she said, 'we'll call on the remaining tenants tomorrow, but we won't need firearms back up, thank you, Commander.'

'Well at least take McAllister with you to be safe,' said James

Upton. 'Just because these others appear to be British doesn't mean they're not something else.'

'Very well, if you think I should,' agreed Harriet.

'And you go armed, McAllister,' said Upton to Duncan.

'Yes, sir.'

'Back to headquarters, everyone,' said Charlie, 'time for lunch.'

Officers returned to their vehicles and made their way back to the police station where everyone gathered in the Incident Room. They began wriggling out of their bullet-proof jackets and Harriet suggested they had lunch before doing anything further. Jack had put his findings on the board and Harriet thanked him for his speedy checks.

'No problem, ma'am,' he said, 'I'm getting pretty good at this kind of thing.'

'You've always been the expert, Jack,' said Charlie coming over to him.

'Well, I haven't managed to track down this Victor Peters, Ann Peter's husband,' said Jack.

'The Pegasus House receptionist?' said Earl Cassells joining them at Jack's desk.

'Yes. They live at fourteen Lambourne Road,' replied Jack. 'According to records, she's there but I can't find him anywhere.'

'He must be on the Electoral Register,' said Harriet.

'That's just it,' answered Jack, 'he's not. All the utilities are in the name of Ann Peters'

'Do we know where he works?' aske Earl.

'Can't find that either.'

'We'll pay Mrs Peters another visit,' said Harriet, 'there must be a simple explanation, perhaps her husband is away on business overseas or something. Grab a coffee and something to eat, Charlie and then we'll go over to Pegasus House.'

'We were going to visit the Gilberts to check on Sophie Gilbert's husband,' said Charlie.

'Earl, will you do that,' said Harriet, 'take Duncan with you and both of you keep your flak jackets on, and don't forget you're attending the post-mortem of Ursula Blackwell this afternoon. One other thing, before anything can you send someone to Leicester to tell Mrs Hemmingway about the death of her sister; the murder won't be in the morning papers, but it might be mentioned on the news.'

'Yes, ma'am, but I thought you and DCI Marlow were going home, you must be shattered.'

'We'll go as soon as we've spoken to Mrs Peters, but call me if you have any problems,' said Harriet.

Earl went over to Duncan and told him to put his jacket back on. 'Have your lunch as quickly as you can,' he said, 'and then we're to pay the Gilbert's a visit after which we are attending Mrs Blackwell's PM.' The inspector then asked Sally to go to Leicester with Narinder to speak to Connie Hemmingway.

Harriet went to her office and Charlie offered to make them coffee before leaving. His eyes were stinging due to lack of sleep and he guessed Harriet was feeling the same. The coffee might help them stay awake.

Travelling in Charlie's car they drove to Pegasus House and parked in the carpark where George Blackwell had met his demise. Entering the building they went to the reception window and rang the bell. A woman they had never seen before rolled back the glass and smiled. 'Yes, how can I help you?'

'We'd like to speak to Ann Peters please,' said Harriet.

'I'm sorry, she hasn't come in today,' said the woman, 'but I'm sure I can help you.' Harriet produced her warrant card. 'It's police business,' she said, 'is Mrs Peters ill?'

'I really don't know, she just didn't turn up this morning.'

'Thank you,' said Harriet and moving away from the window

she turned to Charlie wrinkling her nose. 'Fishy or what?' she said.

'To Lambourne Road?' asked Charlie.

'Yes, number fourteen. Let's go.'

Charlie drove to the address they had for Ann Peters and pulled up outside the house they were interested in. Lambourne Road was a quiet road of terrace houses with several cars parked half on the road and half on the pavement. There was no car outside number fourteen and hurrying up the path Harriet knocked on the front door. There was no response and she knocked again. Charlie went around to the back of the house and peered through the kitchen window. The place was neat and tidy with nothing on the surfaces and no litter anywhere. He tried the back door and found it locked. Harriet joined him and asked him what he thought.

'I think we have grounds to force an entry,' he said, 'we obviously think Ann Peters might be lying in the house ill as she hasn't turned up for work and hasn't contacted anyone.' He raised an eyebrow as he spoke, and Harriet nodded.

'Go ahead, Charlie.'

Charlie used his elbow to smash the kitchen window, and knocking out the broken glass, he leaned in and opened it. He climbed through into the kitchen and unlocked the back door for Harriet. 'We check the rooms together, Harry,' he said, 'we have no idea who or what this woman is.'

Harriet nodded and together they made their way to the front room. It was sparsely furnished, cold and uninviting. 'There's no heating on in the house,' said Harriet, 'and it's November.'

'The place doesn't feel lived in' said Charlie. 'Let's see what's upstairs.' He quickly stepped in front of Harriet to lead the way. There were two bedrooms and a bathroom all quite cold and bare. They opened cupboards and drawers all of which were empty.

'Has she done a runner?' said Charlie.

'If she's the Russian hitman's assistant, then I think the answer is yes.'

'I'll call Forensics,' said Charlie, 'see what they can turn up.' He took out his mobile and pressed in the number.

'I take it there is no Mr Peters,' said Harriet, 'and that's why Jack was unable to trace him.'

'Looks like it,' agreed Charlie, 'living as a couple was a front.'

'But she's not the killer of Blackwell,' said Harriet, 'she never left the building when he was shot, the security man said no one left and all the other clerical staff in reception agreed with this.'

'No, the hitman is a guy,' said Charlie, 'but his sidekick is the person who passes on his instructions no doubt.'

'I can't believe this is happening in Torreston,' said Harriet, 'it's quite alarming.'

They waited for Forensics to arrive and as the Scientific van pulled up, Charlie unlocked the front door to let them in. While Fraser Overton and his men went over the house Harriet and Charlie sat down in the front room. Harriet's head was spinning, and she was having difficulty keeping her eyes open and she guessed Charlie felt the same. An hour passed with Harriet and Charlie sitting in silence and nodding off from time to time. Suddenly the door opened, and Fraser Overton appeared.

'Just this room to check,' he said, 'and may I suggest that you two go home and I'll ring in any result later today. You both look dreadful.'

Charlie got to his feet. 'Fraser's right, Harry,' he said, 'we'll be useless tomorrow if we don't get some sleep, come on I'll drive you home.'

Harriet knew he was right, she couldn't remember when she had last slept properly and rising she nodded. 'Let's go, Charlie, and thank you, Fraser I'll read your report in the morning.'

They left Lambourne Road and twenty minutes later Charlie pulled up outside Magnolia Cottage. Harriet thanked him and hurried into the cottage. As tired as she was she knew she had to ring headquarters and doing this she told Jack about Ann Peters and asked him to pass this information on to Earl Cassells. 'Circulate a description of this woman, Jack,' said Harriet, 'and make sure airports are alerted.'

'What about Eurostar?' asked Jack.

'Alert anywhere you think she might use as an escape route,' said Harriet.

'Yes, ma'am.'

'I'll be in in the morning, Jack,' said Harriet, 'but I am to be called if there is an emergency.' She hung up and barely able to walk she crawled up the stairs and kicking off her shoes she fell into bed just as she was.

Inspector Cassells and Duncan called at the home of Sophie Gilbert, or as they now knew her to be, Sofija Adamkute. The door was answered by a well-built man in his thirties, with short cropped fair hair and grey eyes. 'Yes?' he asked.

Earl held up his warrant card. 'Inspector Cassells,' he said, 'and this is Sergeant McAllister.'

'Oh, God, is Sophie's all right?' gasped the man.

'Yes, yes,' said Earl quickly, 'may we come in for moment, you are Charles Gilbert?'

'I am, what's this all about?'

They followed Gilbert into the house where they were invited to sit down. 'Now how can I help you?' he said.

Earl decided it was pointless beating about the bush and so he explained how they were checking on everyone who worked at Pegasus House who was of foreign origin.

'This is to do with Blackwell's murder I take it,' said Gilbert.

'We have to check everyone,' said Duncan, 'and of course we learned that your wife's name was Sofija Adamkute before she married you, so we have to make sure you really do exist.'

'Would you like to check our marriage certificate?'

'That won't be necessary,' replied Earl not adding that Jack had already done so.

'She spells her name Sophie now simply to belong, she felt she would be less conspicuous with an English name,' said Gilbert, 'you know how hateful some people can be towards foreigners.'

'We understand,' said Duncan. 'Your wife has left Pegasus House now, hasn't she?'

'She has, should have left months ago, Blackwell was a bully and didn't deserve having Sophie work for him. She's at an interview this very moment and she'll be snapped up, I can tell you.'

'That's good news,' said Duncan.

'You are an exporter, we hear,' said Earl.

'Yes, I deal mainly in tea and exotic coffee and do much of my work from home.' He went to the sideboard and picked up a pile of cards. He handed one to Earl. 'My business address should you wish to contact me in the future. Was there anything else?'

'No, thank you, that's everything,' said Earl, 'and we hope Sophie is successful with the new job.'

They left the house and returned to the car. 'Now for the post-mortem,' said Earl, 'have you attended one before, Duncan.'

'Yes, sir, but only one and I can't say I enjoyed it.'

'I agree with that sentiment,' replied Earl, 'but if you feel the slightest bit queasy just walk out, no one will think any the less of you. I can honestly say I have done just that in the past.'

'Thank you, sir. I'll do my best to hold up, but it's good to know you won't mind if I leave the room if I don't feel up to it.' With Earl driving they headed for the mortuary and Ursula Blackwell's post-mortem.

Ed arrived home at six and found Harriet fast asleep on top of the bed. Although he too had been up most of the night he had stayed in bed late that morning and not arrived for duty until midday. He looked at the sleeping figure of his wife and then gently pulled her sweater over her head and then carefully removed her trousers before lifted her and placing her under the duvet. Harriet murmured but did not wake. Ed kissed her on the cheek and quietly left the room.

Chapter Fifty-Two

Harriet awoke to find Ed standing by the beside holding a tray with a cup of tea and a plate of toast and marmalade. She sat up and rubbed her eyes.

'What's the time?' she asked.

'Six thirty, Thursday morning.'

'No!' Harriet was incredulous. 'I can't believe I've slept since yesterday afternoon.'

'Well, you have,' said Ed, 'you must have been shattered.' He leaned over and kissed her.

'I think I was,' agreed Harriet. 'And I see you half undressed me.'

'I thought you'd roast in a sweater and trousers in bed,' said Ed smiling, 'so I took my life in my hands and removed them.'

'Thank you, Ed, and thank you for the tea and toast.' She took the tray and Ed placed another pillow behind her back.

'I'll leave you to it, Harry,' said Ed, 'I think I heard the cat flap which means Feather will be wanting her breakfast too.' He left the room and as Harriet sipped her tea she could hear him talking to their cat downstairs.

Harriet arrived at the police station at eight o'clock. She was eager to hear how things had gone yesterday afternoon and was pleased to see that Inspector Cassells was already in the Incident Room with Jack.

'Good morning, Earl, Jack,' she said as she came into the room.

'Good morning, ma'am,' they both replied.

'I hope you slept well and are feeling better this morning, ma'am,' said Earl.'

Harriet smiled. 'I slept like a baby,' she said, 'and I hope Charlie managed to do the same.'

'You certainly look better than you did yesterday,' said Earl, 'we were all quite concerned about you and DCI Marlow.'

Charlie came into the room at that moment. 'Did I hear my name mentioned?' he asked.

'I was just saying how worried we were about you and the superintendent yesterday,' said Earl, 'seeing how tired you both were.'

'We're survivors,' said Charlie with a grin. 'How did the post-mortem go?'

'It was interesting,' replied Earl, 'Duncan held up very well and Doctor Boston removed the bullets from the deceased and they have gone to Forensics. We discovered that Mrs Blackwell had several old injuries on her body which Doctor Boston thought was abuse.'

'Well knowing what a bully her husband was, I don't suppose we're surprised,' said Charlie.

'Sophie, his secretary, told us she thought he hit her,' said Harriet, 'and I should think this confirms it.'

'I got your message about Ann Peters,' said Earl, 'and Jack and I put out warnings to all ports and airports asking them to check in case she tried to leave the country.'

'And Eurostar,' added Jack.

'Anything?' asked Charlie.

'Nothing so far.'

'How did Mrs Hemmingway take the news of the death of her sister?' asked Harriet.

'Surprisingly very calmly,' replied Earl, 'Sally said she had almost expected it.'

'I presume she'll let us know when the funeral is?'

'Yes, she told Sally she would organise it straight away.'

'Good,' said Harriet, 'we'll get briefing over, and then decide what to do next.'

Officers began arriving and Harriet and Charlie went to the front of the room. Harriet began by telling them about Ursula's murder and that they had brought back her laptop and various letters and documents found at her house. 'The laptop is with Doctor Chong,' she said, 'and we will await his report on that. Inspector Cassells and Duncan attended her post-mortem, so I'll let them advice you on that.'

Earl stood up and told them about the bruises Doctor Boston had discovered on Ursula and the fact that she thought it had been abuse. 'The bullets were removed and have gone to Forensics,' he added.

'I saw the bullets,' said Duncan, 'and I'm pretty sure they're the same as the ones that killed George Blackwell and Freddie Fingers, they were definitely nine millimetres.'

'Forensics are going to rush things through for us,' said Earl, 'and we should have the results back by the end of the day.'

'Today we must visit the other rental properties,' said Charlie, 'all appear to be British and we don't think they hold any problems, however you wear flak jackets and always go in twos.'

'Anything suspicious, you back off and call in for back-up,' said Harriet, 'and, Duncan you have permission to go armed but please don't make it known to the public.'

'Right, ma'am my weapon won't be on view.'

'Good luck everyone,' said Charlie, 'see you back here later.'

Officers left the Incident Room and Harriet and Charlie went to Harriet's office. On her desk was an assortment of newspapers and picking up the local one she winced as she saw the photograph of herself and Charlie on the front page. They were walking down the steps at the front of Copper Beeches and the headline read: WIFE OF MURDERED BUSINESSMAN SLAIN IN OWN HOME. The article went onto say that armed police were called to the Blackwell house late Wednesday night to discover the murdered body of Ursula Blackwell who had been shot.

'Blasted reporters,' said Charlie, 'we know they listen in to the police wavelength and it doesn't seem that we can do anything about it.'

'It is an offense if they're caught of course,' said Harriet, 'but on the other hand I suppose they have a job to do.'

'It's that obnoxious Beefy Cavendish that I can't stomach,' growled Charlie, 'It's not just a story he wants but he does his best to knock us down.'

'He doesn't have a great deal to say about Ursula's murder,' said Harriet reading he article, 'but hints that we think she was killed by the same person who killed her husband.'

'Well he got that bit right.'

Don Underwood too read the article on the murder of Ursula. His stomach churned, and he felt quite sick. They'd had some good times together but on reflection he had been right to distance himself from her and her activities. He was a car dealer, albeit in stolen vehicles, but murder, oh no, he drew a line at killing, and thank goodness for that if now Ursula herself had been killed. He folded the newspaper, finished his coffee and put on his coat. He would put the murder of Ursula out of his mind however sorry he felt for her, he would go to the yard and keep himself busy.

A knock on the door announced the arrival of Doctor Chong who hurried into the room carrying Ursula's laptop. 'Good news,' he said eagerly, 'Mrs Blackwell's laptop has the Cerberus website on it and it has been used recently, and not only that, but she recently withdrew ten thousand pounds from her bank account.' He placed the laptop on the desk in front of Harriet and Charlie and ran his fingers over the keys. The website CERBERUS came up. 'I still haven't managed to open it, I'm afraid,' he said.

'So, we just need a password, do we?' asked Charlie.

'Yes, I'm still working on it.'

Harriet looked at the screen in front of them. 'Try Hercules,' she said.

Chong typed in HERCULES and he and Charlie gasped as the website opened. In the middle of the screen appeared. Cd. 4

'Well done, ma'am,' said Chong, how did you know that?'

'Greek Mythology,' replied Harriet.

Charlie grinned. 'So, your three-headed dog has leaped to the fore,' he said.

'Cerberus, the twelfth and final labour that Hercules had to perform,' said Harriet. She opened he desk drawer and took out the piece of paper that had been found at Freddie Finger's house. She read out what was written there. 'CERBERUS -12-Cd 2. So, Cerberus is the website,' she said, '12 indicates the labours of Hercules which gives us the password and the next thing is Cd, whatever that means.'

'Code, do you think,' suggested Henry Chong.

'So, we now need a code to put in,' said Charlie, 'Code 4 by the look of things, on the original paper the code was 2.'

Harriet wrinkled her nose. 'So, the code changes. I have a feeling I'm not seeing what I should be seeing,' She suddenly smacked her hand against her forehead. 'The book, Charlie,' she said.

'What book?'

'The book in Ursula's sitting room, I picked it up, it was on the sofa and she had most probably been reading it.'

'What was it, Harry,' stressed Charlie.

'A book on Greek Mythology, not the sort of book Ursula Blackwell would read surely. Send someone over to Copper Beeches straight away, Charlie and ask them to pick it up.'

Charlie jumped to his feet. 'Everyone is out,' he said, 'so it will have to be Jack and we do have the keys to the house here.'

Harriet produced the keys to Ursula's house and handed them to Charlie. 'Ask Jack to go now,' she said, 'I really think we may have cracked this.'

Clutching the keys Charlie hurried to the Incident Room.

'I'll be in my lab should you need me,' said Doctor Chong, 'but do let me know how this develops, superintendent,' he said.

'I will, Henry and thank you for your help.'

Duncan accompanied the CID Team in the van as they set off to do the checking on the other houses that had been rented in the last six months. Although all the names on the leases were British they had been warned to be on the alert. All were wearing bullet- proof jackets and in a pocket of his anorak, Duncan was carrying a Glock 17. Luke and Ben sat together at the back of the van feeling very excited. This is what police work was all about and they couldn't wait to see some action. The driver pulled up outside the first house and Inspector Cassells instructed Ben and Luke to wait outside the house while he approached the door with Duncan. Sally and Narinder were to stay in the van for the time being. Narinder muttered her dissent but Earl told her it was nothing to do with them being female but as the second house they were to visit was rented by two females he thought it prudent that they accompany him on that visit.

Earl knocked on the door which was opened by a heavily pregnant woman in her late twenties. He held up his warrant card assuring her that there was nothing wrong and they were making general inquiries.

'You are Mrs Bottrell?' he asked.

'I am.'

'We're looking for someone who has recently rented a property in this area,' he said, 'so we are visiting everyone who moved here in the last six months.'

The woman nodded. 'Yes, we came here six months ago.'

'Where were you before that?' asked Earl.

'Corby.'

'Could we have your last address please.'

'Of course,' replied the woman and reeled off the address.

'Thank you,' said Earl, 'there's nothing to worry about, sorry to have troubled you.'

They returned to the van and Ben and Luke joined them. Earl gave the driver the next address and the van moved off. As they headed for the next house Ben spoke to Luke.

'If we get off duty at a reasonable time tonight, would you come with me to look at a flat?'

'Course I will. Where is it?'

'Back Lane, Torreston.'

'Very nice,' replied Luke, 'isn't it going to be expensive there?'

'It's a private letting,' said Ben, 'I saw it advertised in the paper and gave the owner a ring. She's a widow lady who has divided her house into two flats and she lives in one of them.'

'Sounds okay,' agreed Luke, 'yep, we'll go after work all being well.'

Sally and Narinder accompanied Inspector Cassells to the next house. Duncan was close behind with his hand in his pocket touching his gun. There was no one at home and Sally knocked at the house next door. The elderly lady who lived there told her that both women worked, and she thought one was a hairdresser at Goldilocks in the High Street but was unsure where the other one worked. Sally thanked her and reported back to Inspector Cassells.

'We'll call at the hairdressers,' he said, 'but I have a feeling that these two have nothing to do with our investigation.'

Sally was inclined to agree but knew that all these people had to be checked. Officers returned to the van and set off for the High

Street.

A telephone call from West Midlands Police was put through to Harriet's office and the news she received was enlightening. She called Charlie who appeared within minutes.

'Charlie,' she said as he came into the room. 'We've information from West Midlands giving us the name of the Russian woman they think is the hitman's side-kick.'

'Great, who is she?'

'Anna Petrov, and how much closer to Ann Peters can that be.'

'It looks as if we have the right woman in our sights then,' said Charlie. 'I don't suppose they have the name of the actual hitman?'

'They're still working on it.'

'Not that having his real name will help us catch him,' said Charlie, 'no one knows what he looks like.'

'That's true. At least we do know what Anna Petrov looks like and with her description being circulated we stand a chance of catching her.'

'She must have a passport,' said Charlie, 'I'll get onto Boarder Control and see when she came into the country.'

'She will have had a phoney passport in the name of Ann Peters,' said Harriet, 'but check on both names just in case.'

'I'll do that straight away as Jack isn't back from Copper Beeches yet.' He left and hurried to the Incident Room.

Chapter Fifty-Three

Jack arrived at Copper Beeches and ducking under the blue police tape he unlocked the front door and entered the house. The building felt strangely cold and eerie and Jack shivered. He went to the front room and looked around. He saw the book on the sofa and picked it up. Yes, Greek Mythology, this was the book the boss said he would find here. Jack put the book in his pocket, not sure of its significance and oddly uneasy he hurried from the room and out of the front door locking it behind him. The sergeant was a solid, confident officer, who rarely lost his cool, but on this occasion, he felt anxious and ill at ease. He wondered if it was all the talk of this Russian being a killer and they should all wear bullet-proof jackets when attending an incident. He wasn't wearing such a jacket, having been asked to collect the book as quickly as possible and leaving the station in a rush. He reached the car and looked around. He had a weird feeling he was not alone and unlocking the car door he jumped inside and started the engine driving down the drive as fast as he dared go.

Don Underwood, crouching in the bushes, watched the portly sergeant drive away and breathed a sigh of relief. He could do without being seen here, but he had been drawn to Copper Beeches having read of the murder of Ursula. He was saddened by her death, but his business mind soon overtook these feelings. One of his workers had driven him to Copper Beeches and dropped him off and now he knew what he was looking for. Ursula's red Audi! It was worth a bob or two and having obtained it for her felt he had the right to take it back. He found the car at the side of the house and taking his spare set of keys from his pocket he unlocked it and climbed inside.

Earl and the team completed their visits to the rest of the people renting properties in the area convinced that none of them had anything to do with the shootings they were investigating.

Those they had spoken to this morning would still be checked on the system on their return to the police station, but Earl was confident that this would only be a formality.

Jack arrived back at headquarters carrying the book which he took immediately to Harriet's office.

'Now explain,' said Charlie picking up the book on Greek mythology.

Jack was intrigued and waited to hear what the boss had to say.

'If Cerberus is the website,' she said, 'and twelve being the number of labours put to Hercules, hence Hercules is the password to open the site, then my thinking is that the codes are the other labours of Hercules.'

'So, in the case of Blackwell's killing the code was two,' said Charlie.

'Yes,' replied Harriet flicking through the pages of the book. 'Here we are, the twelve labours of Hercules, and the page is well thumbed.' She opened out the book at the page mentioned and pointed to the list labelled: The Labours of Hercules.'

'Good Lord,' exclaimed Jack.

Charlie ran his eyes down the page. 'The second labour was Lernaean Hydra, whatever that means,' he said.

'This was a nine-headed creature that Hera, the Queen of the Gods, raised simply to slay Hercules,' said Harriet, with a slight smile. 'But Hercules killed the creature by firing flaming arrows into the Hydra's lair.'

Charlie grinned. 'I forgot this was a pet subject of yours,' he said, 'so what do you think the significance of this is?'

'I think you type in the name that fits the code matching the labour of Hercules and the site opens up,' replied Harriet.

Jack was standing watching in amazement. This was over the top of his head, but even so he was fascinated.

'Okay,' said Charlie, 'so the code from Ursula's lap-top is four. Which labour is that?' Harriet checked with the book. 'The Erymanthian Boar,' she said.

'A wild pig?' asked Jack.

'Well, yes, sort of,' answered Harriet. 'Hercules was told to capture the vicious beast and he was advised to drive it into the thick snow which he did and was able to catch it. He bound the boar and brought it back as he had been instructed.'

'So, do we try and open this site by typing in Erymanthian Boar?' asked Charlie.

'Why not,' agreed Harriet.

Charlie opened up the website again and on reaching the code, he put in Eerymanthian Boar. Nothing. There was no response at all.

'Damn,' said Charlie, 'I really thought we had it.'

'Don't give up,' said Harriet, 'supposing the code changes regularly, we know it was two when we first saw the clues, and now according to Ursula's laptop it's four, so let's try five.'

'Which is?' asked Charlie.

Harriet consulted the book again. 'Augean Stables,' she announced.

'For, heaven's sake,' muttered Charlie, 'what in the world is that?'

'Hercules was instructed to clean the stables of King Augeas,' said Harriet. 'The task was meant to humiliate him and was near impossible as over a thousand animals lived there and the stables had not been cleaned for over thirty years. I won't go on,' she added, 'as it's long story, but as you will guess Hercules was successful.'

'I'm beginning to enjoy these stories,' said Jack, 'I never did any Greek Mythology in my younger days.'

Charlie was already typing in the labour of Hercules that was number five. He pressed "enter" and there was a gasp from Jack as a number appeared on the screen.

'That's a mobile number,' said Harriet. She picked up the original paper found at Freddies and held it for Charlie and Jack to see. 'As on this paper the password and code is followed by the mobile number, written in a different hand, so probably added by whoever opened the site.'

'That person being Ursula Blackwell we now think,' said Charlie.

'It's beginning to look that way,' agreed Harriet, 'especially as we now know she withdrew ten thousand pounds just before the attempt on Rosalind's life.'

'So, she had her husband killed and nearly did the same to her step-daughter,' said Jack.

'I think so,' replied Harriet, 'she wanted to be with Don Underwood and didn't want Rosalind to get her hands on the money or have her sell Copper Beeches and lose the profit.'

'Nice woman,' said Charlie, 'so why was she killed.'

'I think the hitman began to think she was a liability with Freddie finding the paper with the code clues on it. He was in the newspaper as having robbed Copper Beeches and I wonder if Ursula let it slip that the paper was taken as well.'

'Don't suppose we'll ever know that,' said Charlie.

'Well it appears she got her comeuppance,' said Harriet.

'Back to the codes,' said Charlie. 'That original mobile number was discontinued according to Henry Chong, it's all very cloak and dagger.'

'Something we're not used to here in Torreston,' said Harriet.

'Then, this mobile number changes as the codes do?' asked Charlie.

'Absolutely, they cover their backs very efficiently.'

'Crikey,' muttered Jack, 'Is this really happening in Torreston.'

'Do I ring this number?' asked Charlie.

'Not yet,' replied Harriet, 'we'll get Henry to set up the means of tracking the call and put it in operation as soon as that's done.'

'This is quite amazing' said Jack, 'it feels like a spy thriller.'

'In a way I suppose it is,' agreed Harriet, 'but all pretty nasty and something we can do without on our patch.'

'I'll get this down to Henry,' said Charlie, 'and get the ball rolling for the call we make to be traced.' He jotted the number down in his notebook and made for the door.

'We'll need to have you primed and ready to speak to whoever answers the phone tomorrow,' said Harriet. 'As soon as you've spoken to Henry come back and we'll work something out.'

'I'll be fifteen minutes,' said Charlie, and left the room with Jack on his heels.

Harriet sat at her desk and thought about how they should proceed the following day. They had to be careful so as not to alert the killers and to do this they needed to be well prepared. She picked up the telephone and called Phillip Hewitt asking him and his SOCO team to help out tomorrow. She told him what she wanted him and his men to do and satisfied that the sergeant would organise things she thanked him and hung up. Charlie returned, and Harriet told him what she had done.

'That's a great ides' he replied, 'and knowing Hewitt the plan will be more than perfect.'

'Let's hope so. Now, Charlie you will have to think of a fictitious name of the person you want killed as you will surely be asked for it. And and if you are asked for a workplace you need to be ready to answer without hesitating, after all Blackwell was killed at his place of work. As we have just organised with Phillip, you state you work on the canal in Wharf Lane. Your company deals in pallets and containers so see that you know something about that business, just in case.'

'Oh, great thanks, Harry,' said Charlie, 'do you expect me to sleep tonight worrying about this? It'll be like swotting for an exam.'

Harriet smiled. 'Comes with the job, Charlie and you're more than capable of carrying this off. Phillip is organising a delivery of pallets to Wharf Lane in case whoever it is answering these mobile calls, decides to check you out. We have to be prepared.'

Charlie pulled a face. 'I'll be a nervous wreck. Is there anything else I need to know?'

'We'll sort everything else out tomorrow at briefing when we discuss the operation with the team.'

'Do we grab this guy if he turns up?'

'Absolutely not. It's the hitman we want, and I think all these preliminaries, like collecting the money and so on, are done by the organisation.'

'Part of which was Anna Petrov,' said Charlie, 'and that's what Mrs Blackwell was doing the day she visited Pegasus House, delivering the ten thousand to have Rosalind De Luca killed.'

'Exactly. And that's the one thing that worries me,' said Harriet. 'Has Anna informed anyone that she's done a runner?'

'Probably not, they wouldn't look too kindly on her doing that, so she has most probably taken it upon herself to hide away.'

'We'll soon know tomorrow,' said Harriet, 'but if our plan goes pear-shaped, heaven knows how we'll track down the hit-man.'

'I'll have a word with Jack and see about organising some more cover on Wharf Lane,' said Charlie. 'I only hope this guy does decide to check us out or we've done a lot of work for nothing.'

'Rather that than not be prepared at all,' replied Harriet. 'What name are you going to use for the victim tomorrow?'

'Fred Biggins,' replied Charlie with a grin.

Charlie headed off to speak to Jack and Harriet continued to ponder over the plan for the following day.

Earl returned and put the names and addresses of the people they had just visited on Jack's desk. 'I won't tread on the sergeant's toes,' he said with a smile, 'I know he likes doing these checks and he's very thorough, so I won't attempt to have a go myself.'

'More than your life's worth, sir,' said Narinder.

Jack bustled into the Incident Room at that moment and saw the paper on his desk. 'I take it these are the last tenants you've just visited?' he said. 'Another job for me I see.'

'If that's all right, Jack,' said Earl.

'Of course, of course, I'll get on to it straight away.' He fired up his computer and began typing.

'It's well after lunch time,' said Earl to the team, 'so do go and have your lunch and I'll go and see the boss and tell her how we got on.'

'I'll have to go and stash my gun away,' said Duncan, 'but I'll be as quick as I can.'

Charlie came into the room and asked Jack if they could talk. As Jack nodded Charlie pulled up a chair and sat down beside him.

Earl reported to Harriet's office and explained what had happened and how he thought the people they had visited were all in the clear. 'We're playing safe though, ma'am,' he said, 'and Jack is tracking back on their previous addresses and where they work, but I really don't think they have anything to do with the shootings.'

'Thank you, Earl,' said Harriet, 'now as everyone has worked such long hours lately, without much of a break will you see they get off at a reasonable time today and ask them to be in by eight tomorrow. We've had a breakthrough in the coded message, which I will tell you about, and tomorrow we're going to try and track our Russian through a mobile number.' She went on to explain about the Greek mythology and the codes that they thought were being used to unlock a mobile phone number which in turn gave them access to the hit-man. Earl went back to the Incident Room and advised everyone that as soon as they had completed their notes and written everything up, they could go home. 'The superintendent would like you all here tomorrow at eight,' he said, 'she has some interesting news for you, news that hopefully might help us track down our hit-man.'

Charlie looked up. 'Fingers crossed on that,' he said, 'we have to wait for Doctor Chong to set up a tracking device and having just spoken to him he's going to make sure he has it ready for us by tomorrow morning.'

'Brilliant,' said Narinder, 'I'd really like to see what this Russian looks like. Has there been any news on Anna Petrov?'

'Not yet,' replied Jack, 'I should think she's doing her best to keep a low profile as by now she will know we're on to her.'

'So, won't the hit-man know we're onto him as well?' asked Sally.

'Not necessarily,' said Charlie, 'the two of them most probably have no contact with each other. The hit-man will be convinced he's safe and there's no way his cover can be blown; he'll think he's invincible. So, not a word to anyone about any of this,' he added, 'it would be a disaster if our plans leaked and the Russian was warned off. We want to catch him.'

'The boss want's us all in by eight tomorrow,' said Earl, 'so that we can be ready when Doctor Chong produces his tracking equipment.'

'Good,' said Charlie, 'I take it everyone knows?'

'Yes, sir,' replied Earl, 'they're just finishing off their notes before they leave.'

Chapter Fifty-Four

The CID tem was busily writing up their notes eager to have an early finish for once. Ben and Luke had agreed to meet up at the end of the day and visit the flat that Ben wanted to look at. Luke came across and asked Ben if he was ready and putting away his papers Ben jumped to his feet.

'Thanks, Luke,' he said, 'I can't wait to see this flat. I'm already getting quite excited about having a place of my own.'

'Have you told your parent's yet?'

'Er, no,' replied Ben, 'I thought I'd wait until I actually had a flat before I broke the news.'

Luke grinned. 'I know how you feel,' he said, 'it took me ages to pluck up the courage to tell my mum I was leaving home.'

'Perhaps it's a mother and son thing,' said Narinder hearing the two men talking. 'I had no problem telling my parents I was off, in fact I think they were happy to see the back of me.'

'I can't believe that, Narinder,' said Luke, 'I thought Asian parents wanted to hang onto their children.'

Narinder gave a wicked smile. 'Not all of them, and anyway I wasn't going to miss the chance of having a share in a real house.'

'That's the one in Wicken you bought with Sally, is it?' asked Ben.

'It is,' said Narinder, 'we have this fabulous cottage in a lovely village. You two ought to consider doing the same. It's certainly one way of getting on the housing ladder.'

'It's a thought,' agreed Luke.

'Well let's look at this flat,' said Ben, 'and that will be a start for me.' They left the Incident Room and Narinder went over to see if Sally was ready to leave.

With Ben driving his car the two men made for Back Lane. It was a secluded road lined with trees and with wide pavements. The houses wre mostly Victorian with neat gardens and shiny windows and paintwork. Ben pulled up outside number twelve which was one of the smaller residences.

'It's a jolly posh area,' said Luke, 'are you sure you can afford this, Ben?'

'The rent is no more than those terrace houses in the centre of Torreston,' replied Ben.

'I can't believe that, perhaps she made a mistake when she gave you the price.'

'We'll soon see, but I'll be very disappointed if I miss out on this, it looks great and would suit me down to the ground.'

They left the car and walked up the short drive to the house. The dark blue door looked newly painted as did the framework of the windows. Ben rang the bell and the door was opened by a small, thin woman who appeared to be in her late seventies. She smiled brightly at the two men and stuck out her hand.

'You must be Ben,' she said as Ben shook her hand. He introduced Luke and again the woman offered her hand which Luke took. 'I'm Agnes Wilmot,' she said inviting them into her house. Sitting in the front room Mrs Wilmot offered them tea which they both declined. 'If I could just see the flat,' said Ben eagerly.

'I am having to be a bit careful here,' said the woman, 'the present tenant doesn't leave for a few days but as his car is not on the drive I know he is out, so I think it will be in order for me to give you a quick look round.'

'Great,' said Ben rising to his feet desperate to see the apartment.

Mrs Wilmot told them to follow her. 'It's the upstairs flat,' she said, 'I suffer from arthritis in both hips so keep the downstairs flat for myself. My husband died two years ago and rather than sell the house I had it converted into two flats, one for me and the other to bring in some money.' She climbed the stairs slowly holding onto the handrail. At the top there was a small square landing where a door had been fitted. She took a key and unlocked the door. Ben and Luke followed her inside. The flat was immaculate. The large sitting room they were in was as clean as a new pin and void of any clutter. There was nothing on the worksurfaces other than a book on the coffee table. The present tenant was presumably packed ready to leave in a couple of days.

'He's a wonderful tenant,' said Mrs Wilmot, 'no trouble at all very polite and gentlemanly. Quite honestly, I hardly know he's up here he's so quiet. I think he's from Birmingham, he has that accent, that sometimes I have difficulty understanding.' She showed them two bedrooms, one quite large and the other slightly smaller, a bathroom and kitchen. Ben's eyes were getting wider and wider as he looked around.

'It's terrific,' he said, 'could I just check the rent you are asking.'

Mrs Wilmot quoted the same figure she had given Ben over the telephone and he didn't dare look at Luke he was so excited. 'I'd really like to have it, Mrs Wilmot,' he said.

'You told me you are a policeman,' said the woman, 'I think that would be really nice to have you in the house. As you can see I don't ask for exorbitant rents, but I do like to have excellent tenants and I think you fit the bill.' She left the flat with the two men following and downstairs she asked for Ben's details. 'I will need a reference,' she told Ben, 'your superior officer would be ideal.'

'That's no problem,' said Ben hardly able to contain himself, 'I'll get it to you straight away. When will I be able to move in?'

'Mr Harris is leaving in a couple of days, and then I shall have the flat cleaned, so you can move in on Monday if you like. You can sort out the standing order for your rent with your bank and I'll give you my bank details so that you can get that up and running. I do ask for a month's rent in advance.' Mrs Wilmot took a notebook from the sideboard and a folder which she opened before writing her bank details down for Ben. She handed him the paper 'No problem,' said Ben taking the paper. 'And thank you, Mrs Wilmot, I promise to be a good tenant.'

The woman smiled. She felt quite happy that she would be having a policeman in her house; a bit of extra security.

Harriet arrived at the police station early Friday morning surprised to discover Constable Ben Granger waiting for her in the Incident Room.

'Anything wrong, Ben?' she asked.

'No, ma'am, but knowing how busy we're going to be this morning I thought I ought to catch you before everyone arrived.'

'So how can I help you?'

Ben explained about the flat he was going to rent and that he needed a reference. 'Mrs Wilmot said my superior officer would be fine,' he said, 'she just needs to know that I am who say I am and that I'm trustworthy.' He smiled sheepishly.

'I can vouch for both of those, Ben,' replied Harriet, 'when do you need this reference.'

'I don't think she'll chase me for it, but in the next two days would be brilliant.'

'Leave it with me,' said Harriet.

Doctor Chong arrived at that moment carrying a box in his arms. 'All set, ma'am,' he said placing his equipment on the table.

'Can you put it on speaker, Henry?' asked Harriet, 'so that all the team can hear what's being said.'

'Absolutely. When do you want to start?'

'As soon as everyone is here. We're not sure what time this phone number will respond,' said Harriet, 'but being a mobile number, time probably doesn't matter.'

Officers began arriving, all eager to hear what it was the superintendent had to tell them. By ten to eight the team was complete, and Harriet and Charlie moved to the front of the room. Harriet told them she had received the result of the ballistic test on the bullets that killed Ursula and it was no surprise that they matched the weapon that had killed George Blackwell and Freddie Fingers. She then went on to explained about the breaking of the code and how this code changed to give a new mobile number. 'The Labours of Hercules, is the secret,' she said, 'sorry, Luke that it wasn't your warship but thankfully we have managed to get into the website that we think is the way to contact the hit-man.'

'Are you saying that people can contact a hit-man on line?' asked Sally.

'Only if they are in the know,' replied Harriet.

'So, did Mrs Blackwell have her husband killed?' asked Duncan.

'She did,' answered Charlie, 'we have her laptop and all the evidence is there.'

'But how did she know about the hitman?' asked Narinder. 'If I wanted to knock someone off I wouldn't have the faintest idea how to go about it.'

Ripples of laughter ran around the room and Harriet held up a hand. 'We now believe the link to all this was the receptionist at Pegasus House, Ann Peters,' she said.

'Her real name,' continued Charlie, 'is Anna Petrov, a Russian who has only been in the country six months, the time line we have on this business.'

'We were told by Blackwell's secretary that once when Ursula Blackwell had been rowing with her husband, he struck her and was later comforted by Ann Peters in reception,' explained Harriet. 'We can only presume that the woman we now know to be Anna Petrov gave her the idea of having him killed and gave her the website name Cerberus and how to access it. We can only presume that she was given a cut from the payments for these killings.'

'Anna Petrov has now vanished,' said Charlie, 'and we have an alert out for her at all ports and airports.'

'But we still need to catch the killer,' said Harriet, 'and that's what we are going to attempt to do this morning. We have the latest mobile number, which we found using the fifth Labour of Hercules, so this is the number we are going to call now. Doctor Chong will be tracking the call so that hopefully we can trace the mobile to where the headquarters of this gang is.'

'I'm ready when you are,' said Henry Chong.

'We need absolute silence in here,' said Harriet, 'we can't afford to let this chance slip through our fingers.' She nodded to Chong who put on his earphones and nodded in return.

Charlie picked up the pay-as-you-go mobile Harriet had given him and dialled the number they had taken from the website yesterday. Officers waited almost holding their breath. A loud droning noise came over the loudspeaker and everyone waited.

'It's a dead number,' said Henry taking off his headphones. Officers groaned, and Charlie looked at Harriet in dismay.

'The code must have changed again,' she said, 'where's the book; we need to put in the next code.'

Jack picked up the book from the desk and handed it to Harriet. She flicked through the pages and found the chapter on the Labours of Hercules. 'The last one used was the fifth labour so let's try the sixth,' she said.

'Which is?' asked Charlie with his laptop open and ready. The Slaying of the Stymphalian Birds,' read out Harriet.

'Crikey,' muttered Luke, 'what's that when it's at home?'

'We haven't time to go into the full story now,' replied Harriet, 'but the Stymphalian birds were man-eating creatures with beaks of bronze and sharp metallic feathers.'

'Deadly in other words,' said Charlie. 'like the other creatures and I reckon that's why these killers picked the subject they did. It's all to do with killing. What do I type in, ma'am?' he asked turning to Harriet.

'Just Stymphalian Birds, I should think,' she replied.

'And how's that spelt?'

Harriet pushed the book in front of Charlie and everyone waited as he typed in the words and pressed enter. A number came up on the screen and people gasped. It had worked.

Charlie wrote the number on a piece of paper. 'Ready, Henry?' he asked. Henry Chong nodded and put on his earphones.

Charlie dialled the new number and over the loudspeaker came the familiar sound of a number ringing. Harriet let out her breath feeling relieved. Suddenly the call was answered by a thick, deep voice with a strong foreign accent.

'Solid Security, how can I help?'

Charlie felt his heart racing and he caught the eye of Henry Chong who wound a hand round indicating he wanted him to keep the man on the line talking.

'I need some help,' said Charlie feeling his throat drying up.

'What kind of help?' asked the voice.

'I need someone eliminating.'

'Name and address of this person.'

'Fred Biggins,' said Charlie desperately hoping that Henry wouldn't take long tracing the call.

'Workplace or address?'

Charlie was panicking remembering what he and Harriet had discussed yesterday. He wasn't sure he had sufficient information to fob off the man on the line. He looked across at Henry and widened his eyes. Henry wound his hand round again. 'He works at the woodsheds down by the canal on Wharf Lane,' said Charlie confidently.

'Ten thousand pounds. I have your number and you will be contacted as to where the money, cash only, has to be delivered.' The line went dead.

Chapter Fifty-Five

There was silence in the room and then everyone began talking at once and Harriet asked for quiet. 'Any luck, Henry?' she asked.

'Some,' replied Doctor Chong, 'I haven't pin-pointed the exact place but it's north of Market Harborough.'

'The Innovation Centre I bet,' called out Sally. 'We always thought there was a connection with that place.'

'We can't be positive that's where the call came from,' said Charlie, 'but I reckon Sally could be on to something.'

'This person you spoke to,' said Harriet to Charlie, 'was he foreign?'

'Certainly was,' replied Charlie, 'I've never been so nervous in all my life.'

'You were fine' said Harriet. 'Now I should think this organisation will check the victim out before he does anything, which means we could be in trouble if we are not fully organised at Wharf Lane.'

'There are definitely sheds there,' replied Charlie, 'and still in reasonable order, I checked them on my way home last night. No one has worked there for years and the place does look a bit run down.'

'We're putting that right' said Harriet. 'Nothing's going to happen to Fred Biggins,' she smiled as she said the name, 'until the money has been handed over so if the place is going to be looked at by someone in advance of the killing, then we need to put workmen in the sheds. I have spoken to Sergeant Hewitt and he and the SOCO team are already down there sorting things out.'

'When do you think they may take a look at the sheds, ma'am?' asked Jack?

'Today, I should think.'

'Right,' said Jack, 'I've organised the trucks and lorries DCI Marlow asked for and I'll see that they go there straight away.'

'Sergeant Hewitt has the pallet company standing by as well,' said Harriet, 'I'll give him a ring and tell him we're on. We need CID there, and someone has to be Fred Biggins.'

'That'll be me,' said Charlie, 'I'll go and speak to Phillip and get myself some overalls. We need to get over there as soon as possible to sort the place out and make it look like a working company.'

'Before you go,' said Harriet, 'you may need these, courtesy of the Tech department.' She handed Charlie a small pack of business cards. 'Just in case our visiting crook asks for something positive,' she added.

Charlie took the cards and smiled when he saw what was printed on them. Fred Biggins, Pallets and Boxes Supplier. The Sheds Wharf Lane. 'That was quick,' he said.

'When you decided on the name last night,' said Harriet, 'I gave the department a ring and they worked late to produce those. Not only that, but if Googled, Fred Biggins turns up on line as well, all very convincing, don't you think?'

'Brilliant,' replied Charlie dourly.

'And everyone wears bullet-proof vests,' said Harriet casting her eyes around the room.

'The surveillance van is being set up, as you asked, ma'am,' said Earl Cassells, 'do you want me in that?'

'No, you and Duncan can be part of the working team, keep your eyes and ears open and Duncan has permission to be armed. A couple of the armed-response team will be hidden away in the sheds as well but be careful.'

'I'd better go and collect my weapon, then, 'said Duncan and Harriet nodded. 'Wait for Inspector Cassells at the front of the building,' she said. 'I will be in the surveillance van with some of you and we will need the long-lens camera; Sally you can be in charge of that.'

'Yes, ma'am I'll go and get it.'

There was an air of excitement in the room and as the officers assigned to the operation left, Jack picked up the phone and began dialling. He was to remain at the station at the end of a telephone in case needed.

The canal sheds in Wharf Lane that had been unused for so long had now come alive. Twenty men in overalls were gathered there and several vans and lorries were parked; one open-backed lorry fully laden with wooden pallets. It was a cold November morning and officers clapped their hands together to keep them warm. Charlie gathered them together and explained what needed to be done. 'Get some of the pallets off the lorry and put them in the first shed,' he said.

'Once that is done we wait. As soon as we see a vehicle coming down the lane you start working like bees, by collecting the pallets and loading them back on the lorry. We have to look like a proper company.'

'If this guy does turn up,' said one of the officers, 'is he likely to be armed?'

'We doubt it,' replied Charlie, 'but we're playing safe that's why we're all wearing flak-jackets. There are two armed officers in the first shed where you will be working, and Duncan here is also armed.'

The man nodded looking satisfied as Duncan pulled back his jacked disclosing his Glock tucked in his belt. Charlie turned to Phillip Hewitt. 'I'll give the signal when I want your men to act like pallet company workers,' he said, 'so you stay close to me.'

'Yes, sir.'

In the dark grey Transit van parked at the end of the lane but close to the sheds Harriet was watching proceedings through binoculars. Narinder was doing the same and Sally was poised with the camera, two uniformed officers were with them. All were wearing bullet-proof jackets as were the officers acting as workmen. The minutes ticked by and people were becoming restless; it was already ten thirty. Suddenly the engine of a nearing vehicle was heard, and Charlie nodded to Sergeant Hewitt who hurried over to his men and told them to start work. They began carrying the pallets from the shed and loading them back onto the lorry. A car came down the lane and parked close to the surveillance van. Inside the van Sally took the first photograph of the man who stepped from the car.

'Oh, no!' she cried, 'It's Beefy Cavendish.'

Harriet's heart sank as she saw the scruffy reported making his way towards Charlie and the officers acting as workmen. Was he going to give their operation away? Charlie saw who it was approaching and called to Phillip Hewitt to stop the men working. He then went up to Beefy and asked him what on earth he was doing.

'I knew you lot were up to something,' said Beefy smirking, 'I keep an ear to the ground and an eye on you and when I saw all this activity I guessed something was afoot.'

Charlie's pulse was racing. 'For God's sake, Beefy,' hissed Charlie, 'this is a vital under-cover operation, were hoping to catch a killer and if you mess it up I can promise you, you will spend a very long time behind bars.'

'Then you should have told me.'

'I'm telling you now.' Charlie was fuming, and he couldn't hide his anger. 'We're expecting a dangerous criminal to arrive at any time now and we are supposed to belong to a pallet company. If this guy suspects for one moment we are the police, then it's all over and you will be to blame.'

'No need to be hateful,' grumbled Beefy, 'I didn't know.'

'Just go,' said Charlie.

'All right, but if I keep quiet about this, can I have an exclusive?'

At that moment another car was heard approaching and quickly Phillip Hewitt hurried over to his men and instructed them to begin work again. Charlie thrust one of his business cards at Beefy. 'If you want to live, Beefy, be very careful what you say if the guy arriving speaks to you.' He pointed to the card. 'Fred Biggins,' he hissed, 'that's me and I sell wooden pallets and boxes, now get out of here.'

'How about that exclusive?' insisted Beefy.

'All right, all right so long as you don't blow it.'

Beefy grinned and began walking back to his car. The BMW that had come down the lane stopped in front of the reporter and a stocky man in his forties climbed out and came over to him. Charlie felt sick as he watched and in the van Harriet and the others held their breath. For all his arrogance and nastiness, Beefy was no fool and he looked up as the man spoke to him. Harriet watched, and Sally continued clicking away with the camera. She had some clear photographs of the man they were interested in. The two men outside the van were very close and they could be heard talking.

'You deal with this company?' the man asked Beefy.

'Yeah,' answered the reporter, 'I've just ordered a new load of pallets from Biggins. He always gives me a good deal, I wouldn't go anywhere else.'

'Which one's Biggins?'

'The tall guy in the blue baseball cap,' said Beefy. 'Good luck.' He went to his car got in and drove away.

Harriet let out her breath hardly able to believe they had got away with it. Narinder suppressed a giggle and muttered, 'well done Beefy'.

The driver of the BMW went over to Charlie. 'Fred Biggins?' he asked in a deep throaty voice.

'Yes,' replied Charlie, 'can I help you?'

'I need some wooden pallets and I'm just checking on prices and delivery times before I make an order.'

'No problem,' said Charlie his stomach churning, 'we do next day delivery and our prices are very competitive.' He handed the man a paper with the prices on it but with the heading changed to show Fred Biggins at the top and not Torreston Pallet Company.

'Will you be here all day?' asked the man.

'Fraid not,' replied Charlie quickly, 'we're here from eight thirty until one every day.'

'I'll be in touch,' said the man.

Charlie handed him a card which the man put in his pocket. He nodded and returned to his car. As the BMW disappeared down the lane Charlie held up his hand and the officers stopped work.

'We'd almost run out of pallets in the shed,' said Phillip Hewitt, 'I was beginning to wonder what we did next.'

Charlie sat down on a pile of logs. 'Phew, that was pretty scary I can tell you,' he said, 'I thought Beefy was going to blow it, but it seems he turned up trumps.'

Harriet came up to them. 'Beefy probably convinced the man you were genuine,' she said with a smile, 'he said he always bought his pallets from you because you gave him such a good price.'

Charlie smiled weakly still feeling shaky. 'I promised him I'd have him in prison if he mucked up the operation,' he said, 'but I did also have to promise him an exclusive if it all went well.'

'We'll cope with that,' said Harriet, 'and well done everyone. Thank you, Phillip,' she said to Sergeant Hewitt, 'can we leave you to have the pallet lorry returned to its rightful owners.'

'Yes, ma'am I'll see to the clearing of the site, and do you want the same again tomorrow in case this guy reappears?'

'We're not going to let it get that far, Phillip,' said Harriet, 'we can't afford, Fred Biggins getting shot.' She smiled, and Phillip did his best to smile in return. He was always rather in awe of the superintendent and often found himself tongue tied in her presence. He made his way back to his men happy that his team had helped in a successful operation.

Charlie got to his feet and told Harriet he would see that everyone was thanked and told they could return to their various units. 'I'll meet you back at HQ,' he said, 'I'm interested in the photos Sally took.'

In the Incident Room later all the talk was about the operation at Wharf Lane. Charlie was now calm although he hoped he wouldn't have to meet the stranger from the BMW again. 'He actually made me feel quite nervous,' he said to Harriet, 'his eyes seemed to go right through me.

'I take it he was foreign,' said Harriet.

'Definitely,' said Charlie, 'and at a guess I'd say Russian.'

'Sally is sorting out the photographs,' said Harriet, 'and she is going to put them up on the screen as quickly as possible.'

'Good,' said Charlie, 'we can then send them to other forces and see who can identify this guy.'

'We've given Jack the registration number of the BMW,' said Narinder coming over, 'and he'll let us know the name of the owner in a few minutes.'

'All done,' called Jack from behind his computer, 'the BMW is a hire car and I have the rental company name.'

'Things are coming together at last,' said Charlie, 'If necessary I'll visit the car company when we've looked at these photos from Wharf Lane.'

'Good,' replied Harriet, 'and then we need a plan to catch our Russian before tomorrow.'

Chapter Fifty-Six

Sally dashed into the Incident Room eager to show the photographs. The screen on the wall came alive and the first of the pictures appeared.

'Great one of Beefy Cavendish, Sally,' called Luke.

'And the car number plate,' said Ben.

'An even better one of our Russian,' said Charlie.

Narinder let out a squeal as the photograph of the man in the BMW appeared on the screen. 'We know him, Sally, we've met this guy, where was it?'

Sally too recognised the man in the photograph and frowned trying to remember where they had seen him. 'Was it Pegasus House?' she mused.

'It has to be somewhere like that,' agreed Narinder.

'I've got it,' exclaimed Sally excitedly, 'it was at the Innovation Centre in Market Harborough.'

'You're right,' agreed Narinder, 'it was the day we were there interviewing everyone who had met Conrad Winston and he rushed out of his office next door to Ramesh and nearly collided with us.'

'So, the Innovation Centre is the link we're looking for,' said Harriet.

'Do we go and get him?' asked Charlie.

'We do,' answered Harriet, 'but we carry out a few tests first. Sally could you ring your friend at Innovation and ask him if the

Russian is back yet, and if he isn't would he call you when he is.'

'The reception will have this guy's car reg,' said Narinder, 'they all have to register their cars.'

'Good thinking, Narinder,' said Charlie, 'will you see to that.'

'Straight away.' Narinder took out her mobile and moved to a corner of the room to phone.

'I'll call Ramesh,' said Sally and followed suit.

'When do you think the Russian will call to tell us where to leave the money?' asked Earl.

'As soon as he gets back to Market Harborough, I should think,' replied Harriet, 'now that he knows who Fred Biggins is and where to find him'.

'He certainly won't arrange anything with the hit-man until the money is handed over,' said Charlie.

'If the money is always given to Anna Petrov,' said Duncan, 'surely the Russian we've just seen at Wharf Lane will find out she's done a runner.'

'That's a point,' agreed Harriet, 'so the sooner we pull him in the better.'

Narinder came over and told them the car registration on the photo belonged to a John Patterson and yes, he did occupy the office next door to Ramesh Chowdhury.

Sally joined them and confirmed that Ramesh agreed that the occupant of the office next to him was John Patterson and as yet he had not arrived. 'Ramesh will ring as soon as he comes in,' said Sally.

'Do we evacuate the building?' asked Earl.

'If we do that the Russian will know immediately what's happening,' said Harriet. 'No, I think we just arrive out of the blue and arrest him but I'll ring the Centre Manager before that happens.'

'Do we notify Harborough Police?' asked Charlie.

'Yes, I'll do that as well,' said Harriet, 'but I shall ask them that they allow us to go in with our Armed Response Team.'

'They might insist we evacuate the building before we go in,' said Earl, 'that is the procedure, isn't it?'

'Sometimes we have to go around procedure,' replied Harriet, 'but we will have to be careful, we must play safe.'

'Suppose I ask Ramesh to discretely invite his immediate neighbours to go down to coffee when we arrive at the building,' suggested Sally.

Harriet wrinkled her nose. 'Let me think about it,' she said, 'meanwhile we prepare to leave. Duncan will you alert Firearms and explain what we're doing, and you must join them.'

'Yes, ma'am.' Duncan grabbed his mobile and called his Armed Response boss.

Ben picked up the book on mythology and came over to Harriet. 'Ma'am,' he said hesitantly, 'I don't know if this means anything but that flat I was telling you about that Mrs Wilmot showed us round.'

'I haven't forgotten the reference,' said Harriet, 'you will have it by tomorrow at the latest, I promise.'

'No, ma'am, that's not what I was about to say,' said Ben now feeling foolish.

'What is it, Ben?' asked Harriet rather sharply, anxious to get the team organised for the raid on the Innovation Centre.

'It's this book,' said Ben. 'When we were in the flat this same book was on the coffee table and not only that, but Mrs Wilmot said she couldn't always understand what the man said because of his strong accent. She thought he was from Birmingham but suppose he's Russian.'

Harriet was now alert. 'Did you see the man?' she asked.

'No, ma'am he was out, that's why Mrs Wilmot thought she could give us a quick look round.'

'Well done, Ben do you know this man's name?'

'Peter Harris, ma'am, sounds very British doesn't it.'

'They all seem to change their names to sound British,' said Harriet, 'when does this man leave?'

'In two days' time, that's why I can move in on Monday.'

'Good, we have time to arrest the Russian at the Innovation Centre before we tackle Mr Harris.' She was eager to get going but knew she needed to contact Leicestershire Police to advise them on the operation that was about to take place in Market Harborough. She dialled the number of the headquarters at Enderby and asked for the senior officer there. She spoke to Superintendent Josh McNab and talked for about ten minutes. Satisfied that she had the "all clear" to carry out their planned operation she replaced the receiver.

Sergeant Pete Yates rang to say that a reporter by the name of Tom Cavendish was downstairs asking to speak to DCI Marlow. 'You'd better see him, Charlie,' said Harriet.

'Explain that the operation is ongoing, but he will be the first person we contact when we have any news, we'll meet you downstairs.'

Charlie nodded and hurried from the room. Trust Beefy to turn up when they were so busy organising something as important as arresting the Russian.

Commander Upton contacted Harriet to say his men were ready and waiting in the van at the front of the building. 'Thank you, James,' said Harriet, 'we'll be with you straight away.' Replacing the receiver, she turned to the team. 'Right, we're off. No police cars just our un- marked vehicles, and is everyone in a bullet-proof jacket?'

There were murmurs of agreement and Harriet nodded and led the way from the room. As usual Jack stayed at his desk ready to man the telephone or to dive into his computer if need be.

Charlie took Beefy Cavendish to one side and explained that

the operation was in full swing but as soon as it was concluded he would be contacted and given the exclusive he'd asked for. Beefy appeared satisfied with this and left the building. As he went down the steps he saw the parked van and noted officers in full riot gear, something was definitely afoot. He wondered if he dared to follow the van to see what happened at first hand. If he kept well out of sight he wouldn't cause a problem, and he had been promised an exclusive. He went to his car and sat in the driver's seat waiting.

Harriet checked that everyone was ready and then gave the order to set off for Market Harborough. She was in the lead car with Narinder driving. Sally sat in the back with her mobile phone in her hand; Ramesh was going to call her the minute the Russian arrived in his office. Harriet had been concerned that the Russian might see the convoy of police vehicles arrive, but Sally was adamant that they wouldn't be seen as the man's office was on the other side of the building with no view of the road leading to the Innovation Centre. As they drove into Market Harborough Sally's phone rang. She spoke briefly to Ramesh.

'We'll be there in about ten minutes,' she said, 'could I ask a big favour of you?'

'What now?' asked Ramesh.

'Could you loiter in the corridor outside your office and ring me if John Patterson comes out of his room.'

'Crikey, Sally, I'm not a member of your police team.'

'Please, Ramesh it would really help us. We're nearly with you, will you do it?'

'All right, but you owe me.'

'Thanks, Ramesh.' Sally closed down her phone and spoke to Harriet. 'We need to know where the Russian is when we arrive,' she explained, 'if he leaves his office and goes somewhere else we could be in trouble.'

'Well done, Sally,' said Harriet, 'and I must thank your friend when this is over.'

Narinder drove into the Innovation car park and Harriet told Sally to ask everyone to wait in their vehicles until she had spoken to the people in reception. She jumped from the car and hurried into the building. She had telephoned earlier and spoken to Liza Menzie and promised she would speak to her on arrival at the centre. .At the reception desk she held up her warrant card. 'Superintendent Love of Torreston CID,' she said, 'the manager is expecting me.'

Liza appeared from her office looking rather apprehensive.

'We are about to carry out a vital operation,' said Harriet, 'which involves the arrest of one of your clients and to play safe we would appreciate you stopping anyone from this floor going upstairs.'

The woman looked anxious. 'What do you want me to do?' she asked.

'Just keep yourself and colleagues down here. There will be a police officer in the lobby outside this floor keeping people back. The arrival of policemen in riot gear might be rather alarming,' said Harriet, 'but I can assure you we will see that no one in the building is harmed. You will be told when it's all over.'

Liza looked worried; it was her responsibility to ensure the safety of her colleagues and she could only hope that this senior police officer knew how to handle the situation.

Harriet left the building and waved to the officers waiting in the car park.

Upstairs on the first floor where he had his office, Ramesh was leaning on the wall holding his mobile phone in his hand and hopefully, he prayed, looking casual. There had been no movement from the office next to his and so he'd had no need to contact Sally. Ramesh felt decidedly nervous and was glad he was not in the police force.

Downstairs a uniformed officer stood in the doorway ready to keep people back as firearms officers in their riot gear and holding guns climbed the stairs. Charlie and Harriet followed close behind. As they reached the first floor a young woman came out of her office and gasped when she saw the men. The officer at the front put a finger to his lips and indicated to her to go downstairs.

Charlie stepped forward and took her arm. 'Go to the café and wait there,' he said, and the woman scurried away to be met on the ground floor by the uniformed officer who explained what was happening and that there was no need for her to be afraid. 'It will all be over very soon,' he said, 'and I'll let you know when it's all clear.'

The woman hurried through the double doors to the café and went over to the counter where Karen and Donna stood wondering what on earth was going on.

Ramesh saw the armed officers arrive and pointed to the door that was the Russian's office. Commander Upton nodded, and his men assembled outside the room. Swiftly he opened the door and the men rushed in. The stocky Russian was sitting at his desk with a mobile phone pressed to his ear. He looked up in horror as he police entered. He had a fleshy, pot-marked face with a bulbous nose and deep set, hard, grey eyes. He quickly closed down the phone and Upton snatched it from him. Two officers pulled the man's arms behind his back and handcuffed him.

'What is this?' shouted the Russian, 'how dare you handle me in this way.'

Charlie and Harriet entered the room recognising immediately the man from the photograph at Wharf Lane. They were joined by Sally and Narinder who pulled on latex gloves and immediately began going through the desk drawers.

'Oh, yes!' cried Narinder as she opened a drawer full of cheap mobile phones. 'Plenty of phones to use for the Cerberus website.'

'I don't know what you talk about,' said the man, 'what is this Cerberus.'

'You've never heard of it?' asked Harriet.

'No, never.'

Harriet took out her mobile phone and called Jack telling him to do as she and he had planned before they left the police station.

Jack had his computer open at the Cerberus website and now he tapped in the name, Stymphalian Birds, a phone number appeared at once. In John Patterson's office the mobile phone that Upton had confiscated from the Russian rang out. The Commander handed the phone to Harriet who answered it. 'Thank you, Jack,' she said, 'this confirms everything.' Closing down the call she tuned to the Russian. 'That was my colleague using the Cerberus website to contact you,' she said, 'the website you know nothing about.'

The Russian scowled but made no reply. Sally opened another drawer and caught her breath. Gingerly she took out a hand gun. 'And I suppose you have permission to carry a firearm,' she said, holding it up.

'I don't know this,' said the Russian, now looking quite aggressive.

James Upton took the weapon. 'This is a Makarov eighteen-millimetre pistol with integral suppressor,' he said, 'and not your everyday weapon by any means. It's not, may I add, Superintendent the weapon that killed Blackwell and the others.'

'Who would want a pistol with a silencer attached,' said Charlie, 'unless that person was up to no good.'

'I'm sure Mr Patterson has never seen it before.' said Harriet. 'Bag it, Sally and we'll get it back to forensics.'

Sally held out an evidence bag and Commander Upton dropped the gun in it. 'You'd better have this as well,' said the commander holding out the mobile phone he had taken from the Russian. Sally opened another bag and Upton gave her the phone.

'Take him away,' said Harriet to the officers holding the prisoner.

Chapter Fifty-Seven

Crouched behind a car close to the main entrance of the Innovation building, Beefy Cavendish could hardly believe his luck as he watched the activities of Torreston police. He had driven in behind the police vehicles and parked a short distance away from them. He watched as Superintendent Love entered the building and then minutes later appear at the door and waved. As if by magic the doors of the grey police van opened, and several heavily armed officers rushed into the building. They were followed by officers he knew from CID and risking all, he took some quick photographs. Now all he had to do was wait and see what the outcome of this raid was. It had to be serious, you didn't see armed police very often. Was this about terrorism? he wondered. The minutes ticked by as he sat in his car hardly able to believe he had a grandstand seat for such a momentous occasion. Suddenly the door of the Innovation Centre opened again and two officers in riot gear emerged holding the arms of a man in handcuffs. Beefy wound down his window and clicked away on his camera. This was fantastic, his exclusive if ever there was.

In the office of the Russian, Sally and Narinder had bagged everything they could lay their hands on, which was not an enormous amount. The laptop was the most important item, but apart from a couple of folders and the mobile phones the office was pretty bare. The gun of course was a vital piece of evidence and carrying the bags the two women left the room. Ramesh was waiting in the corridor and he grinned when he saw Sally.

'A success then?' he asked.

'Absolutely,' answered Sally, 'and thank you so much for your help, Ramesh.'

'Are you able to tell me who this guy is?'

'Not at the moment, I'm afraid,' said Sally, 'but his names not John Patterson. As soon as we're cleared to speak about it we'll be in touch.'

'Over dinner,' suggested Narinder.

'That'd be good, because as I said, you owe me.'

Harriet appeared behind them and heard the end of the conversation. 'We owe you a great deal,' she said holding out her hand, 'I'm Superintendent Love and I've heard a great deal about you Mr Chowdhury.'

Ramesh shook her hand. 'Happy to help,' he said, 'not that I think I had any choice.'

Harriet smiled. 'I know how persuasive these ladies can be,' she said, 'so see that you hold them to their promise to see you right.' She turned away and went down the stairs to report to the centre manager that the operation was over, and people could return to their offices.

Sally and Narinder promised to make a dinner date with Ramesh, said goodbye and followed Harriet down the stairs.

From his vantage point, Beefy watched as officers began appearing from the building and returning to their vehicles. He took more pictures very happy with the one of the two female offices carrying what could only be evidence from a crime scene.

The convoy of police vehicles returned to Torreston where the Russian was signed in and placed in a cell. So far, he had refused to give his real name insisting that he was John Patterson, a business man.

'Get Earl to formally arrest him,' said Harriet to Charlie, 'and take his fingerprints, that will tell us who he really is. Ask him to get all the bank statement of John Patterson as well would you, they could prove to be very interesting. When you've done that get back here as soon as possible as we have another serious matter to discuss.'

'That sounds ominous.'

'We could have a lead on the hitman,' said Harriet.

'Good Lord, how'd that come about?'

'I'll explain as soon as you get back', said Harriet.

Charlie dashed off to speak to Earl Cassells eager to get back to Harriet to discover what this new information could be. When he had gone Harriet rang the Incident Room and asked Ben to come to her office.

A nervous Ben knocked on Harriet's door and entered at her request. 'Ma'am,' he said as he stood in front of her desk. He felt like he had once some years ago when summonsed to the headmaster's office and made to stand in front of him. The only difference now was that on this occasion he wasn't going to be reprimanded for smoking behind the bicycle sheds.

'Sit down, Ben,' said Harriet, 'and tell me all about this man in the flat you are interested in.'

'Could we have Luke in here as well, please, ma'am,' said Ben, 'he was with me when I was shown over the flat.'

'Is he in the Incident Room.'

'Yes, ma'am.'

Harriet picked up the phone and asked Luke to join them. He arrived minutes later and was invited to sit beside Ben.

'Now,' said Harriet, 'tell me everything you know about this man.'

'Mrs Wilmot, said she had difficulty understanding him at times,' began Ben, 'because of his strong accent. She said she thought he was from Birmingham, but I wonder if he might be Russian.'

'And the book?' asked Harriet.

'It was the book that made me think,' said Ben, 'it was on Greek Mythology, the same book you held up at briefing.'

'Did you see the book, Luke?' asked Harriet.

'I saw a book, but I can't say I read the title, but, Ben's right, Mrs Wilmot wasn't really sure about the man's accent, she's probably only ever heard a Birmingham accent so thought that's what it was.'

'Was there anything else in the flat?'

'It was surprisingly bare,' replied Ben.

'Mrs Wilmot said he was leaving in two days,' said Luke, 'so he was probably packed ready to go.'

There was a light knock on the door and Charlie came in. 'Inspector Cassells is dealing with the prisoner,' he said, 'and Sally has sent the gun to Forensics.'

'And the laptop?' asked Harriet.

'The laptop and mobile phone are with Doctor Chong.'

'Good.'

'Now, what's all this about a lead to the hit-man?' asked Charlie.

Harriet told him about the man in the flat that Ben and Luke had visited the previous day and Charlie puffed out his cheeks.

'Phew, if it is the Russian, it could be "case closed",' he said.

'We have today and tomorrow to decide what to do,' said Harriet, 'and then this man is off.'

'I take it you're convinced he is the man we're after?' said Charlie.

'Who else would want a book on Greek Mythology other than our killer?' asked Harriet.

'Good point,' agreed Charlie.

'You say the mobile phone Commander Upton took off the Russian is with Henry,' said Harriet.

'It is.'

'The Russian was talking to someone on it as we arrived,'

said Harriet, 'we need to check who that was.' She picked up the telephone receiver and called Henry Chong.

Henry gave Harriet the number of the last call made by the Russian and she jotted it down. 'Henry tells me it's another mobile so probably another throw-away,' she said.

'Supposing the Russian discovered Anna Petrov had gone and was warning the hit-man to leave?' suggested Charlie.

'I was wondering about that,' agreed Harriet. 'I suppose the Russian would have had to advise her on another payment arriving and Pegasus House would have told him she hadn't been in.'

'Mrs Wilmot said her lodger was leaving in two days,' said Ben, 'but if he's been warned he could be off today.'

'He will still be confident that we don't know who he is,' said Harriet, 'but I think we organise picking him up as soon as possible.'

The telephone rang at that moment and Harriet picked up. She said very little other than good, excellent, and thank you, Jack. Replacing the receiver, she smiled. 'Anna Petrov was picked up at Gatwick Airport a few minutes ago,' she announced, 'she was attempting to book a flight to Moscow.'

'Great,' said Charlie, 'two down one to go.'

'Get everyone together in the Incident Room, Charlie,' said Harriet, 'and I'll call Commander Upton and ask him to join us, the last Russian is the most dangerous. We'll ask the Commander how he thinks we should go about catching Mr Peter Harris.'

Charlie stopped in his tracks as he made for the door. 'Did you say Peter Harris?' he asked.

'Yes,' replied Harriet, 'that's the name of the tenant at Mrs Wilmot's house, and are you wondering like me why the name rings a bell?'

'Exactly! Its also the name of the guy who registered at the Glebe Hotel the night the attempt was made on Rosalind De Luca's life.'

'Of course.' Harriet held a hand to her head. 'Well done,

Charlie I've been puzzling the name since Ben mentioned it and just couldn't place it. Well, we've got him then,' she said, 'at last we're going to catch the hit-man.'

Charlie just nodded and dashed from the room.

The Incident Room was packed, and Harriet and Charlie stood at the front with James Upton. Harriet thanked everyone on the success of the operation at the Innovation Centre and then explained about the tenant who had a book on Greek Mythology. 'Thanks to Ben's sharp eyes,' she said, 'he spotted this book in a flat rented by a man, called Peter Harris who has a strong accent that we wonder might be Russian. A man who incidentally was at the Glebe Hotel the night Mrs De Luca was shot at.'

'Well done, on the book, Ben,' called someone.

'We can't believe someone else might just be reading a book on Greek Mythology,' said Charlie, 'too much of a coincidence, and now that we know his name is Harris we're sure we have our killer. We are considering raiding this house sooner rather than later.'

'Ben tells us the landlady said this man is leaving in two days' time,' said Harriet, 'so we dare not let an opportunity to catch him slip through our fingers.'

'What about Mrs Wilmot?' asked Ben, 'she lives in the ground floor flat, Harris is in the flat upstairs.'

'We'll have to get her out before we go in,' said Commander Upton, 'we can't have a member of the public in danger.'

'Do we do this tonight or tomorrow morning?' asked Earl Cassells.

'Tonight, I think,' replied Upton. 'The longer we leave him the more chance there is of him escaping.'

'The trouble is,' said Harriet, 'we're not sure if he has got wind of Anna Petrov getting away alerting him to us closing in.'

'Also,' said Charlie, 'did John Patterson, or whatever his Russian name is, contact the hit-man and warn him to get out?'

The door opened at that moment and Henry Chong hurried in. 'Your John Patterson is a hardened Russian criminal by the name of Vitali Vasiliev,' he announced excitedly, 'and not only that but all the information you need is on his laptop. Luckily, he had no time to delete anything and he still has the name George Blackwell on file, with all his details, place of work and time he usually left Pegasus House. Mrs Blackwell is there too, with all her requests including the one to kill Rosalind De Luca.'

There were gasps around the room followed by clapping. Harriet was overjoyed, they were going to close this case after all. She held up her hand. 'We still have to get the hit-man,' she said quietly. 'Commander Upton, what do you suggest?'

Vadim Kuznetsov, or Peter Harris as Mrs Wilmot knew him, had finished his packing feeling anxious about the phone call he had received from the Master as he was known. He suggested to the boss that he leave immediately but had been instructed to wait until the morning. It seemed Anna Petrov had already gone, wise woman, he only hoped she had reached Russia by now. He also hoped the money he had been promised had turned up in his bank account but decided to play safe and not open up any Russian websites, as he was now wondering what sort of surveillance the British police had on them. The Master had been concerned that their cover had been blown and was blaming Anna for doing a bunk without permission. She would no doubt be in trouble when she arrived home in Moscow. Kusnetsove had been ordered to stay put until morning when he had air tickets for Moscow. He had been instructed to leave his hire car at the airport; when it was discovered he would be long gone. On the way to Heathrow he was to drop his Barretta in the rubbish bin at the children's play area at the end of his road where it would be collected by the Master. No way could guns be smuggled through airport security these days, but easy-come, easy-go, he had been given this one on arriving in Britain and he would soon be given another once he was home. He fingered his Barretta lovingly and gave a sinister smile. He'd done well and certainly earned his money, he'd soon be able to retire.

Chapter Fifty-Eight

By seven o'clock a plan had been devised. Commander Upton had briefed his men and Harriet had contacted the assistant chief constable to inform him of their intention to arrest the man in Back Lane. She explained that she was convinced this man was the Russian hitman and with Commander Upton they had worked out a plan. Liam Fenshaw was unsure about armed officers going to a house when there was no definite evidence that the wanted man was there, and he began huffing and puffing. Harriet insisted they had to make an immediate decision and she would take full responsibility for the raid and reluctantly the ACC gave the go ahead. Ben was concerned about the safety of Mrs Wilmot and asked Harriet if he could go the house before the raid and get her to leave.

'Mrs Wilmot knows me, ma'am, and that I'm a policeman,' said Ben, 'so I'm sure I could get her to leave the house.'

Harriet turned to James Upton. 'What do you think?'

'We certainly need her out of the house,' he replied. 'If this guy is armed as you think he is we can't afford to get this wrong.'

'Put on a bullet proof vest, Ben,' said Harriet, 'and wait to be told what to do and do you have Mrs Wilmot's telephone number?'

'Yes. ma'am.' Ben took his notebook from his jacket and scribbled the number down for Harriet which she took and pushed in her pocket.

As CID officers didn't wear uniform Ben took off his sweater and pulled on the protection feeling quite excited to be playing an important role in the capture of the Russian. He replaced his sweater and put on his anorak ready for action. Luke came over and sat beside him. 'Good luck, mate,' he said, 'just be careful.'

'I will,' replied Ben, 'I'm sure Mrs Wilmot will leave if I ask her to and then the armed guys can go in.'

'Have you told your mum you're working late?'

'I have,' Ben gave a weak smile, 'but I haven't told her what I'm doing.'

Charlie called everyone together. 'We're about to go,' he said. 'No one moves until Ben and the woman are out of the house and Commander Upton has been in and given us the all clear.'

'We stay in our vehicles until the call comes,' said Harriet. 'Inspector Cassells will be in charge of the van with the radio equipment; Sally, Narinder and Luke that includes you. The rest of you stay in your cars until needed. I will be in the first car with DCI Marlow and Ben but will stay well back from the house.'

'I will notify you when my men are in position,' said Upton. 'We will surround the house and I will advise over the radio as to what is happening. Is DC Granger wired?'

'I am sir.'

'Good, then let's go.' Commander Upton strode from the room to join his men in the van at the front door. Duncan had already left to get into his riot gear and collect his weapon.

Harriet looked at the officers left in the room. 'Good luck, everyone,' she said quietly, 'and no hero's please.'

It was quite dark when the police vehicles arrive in Back Lane and parked at the end of the road and out of sight of number twelve. Everyone sat and waited in silence. Sally had the camera and both she and Narinder were wearing earphones listening to what was going on. Harriet had an earpiece so that she could hear Commander Upton, and Ben once he went to the house.

Ben was feeling sick, although he wasn't going to tell anyone. He had a job to do and he wanted to do it well. His stomach churned when he heard the voice come over the radio.

'We're in position, tell the DC he can go to the house.'

'Ready, Ben?' asked Harriet.

'Yes, ma'am.' Ben climbed from the car and began walking slowly down the lane. He had been instructed to act in a casual manner in case anyone was watching but as he found his legs were shaking, walking slowly was all he could manage.

Vadim Kuznetsov was feeling agitated and wasn't sure why. He had wanted to get away tonight and was annoyed that the Master had instructed him to stay until morning. He'd been told that Anna had vanished, and this had alarmed him. Had she already left the country and was now safely back in Moscow? Although his air tickets were for the following day he could have lain low at the airport until his scheduled departure, or even requested a change of flight. Perhaps this is what Anna had done. The Master had told him this might draw attention to him and so he had had to comply. You didn't disagree with the man at the top. Now he paced the floor. It was only eight thirty, not even time for bed. He went to the window and looked out. The lane was quiet and still. He was about to turn away when he saw a figure approaching. The figure turned in at number twelve and the Russian caught his breath. Opening the door of his flat he crept down the stairs and crouched behind the bannister listening. Mrs Wilmot opened the door and he heard her say 'Ben, how nice to see you, do come in.'

Kuznetsov relaxed. The landlady knew this man, a relative perhaps. He was about to go back up to his flat when he heard the man speak.

'Mrs Wilmot, I need you to come with me.'

'Whatever for?'

'I need you out of the house' said Ben, 'you could be in danger.'

The Russian froze then hurried back up the stairs to his flat where he grabbed his gun and returned to the staircase. The young man had come into the house and was standing with the woman in the hallway. He crept down the stairs his gun at the ready.

Sitting in the car at the end of the lane Harriet and Charlie listened to Ben talking to Mrs Wilmot. 'Why do you want me to come with you, Ben?' she asked, 'whatever do you mean about danger?'

'I'm a police officer, Mrs Wilmot, please trust me.'

'Very well, but this is very alarming, I'll get my coat.'

Harriet and the others in the van sat waiting, almost holding their breath. At least the woman was going leave with Ben. Suddenly another voice was heard, a voice with a strong foreign accent.

'No need to get your coat, Mrs Wilmot you won't be going anywhere. And you, officer shut the door and stay where you are.'

Ben's voice was heard. 'Put the gun down, there's no need for that, I'm not armed.'

Harriet's heart sank, the Russian was there, and he was armed. She contacted Commander Upton. 'You heard that?' she asked.

'Yes, your lad was tipping us off to the fact that the guy had a gun.'

'We can't risk him or Mrs Wilmot getting hurt,' said Harriet.

'Do we have a phone number for the house?'

'Yes, I have it here.' Harriet took the number from her pocket and read it out for James Upton.

'I'm going to ring the house and ask for the Russian,' said the commander, 'pity we don't know his name.'

In the house Kuznetsov ushered Ben and Mrs Wilmot into the front room where he told them to sit down. He addressed Ben. 'How many police are there out there?'

Ben hesitated. Should he tell this man that the place was surrounded, or should he stay quiet and pretend he was alone. The situation was answered for him when the telephone rang.

'Answer.' Instructed the Russian to Mrs Wilmot. The woman looked terrified not understanding what in the world was going on. This nice quiet man had changed completely and was now aggressive and quite hateful. She picked up the receiver.

'Hello,' she said her voice trembling.

'This is Commander Upton of the Quick Response Firearms division, is that Mrs Wilmot?'

'It is, can you tell me what all this is about?'

'We are going to keep you safe, Mrs Wilmot,' replied the commander, 'let me speak to the Russian,'

'Russian!' squealed Mrs Wilmot.

'The man with the gun,' said Upton.

'Is he a Russian?' gasped the landlady beginning to shake.

'Please give him the receiver, Mrs Wilmot,' said Upton keeping his voice calm.

Mrs Wilmot turned to Kuznetsov. 'He wants to speak to you,' she said in a shaky voice handing him the receiver.

The Russian took it and said, 'Yes?'

'This is Commander Upton of Torreston Police, the house is surrounded so come out with your hands in the air and without the gun and no one will be harmed.'

Kuznetsov frowned. So, they knew he had a gun, did they. It was time to put it to good use. 'Anyone coming near the house I shoot the lady and policeman,' he snarled.

'That won't do you any good,' said Upton, 'if you do that we will come in and shoot you.'

'So, you are happy that two people die?' asked Kuznetsov, knowing full well this was not how the British police behaved.

'What do you want?' asked Upton.

'To leave unharmed.'

'Your colleagues are both in custody,' said Upton. 'Vasiliev and Anna Petrov have both been arrested.'

The Russian was silent. This was not good news, he needed to get out of the country, but if this was not to be the case and the police were going to shoot him then he would make sure he took others with him. He could start with one of their own. 'Your man will be the first to die,' he said, 'if I don't get safe passage out of here. Let me know how you are going to do this.' He slammed down the receiver.

Sitting in the car with Charlie, Harriet felt sick. Ben was in that house with a madman and they needed to get him and the woman out. She called Upton. 'We're driving up to the front of the house,' she said. 'No need to keep our presence a secret as he knows we're here.'

'I'll join you there,' replied Upton.

'Let's go, Charlie,' said Harriet her heart pounding. 'Stop in front of the house where we can be seen but on the other side of the road.' She then instructed the van driver and the officers in the other cars to do the same. 'When you're there,' she added, 'stay back but be alert.'

The convoy of police vehicles moved down the lane and parked a short distance from number twelve. Inside the house Ben was frantically trying to think what to do. He was very frightened but the policeman in him was holding him together. His one thought was for the safety of Mrs Wilmot and with this in mind he walked up to her where she sat in an armchair looking terrified.

'Don't worry, Mrs Wilmot,' he said quietly, 'we'll get you out of here safely.'

'What's all this about, Ben?' she asked in a quavering voice.

'I'll explain about it later. Just do as I tell you.' he looked at the Russian and spoke firmly. 'Let Mrs Wilson go, this has nothing to do with her, you can keep me as hostage.'

'Sit down and be quiet,' hissed Kuznetsov.

Ben remained standing. 'How very brave of you,' he said, 'using an elderly lady as a hostage. Make you feel big does it?'

The Russian hit Ben with his gun. 'Shut your mouth,' he shouted almost hysterically.

Ben grunted with the pain and put his hand to the side of his head where he had been hit. It came away covered in blood. Mrs Wilmot cried out. 'Oh, Ben you're hurt.'

'Just a scratch, Mrs Wilmot, but come with me.' Ben took her arm and she rose from the chair.

'Stop,' screeched Kuzetsov, 'what are you doing?'

'Mrs Wilmot is leaving,' said Ben firmly keeping himself positioned in front of the gun man. He opened the door and all but pushed the trembling woman through it keeping himself between her and the Russian.

Kuznetsov waved the gun. 'Stop, stop, or I'll shoot.'

'Go,' hissed Ben to Mrs Wilmot slamming the door shut behind her. The woman scurried down the passageway, and Ben kept himself in the doorway pressing his back to the door. 'You have me as your hostage,' he said to the Russian, walking bravely towards him, 'let Mrs Wilmot go.'

Chapter Fifty-Nine

Siting the car Harriet and Charlie were listening to Ben. They had heard the thud and cry of pain from him when the Russian had struck him, and now here was the young constable standing up to a killer. As they heard Ben insisting that Mrs Wilmot should be allowed to leave and he would be the hostage, the front door of number twelve opened and the slight figure of an elderly woman appeared. Sally was out of the van like lightening. She ran across the road and took the woman by the arm guiding her to one of the police cars.

'Are you all right, Mrs Wilmot?' asked Sally, helping her into the car.

'I think so,' she answered tearfully, 'but please help Ben, Mr Harris has gone mad, he has a gun.'

'We'll get Ben out,' replied Sally, 'just stay here, you're safe now. Can you give me a description of this Mr Harris?'

'He's tall with a lot of greying hair and moustache, in fact I always thought he looked like Albert Einstein, younger of course but rather like him.'

'Thank you,' Mrs Wilmot, that's a great help.' Sally left the woman in the car and hurried away.

Police officers had been down the lane knocking on doors telling the occupants to stay inside as there was a police incident in the road and they would be informed as soon as it was over. Curtains in the neighbouring houses had been twitching for some time and it was no surprise that someone had telephoned the newspapers. Cars began arriving and reporters were having to be held back by uniformed officers at the top of the lane.

'We need to know what's going on,' demanded Beefy Cavendish, 'is this to do with the arrests made in Market Harborough?'

'What arrests in Harborough?' asked Colin Bragg of *The Tribunal*.

Beefy wished he'd kept his mouth shut about that but answered casually. 'Oh, I heard some guy had been arrested there and I wondered if there was a connection.'

'Oh, yeah,' said Michael Dellaware of *The Herald* sarcastically, 'we all believe that one, Beefy, what do you know that the rest of us don't?'

Before anything further could be said the group standing there saw activity at number twelve. They watched as the tall figure of a woman leaped from the police van and ran to the house and where an elderly lady had just come through the front door. The young woman. who had to be a police officer, escorted her to a waiting police car.

'Can you tell us what this incident is?' asked Dellaware.

'I'm afraid I can't,' replied the officer, 'but you will be told in due course.'

A car pulled up at that moment and the constable went over to confront the driver. 'Oh, good evening, sir,' he said when he recognised Chief Inspector Harrington.

'Any news?' asked Ed.

'Not yet, sir, but I think the woman is out of the house.'

Ed moved away and suddenly felt his arm pulled. He looked across to see Beefy Cavendish lurking behind a car.

'Chief Inspector,' hissed Beefy, 'could you remind DCI Marlow that he promised to give me information on this case as I've done what he asked me to.'

Ed had little regard for this man but nodded. 'I'll give him your message, Beefy,' he said, 'but I'm sure he's very busy at the moment.'

'A promise is a promise,' growled the reported as Ed strode down the lane. He found the car with Harriet and Charlie in it and tapped on the window. Harriet looked up and gave a weak smile. Ed opened the door and slipped inside. 'Hi, Harry, Charlie,' he said sitting beside his friend.

'Good to see you,' said Charlie.

'Thank you for coming, Ed' said Harriet, 'we have a dreadful situation here.'

'I heard on the news, is it the Russian in there?'

'It is, and the awful thing is he has Ben Granger with him.'

'Not so good,' agreed Ed.

'Have you been home?' asked Harriet.

'I nipped home to feed Feather as I thought you may well be here for some time, and then drove back to the station to finish off my paper work.'

'So, you can stay?'

'For as long as you like, Harry.'

'Thank you, Ed,' said Harriet pleased to have her husband with her.'

'There's a friend of yours at the top of the lane, Charlie,' said Ed. 'Beefy Cavendish, said you owed him information on this case.'

'Blast,' muttered Charlie, 'trust him to get here. I'll nip and have a word with him as we don't want him going off at the deep end.' He slipped from the car and hurried off up the lane.

Sally came over to the car to report that Mrs Wilmot was unharmed and safely in a police car. 'She's very worried about Ben, ma'am,' said Sally, 'she said his head is bleeding from where the Russian hit him.'

Harriet winced. 'Thank you, Sally, I'm going to try and speak to this man myself.'

406

'I have a description of the Russia,' said Sally, 'which might help us.'

'Well done, Sally,' said Harriet, 'and is Mrs Wilmot all right?'

'Unharmed,' replied Sally, 'but very shaken.'

'Give me the description of the gunman, Sally,' said Harriet taking out her note pad, 'and I'll distribute it to everyone.'

Sally did as she was asked and then returned to the CID van.

Charlie returned and confessed that he had promised Beefy he would contact him when all this was over and give him a story.

'Don't worry, Charlie,' said Harriet, 'you had to do that, Beefy did after all keep his side of the bargain.'

'I suppose so, the little creep.'

Harriet took her mobile and dialled the number of Mrs Wilmot's house. The Russian answered immediately.

Harriet spoke to him in perfect Russian. 'This is Superintendent Love of Torreston Police,' she said, 'you have no chance of escaping so please come out with your hands up.'

'Ah, a Russian speaker,' replied Kuznetsov in Russian, 'but not a Russian I fear.'

Still speaking in Russian, Harriet again asked him to leave the house. The man simply laughed and hung up. Commander Upton came over to the car and Harriet wound down the window.

'I have men positioned around the house,' he said, 'and two highly trained marksmen positioned in places where they may be able to get a shot in. McAllister is in an upstairs window of the house directly opposite and Hobbs is across the road in the bushes. McAllister's one of our best shots and hopefully from the upstairs window he'll have a good view of the target. I've given instructions to the men to shoot if they get a clear shot. I shall be in our radio van,' he added.

Harriet shuddered, her big fear being the safety of Ben Granger. 'Thank you, James,' she said.

In the CID van Narinder raised her eyebrows as she listened to Harriet speaking in Russian. 'Didn't know the boss spoke Russian,' she said.

'We knew she did French and Italian with her law degree,' said Sally, 'she must have taken Russian as well.'

'That must have given the hitman a shock,' said Narinder.

'I doubt it,' said Earl Cassells, 'people like that don't shock easily.'

'I hope he doesn't hurt Ben,' said Sally, 'it was jolly brave of him to get Mrs Wilmot out.'

Ben sat down, his head throbbing from the blow he'd received. He was relieved that Mrs Wilmot had escaped and a bit surprised that the Russian hadn't shot him. He began to realise that he was the bargaining chip and this killer needed him alive. Although he was still scared, Ben was feeling positive, he was not about to cower to this man, he would do his bit in getting him caught. He listened as the Russian answered the telephone and spoke only in Russian. Was this an accomplice or had the police called in an interpreter? He heard the Russian laugh and watched as he slammed down the receiver.

'Why don't you give yourself up?' asked Ben, 'you don't stand a chance you know.'

'Shut up,' snarled the man holding the gun

'Why did you kill Mrs Blackwell?' asked Ben knowing the team was listening in. 'We know you killed her husband for her, but why kill her?'

Kuznetsov gave a sneering smile. It didn't matter now if he spoke about his handiwork.

'She was trouble,' he said, 'and I blame Anna for telling her about our organisation.'

'So, you killed her,' said Ben.

'Yes, I kill her.'

'And was it she who paid to have Rosalind De Luca, killed?'

'Yes, she pay.'

Ben was feeling braver with each minute and hoping someone outside was getting this recorded. 'And what about Freddie Fingers?' he asked.

'The Blackwell woman tell Anna that this man had stolen the code and this could put us all in danger, so he had to die.'

Ben shivered. This man had no compunction about killing, but please God don't let him shoot me.

In the car Harriet had the conversation on speaker so that they could all hear. Ben was being very brave, but he needed to be careful.

'Ben's got us all the information we need on the killings,' said Charlie.

'I hope he doesn't push his luck,' said Harriet.

Commander Upton spoke on the radio to his marksmen. 'Any sightings?' he asked.

'Not yet, sir,' replied Duncan.

'None here,' answered two other firearms officers.

Both marksmen were carrying Heckler and Koch 417's and both were highly trained.

A knock on Harriet's car window made her jump and looking up she saw the ACC standing there. Liam Fenshaw didn't look too happy and tentatively she lowered the window.

'Sir,' she said.

'What's happening?' asked the assistant chief constable.

'The Russian is holding DC Granger hostage,' replied Harriet, 'and at the moment we are trying to negotiate with him.'

'So, it was the person you thought it was in this house.'

'Yes, sir.'

'I'll be in the firearms van,' said Fenshaw, 'I presume I can listen in to what's happening.' He strode away to find the commander.

Kuznetsov was desperately thinking how he could leave the house without getting shot. He had a hostage, but how could he make sure he himself was well covered as they left the building. His BMW was on the drive not many metres from the front door, so he needed a way to remain shielded so that he could reach it. He had an idea and poking the gun in Ben's ribs he told him to walk in front of him as there were things he needed to collect before they left the house.

'So, we're leaving, are we?' asked Ben.

'We are, and we are taking my car.'

'Where are we going?'

'That does not concern you,' replied the Russian, 'just come with me.' In the hallway Ben was told to take off his coat and put on a raincoat that was hanging on the hallstand. Ben hesitated and Kuznetsov poked him with the gun. 'Take off coat,' he insisted.'

Ben began unzipping his anorak knowing he would disclose his wire and microphone. The Russian became impatient and dragged the zip down himself. He cried out in Russian when he saw the wire and instinctively hit Ben across the head with the gun. Ben went down with a groan, blood spurting from another wound.

Officers outside the house were listening to the conversation and Harriet prayed that no harm would come to the constable. 'Ben's been putting himself at risk keeping us informed as to what's going on,' she said, 'he's been extremely clever, but I worry he's now in danger himself.' Her heart sank when she heard the Russian shouting abuse in Russian. He had discovered the wire.

'Very clever, Russian speaking superintendent,' came the killer's voice, 'but you have this communication no longer.' There was a crunching sound and the line went dead.

'The Russian has crushed the microphone we had on Ben,' she announced, 'I pray he won't harm him.'

Commander Upton called up the marksmen again and told them that the Russian and DC Granger were leaving the house and they were only to shoot if they had a clear view of the hitman. 'No harm must come to the constable,' he insisted.

The ACC sitting in the van was feeling anxious. He had after all given the go ahead for this operation and if anything went wrong it would be he who carried the can.

Chapter Sixty

Everyone waited. Six minutes went by with nothing heard from inside the house. Suddenly the door opened and watching officers were amazed at what they saw. Two figures emerged, but they were completely shielded by two large umbrellas.

'I can't tell who's who,' called Duncan from his vantage place at the upstairs window in the house opposite.'

'Nor can I,' said the other marksman.

'Do not shoot,' ordered Upton, 'I repeat do not shoot.'

'They're in the car,' announced Duncan, 'but I can't tell who's in the driving seat because of the tinted windows.'

'Stand down,' instructed Upton, and leaving the radio van he went over to Harriet's car.

'Do you want us to follow him when he drives off?' he asked.

'Ben has a tracker on his mobile phone,' said Harriet, 'and if the Russian doesn't take it off him we could be in luck and be able to follow them.'

'I've spoken to Jack,' said Charlie, 'and he's tracking Granger right now and will keep us posted.'

'Good,' replied Upton, 'I'll organise a car with some of my guy's in it and I take it you will be in this car?'

'Absolutely,' agreed Harriet. 'Jack will contact us on the same line, so we can be independent.'

'The firearms van can follow at a distance,' said Upton.

'The BMW is leaving,' called Duncan.

'We're ready,' replied the commander, 'get back here, McAllister and you Hobbs as we will be following.'

Kuznetsov shoved Ben into the driving seat and climbed into the seat beside him. 'Drive,' he hissed.

Ben was feeling dizzy after the second blow to the head and his vision was definitely blurred. He started the engine and pulled out of the drive. 'Where to?' he asked.

'Head north.'

Ben did as instructed but was wondering if he was going to be able to drive he felt so dreadful. With blood running down his face from the deep cut in his temple, he drove out of the drive, up Back Lane and onto the main road.

With Charlie driving the unmarked police car, and carrying Harriet and Ed, he turned around in the lane and followed. Behind him was another car driven by Upton himself and with Duncan and Sergeant Hobbs on board. The Firearms van brought up the rear with the CID van close behind. Jack was tracking Ben's mobile phone and was in constant contact giving them the direction of the BMW. The hitman was heading north.

Now on the M1 Kuznetsov told Ben to put his foot down, but Ben was feeling sick and dizzy and knew he shouldn't be driving at all. 'I feel faint,' he said, 'I'm going to have to stop.'

'Do not stop,' shouted the Russian.

Ben carried on and at the A453, the East Midland Airport turn off the Russian told Ben to come off the motorway. Ben obliged but suddenly feeling very faint he swerved into a lay by and stopped placing his head on the steering wheel feeling very sick. He desperately wanted to do something to let the boss know where he was going and realising he was either going to be thrown out of the car, or worse, shot, he suddenly thought of one thing he could do. 'I've had it' he croaked, his head still on his hands, 'I'm going to be sick, I can't go on.'

Kuznetsov cursed in Russian and jumped from the passenger seat and came around to Ben's door. Opening it he dragged the constable from the car and flung him onto the grass. Ben was only semi- conscious and lay where he had landed. The Russian was still swearing in his own language as he climbed into the driver's seat. Before closing the door, he took his gun pointed it at Ben and fired.

Jack's voice came over the radio. 'Ben's tracker has stopped,' he announced, 'he's just come off the M1 at junction 23A and is on the A453, it looks as if they might be heading for East Midlands Airport.'

'Make sure the airport is alerted for this man, Jack,' said Harriet, 'we now have a description of him, so pass it on.' She gave it out, adding; 'we're still on the motorway, we'll slow down so as not to catch them up.'

Charlie slowed and waited for Jack to tell them what was happening.

'Hang on,' said Jack, 'They're moving again, looks as if I'm right in where he's going.'

Charlie continued and as the A453 turn off loomed he asked if he should exit.

'Yes,' said Harriet, 'we need to keep reasonably close to them, but at least we know the car registration so should be able to find it.' She contacted James Upton who informed her that he was not that far behind and had heard what Jack was saying.

Charlie pulled off the motorway and headed for the Airport. They passed a lay by where a great deal of activity was taking place. A police car it's blue light flashing and siren screaming came towards them and as Charlie went by they saw it swing into the layby.

'Another incident to be dealt with,' said Ed, 'that was a Derbyshire car.'

'I'll ask Jack to contact Derbyshire police to let them know what's happening,' said Harriet. 'When we finally discover where this Russian is going they may like to join us. I'll also give them the registration number of the BMW, you never know one of their patrol cars might spot it.'

'That's a good idea,' said Ed, 'the more people looking for it the better chance we have of finding it.'

Harriet opened up her mobile and called Torreston police headquarters. At that moment an ambulance raced by its lights flashing and siren wailing. 'Going to that layby I should think,' said Charlie, 'wonder what's going on there?'

Harriet finished her conversation with Jack who had told her the tracker on Ben's phone showed the car was on still the A 453. She had asked Jack to send someone to the Granger house to tell Ben's parents what had happened but to try not to alarm them too much. 'See that a liaison officer goes with whoever you send to speak to them, Jack,' said Harriet, 'and ask this officer stays with the Grangers until we have good news about Ben. I'm going to send Inspector Cassells and the others back to headquarters.'

'Right, ma'am.' replied Jack suppressing a yawn. It was already eleven o'clock.'

Harriet contacted the CID van and asked Earl to return to Torreston, and although she knew Sally and the others would be disappointed she knew that having too many police vehicles on the road might hinder the operation rather than aid it.

Charlie continued driving at a steady pace, now waiting for directions from Jack. 'The car's making for Diseworth, ma'am,' said Jack over the speaker, 'I wasn't expecting that, it's a small village on the right of the road you are on.'

Charlie turned down the Diseworth road not sure where he should be going.

'The tracker has stopped,' said Jack, 'it's in Burnstock Road, that's about a mile from where you are at the moment. When you reach Highcroft Road on your left, go down it and Burnstock is the second road on your right.'

'Thank you, Jack,' replied Harriet, 'we'll soon spot the car if we drive down the road. What did Derbyshire police say about this?'

'They thanked us for telling them we were working on their patch and said go ahead but tell them the outcome of the operation. If we need their help we're to contact them, but they will keep their eyes open for the BMW.'

'Good,' said Harriet. 'Have the others returned to the station.'

'Not yet, ma'am.'

'When they arrive tell them to go home and hopefully we will have something positive to tell them in the morning.'

'Yes, ma'am.'

Harriet gave Charlie the directions that Jack had given her and five minutes later Highcroft Road appeared. Turning into it they soon spotted Burnstock road and driving into it they cautiously scanned it for the BMW. There was no sign of it. Burnstock Road was a street of Victorian terrace house, none had garages and so if the car was here it should be outside the house.

'Parked in a garage somewhere do you think?' asked Ed.

'There are no garages on this road,' said Ed.

Harriet called up Jack. 'No sign of the car, Jack,' she said.

'The tracker is stationary,' said Jack, 'so I'm presuming the car is too.'

'Let me know if it moves,' said Harriet and to Charlie she said. 'Cruise slowly down the street, I'll look to the left, Ed if you'll take the right side, we might spot the car.'

Charlie drove the length of the street but there was no sign of the BMW. Commander Upton stayed at the top and waited to hear if the car had been spotted. Jacks voice came over the radio.

'Ma'am, the tracker hasn't moved, it's half way along the street so must be in one of the houses.'

'So, he's dumped the car somewhere and has taken Ben into one of the houses,' said Charlie.

'It can't be far away,' said Ed, 'we weren't that far behind him.'

'If we can find the house,' said Harriet, 'it doesn't matter about the car, we want the Russian, and Ben safe.'

Kuznetsov had driven into the cul-de-sac of lock up garages and quickly unlocked the padlock on the door of last one in the row. Having driven the BMW into the garage he snatched his holdall from the boot and left, relocked the garage door behind him. Moving swiftly along the street he hurried up the path of number thirty-three. He'd laughed when told about this safe house and lock-up garage rented especially for an emergency such as this, but now he felt relieved, as according to the Master there would be food and other useful things in the house. He took the key he'd been given, from his pocket, unlocked the door and hurried inside. He took off his overcoat and flung it on a chair before going into the kitchen and opening the fridge door. There was not lot in the fridge, but the freezer was well stocked including milk in plastic bottles, and bread. This made sense as no one would have known if the house was to be used and anything not in the freezer would soon go off. They had been scheduled to be in the country for only six months. Kuznetsov took milk and bread from the freezer and a ready-made dinner.

He couldn't remember when he had last eaten but these items would soon thaw if he put them in the micro wave. This he did and then went upstairs to the small bedroom where he looked for the trunk he had been told would be there.

Charlie returned to the top of the road where the Firearms van was waiting and pulled up behind it. Harriet's phone rang and quickly she answered it.

'Yes, Jack, hello,' she said, 'any news?'

'The worst, ma'am, Derbyshire police have called to tell us that a young man was found injured in a lay by just off the M1 and they say it's Ben. They found his warrant card in his pocket.'

'Oh, no,' gasped Harriet, 'is he badly injured.'

'A nasty gash to the head and he has concussion,' said Jack, 'he's been taken to the Royal Derby Hospital.'

Earl Cassells came on the line. 'Is there anything you'd like me to do, ma'am,' he said, 'I've sent everyone home, but I shall remain here with Jack.'

'Thank you, Earl, could you speak to the liaison officer at the Granger house and tell her to explain to them what has happened. Tell them which hospital Ben is in as they will want to get over there I'm sure.'

'I'll see to it ma'am,' said Earl.

Jack came on the line again. 'If Ben was dumped in that lay by, ma'am,' he said, 'how come I've been tracking his mobile?'

'He's been very clever,' replied Harriet, 'he obviously slipped his phone into the Russian's pocket knowing we'd be tracking it. We need to know which house he's in, Jack, and as quickly as possible.'

'Drive back down the road slowly,' said Jack, 'and I'll shout when you're by the house.'

'Right,' said Charlie turning the car around, 'here we go.'

Kuznetsov opened the lid of the trunk and smiled. He was faced with an assortment of clothes, wigs and other gadgets. He pulled off the wig he was wearing and the moustache and added them to the collection. He wasn't sure what he was supposed to do with the Barretta now that the original plan had gone haywire. This house was to be abandoned, so perhaps he should leave the gun here in the trunk where it would eventually be found, but not yet, he felt safe having it on him. He would dump it as he set off for the airport in the morning; he would soon be out of the country. He felt at the bottom of the trunk and pulled out a box. In it he found the passport he wanted and a wad of English currency and Euros. The passport was French and in the name of Louis Moreau but there was the photograph of the him, hairless and minus the moustache. No one would recognise the Peter Harries that once lived at Mrs Wilmot's house. He put the passport and money in his jacket pocket and went downstairs to see if his dinner had thawed.

Chapter Sixty-One

Charlie drove slowly down Burnstock Road waiting to hear from Jack. Half way down the road the sergeant called out. 'Hold it there.'

Charlie braked. 'You're outside the house,' said Jack.

'Number thirty-three,' read Harriet, 'and there's a light on inside.'

Charlie continued down the road and turned at the bottom retuning to where Commander Upton and his team were waiting. Harriet jumped from the car and went to the van. 'He's in number thirty-three,' she said when Upton opened the door.

'Right,' said the commander, 'now you leave this to us, Harry and stay in the car till we have him, there may be bullets flying about and we don't want anyone hurt.'

Harriet nodded and returned to where Charlie and Ed were waiting. She got into the car suddenly realising she was shaking. Ed leaned over from the back seat and put his hand on her shoulder. 'You're nearly there, Harry,' he said softly, 'let the armed guys take over now.'

Harriet nodded, she just wanted it over but at the same time she wanted all officers to be safe.

Commander Upton gathered his men together, instructing four of them to go down the alley between the houses and find the back of number thirty-three. The rest of us will wait here until you let me know you are in position,' he said, 'at which time we will go to the front of the house. We don't ring the door bell,' he added, 'bring the battering ram, we're entering uninvited.'

Four officers left the van and went down the road to find an alley way between the terrace houses. Upton and the rest of his team waited. It was eleven thirty, dark, cold and quiet.

Luckily there was no one about. In the unmarked police car Harriet with Charlie and Ed also waited. The radio crackled and then a voice was heard.

'We're behind number thirty-three, sir. There's a light on in the kitchen and a guy appears to be making a meal. This guy doesn't match the description we were given of the Russian though.'

Harriet's heart sank as she heard this. Surely, they had the right house and therefore the right man.

The officer spoke again. 'This guy is pretty tall but he's as bald as a coot and has no moustache.'

'In which case we will have to play safe,' replied Upton. 'I shall therefore ring the doorbell and announce that we're police and we'll take it from there. If he's innocent he'll open the door, if not we need to be ready for fireworks. If possible, we want this guy alive. So, don't aim to kill if you have to shoot.'

Harriet shivered. This was not what she'd wanted. She'd thought it was a cut and dried case and they would just grab the Russian.

'We're going down the road,' said Upton, and the dark figures of the men in full riot gear carrying MP5SFAs semi-automatic carbines with EO Tech 512 holographic sights attached, made their way down to number thirty-three. At the gate of the house they stopped, and Upton gave instructions. He then spoke to the officers at the back of the house who confirmed that the man in the kitchen was sitting at the table eating.

'Right,' said Upton, 'I'm knocking on the door.'

Sitting eating the meal he had cooked in the microwave Kuznetsov was feeling relaxed for the first time in days. This would soon be at an end and once he made his getaway to France he could begin his cross-county trip home. A loud knocking on the front door made him jump and instinctively he grabbed his Barretta. He waited. Another knock, louder this time and then to his horror he heard a voice shouting. Police. Open up.

The Russian jumped to his feet; this couldn't be happening; how could they have discovered the safe-house? Clutching his gun, he went to the kitchen door and switched off the light standing with his back flat against the wall. He began edging his way to the back door and then realised there were shady figures out there in the dark. He was trapped! His only option was to shoot his way out, he had nothing to lose. Going onto his hands and knees he crept out of the kitchen and made his way down the passage where through the glass panel on the front door he could see figures on the doorstep. A crash on the door made him realise the police were going to break in; he had to do something.

Commander Upton gave the order to break the door down and two of his men stepped forward and raised the battering ram. The door swung open on the second bang and Upton held up a hand. His men waited. Nothing happened. The commander stepped into the hallway followed by his men with their guns at the ready. The house was quiet, and Upton switched on the light. The hallway was empty. One of the men opened the door of the first room and entered.

'All clear,' he called.

Upton spoke to his men at the back of the house. 'Any movement?' he asked.

'Nothing,' came the reply, 'and no one has left the building.'

'He's in the house somewhere,' said Upton, 'start searching men.'

Two officers went upstairs, and the others made their way cautiously to the kitchen where Upton kicked open the door. The officers rushed in, but it was obvious there was no one there. A noise in the hallway made them turn and dash out just in time to see a figure go through the front door. A loud crack of a gun was heard, and the Russian fell to the ground grasping his thigh. As Upton ran towards him Kuznetsov rolled onto his back and raised his gun pointing it at hm. Another shot rang out, but it was not from the Russian's gun. Across the road leaning over the wall of the house opposite, Duncan lowered his carbine and walked towards them.

'I did my best not to kill him, sir,' said Duncan, 'but I had to take the second shot before he shot you.'

'You did well, lad,' said Upton quite shaken by his narrow escape, 'the blighter must have been hiding in the cupboard under the stairs.' He bent down and felt for a pulse in the Russian's neck. He looked up and shook his head.

Hearing the shooting Harriet, with Charlie and Ed came down the street relieved to see that Upton and his men were standing and unharmed. The figure of a bald-headed, clean shaven man lay on the path. Looking not at all like Einstein. An officer came out of the house carrying a wig and false moustache and held them up.

'There's a whole box full of clothes and disguises upstairs,' he said, 'and several passports and currencies of different countries.'

'They were very well organised,' said Harrier, 'thank goodness it's over. Well done everyone.'

'I've contacted Derbyshire police,' said Charlie coming up, 'and they're sending their coroners van and pathologist and want to know if you're happy with this?'

'Absolutely,' said Harriet, 'all his happened on their patch, so we'll let them finish it off. Make sure we have the gun the Russian was holding and his mobile phone and whatever else he has on him.'

'A DI Johnson will be her soon,' said Charlie, 'and he's offered to take over so that we can get off.'

'Even better,' said Harriet. She looked at her watch, it was twenty past midnight.

'We still have no idea who he is,' said Charlie, 'the passport in his pocket says Louis Moreau and that's a likely name. I'll take his finger prints before we leave and try and get a name when we get back.'

Commander Upton instructed the rest of his men to join them from the back of number thirty-three. He picked up the gun the Russian had dropped and put it in an evidence bag. 'It's the right sort of weapon,' he said, 'we thought it might be a Barretta and it has the silencer attached. I'll get it to Forensics, if you like.'

'Thanks,' said Charlie.

The commander went through the dead man's pockets and held up two mobile phones.

'We think one of these belongs to PC Granger, don't we?' he said.

Charlie took out his own phone and punched in a number. The mobile in Upton's left hand rang. 'That's Bens,' he said, 'it's thanks to that clever move of his that we got our killer.' He put out his hand for the mobile which Upton handed him.

As they all stood there talking a Derbyshire police car pulled up and a stocky man in his forties jumped out and came over to them. 'DI Johnson,' he said, and looking at Harriet added; 'you must be Superintendent Love.'

They shook hands and Harriet introduced the rest of the team. It was agreed that Commander Upton would write the report on the house raid and the shooting of the Russian and Harriet would submit her report on how he was traced and followed to Derbyshire. The coroner's van arrived, and the dead Russian was put on board.

'I'll get my men to secure the house,' said Johnson, 'and we'll go over it tomorrow.'

'The Russian has a black BMW tucked away somewhere close by,' said Charlie, 'it would help if you could find that for us.'

'Leave it with me.'

'Thank you,' said Harriet, 'and I'd be grateful if you could let us know if you find anything significant. It seems this is some kind of safe-house the Russian's had.'

Johnson whistled. 'All very clandestine,' he said, 'but leave it to us, Superintendent, we'll keep you posted.'

'I'll ring headquarters and let Cassells and Jack know it's over,' said Charlie, 'and I'll tell them both to go home. Do you realise it's almost one?'

Harriet gave a weary smile. 'There's one thing you need to do, Charlie, contact Beefy Cavendish and give him the news. You did promise him, so we need to keep our side of the bargain.'

Charlie grinned. 'Yes, I suppose I'd better do that,' he said. 'I won't give him all the gory details, but I'll let him know he is having the exclusive he was promised.'

'He may be lucky enough to get it in the morning paper,' said Harriet, 'that would really give him a boost.'

'Not that I think he deserves it,' growled Charlie, 'he's always such a thorn in our side.'

He opened up his mobile to call the reporter.

The group dispersed and with Charlie driving, Harriet sat in the back with Ed feeling relieved and very tired. 'Charlie,' she said, as they drove away from Burnstock Road, 'do you know where the Royal Derby Hospital is?'

'I do, I take it that's where you want to go.'

'Yes, we must see how Ben is.'

Ed took Harriet's hand and squeezed it. 'He'll be fine, Harry, Jack said he had concussion, and he's a young man and pretty tough.'

Harriet smiled weakly. 'I hope so, he's the second young officer to be shot.'

'We all know the risk,' said Charlie as he headed for Derby, 'and we knew the risks when we joined, don't forget we were all young officers once.' He laughed, and Harriet had to smile. She felt comforted holding Ed's hand and wondered how she had ever coped with such nasty situations before she had married him.

At the Royal Derby Hospital Ben Granger sat up in bed feeling pretty woozy but otherwise all right. His head felt heavy, but the nurse convinced him the medication he had been given had dulled the pain leaving this odd feeling. He looked at his parents who sat at his bedside and smiled.

'I'm okay, really I am, you needn't worry, the police look after their own.'

'You could have been killed,' wailed his mother looking distressed.

'Well I wasn't, mum, so please don't fuss, I'm doing exactly what I want to do.'

His father patted his arm. 'Course you are, son,' he said, 'and I bet they're all proud of you at the station.'

Ben suddenly pulled himself up straight in the bed and gasped. His parents looked around and saw a tall, handsome woman with an equally tall man walking towards them.

Harriet and Charlie stopped at Ben's bedside. 'Mr and Mrs Granger?' asked Harriet, and as they nodded she introduced herself and Charlie. 'How are you, Ben?' asked Harriet.

'Fine, ma'am, I had a bit of a headache where the stitches are, but the nurse has given me an injection, so I can hardly feel it now.'

'I'm so glad,' said Harriet, 'and we have to congratulate you on your clever move of leaving your mobile phone with the Russian.'

'It's all thanks to you we were able to track him to a house in Derby' said Charlie.

'Did you get him?' asked Ben eagerly.

'We did,' replied Harriet, 'and as Chief Inspector Marlow said, it was all down to you.' Ben grinned. 'I thought he was going to kill me, so I slipped my phone in his coat pocket, I guessed you'd be tracking me.'

'You were very brave, Ben,' said Harriet, 'we're all proud of you.'

'Is Mrs Wilmot all right?' asked Ben.

'She's fine,' replied Charlie, 'and she was very concerned about you.'

'She's a nice lady.'

'The nurse told us there's a bullet shot in your flak jacket,' said Charlie, 'you had a narrow escape.'

Mrs Gordon clasped her hands to her head and cred out in horror.

'My number wasn't up,' said Ben.

'Obviously not,' said Harriet smiling. 'We'll leave you now but will send a car for you tomorrow. You have to stay in overnight because it's a head injury.'

'Yes, I was told, and thank you, ma'am.'

They said good bye to Ben and his parents and quietly left the ward.

Chapter Sixty-Two

Beefy Cavendish was at the offices of the Chronical waiting with the night staff. He had persuaded the editor to hold the front page as he was expecting an exclusive report to do with the murders of George Blackwell, his wife and Freddie Fingers. He had printed off the photographs he had taken in Market Harborough and the editor had been very impressed with them. It was because of this that he had held the front page. Midnight came and went, and the night editor began to be concerned.

'If we don't get this story soon, Cavendish we're going to be in real shit as at the moment we have a blank front page.'

'Hang on, boss,' said Beefy, 'I was promised this story and I don't think I'll be let down. We have the photos I took so if the worse comes to the worse we'll go ahead and print with the story that this guy was arrested at the Innovation Centre and we're awaiting information as to who he is.'

'Hmm,' muttered the editor not feeling at all sure about this, 'what exactly did the police tell you about all this,'

'Not a lot, but they owe me one, so hang on a bit longer, boss cos I know the story will come.'

Jack and Inspector Cassells were relieved to hear the news that the Russian had been captured and there had been no police casualties. It had not been announced that the Russian was dead having been shot by a member of the firearms team.

'Time to go home, Jack,' said Earl, 'we'll all be yawning tomorrow.'

'It'll be worth it,' said Jack. 'I'll text Sally to give her the news,

I won't ring in case she's in bed but knowing her and Narinder I doubt that very much.' He typed in the message and pressed send. He closed down his computer and put on his coat to leave when his mobile rang. It was Sally.

'I rather thought you might still be up,' said Jack, 'I wanted you and Narinder to hear the good news.'

'Is Ben all right?' asked Sally anxiously.

'Yes, he's recovering in the Derby Royal,' replied Jack. 'The other news, although we don't have all the details, is that the Russian has been caught and there have been no casualties.'

'That's fantastic,' said Sally, 'and what's going to happen to Ben if he's in Derby?'

'The boss and DCI Marlow have been to the hospital and spoken to him and he appears none the worse for wear apart from butterfly stitches in his head but has to stay in overnight. His parents are with him.'

'Thank heavens he's okay,' said Sally, 'we can go to bed now. Thanks for letting us know, Jack, see you in the morning.'

Sally closed down her mobile and grinned at Narinder and the two men in the room and held up a victorious thumb. They were all dressed for bed and sitting huddled together in their dressing gowns on the sofa, none of them wanting to go to bed without knowing the outcome of the chase of the Russian.

'Well,' said Narinder stretching her arms above her head. 'Ten cups of coffee later we have a success story. I take it the thumbs up means Ben's okay?'

'He is,' replied Sally, 'he's in the Derby Royal with a stitched head and will have to stay there overnight, but he's okay. The boss and DI Marlow have been to see him.'

'Brilliant,' said Narinder.

Gerry looked at his watch. 'It's two thirty, none of us will be very bright tomorrow morning and I have a rehearsal at nine for the end of term Christmas play.'

Dave laughed. 'Don't know how to tell you all this,' he said, 'but I have the day off tomorrow. You do realise it's Saturday.'

Narinder hit him with a cushion. 'We can't remember the last time we had time off,' she said.

'Knowing the boss, she'll send us all home early tomorrow,' said Sally, 'but come on, guys, bed.' She jumped to her feet and made for the stairs. 'Can't wait to hear all the details about tonight though,' she added, 'I bet it was exciting.'

Charlie pulled into Torreston Police Station car park at three thirty and stopped beside Harriet's little red Lotus. 'Where's your car, Ed?' he asked.

'Left it at our station,' replied Ed, 'and got a lift to Back Lane with one of the guys on patrol in that area. It can stay there, and I'll collect it in the morning.'

He got out of the car and offered a helping hand to Harriet. 'You look done in, Harry,' he said. 'Give me the keys and I'll drive.'

For once Harriet didn't argue and willingly handed over her car keys. They said good bye to Charlie and waved as he left. Ed folded himself into Harriet's little car and she slipped in beside him. Fifteen minutes later they were at Magnolia Cottage.

The Incident Room was noisier than it had been for some time. It was Saturday, but everyone had turned up. Harriet had dropped Ed off at Central as he had left his car there the day before and he told her he would be home soon after lunch and hoped she would be able to do the same. Harriet agreed to do her best but told him she had to tie up a few loose ends before she could leave. All officers in the Incident Room were elated at the news that the Russian had been caught and Ben was recovering in hospital. Harriet and Charlie stood at the front of the room and Harriet thanked everyone for all the hard work they had put into the case over the last few weeks.

'It was a tough one,' she said, 'Russian hitmen just don't turn up in Torreston every day.'

Ripples of laughter ran around the room. 'And probably never will again,' said Charlie.

'Although a difficult case,' continued Harriet, 'we got there in the end. What hasn't been disclosed is the fact that the Russian was shot and killed last night, but so far we still have no name for him.'

'His fingerprints are being analysed at this moment,' said Charlie, 'as are the bullets taken from the man's Barretta that he was holding when shot. The nine-millimetre bullets in it do fit the bill as far as the killings go so we're pretty confident that we have our hitman.'

It was policy not to name the officer who killed someone and as they spoke Harriet avoided looking at Duncan, who like her, and Charlie looked extremely tired. She explained about the safe house in Derby and the box of disguises, passports and currencies that were kept there. 'We have to congratulate Ben,' she said, 'he stood up to the gunman and managed to get Mrs Wilmot out of the house, that took courage as he could have been shot. And later when a hostage and although injured, he had the presence of mind to slip his mobile phone in the Russian's pocket knowing we'd be tracking him.'

'The blighter dumped Ben on the side of the road,' said Charlie, 'and as he left he shot him.'

'Thank God he was wearing his bullet-proof jacket,' said Harriet. 'it saved his life. But thanks to Ben we managed to track the Russian to a house in Diseworth and that's where we got him.'

Earl held up *The Chronical*. 'Don't know if you've see this, ma'am,' he said, 'but you are on the front page.' He handed Harriet the newspaper which she looked at and passed it to Charlie.

'Well, Beefy got his exclusive,' he said, 'I did as I had promised, and called him from the safe-house last night.'

On the front page of the paper was a photograph of Harriet coming out of the Innovation Centre in Market Harborough. Two police officers in full riot gear were also coming out of the building holding the arms of a man. The headline read.

TORRESTON POLICE CAPTURE WANTED MAN A

SECOND SHOT DEAD. The article went on to say that the second man, a Russian had been traced to a house in Back Lane but had escaped using a policeman as hostage. The story told of the chase up the motorway to Derbyshire and the eventual shooting of the man. Beefy had elaborated on much of the story and made the most of Ben's injuries saying that a young DC was in the Derby Royal having nearly been killed by the Russian.

Charlie put the paper down. 'We'll allow Beefy his short time of fame,' he said, 'but I might just be asking him how he got the photographs at the Innovation Centre.'

'We all know what a creep he is,' said Narinder.

'But he did cover well when we were at the canal sheds,' said Sally, 'he could have given DCI Marlow away.'

'True,' agreed Charlie, 'and that's why we allowed him his exclusive.'

'He'll be back to his obnoxious self next week,' said Harriet, 'but enough of Beefy Cavendish, the main thing is, we've closed the case. I telephoned the ACC late last night to give him the news and for once he was very complimentary.'

'One other bit of good news,' said Charlie, 'is that Roy Franks was discharged from hospital yesterday, and will be taking a further week off duty to fully recover.'

'Yes, that is good news,' agreed Harriet, 'now, unless you want to hang on until the results come in from Forensics on the Russian's gun and the fingerprints, you can all to go home, and not appear here until Monday morning.'

Everyone cheered and began putting their things away. Luke came up to Harriet and asked how Ben was getting back to Torreston.

'His parents stayed in Derby overnight,' said Harriet, 'and are going to bring Ben back this morning.'

'Do you think it would be in order if I went to see him when he gets back?' asked Luke.

'I'm sure he'd be very pleased to see you, Luke,' replied Harriet, 'he'll be able to tell you all the details of his scary ordeal.'

Within ten minutes the Incident Room was empty apart from Harriet, Charlie and Earl. There was a knock on the door and it opened to disclose the chief constable himself. He came into the room smiling.

'Well done, Harriet,' he said. 'I knew you'd do it, and you two, of course,' he said nodding at Charlie and Earl. 'You got thrown in at the deep end, Cassells,' he added, 'but you look as if you've survived. We have quite a team here.'

'They're certainly that, sir,' replied Earl, 'the best I've ever worked with.'

'That's exactly what it is,' said Harriet, 'team work, no one person does more than anyone else but together we manage to put things together to find the answer.'

Brian Nattrass smiled, he was a great admirer of Harriet Love and it was his deciding vote that got her the position of DCI at Torreston some years ago. 'I've heard about the bravery of the young constable,' he said, 'and your suggestion he is awarded the Queen's Gallantry Medal.'

'He not only managed to get the landlady out of the house safely,' said Harriet, 'but without his clever move in putting his tracker in the Russian's pocket, we might well still be looking for him.'

'And whilst doing that,' added Charlie, 'the lad had a nasty gash to his head and must have been feeling dreadful.'

'Right,' said Nattrass, 'I'll put the wheels in motion.' He shook hands with all of them and again saying congratulations, he left the room.

Chapter Sixty-Three

Luke drove to his friend's house and was pleased to see that Ben's parent's car was on the drive. He knocked on the door and it was opened by Ben himself looking pale.

'How are you mate?' asked Luke.

'I'm fine, still got a sore head and feel a bit bruised but apart from that I'm okay.'

'The boss told us the Russian shot you and you were saved by your flak jacket.'

Ben grinned. 'Yes, thank God he didn't aim at my head. When I came to in the hospital I couldn't understand why my ribs hurt so much, I thought the Russian had probably kicked me, but I was told it was because of the bullet that hit my flak jacket.'

'Crikey,' muttered Luke, 'you were damn lucky, Ben.'

'So I've been told. But come in and have coffee with us, Mum has just made it.'

'Have you told her about your new flat yet?'

'Not yet, still waiting for the right moment.' Ben smiled sheepishly. 'But I'll tell her today as I'm moving in on Monday.' They went into the living room where Ben greeted Luke's parents. Mrs Granger poured the coffee and offered a plate of cakes. The doorbell rang, and Mr Granger left the room to see who was calling. He returned with Harriet beside him and both Ben and Luke leaped to their feet.

'Sit down, sit down,' said Harriet, 'I'm not stopping I just wanted to see how you are Ben.'

'How kind of you Superintendent,' said Mrs Granger, 'It's wonderful to have Ben home safe and sound.'

'Yes, ma'am,' said Ben, 'I'm fine thank you, I'll be back at work on Monday.'

'I'm glad, Ben, and on Monday we have a nice surprise for you.'

'Oh, what's that Superintendent?' asked Mr Granger.

'You can both feel extremely proud of your son,' said Harriet, 'he is to be awarded the Queen's Gallantry Medal in recognition of his bravery in the capture of a very dangerous criminal. The chief constable sanctioned this award a few minutes ago.'

Mrs Granger covered her face with her hands and wept and her husband put his arm around her. Ben puffed out his cheeks in amazement and Luke patted his friend on the back.

'Well done, mate,' he said.

'I'll see you both on Monday,' said Harriet turning to leave, 'I'm going back to headquarters as the results of the bullet and fingerprints are due. Once I have those I will be able to relax.' She smiled, 'and have a restful day all of you,' she added.

Harriet left the house and climbed into her car. Back at the police station she entered the Incident Room and was amazed to find Jack in the room with Charlie and Earl.

'I wanted to be here when those results came through,' said Jack, and Earl nodded in agreement.

'Couldn't let you have all the excitement on your own, ma'am,' he said, 'and anyway, I thought I'd stay a while and get all this stuff off the boards now that the case is over.'

'Until the next one,' said Charlie.

'Thank you all,' said Harriet quietly, 'now I shall make the coffee and hopefully we will get those results very soon. She hurried from the room feeling foolish that her eyes had welled up. It was partly because she was so tired but mainly because she was so grateful to her team who were always so supportive. She made the coffee and carried the tray back to the Incident Room. As they sat drinking coffee Pete Yates arrived carrying a sheet of paper which he handed to Harriet. 'The results you need,' he said, 'and may I add my congratulations, ma'am.'

'Thank you, Pete,' said Harriet taking the paper. She read what was there and looked up. 'As we thought, the bullet from the Russian's Barretta matches the bullets from the other killings so thank goodness we have out hitman.'

'I don't think we doubted that,' said Charlie, 'and the fingerprints?'

'Yes, they have a name,' said Harriet, 'Vadim Kuznetsov a well-known gangster according to Interpol.'

'How do such crooks get into the country,' growled Jack.

'And how do they get out?' said Earl. 'This safe-house is like something out of a spy book.'

'Well, this is one Russian criminal who won't be going back to Moscow,' said Charlie.

'Charlie,' said Harriet, 'would you telephone Rosalind and inform her of the death of Ursula, as she of course will now inherit everything.'

Charlie hesitated before answering. 'I think we should let Bardwell-Fox do that,' he said, 'let him earn his money, the creep.'

'If you think that's what should be done,' replied Harriet, 'but check with him on Monday to see that she is told.'

'I'll do that,' said Charlie, and changing the subject quickly he said; 'I've just realised, I have the Russian's mobile in my pocket.' He went over to his overcoat hanging on the back of the door and took the phone from the pocket. 'Give me a few minutes to go through this,' he said, 'it might tell us a bit more about the organisation.' He clicked away for several seconds before beginning to smile.

'What is it?' asked Harriet.

'Guess whose number is in his phone?' replied Charlie, 'and

who obviously sold him the BMW.'

'Not Don Underwood?'

'The same. Here it is, the Yard Garage.'

'No surprise there,' said Jack, 'and it will have been a cash deal with no questions asked.'

'And no doubt stolen,' said Earl.

'We'll deal with that on Monday,' said Harriet, 'we will have a few things to attend to then. It's Ursula Blackwell's funeral at two, her body was released yesterday, and her sister has told me the funeral will be at the same church as her husband.'

'Am I to go with you?' asked Charlie.

'Yes please, and perhaps you would join us, Earl,' she said, 'it will show our support.'

'Of course, ma'am.'

The telephone rang, and Jack picked up. He handed the receiver to Harriet, 'Inspector Johnson of the Derbyshire Police,' he said.

Harriet spoke for several minutes and hanging up she announced that the Derby police had found the BMW. 'It was in a lock-up garage not far from the house where the Russian was caught,' she said. 'There was an agreement in the glove compartment stating that the car was hired for six months from The Yard Garage in a cash deal, and would be returned there when the purchaser, Peter Harris, returned to his own country.'

'Don Underwood has lost out on that then,' said Earl, 'as I don't suppose he'll be getting the car back.'

'Let Derbyshire sort that one out,' said Charlie, 'but I think we should let Sally and Narinder tell Underwood about it on Monday.'

'Good idea,' said Harriet, 'but now I think we've done enough. Thank you all for everything you have done, I was beginning to think we weren't going to make it.'

'Never that, ma'am,' said Jack, getting to his feet and putting on his coat. 'Never that!'

They left the Incident Room and went down the stairs to reception where a group of uniformed officers stood. Vic Baldwin was with his men and instinctively they clapped. As they went by Harriet thanked Inspector Baldwin and said how happy she was that Roy Franks was on the mend.

'He'll be back in a couple of weeks,' said Baldwin, 'I've been to see him, and he told me you'd called in at the hospital, he was very touched by that.'

'That was the least I could do,' replied Harriet. 'We're off now but I'll see you on Monday, Vic.'

They left the station and saying goodbye to each other they made for their cars. Harriet felt as if a great weight had been lifted from her shoulders and starting the engine of her car she headed for home. Ed would be waiting for her, at last they could have some time together after weeks of little sleep and little social life. As she pulled up at Magnolia Cottage she saw Ed's car in the drive way; he was home. She jumped from the car and as her husband came through the front door to greet her she ran into his arms hugging him. The case was over; it had been a long and difficult one. The two injured officers were on the mend and the threat of a killer on the loose eliminated.

'Come on, Harry,' said Ed softly, 'time to switch off.' He led her into the house his arms still firmly around her, and kicked the door shut behind them.

My Thanks to all The Innovation Centre who helped me, especially Gary Lunt of Customer Attuned. My thanks also to Rose Andertson in helping me to proof the manuscript.